The Bronze God of Rhodes

THE BRONZE GOD OF RHODES

L. SPRAGUE DE CAMP

PHOENIX PICK
an imprint of
ARC MANOR
Rockville, Maryland

ISBN: 978-1-61242-144-5

Published by Phoenix Pick
an imprint of Arc Manor
P. O. Box 10339
Rockville, MD 20849-0339
www.ArcManor.com

Contents

Harry Turtledove

INTRODCUTION

Alexander the Great flashed across the political landscape of the ancient world like a comet. When he succeeded his father, Philip, as King of Macedonia in 336 BC, the Persian Empire, though creaky, was still far and away the largest power in the Near East. At his death--astonishingly, only thirteen years later--Macedonian rule stretched from Greece all the way beyond the Indus River. Macedonians and Greeks swarmed east into the newly conquered lands in hopes of making a fortune.

Alexander was only thirty-three when he died. He left no obvious successor, only a half-brother who was also a halfwit and a posthumous son by Roxane, the Persian princes he had married. While he was alive, his generals--rather like those of Napoleon more than 2,000 years later--danced to his tune. As soon as he was gone, they all started grabbing with both hands. For the next forty years, the Greek-speaking world echoed with the tramp of armies on the march as the generals tried to reunify the quickly built empire. In the generation right after his death, the four major players were Lysimakhos in Macedonia, Antigonos in Asia Minor and Syria, Ptolemy in Egypt, and Seleukos off in the East, in Iraq and Iran. They warred on one another and made and broke alliances with astonishing speed, skill, and treachery.

Dwarfed by these new military kingdoms yet not gone and not quite forgotten were the Greek city-states (poleis) that had been trading and squabbling for many years before the Kingdom of Macedon rose. Two of the most important of these in the late fourth century BC were Athens and Rhodes. Athens we know from its cultural glories of the previous century. When we think of Athens, we think of democracy. We think of Pericles and Alcibiades, Socrates and Plato, of Thucydides, of Aeschylus and Sophocles and Euripides, of Aristophanes. We think of the Parthenon. When we think of Rhodes, we think of . . . well, what exactly?

The polis of Rhodes lay near the northern tip of the largish island of the same name, off the coast of southwestern Asia Minor. Rhodes itself was a new city, built in 408 BC by the citizens of the three older towns on the island, Lindos, Kamiros, and Ialyssos. It was a planned city, built on a grid, a novel and exciting idea at the time. Like Athens, it was a democracy. Rather than being led by a king or a tyrant (to the Greeks, a tyrant was a sole ruler who didn't hold power by right of descent, and could be good or bad), it was ruled by the people--well, by the property-owning male citizens. Thanks to its location and its enterprising populace, it was a major trading center at this time. Its navy worked hard to put down piracy, which was worse in the Eastern Mediterranean then than it is in the Red Sea and Indian Ocean now.

Rhodes was friendly toward Ptolemy, the ruler of Egypt. Considering how much business Egypt did through the port there, Rhodes had excellent reasons to be friendly to him. And Rhodes also wanted to stay on good terms with Antigonos, who held the nearby mainland. If Rhodes did not stay on good terms with him, he was much too likely to want to gobble it up.

Antigonos tried to persuade and to browbeat Rhodes into allying with him and abandoning Ptolemy. When that failed, he went to war against the city-state. The siege led by his son, Demetrios, is one of the most famous of antiquity. Demetrios and the engineers attached to his army devised an astonishing array of siege engines and siege towers designed either to break through Rhodes' walls or to put soldiers on top of them and get down into the city that way.

The Rhodians were every bit as ingenious in countering his devices. Because of this campaign, Demetrios earned the nickname--almost the title--*Poliorketes*: the Besieger.

The events leading up to the siege of Rhodes, the conflict itself, and its aftermath are, so to speak, the background for L. Sprague de Camp's *The Bronze God of Rhodes*. The foreground is the struggle by the sculptor Chares (pronounced, roughly, "Carey's") of Lindos to create a (hollow, of course) bronze statue roughly the size of the Statue of Liberty in Rhodes.

Little is known about Chares except that he did exist, that he studied under the famous sculptor Lysippos, and that he succeeded in erecting the statue that became known as the Colossus of Rhodes. This makes him an ideal subject for historical fiction. An author can play with what is known yet also freely invent without fear of being caught up by some inconvenient fact. De Camp does exactly that. His Chares is short-tempered and egotistical: not always a man who would be pleasant to know--a lot of de Camp's protagonists have flaws. But the character never fails to be interesting, and he certainly lived in fascinating, exciting times, all of which de Camp vividly depicts.

The Colossus of Rhodes promptly became recognized as one of the Seven Wonders of the ancient world. Ironically, it stood for less than a hundred years before an earthquake knocked it down. The wreckage remained on the island of Rhodes for more than 800 years longer; we may guess that the toppled statue became a minor tourist attraction in its own right. At last, after the Muslim conquest of Rhodes, a Jewish merchant loaded the bronze on a great many camels (as de Camp discusses in his afterword) and carted it away.

Finally, I'll note that *The Bronze God of Rhodes* helped inspire me to write four historical novels set on and near Rhodes in 310-307 BC, a little before the great siege. *Over the Wine-Dark Sea, The Gryphon's Skull, The Sacred Land*, and *Owls to Athens* will soon be back in print from ArcManor/Phoenix Pick. And, after this brief commercial message, we now return you to our regularly scheduled novel.

THE BRONZE GOD OF RHODES

Book I

KALLIAS

I am Chares of Lindos, who built the Colossus of Rhodes. Stranger, as you look upon this mighty eidolon of glowing bronze, you may think: Happy Chares! As long as that great statue stands, the glory of his name will remain green.

But will it? Time buries all. Who now knows the name of him who built the gigantic pyramid of King Souphis, which rises in gleaming majesty from the desert sands above the Nile?

Nor is the question solely one of my personal credit. My statue also honors the people of Rhodes for their heroic resistance to the forces of lawless greed and tyrannical power. It honors them for proving that, in this world of sprawling empires and royal rapacity, the spirit of free, self-governing Hellenes, living under laws that they themselves have made, still lives.

With the ever-widening spread of letters and libraries in the world, it has become the fashion for men of mark to set down their personal recollections. Therefore, lest the honor due my city-state and my statue wither like an anemone in the summer sun, I shall write an account of the deadly struggle that led up to the construction of the Colossus. Perhaps when, as the Chaldeans prophesy, Rhodes shall have sunk back into the sea which gave her birth, this memoir shall still be copied by scribbling slaves, and the glory of Chares the Lindian and of the city which he adorned shall live on in the minds of men.

Sixteen years after the death of the divine Alexander of Macedon, I returned to the Isle of the Three Cities from seven years' study abroad.

These were restless times. The Successors still contended over the corpse of Alexander's empire, none being strong enough to possess himself of the whole, none willing to content himself with less. Kasandros ruled Macedonia; Lysimachos governed Thrace; Antigonos held sway over Anatolia and Syria; Ptolemaios held Egypt; and Seleukos controlled Babylonia. As they shamelessly pursued their selfish interests, the world resounded to the tramp of armored men. Great cities were sacked and burnt by mercenary hordes, and the flames that consumed them were reflected redly in the scarlet streams that ran through the streets.

Few of the city-states of Hellas retained their independence, however ardently they connived, dodged, and sought by secret plot and frantic flattery to fend off the Macedonian warlords. But my beloved Rhodes, though briefly invested with a Macedonian garrison in the days of Alexander, now stubbornly maintained its liberty. Although, in the first war of the Successors, the Macedonian general Attalos, of Eumenes' faction, had attacked us, our small but superbly trained navy had roundly trounced him.

On a fine summer morn in the second year of the 118th Olympiad, the trading ship *Galatea*, of Kition in Cyprus, entered the harbor of Rhodes. Standing on the cargo-cluttered deck and braced against the roll by leaning against an oil jar, I watched the sailors furl the yellow sail and put out the oars. Slowly we pulled around the North Mole, which shields the Little Harbor from Boreas, and steered for the quays.

Before me lay the City of Roses. Red-roofed houses, with gleaming whitewashed walls, rose tier upon tier, like the curving seats of a theater. Along the waterfront, emerald palms waved languid fronds in the gentle breeze, while farther back the dark green spearheads of cypresses stood in soldierly rows. On the left, in the middle distance, rose the tawny slopes of the akropolis, crowned by the golden-marble temple of Helios-Apollon, our ancestor and tutelary deity.

Above all glowed the bright blue bowl of the luminous Rhodian sky. Perhaps the brilliance of the colors made my eyes smart; perhaps it was the sight of my homeland that brought the tears, in spite of the fact that I had embarked unwillingly, brought to heel by my father's threat to cut off all support.

Beside me, Zenon said: "It looks more like a painting than an authentic city. The gods grant that the warlords destroy it not."

Zenon was a tall, swart, stoop-shouldered, gangling young Phoenician of my own age, with a great hooked beak of a nose. He was returning home to Kition from a trading voyage to Argos. We chatted as fellow travelers will, although to tell the truth I found him a dour and somber companion.

Bemusedly, I replied: "Yes, Protogenes the artist used to say that, given the colors of Rhodes, what painter would look elsewhere for a background? Can't you see a colossal statue of Alexander, like the one I have dreamt of building, towering over the waterfront?"

"I can imagine a colossal statue readily enough, but why of Alexander?"

"Why not? For all that he was a little fellow, didn't he achieve the greatest deeds of any mortal since the beginning of time?"

Zenon spat over the rail. "Such as massacring and enslaving the Tyrians? You are part Phoenician yourself; you should weigh such monstrous crimes before ascribing godhood to that backwoods butcher."

"I don't approve of all that he did; but, if not Alexander, whom? Who is great enough to stand beside him?"

Zenon shrugged. "I am neither artist nor historian."

My slave Kavaros leaned against the rail, moodily tugging his long red mustache. He was a Kelt, one of those tall, pale-faced, warlike barbarians who, swarming out of the trackless northern forests, have overrun the Getic country and raided deeply into Thrace and Macedonia. He turned his head to say:

"Ah, if I was only a free man, young master, I would be finding that city as beautiful as you do. Why do you not let me work a bit for myself in my off time, now? I would soon be buying myself back, so you would not be the loser at all."

"We tried that on the mainland," said I sharply. "As soon as you had a few drachmai, you either gave it away to beggars or got drunk and went around breaking people's heads, and I had to pay your fines. Is all the gear packed?"

"It is that, sir."

We tied up to a quay. I thanked the captain for a safe voyage and said to Kavaros:

"Let's get the gear ashore. Take that end of the chest."

A sculptor cannot travel light. The box with my hammers, chisels, gouges, rasps, files, knives, modeling tools, calipers, scales, square, plumb bob, brushes, and whetstones weighed nearly three talents.[1] There were also our bags of clothes and effects and a special workstand that my fellow pupil Eutychides and I had invented, with a top pivoted to turn like a potter's wheel, so that the sculptor could spin his model any way he liked instead of trotting round and round his stand.

Kavaros raised his end of the chest with a grunt, his great arm muscles rippling. "A pity it is, sir, that you could not have picked a profession like the gentleman in Athens who collects butterflies. Your gear would make easier carrying, I am thinking."

I helped Kavaros to carry the stuff down the gangplank. A sculptor cannot be snobbish about using his hands. Kavaros set down his end of the chest on his toes and clove the luminous Rhodian air with a howl. While he cursed in Keltic, I sought for bearers, knowing Kavaros to be useless in any mission that called for chaffering.

Many dockside loafers lounged in the sunshine, but none offered himself. I suppose our liturgies, whereby the rich are made to feed the poor, are better than the class warfare that once ravaged the island. But it does give us a group of idlers who will not work though work be proffered.

I accosted a pair with a carrying pole. Doubtless my Argive tunic made them take us for strangers, for one said:

1 A talent = about 60 pounds.

"Five drachmai will do, young sir."

I let my temper boil over. "Dog-faced temple thieves!" I shouted. "D'you think that as a stranger I'm fair game?" I laid on my strongest Rhodian Doric, the dialect of Lindos, and after a bit of bargaining they cut the price in half.

When the chest had been lashed to the pole, I said: "Kavaros, pick up the rest and follow me."

Zenon was at my elbow. "Are you taking me to your cousin's house as you promised, O Chares?"

"Certainly. Come along."

The Phoenician tipped the watchman to ward his cargo against pilferage and followed us like some melancholy marsh bird. We picked our way among bales and bundles and jars of many shapes and hues, which littered the flagstones of the waterfront: oil, honey, and marble from Attika, pitch from Macedonia, salt fish from Byzantion, cheese from Bithynia, nuts and rare woods from Pontos, wool from Miletos, figs from Syria, dates from Babylonia, raw silk from India, spices from Arabia, and papyrus, linen, and wheat from Egypt.

We crowded through the fortified gate in the harbor wall and passed on into the city. A broad thoroughfare, wide enough for a four-horse chariot, led from harbor to marketplace. It was thronged by a mixed multitude: bearded Phoenicians in bright-hued kilts, jerseys, and little round caps; clean-shaven Egyptians in white linen; Syrians in tall spiral hats and shimmering robes; men with the long hair and flapping trews of the sunrise lands; slaves of all shapes and hues, from Keltic pallor to Ethiopian black. And, of course, the native Rhodians, in cloaks and shirts of sober hue, pacing sedately and punctuating their rolling periods with graceful gestures.

"*Phy!*" said Zenon. "I hate crowds."

"Oh?" said I. "I like them. I like anything with color and contrast."

Instead of heading straight for home, I went first, at Zenon's behest, to the house of my mother's cousin. Giskon and his brother Pymiathon, in Cyprus, were shipowners, in whose ships my father imported most of the copper and tin for his foundry.

We found Giskon amid his accounts. I said: "Rejoice, O Giskon! Do you remember me?"

My kinsman raised his bushy black brows. "Certainly, Chares. Have you been away?"

He roared with laughter at my expression, jumped up, and came around the table to hug me like a great bald bear. "Don't take it so hard, boy. I knew you would be home soon. Let's look at you. It's a shame you never grew any larger."

I hid my vexation at this remark, for I was touchy about my size. Giskon went on:

"And handsome as a god! Watch yourself, or every boy-lover in Rhodes will be chasing you."

"Never fear. I don't care for those games."

"Thank the gods for that! But, with your size, you might not be the one to decide."

"Indeed?" I took his swart, hairy paw in mine. "I can handle most men of half again my own weight." I squeezed.

"*Io!*" he cried, wringing his hand. "Wrestling with clay and marble has given you a grip like that of the serpents of Laokoön."

"I've also been trained in the Argive mode of wrestling. It sometimes comes in useful with middle-aged admirers."

"Good boy! Will you tarry for a bite and a swallow of wine?"

"I thank you, but I must get on home. I only stopped to present Zenon of Kition, who asked to make your acquaintance."

"Rejoice!" said Giskon. "Whom in Kition do we know in common?"

"I am the son of Mnaseas the trader," said Zenon, "of the firm of Mnaseas and Demeas."

"My brother does business with them all the time," said Giskon. "Use my house as your own while you are here." He turned to me. "Chares, will you be free the evening of the day after tomorrow?"

"As far as I know. Why, what is doing, cousin?"

"My dinner club meets here that night, and I should like you to be my guest."

"You're very kind, Giskon. I shall be there."

As I departed, the voices of Giskon and Zenon rang out in the harsh sounds of the Punic tongue. They had spoken Greek out of politeness, although in fact I know enough Phoenician to get along with. I resented my Phoenician blood in a way, because it greatly diminished my chances of ever attaining full citizenship; although, paradoxically, I liked my Phoenician kinsmen better than my father's people. Punic influence has always been strong in Rhodes, ever since the settlements of Kadmos and other Phoenician chiefs before the Trojan War.

In the marketplace, as of yore, hucksters cried their wares from folding booths amid the statues and memorials; businessmen chaffered; politicians orated; sophists lectured; idlers gossiped; and charlatans beguiled. I paused to look once more upon Lysippos' great bronze of the sun god driving his four-horse chariot across a copper cloud. It was love of that statue, now green with the patina of years, that had led me to seek out Lysippos for my teacher.

We breasted the slope of one of the narrow cobbled streets that run back from the marketplace, where business establishments give way to a mixture of small shops and middle-class residences. The sounds of hammer and saw in the workshops mingled with the whir of querns and the clack of looms in the dwellings.

My route took me past the shop of Makar the stonecutter. Although other artists looked down upon Makar as a mere mechanic, I esteemed him, for he had taught me the rudiments of stonecutting and had set my feet upon the path to the practice of sculpture. He was there in the yard before his shop, a dwarfish brown figure, working on a kind of marble bowl. Another was being roughed out by one of his slaves, while a third, gleaming whitely, stood finished atop a marble post.

"Be of good health, O Makar!" I said.

"O Chares!" he cried. "Welcome home! When I heard you were apprenticing under Lysippos, I thought you'd sure stay on the mainland."

I smiled. "Why compete with the greatest sculptor of the age on his own grounds?"

"I would think he'd have taken you for his successor."

"No, Lysippos has three strapping sons, all sculptors, and he naturally favors his own kin. But now that I've mastered his methods, I will put them into practice here. The art shall be revolutionized."

"I suppose you're one of these new realists, who carves old beggar women instead of immortal gods?"

"More than that, O best one. Lysippos and his brother have invented a new method of casting. You'll be struck dead with astonishment when I tell you about it, but now I must get along home." I started to leave but paused to look into the finished marble bowl. Its milky inner surface was divided into zones by inscribed lines, and a bronze pointer jutted from one side out over the center of the depression. "What is this?"

"It's a new kind of sundial," said Makar. "I make them for a Babylonian refugee, who sells them to rich Rhodians."

"Very interesting; I must know this fellow. When does the Artists' Guild meet next?"

"Tomorrow evening, as it happens. Shall I put you up for membership?"

"I was about to ask you to. I have a letter of commendation from Lysippos, and I can explain the new method of bronze casting at this time. These ought to get me in, don't you think?"

"Oh, sure. Be at the Town Hall at sundown."

I plodded on up the hillside. Once I lost my way. Although I was born in Lindos, my father had removed to Rhodes while I was yet a small boy. Still, boyhood memories fade in seven long years, and there had been much new building hereabouts since the great flood, which had wrought much ruin three years before I left home.

"Is it that the young master does not know his own country any more?" said Kavaros. "Or have we come to the wrong city?"

"Hold your tongue, you impudent rogue!" I said.

"Now, sir, you will never—"

"I said to stop!" I shouted, aiming a cuff.

Kavaros jerked his head, so that the blow glanced off with little effect, and muttered something into his mustache. I cast about until I picked up the smoke plume from the foundry. From then on, the clang of the bronzesmiths' hammers guided me home.

My father had written that he had bought the house next door to the foundry, so that he no longer had to sleep over the smithy. It was an imposing dwelling, covered with fine white plaster and as large as those of many full citizens. I gave my name to the porter, who called:

"Mistress! A man here says he is your son!"

My mother, a small, dark, birdlike woman, flew into my arms in a whirl of draperies, asking a hundred questions at once. She sent the porter to the foundry to fetch the master.

I was a little nervous about meeting my father, as our last correspondence had been far from friendly. However, his welcome was hearty enough. He was a big, brown-haired man, upright, sensible, determined, and hard-driving.

When I had freed myself from my parents' embraces and paid off the bearers, I followed my mother and father into the court. The house had a fine interior. The larger rooms opening on the court had windows with shutters in which were set sheets of Kappadokian talc, to let in the light even when the shutters were closed.

The court itself was filled by an elaborate flower garden, vivid with roses of scarlet and yellow.

"What's all this?" I asked, indicating the garden.

My father explained: "Oh, growing flowers is the latest fashion. A Persian woman brought it to Rhodes. Your mother won the prize last spring for the best display. You should see it when the violets and narcissi and hyacinths are in bloom. Is this fellow with the horrible red mustache the slave you insisted on buying?"

"Yes, sir. Kavaros is a Tektosagian from beyond the Istros. Don't ask him to do any task that calls for delicacy, for he doesn't know his own strength. Kavaros, these are my parents, Nikon and Elissa. Obey them as you would me."

Kavaros nodded with his lordly air. "It is pleased that I am to meet you, sir and madam. Indeed and your son is a fine young gentleman, and it has been a pleasure to save the life of him."

"When did you save my life?" I demanded.

"Do you not remember, master dear? The last time was on the ship, when we had the little bit of a storm, and I stood by to catch you if you were swept overboard."

I laughed. "Off to quarters with you. The porter will show you where to go."

I knew it would be useless to pin down Kavaros' lies one by one. If I explained that during the storm he had been too seasick to think of saving lives, he would bring up some other tale, equally false. Nor did beating seem to improve him.

"An impudent brute," said my father. "Kelts are better off in mines than in private houses. They're apt to get moody and slay themselves or their masters."

"I can manage him," I said. "If one appeals to his warrior's pride, his strength can accomplish wonders."

My father grunted. "I don't hold with this profligate modern idea that every middle-class youth should have his own slave before he's old enough to shave. I never had one when I was your age."

"As I told you, I need him in the practice of my art. I'm not big enough to move all those heavy weights by myself. Besides, at a pound and a half he was a good bargain. A whole war band was captured on the Macedonian frontier."

"More of that later. Now we must have a banquet to celebrate your return. How about tomorrow night?"

"The Guild meets then, Father. I told Makar I should be there, as I wish to get started at once in my profession."

My father's stern, strong-boned countenance darkened. "Are you determined to go ahead with this sculptural folly?"

I said: "You don't understand, Father. I have a mission."

"To reform the art of sculpture in Rhodes?"

"Why, that's part of it. How did you know?"

He gave me a wry smile. "At your age I wanted to reform the craft of bronze founding."

"Now you mock me. I will not only reform the art of sculpture; I'll do much more than that." I shook a fist. "Do you remember all those abandoned villains, Hippon and the rest, who tormented me when I was a puny little boy? They shall see who's the bigger man! And do you think we are forever barred from full citizenship because mother's mother was a Phoenician? Just watch!"

My mother said: "Chares, don't take life so hard!"

"I'll take it as I'm made to take it!"

My father, in tones of badly tried patience, said: "Let me explain, son. If you want to be accepted among the best people in Rhodes, having no ancient family to boast of, you need two things: money and well-placed friends. The business, well handled, will furnish you with money; but you'll have to spend years learning to run it. As for friends, you have shown little talent for making them; though, if you're as clever as you think you are, I suppose you can learn."

"I care nothing for money or friends," I growled. "Someday I will put up such a magnificent statue that people will have to respect me whether they wish to or not."

"That's an idle boast, I fear. You cannot compel people to like what they are determined not to like. However, we're forgetting our feast. Shall we set the following night then?"

"I'm sorry, Father, but I promised Giskon to attend a meeting of his club."

"Oh, to the crows with you! You fill your days with engagements before you even see your poor parents."

"I deeply regret it, Father. It wasn't very thoughtful of me."

"Never mind, I cannot be angry with you today. We'll make it tonight—you have no engagements tonight, I trust?"

"No, sir."

"Good! I'll send Sosias out with a list of my friends. Elissa, find out what the cook will need."

While my father waited for the slave to bring him writing materials, I asked: "What sort of eating club does Giskon belong to?"

"The Seven Strangers. Originally there were seven members of different nationalities. Although the group is larger now, it is still in the main a club of mixed foreigners. If your taste runs to tales of distant lands and exotic peoples, by all means go to the Seven Strangers."

Five of the six guests at the banquet were my father's long-time friends, as he was a man with a few faithful cronies rather than a wide circle of acquaintances. One was my mother's cousin Giskon, whom I had already seen that day.

Another was Genetor, of the Kameiran tribe, who owned a deposit of bituminous earth that was mined for the use of vine growers. He was a stout man, sumptuously clad, with a grave, formal manner. Though his big-jowled face was that of a man of sixty, he had a fine head of curly hair, as glossy black as my own, which closer inspection showed to be a wig. The lamplight winked on the golden rings upon his fingers.

Other guests were Tryphon son of Anax, a visitor who owned a silk factory in Kôs, and Damophilos, a full citizen and naval officer, just in from a cruise. Damophilos, a small, lean, beak-nosed man, was talking when I joined the group:

"We searched the coasts in both directions for a day's row and stopped a score of merchantmen, but no sign of them did we find."

"Excuse me, sir," I said, "but for whom were you looking?"

"The book thieves. Didn't you know? Three days ago there occurred a most daring robbery. The library was broken into and all its books stolen."

"Library?"

Genetor enlightened me: "Five years ago some of our citizens decided to build a public library. They assembled a nice collection, too: over two hundred scrolls, and they raised enough endowment to hire a full-time librarian. I may say that my contribution was not among the least."

"Last month," continued Damophilos, "a Phoenician ship put in, bringing goods to trade. On this ship were two men calling themselves booksellers. They went around to the houses of the richer citizens and sold them several rare volumes. These booksellers also visited the public library and asked many questions.

"When they had completed their business, they departed without arousing suspicion. Then came this burglary. The navy was ordered out, but to no avail."

Tryphon of Kôs spoke up: "I had not heard of this. Did you know that the same thing happened in Kôs, several ten-days earlier?"

"No!" we cried. "Tell us!"

"The tale is much the same as yours. The two booksellers were a Hellene and an Egyptian."

Damophilos said: "Here one was a Hellene, I think—a big, broad-shouldered man, almost as blond as a Kelt, speaking Kilikian Greek. The other may have been an Egyptian; at least he was very dark and spoke with a curious accent. A small, curly-haired, wiry fellow, like Chares here, with a scar on his chin."

"Yes," said the Koan. "First came the visit of the booksellers; then, a month later, the rape of the library. I fear that with even slaves and paupers learning to read, book stealing is becoming one of the finer arts."

"That is what comes of giving foreigners such a free run of our city," grumped Genetor. "Between those immoral transparent dresses that our friend Tryphon sells, and robbery, corruption, and inflation everywhere, and women demanding the rights of men, we live in a degenerate age."

"At least," said Damophilos, "Tryphon's dresses will keep men so busy looking at the women that they will not have time for reading. So the demand for books will slacken, and the price will fall."

Giskon laughed "Such knowledge of money is a Phoenician trade secret. If it get out, we shall be ruined. But let the stripling talk; after all, the feast is for him. O Chares, what can you tell us of the doings of Demetrios son of Antigonos?"

I said: "The last I heard, he had settled in Athens after driving out Kasandros' men. He was visiting the historic sights, talking with philosophers, and making merry."

"I hear he is a man of lewd character," said Genetor.

"I don't know," I said. "They say that he likes a joke, a wench, and a skin of wine; that is to say, he is not dedicated to war and conquest like another Alexander. But he is withal accounted a most able and formidable general."

"So? One cannot make a lance head from a lettuce nor a soldier from a pleasure-loving debauchee."

I started to protest this harsh description of Demetrios when Damophilos broke in: "But what is he doing now?"

"Before I left Argos," I said, "I heard a rumor that Antigonos had ordered his son back to Asia."

Genetor said: "We must pray to the Sun that he leave Rhodes alone. Let us hope that my many costly offerings will incline the god in our favor."

"He'll loose the polluted pirates," said Damophilos, "just when we are getting them under control."

Giskon added: "Thrice evil to evildoers! This bodes ill for Cyprus. Antigonos has had his one eye on the isle ever since Ptolemaios seized it."

"You can always earn your bread in Rhodes," said another.

"Easier said than done," replied Giskon. "You natives won't let a foreigner like me set up in trade here."

Another guest spoke: "If you would shave off that bush, Giskon, and learn to speak without that foul Punic accent, we could pass you off as a Hellene."

Damophilos: "We might even contrive a pedigree for you, showing descent from Herakles or Helios-Apollon."

"Let us not play fast and loose with the gods," said Genetor. "Life is risky enough without antagonizing the unseen powers."

"I doubt if they bother with mortals," said Damophilos with a yawn. "At least one cannot see any divine pattern to modern politics. You might as well address your prayers to Lady Luck and have done with it."

"That is probably why the gods have withdrawn," said Genetor. "With so many turning away from them for Eastern cults and godless philosophies, they might indeed lose interest in men. What the world needs is a great spiritual awakening, a return to the faith of our fathers.... That reminds me," he said, looking at me. "Chares, my cousin Nereus is high priest of the temple of the Sun. He has a vacancy on his Board of Sacrificers, for which he seeks a sober young tribesman. The citizens' sons, he says, are too spoilt and immoral, while most tribesmen are chary of taking on a responsibility that carries no pay. Are you a registered member of the Lindian tribe?"

My father put in: "He was registered before he left."

"Well, then, would you be interested?"

I said: "That's kind of you, sir; but—"

"But what?"

I could not see myself taking many hours from my art for unpaid rites in which I did not believe. However, that did not seem quite the way to put it. "It's—it's a matter of conscience, sir."

"Conscience? Do not tell me that you, too, have succumbed to this modern unbelief!"

"I had my eyes opened in Hellas, O Genetor. I heard the lectures of Pyrron, who shows the folly of all dogma. I listened to Evemeros, who proves that the gods are but mortals whose deeds have been magnified...."

My father, who shared the couch with me, jabbed my back with his thumb. I would have burst into angry words, but my guardian spirit checked my tongue. I mumbled something about my faith's having been unsettled by travel.

"Ah, youth!" said Genetor, lying back on his couch. "Always running after novelties, always seeking to cast aside the wisdom of their forebears. You will no doubt settle down in time, as the rest of us have; especially when you acquire property. There is nothing like a little hard-earned wealth to give a sound conservative point of view. I know."

I would have given this stuffy old dogmatist an argument, but I felt my father's brown eyes boring into me.

Then the wine was brought and the entertainers came in. These were three girls, one of whom played the double flute while another twanged the Rhodian sambuke and the third danced, wriggling like an octopus on a fisherman's spear. They wore shifts of Koan silk, through which every rosy nipple and raven pubic hair transpired as plain as day. Damophilos cried:

"O Tryphon, this is some of your doing! Who will lay a bet as to what these girls are wearing? How about you, Genetor? We'll make them strip to settle the wager."

"Thank you, but I am not a gambling man," said Genetor. "I prefer sound investments. Besides, my eyesight is not what it was."

"Nor some of your other powers, forsooth," said the naval officer, "or you would show more interest in these little lovelies. Speaking of which, I know a man who claims that the eating of sea food has no effect on the love life of the middle-aged."

"By our lady Persephonê!" said Tryphon. "Then have we been stuffing ourselves with oysters and squids in vain all these years?"

Watching the dancer's supple body through the sheer film of silk, I was moved to desire. But I forebore, as it had hardly been decent to lay a proposal before her openly. My respectable father gave respectable parties, at which nobody vomited or punched a slave or tried to rape the entertainers or seduce his fellow diners. Nor did we auction off the flute girl, a pretty little thing named Doris who belonged to a girlmonger on the waterfront.

The party was, however, merry enough, for a gathering of Rhodians always finds plenty to talk about. We drank from Rhodian pots in which aromatic herbs had been steeped in water before the wine was poured in. This precaution is supposed to arrest intoxication, though I have never seen it stop a man from getting drunk if he really put his mind to it.

When the company had gone, I burst out: "Father, why wouldn't you let me speak my piece to Genetor? Am I not a free Hellene, entitled to say what I please?"

"Son," he said, "you may hold what opinions you like for all of me. But this man is your future father-in-law."

"*What?*"

"Yes, it's all arranged but the signing. Genetor wanted to look you over first."

"Who's the girl?"

"His daughter Io, and you needn't look as if you'd seen a headless specter in a graveyard at midnight. Io is no Gorgon but a thoroughly nice, attractive girl."

"But who said I wanted to wed?"

"Now, Chares, don't be difficult. I hoped you had outgrown that headstrong streak that used to plague us so."

My mother said: "Everybody knows that a man of your age should be married. She's just the perfect age—fifteen—and Genetor is rich."

"As he never wearies of reminding us," I said.

My father added: "He may soon be admitted to full citizenship, and he's related to several citizens' families. We're lucky. We are after all self-made men and tradesmen, and only by such an alliance can we hope to be accepted by gentlemen."

"I tell you I will not marry at all!"

"Why not? Are you in love with some mainland woman? Or some man?"

"No, I'm in love with nothing but my art."

My mother said: "Oh, Chares, what has that to do with your being married, like any decent young man? You can't carve and cast every hour of the day."

My father added: "Moreover, if you insist on going ahead with this impractical sculptural career, instead of helping me to manage the foundry as you ought, you'll need a good marriage connection more than ever."

"You shall see. When I have achieved fame, I may think of marrying, but for now I'm convinced that I shall go faster in my craft without the comforts and distractions of domesticity."

This idea I had picked up in Athens from Pyrron of Elis, the skeptical philosopher, when he lectured there during my first year of study abroad. Once I had asked Pyrron if there was any general rule by which a man might achieve great deeds. Pyrron rubbed his chin in his absent way—he was a tall, gangling fellow of middle age, so woolly-minded that he was always tripping over things if his friends did not warn him—and replied:

"I suspect that a certain amount of solitude and discomfort enters into the formula." When another student asked if this precluded marriage, Pyrron rejoined:

"I am sure that bachelorhood is a help. You know what Diogenes said of the time to marry: for young men, not yet; for older men, never. On the other hand, many great men have been married; whereas I, who hardly rank as great, have never been. However, I would not advise the seeker after greatness to wed a Greek girl in any case."

"Why not?" I had asked.

"They are too subdued by our one-sided rules of familial life, so that there is no stimulation in their company. A man's wife is chosen for him, and serves him well or badly, but he finds his companionship among men or professional entertainers. Now, in some other lands, such as Egypt and Persia, the women have more spirit. For instance, when I was out east with Alexander fifteen years ago, there was a lovely Persian maid. . . ." Pyrron sighed and changed the subject.

My father, however, stuck to his subject like a limpet to a rock, beating his large, work-hardened fist into his palm. "But what shall your parents do for descendants? I'm a nobody; and, besides, I married into a mixed family—now, now, Elissa, I am *not* criticizing your Phoenician relatives. Some of my best friends are Phoenicians. I'm merely pointing out why I can never be a full citizen; nor, I should think, can Chares. But if we handle our tiller with care and craft, there's no reason why his children should not attain the franchise.

"That means," he went on, "you must step into my shoes when I'm gone—and, of course, beget children to succeed you. I've worked like a mine slave to build up the foundry and give you a good start. If I saw you well settled, learning the business and rearing healthy children, I shouldn't feel I had wasted my life.

"Moreover, since poor little Nikon died, you are our only hope. It is your duty..."

The dispute raged on for an hour, with shouts, threats, and tears. I refused to yield a digit from my stand.

"Oh, plague!" said my father at last. "We cannot argue all night. At least, Chares, promise me not to antagonize Genetor. When the lusts of the flesh come upon you, you may change your mind."

I said: "The whorehouse will take care of my lusts and steal less time from my art."

"But promise not to speak out of turn to Genetor!"

"For you I will. I'll treat the pompous old peacock like a piece of Egyptian glass!"

The next day my first concern was to find quarters for a studio. My father, when he saw that I was determined to go ahead with sculpture, said:

"Why don't you work at home or in the foundry? Then you could still help me out when I need you."

"No, Father, it wouldn't do. A sculptor must have not only lots of light but also space in which to stand back from his work. If he sees it at arm's length only, he finds when he has finished that his warrior looks like a monkey and his athlete looks like a frog. And the house and the foundry are much too cluttered and cut up by walls. What I need is some old house out on the edge of town, where I can knock out most of one wall."

"I daresay such places exist," said my father, "but you'll have to pay for any such house yourself. Since you won't help me, there's no reason why I should buy or rent another house for you, and I cannot afford it anyway."

"That doesn't worry me. I shall pay my own way as soon as I get some commissions. But I must get a commission first and then start hunting for a studio. Who is the municipal architect?"

"Diognetos. He lives not far from here. Sosias can show you."

Diognetos was a tall, thin, elderly man, with little red veins in his skin and a long gray beard such as few Hellenes wear today save philosophers and back-country shepherds.

"Yes, yes, my boy, I know your father," he said. "A fine man, Nikon Charetos. So you desire a commission from the city, eh? What of your qualifications?"

"I have a letter from Lysippos of Sikyon, under whom I studied."

"I have heard strange things of Lysippos and his brother. It is said that they make casts of living faces and use them for models."

"Why, yes, they do. It's their own invention and a very ingenious one. What about it?"

Diognetos pursed his thin lips. "Ingenious though it be, it is not *art*. It is reducing sculpture to mere mechanical craftsmanship, such as any clever Asiatic slave can turn his hand to. No, a letter from Lysippos is no recommendation to me. Have you executed any sculptures since your return?"

"No, sir, I arrived only yesterday."

"Then why do you not make some samples in clay to give me an idea of your work?"

I explained about my need for a proper studio, and how I had to have a commission before I could afford to rent and fit out such an establishment.

"*Phy!*" he said. "A real sculptor can work in a corner of a dungeon cell. If you think you need a Persian palace to work in, you have chosen the wrong trade. Then, have you joined the Guild? I should deem that a good recommendation. Our artists are shrewd critics of each other's work."

"Why, I plan to attend their meeting tonight, and Makar will propose me. It will be a mere formality. There is no question of their not admitting me when they hear what I have to offer."

"Indeed? And what have you to offer?"

"I can teach a whole new method of bronze casting, invented by Lysippos and Lysistratos."

"What newfangled nonsense is this?" growled Diognetos, looking like an aged eagle to whom a rabbit was being saucy.

Irked, I spoke in a loud, emphatic tone. "It's an advance on the piece mold of clay. With a model of clay, you must either dig the clay out of the extremities of the mold, often marring the mold, or else failing to get all the clay out, leaving a defect in the cast; or you must make your mold in sections, and in a free-standing figure of any real complication you can never break the mold down into enough pieces. And there is always the difficulty of building up cores.

"Lysippos' method gets around all these difficulties. He makes a model of sandy clay, a little smaller than the final piece. Then he brushes melted beeswax over it until it is built out beyond the surfaces that the final bronze is to have. He works on the waxen surface, shaving the piece down to size and inscribing surface detail.

"Then he applies the sand of the mold to the waxen surface, leaving pipes to admit the molten bronze and allow the air to escape."

"I see nothing new so far," said Diognetos. "Wax has been used for casting patterns since ancient times."

"Ah, but wait! When the mold is finished, instead of taking the mold off the model or digging the model out of the mold bit by bit, he puts the entire thing in an oven. The wax melts and runs out through pipes called sprues, which the sculptor has provided, leaving a thin but continuous space between model and mold. Then this vacant mold is taken out and inverted. The sculptor pours the molten bronze into the sprues, filling this empty space. When the mold is broken off the outside, and the core broken up and shaken out of the inside, he has a hollow casting, perfect save for rods of bronze where the sprues and air vents were. These have to be sawn off and the surfaces finished by hand."

Diognetos had become more hostile with each sentence. Now he shook his fist and burst out:

"Oh, tricks, technical tricks! A plague upon them! That sort of thing is killing the spirit of the arts. A true artist should work without casts and models and measurements. Do not tell me about your wonderful Sikyonians! Mere mechanics, I deem them. Go to a real sculptor if you can find one, somebody who preserves the true spirit of Pheidias and Praxiteles. Learn from him not to lean on tricks of technique.

"At least, if you will take an older man's advice, do not try to bully your way into the Guild by boasting of your technical sleights. And now, if you will excuse me..."

I left Diognetos' house in a fury. Kavaros, who had waited outside, said: "Does the young master be angry, now?"

"I certainly am," I said. "The old dung-eater put me off. He even had the insolence to suggest that I needed another apprenticeship!"

"Shall we break his neck?" said the Kelt, little savage lights dancing in his blue eyes. "I am thinking his head would look fine over your door."

"No, you bloodthirsty savage! Come along."

"It is like the time my great-grandfather called on the king of the Elves," said Kavaros, plunging into another of his many tales of fascinating if improbable adventures, which he employed to put me in a good humor:

"Gargantyos—that was my great-grandfather's name—went into the king's castle and asked for the king's daughter as his bride, for she was more beautiful nor any mortal woman. But the king of the Elves was not pleased. 'A mortal asking for my darling daughter? Be off, you impudent rogue, you!' he said, putting out his tongue at my ancestor to show how he despised him.

"'So that is your Elvish courtesy?' said my great-grandfather. And he caught hold of that tongue and with one jerk turned the king of the Elves inside out. 'Now, my fine lad, we will talk of plans for the wedding,' said he.

"Of course, the king of the Elves was even less pleased than he had been before. He uttered a terrible spell at my ancestor, to turn him into a spider. But, what with being inside out and all, the spell came out backwards and turned a spider into my great-grandfather instead. Then there were two of them, and before the confabulation could go further, they had to find out which was the real one.

"Now, to a Keltic gentleman there is only one way to settle such a question. The two Gargantyoi pulled out their swords and had at each other. But, because they were exactly alike, they fought for three days and three nights without being able to break through each other's guard at all. By then the swords were so notched that they would have made better saws than swords; and, to tell the truth, one of them was used as a saw in building the magical ship *Nadon's Chariot*, which I will be telling you about someday.

"They would be fighting still, except that, when they paused to catch their breath, the king of the Elves called time out for refreshments. 'For,' he said, 'this is the finest fight I have seen since my father fought his shadow, that the witch Morrigana had put a spell on, and I do not want it to stop because the fighters are after getting tired.'

"But when the cakes and wine were brought, one of the Gargantyoi would not eat them. Instead, he leaped upon a cricket that was creeping by and ate it. So the king of the Elves knew that this one was really a spider, and he said to my forebear—the real one—'Quick, Gargantyos darling, turn me back right side out, so I can reverse the spell, and you will be marrying my dear Brigantia as fast as I can fetch the Druid.' So my ancestor caught hold of him by the spleen—which was on the outside, naturally—and jerked him back right side out. And that is how I come to have one part in eight of Elf blood in my veins. And the moral is: Do not despise any man until he has done something despicable, or you may have to own you are wrong."

When I got home, I told my father of Diognetos' refusal and urged him to think again about renting me space for a studio. But he was firm.

"For seven years," he said, "we've been sending you money whenever you wrote that you were short, even though we often disapproved of how you spent it. First, you hadn't been in Athens two years when you left the professors recommended to you and rushed off to Sikyon to take up sculpture under Lysippos. Then you bought that great lout of a slave. Well, now that you're a man, no longer to be bent to your parents' will, you can take care of yourself. If you fall foul of the one man in Rhodes whom you ought to treat with extra care, I don't see why I should pay for your folly. Besides, we cannot afford it."

"It's not my fault if that stupid old Cyprian ox—"

"That will do, Chares. Diognetos may be conservative, but stupid he is not. I've dealt with him and know."

"Well, then, why not let me tear up all these useless flowers and use that as a working space?"

"You would tear up your mother's flower garden?"

"Why not? It's but a Persian fad that will soon—"

"Hold your tongue! I always told your mother she was spoiling you, and this proves me right. The answer is 'no.'"

He turned his back and returned to the foundry. I ate my midday meal in glowering silence, feeling abused by the world.

I spent the afternoon pacing the court and going over the argument I should present to the Guild, while Kavaros brushed my clothes and blacked my shoes. I could not afford to fail again.

I reached the Town Hall at sunset, being the first to arrive except for Makar. The other members of the Artists' Guild straggled in. Some I knew from aforetime, such as Lykon the sculptor, Glôs the engraver, and Protogenes the painter. Glôs, our fattest member, greeted me:

"Rejoice, old fellow! How are the girls on the mainland?"

I said: "The pickings are poor. They expose so many daughters that the men outnumber the women two to one."

Glôs laughed. "The mainlanders so love their sodomy that they'd never notice the lack of women."

Protogenes, as president, led the Artists' Guild in adoration of the Telchines, the demigods who invented the graphic and plastic arts. Dinner was a typical Rhodian meal of assorted sea foods. A Rhodian gentleman proves his refinement by judicious criticism of each finny or tentacled item, but I could not be bothered. Instead, I made much of my work under Lysippos and Lysistratos.

"I have even," I said, "helped in the building of the world's largest statue."

"What's that?" asked Lykon. He was a broad-shouldered man, a few years older than I, with cold gray eyes in a sharply chiseled face; he had lately been elected herald of the Guild.

"The bronze Zeus at Taras," I said. "It stands forty cubits[2] high and took us nearly two years to complete. Lysippos also made a twen-

2 A cubit = about 1½ feet

ty-cubit bronze Herakles for Taras, but that was before my time. I suppose that, in sheer mass, I've handled a greater weight of material for statuary than all of you together."

"By the Dog!" said Lykon. "How can that be, young man, when we are experienced artists and you are a mere beginner?"

"Why, compute it for yourself. The Tarentine Zeus must weigh over a thousand times as much as a life-sized statue, as it's more than ten times as high."

"Is its skin ten times as thick?" asked Lykon. "That, it seems to me, would make an extravagantly costly construction."

"Not quite, but the difference is made up by the internal bracing needed. Someday I shall build an even bigger statue here in Rhodes."

"So?" said Lykon. "The Tarentine Zeus must be near the practical limit. You'll never erect a bigger one, even if you find some city so mad as to pay for the monstrosity."

"I will, too!" said I, smiting the table. "I'll erect a statue twice as tall as the Tarentine Zeus. You shall see!"

Lykon gave a short, derisive laugh. "I shan't want to be standing nearby when you take the scaffolding away."

Protogenes leaned over. "Boys! You are as silly as the old man and his wife who broke every dish in their house, fighting over the question of what they would have named a child if one had ever been born to them. Wait till Chares gets a contract for his superstatue before you quarrel over its design."

"Well," I said with a shrug that was meant to be magnanimous, "let's agree that mere size is less important than the revolutionary new methods of Lysippos and Lysistratos, which I shall tell you about later."

"Oh, pest!" said Strabon the potter. "Isn't it bad enough that we've got to learn this new Athenian trick of decorating pots with reliefs instead of painting, or get driven out of business, without you upsetting things even more?"

When the meal was over and the wine had been brought, Makar formally introduced me. "Chares will say a few words about his qualifications," quoth he.

I ought to have taken Makar at his word. However, I was still so full of my new ideas that I plunged at once into Lysippos' lost-wax method, in even more detail than I had given Diognetos that morning. I insisted that all the other methods of sculpture had been made obsolete, and that all sculptors would have to come to Lysippos or to those who, like me, had learnt from him.

"Were I mean and niggardly," I said, "I would keep this method secret. Instead, I offer it. to all of you, asking but a reasonable payment for my time in teaching you. I advise you to apply soon, for otherwise you'll find yourselves hopelessly out of date."

Then I went on to tell of the various pieces that I had helped Lysippos with, such as his "Man Scraping Oil from Himself." I fear I enlarged on the part I had played in this work, until one might have thought that I had been the master and Lysippos the apprentice. I also boasted of my architectural and engineering studies in Athens.

So full was I of my message that I did not at first notice that my hearers had begun to squirm with impatience. At length their scowling, yawning, and whispering reminded me that I had been speaking longer than was altogether tactful. I finished my speech with a flourish of Lysippos' letter of commendation.

Somebody muttered: "If that's a few words, the gods protect us from a full-blown address!"

I expected that it would be moved that I be accepted into the Guild; that I be asked to step out while the matter was discussed and voted on; and that then all would be over but the congratulations. Instead, Protogenes stood up and said:

"As it is nearly midnight and too late for further business, I adjourn this meeting. Good night, blessed ones."

"But—" I said. "But what about me?"

Protogenes: "We will take up that matter at some future meeting. If we take any affirmative action, we will let you know."

"Don't hold your breath while waiting," said Lykon.

"Your mortal subjects bid you farewell, O god," said another.

"We shall see you again, we hope—after Protogenes has finished his 'Ialysos,'" said yet another.

This brought a laugh, as Protogenes had been working on his huge picture for six years, and nobody thought he would ever complete it. I said to Makar:

"I'll see you home." When we were out of earshot, I asked: "What's wrong? They seem displeased."

"No wonder!" he said.

"But why?"

"Chares, are you out of your mind?"

"I think not. Why?"

"You come here, a young sprout just out of apprenticeship. You harangue the established artists of Rhodes for three hours, like you was a god teaching the first mortal men how to live civilized. You brag about how good you are and what wonderful things you're going to do. Then you wonder why they don't fall all over themselves welcoming you!"

"I only told them the truth!"

"That may be, but what do you suppose they think of your way of doing it?"

"I don't care what they think. I know my own worth and the value of my innovations, so it is for them to change their thinking, not me mine."

"You might as well say to a piece of clay that won't take the shape you want: 'It's for the clay to obey me, not for me to act humble to it.' But suit yourself. It's your life."

I trudged home in gloomy silence while the stalwart Kavaros walked ahead with his link. He said:

"Master dear, if you would only be listening to good advice, now—"

"Shut up!" I cried and aimed a kick at his shin.

The Kelt moved like a shadow. My kick went wide and caused me to stumble. As I recovered my balance, I heard a snicker. Grasping my walking stick in both hands, I swung. The stick struck Kavaros' shoulder and broke with a loud crack. The link fell to the ground and went out.

"*Ara!*" he said. "That hurt, sir. Someday you will be doing that to a free man and it will not be well for you."

Although I was in a mood to kill anybody who crossed me, the quiet menace in Kavaros' tone made me pause. True, he was not likely to risk death by attacking me. But then, one could never tell with these irrational foreigners, and his execution would do me no good if I were no longer there to enjoy it.

With his usual lack of foresight, Kavaros had not brought any tinder to relight the link, so we groped our way home in darkness.

The next morning my father said: "The porter tells me that you came in after midnight. Your amusements are your own affair, but don't expect me to pay for them."

I told him what had happened, without hiding anything. He sighed. "I fear you learn only by the costliest mistakes, Chares. I wonder that Lysippos ever put up with you."

In fact, the Sikyonian had almost sent me packing thrice. My relations with him had been stormy. I exasperated him by my willfulness and by my insistence that I knew everything, while he goaded me to fury by teasing me about my size.

"Sculpture needs a big man with plenty of brute strength," he would say. "You, boy, would be better off as a dancer."

Or he would twit me about my Phoenician blood, saying: "That is Phoenician work, Chares. A Phoenician is all right if you want somebody to run a bank or sail a ship, but they have no more sense of beauty than a turtle. Having no art of their own, they can only make cheap copies of other nations' art."

I grimly stuck to my task, however, despite Lysippos' gibes. When we parted, he said: "You may make a sculptor yet, Chares my lad, if you do not cause someone to murder you first by that overweening manner."

Now I said: "It's unjust, Father. A man's fate should be determined impersonally, on the basis of his virtues and abilities alone, without regard to all these petty personal likes and dislikes."

My father replied: "Perhaps it should be but it isn't. If they like you, they'll excuse your faults; if they dislike you, they'll overlook your virtues."

"Then they're a lot of stupid fools!"

"Are you only just now learning that? But if they are, you won't change them, not in one lifetime. He wrongly Nature blames who suffers shipwreck twice."

"Well, I seem to have lost all my anchors. I can't get a commission from Diognetos until I can show him some work; I can't work without a studio; and I can't get a studio until I get a commission.

Perhaps I ought to sell Kavaros and hire myself out to turn a stone in a gristmill, or take ship to Aspendos and enlist as a mercenary. I can bear my own oil flask if I must."

"It's not so bad as that," said my father, "even if you're pretty small for soldiering and lack the charm to make a good parasite. You know how to handle bronze. I taught you the elements years ago, and you've had practice with Lysippos. Now I need you. I have a contract for fifty mirrors and a hundred lamps, and the trader is pressing me for delivery."

"Otherwise?"

"Otherwise, out you go. Make up your mind."

I gave in, silently swearing never to forgive my father for thus humbling me; but my grudge against him lasted no more than a day. I awoke Kavaros, who was snoring in a corner of the court.

"Come along," I said. "We're bronze founders after all."

"Eh? But I am trained as a warrior, not as a smith!"

"Who spoke of smithing? There will be plenty of lifting and hauling."

He groaned: "Ah, the black shame of it, that the son of a chief should be worked like an ass!"

"Cats always like to sleep soft. If I can dirty my hands, so can you."

Besides myself and Kavaros and Proteus, the foreman, there were two free workers and four slaves. My father put me under Proteus' orders, warning me:

"Now, son, I will not have you bullying and bossing the slaves as you used to do."

"Did I really?" said I in amazement. My father whistled.

"Oh, all right," I said. "I'll be good."

"And no unauthorized experiments with my equipment, either!"

So I avoided putting on airs to the foundry workers, while they were not so rash as to try any tricks on the owner's son. As a result, we got along well enough; some, in later years, I came to regard as good personal friends.

In such low spirits was I because of my failures that I nearly stayed away from the meeting of the Seven Strangers. My father persuaded me to go, saying:

"When have we given up the war because of losing two skirmishes? Besides, the third try is said to be lucky."

At the end of the first day's toil I washed off the grime for the meeting. It took me so long that I arrived late. Giskon led me in, explaining:

"Any member may be president of the club by giving a dinner to all the other members, and it's my turn. The president may also invite guests. Mine, this time, are you and two of my fellow Punics. After the meal you shall be put to the question."

At my startled look he added: "Oh, you won't be tortured, at least not bodily, though the questions the Strangers ask have made some guests wish for the scourge and rack instead. They will do all they can to embarrass you, and judge your worth by the good humor with which you bear their inquisition."

We reached the andron. Giskon threw a hairy arm about my shoulders and roared:

"Behold my cousin, Chares Nikonos! He's just back from apprenticeship under the greatest sculptor of the age. Or so he says, but you know what liars these Hellenes are. He'll talk your ears off about methods of sculpture, or horrify you with skeptical theories of the gods. We will start at the left. Chares, this is Berosos of Babylon, who makes sundials for birds to bathe in and reads your fortune in the stars."

The Babylonian was a short pudgy fellow a bit older than I, with liquid black eyes and soft brown features. He said:

"May your stars be propitious! Not quite the truth does our host impart, O Chares. If you wish to keep birds from bathing in one of my sundials, you need only to pull the plug from the bottom of the bowl."

"So you'd make me out a liar?" said Giskon. "Go howl! Next we have a man from Egypt, land of mystery and magic, as he never wearies of telling us. He is Onas of Sebennytos, gem cutter by trade and dabbler in the higher mysteries by avocation."

The Egyptian was a tall, powerful man, even darker than the Babylonian, with strong, coarse features. A string of beetle-shaped amulets hung around his neck.

"Life to you, O Chares!" he said. "This scoffing skeptic thinks that, because his mercenary mind is deaf to the deeper secrets of the universe, they do not exist."

"Next," said Giskon, "swilling away in Scythian fashion at my best Byblian, is Sarpedon, a Lykian. The fellow in the beard and the trousers is Gobryas of Synnada. He is a Persian who ruled an estate in Phrygia until Antigonos One-eye thought it would look better on one of his Macedonian officers. We all hate Gobryas because his wife has infected our wives with this passion for flower gardens.

"Next, this prim-looking person is Vindex of Rome—Quintus Iunius Vindex, a trader. They have some barbarous custom there of bearing three names apiece."

"That is in Italy, isn't it?" I said.

"So they tell me," said Giskon. "It seems that the Romans have lately extended their sway over much of the central peninsula, and even over the Greek city of Naples."

"Foreigners ruling Hellenes?" I said.

The Roman, a slight, bearded man, said: "Blame us not, O Chares. We are a peaceful little folk who only desire to be let alone, but we must defend ourselves. Nor am I really a foreigner. I had to prove my descent from Aineias of Troy ere your Board of Trade would grant my license."

Giskon continued: "Next we have Zenon of Kition, whom you already know, and Kallias of Arados, a visiting architect."

Kallias, Giskon's other Phoenician guest, was a man of about forty, with a mop of curly black hair flecked with gray; handsome in a florid, fleshy way. With a charming smile he said:

"I rejoice to meet you, O Chares. We must talk of your new methods of sculpture, for I am sure I can learn something of value from you."

He spoke Greek almost perfectly. Giskon continued around the circle until all had been presented. The Strangers did not look so exotic after all, for all but the Persian wore Greek dress, and most were clean-shaven. They spoke Greek, however, in a fascinating variety of accents. The club was mixed not only as to nation but also as to station. They ranged from a rich Rhodian citizen, Nikolaos, to mere mechanics in shabby cloaks and shirts.

However, none heeded rank. All were men of keen and eager minds, curious about everything under Helios. As Giskon served an appetizer of spiced wine and salt fish, the company was already merry.

I was drawn into a dispute between the Babylonian and the Egyptian. Each appealed to Zenon of Kition.

"Heed him not," said Onas. "Berosos means well but he is no Egyptian. We are the oldest race of mankind, to whom the gods directly gave words of wisdom ere they withdrew from the earth. Therefore we must be the wisest—"

"Rubbish!" cried Berosos. "Our records go further back than yours. And what do you with your wisdom? Mumble spells and incantations, concoct potions and poisons, appeal to demons and demigods that, for aught you know, exist not. *We*, now, are scientific. Records of the stars for thousands of years we have kept, to show how by the radiations of these divine bodies the world is governed. There is no chance in the world, no caprice. All—men, spirits, and gods alike—do obey the stars, like the parts of a well-oiled machine."

"A dismal concept," I said. "Why strive to master my art, if the stars decide beforehand whether or not I shall succeed?"

Onas: "He has a good point, Berosos."

"Not good at all," said Berosos. "If you strive, the reason is that the rays of the stars compel you, willy-nilly, to strive."

The sobersided Zenon had stood with eyes bulging, so that he looked even more like a prawn than usual. Now he said: "For my part, I incline to the beliefs of the Babylonians: that all is foreordained by the glittering stars. I find comfort in the thought that, behind the bloody turmoil of this frantic life, calm impersonal forces determine all in advance."

"Determine they nought that an Egyptian wizard cannot upset by a mighty spell," said Onas. "Why, in the terrible *Book of Thôth* there are two cantrips. If you recite the first, you shall enchant the heavens, the earth, the underworld, the sea, and the mountains. If you recite the second, though you be dead in your tomb, you shall rise from the dead and see the sun in the sky, the moon in her courses, and all the company of the ever-glorious gods in heaven."

I said: "How shall I recite this spell when I'm moldering in my grave?"

"If you have the benefit of Egyptian embalming, you will not molder. And your double—or 'soul,' as you call it—will recite the cantrip."

"I have yet to see proof that the soul exists."

"How ill informed you are!" said Onas. "The records of our ancient wisdom, going back a myriad of years, describe not only one soul but at least three per man."

"To the afterworld with your ancient records!" said Berosos. "Our history goes back thirty-six thousand years; that is, to the times before the Flood."

"The chronicle of our kings is longer than that," said Onas. "Would that my cousin Manethôs were here to recite the whole tally of reigns and dynasties!"

I said: "Who cares how far back your records go? Modern science had done away with all your spells and spooks and stargazing prophecies. All those old notions are based upon hearsay and self-serving dogma, as proved by Pyrron and Theodoros—"

Both disputants sprang upon me. I was saved from being torn to pieces, dialectically if not literally, by Giskon's announcement:

"Dinner is served. Move aside, friends, to let the servants set the tables."

Giskon served a veritable Erymanthian boar. The Strangers discussed a wide range of topics; politics, geography, war, philosophy, and the arts all came within their ken. Any one of them was keen to learn about anything. All, too, were eager to show off their knowledge to one another.

I asked Berosos how he came to be in Rhodes. He explained: "I was a minor priest in the Temple of Mardoukos. Five years ago the armies of Antigonos, seeking to overthrow Seleukos, invaded Babylonia and our holy city seized. Their enemies in the citadels they besieged; much of the city they burnt or demolished; many of the people they slew or sold. Now in ruins lies beautiful Babylon, once the world's greatest city. Finding my own temple sacked and my kinsfolk scattered, I fled with the rest. Methought to seek my fortune in the West, by means of the sundial that I had invented in the course of my studies."

"What was the outcome of the war?"

"First, Antigonos his son Demetrios sent, while Seleukos was fighting Antigonos' other generals in Media; but the boy achieved little besides looting and wanton destruction ere to Syria he returned. Then old One-eye himself with a larger force came down. Seleukos, by clever maneuvering amid the canals and watercourses, kept Antigonos from winning a decisive victory, although Antigonos was too strong to defeat in the field. At last Antigonos, hearing of trouble in his western domains, patched up a peace with Seleukos and returned to Anatolia." Berosos sighed. "So here am I, the most erudite scholar on the Research Committee of the Temple of Mardoukos, eking out a living by selling sundials and casting horoscopes. The most pitiful part is that, having just begun a little to prosper, doomed I find myself."

"How, doomed?" I asked. "Have you some wasting disease?"

"Nay, my health of the best is. But the stars say that, ere the year be out, caught again in the hideous claws of war shall I be."

"That's a chance we all take."

"Ah, but worse than that it is. For to become a soldier I am fated. Me, of all people!" Berosos glanced down at himself. "Far too fat and soft am I, and the mere thought of swords and lances thirsting for my blood inspires me with terror. Yet no escape see I. I was born under the Ram, a belligerent sign, with Nerigal—or Ares, as you call the red planet—in the Scorpion. That forces a warrior's career upon me, willy-nilly. I sought to escape my fate in the priesthood, but the Antigonian army drove me out of that. This year Ares reaches its exaltation in the Ram, which is also my house of life. It is, therefore, scientifically proved that I shall soon be wading in gore—I, the most peaceful of men. Of what use should I be to any army?"

Onas licked his fingers and said: "They could always hang you up and use you for an archery target. You do have the shape for it."

"Perhaps your calculations erred," I said.

"That will be his excuse in any case," said Onas the Egyptian. "Whenever their prophecies prove false, these Chaldeans say: 'Oh, I overlooked that little star and must recompute.'"

"I have cast my own horoscope thrice in a ten-day," said Berosos in a voice of doom. "Each time it came out more ominous. With Aphroditê opposed to Kronos—"

I interrupted. "How do *you* come to be in Rhodes?" I asked Onas.

"My case is the opposite to that of Berosos," he said. "A frustrated warrior, I. For I belong to the old warrior class of Egypt, though little chance to show our valor have we had since the Persians drove out our last king. Six years ago, when Ptolemaios contended with Antigonos for Syria, he raised a native corps among my class and marched us along the coast of the land of Sos to fight Demetrios."

"Did you fight at Gaza?" I asked.

"Say that I was there, though we pikemen had but little to do. From where I stood, nought could be seen but clouds of dust, through which came the hoofbeats of cavalry and the squeals of elephants. When Demetrios' elephants were halted by spiked iron caltrops, Demetrios' horsemen fled and his foot were surrounded and captured.

"Like many of my class, I thought we Egyptian warriors had earned quality with all these greasy Gr—excuse me, sir, with these ambitious Hellenes who have swarmed into the land of Chem and taken all the posts of honor and profit. But nay, perhaps the satrap feared that, were we suffered to keep our arms, we might revolt and put one of our own on Egypt's empty throne. So our arms were taken away and locked up, all but some which had vanished. It was said that some Egyptian warriors hid them for their own use. Came word that I was suspected of being in on this plot, if plot there was.

"Or ever all this befell, it was decided that I, as the youngest son, should learn a trade, as my father's allotment was too small to support all his sons. Therefore, I was apprenticed to my father's cousin in Sebennytos. When the matter of the missing pikes made Egypt too warm for comfort, I came to Rhodes and have practiced my craft here ever since." Onas stretched his powerful arms. "Gem-cutting is a good trade, at least whilst one's eyes hold out. But betimes I yearn for something more active."

Later, as we munched dried chick-peas and sipped sweet wine, Giskon said: "The time has come to choose the next president. Who puts himself forward?"

Sarpedon the Lykian said: "I"—here he said a name that sounded like a sneeze[3]—"of Xanthos, name myself to be the next president."

"Anybody who can make noises like that deserves to head the Strangers," said Giskon. "As I hear no other nominations, Sarpedon shall be our next chief. And now comes the inquisition. Chares of Lindos, stand up! Gobryas, begin the questioning."

The Persian, a brawny, balding, blunt-featured man with a deep, rasping voice, who painted his face in the Persian manner, said: "O Chares, how justify you your existence?"

I thought a moment and said: "My existence is justified by my mission."

"What is that?"

"To raise the practice of sculpture to a level higher than it has hitherto known."

"How will you do that?"

"By applying the methods of my master, Lysippos of Sikyon, and his brother, with such improvements as I can devise."

"What are these new methods?"

"There is—let's see—making a small model before beginning a full-sized statue; there is the life mask; there is the lost-wax method of casting. At least, these are the main ones."

"Explain them."

"Do you really wish to hear all about them?" I said, for I feared another disaster.

"Go ahead!" they cried. "We'll stop you when we become bored, fear not!"

So I plunged again into an account of the new techniques I had learnt. When my speech flagged, they shot searching questions at me. Lucky it was that I knew my subject; a poseur would soon have been stripped of his pretensions.

I also defended the modern realistic school of sculpture against the outmoded idealistic school of Pheidias and Polykleitos. "My master always said: 'If you want models, look about you! Be as faithful to nature as you can, and do not worry about how you compare with

3 Sppntaza

Pheidias.' But alas! Things being what they are, I don't know when I shall have a chance to practice these fine ideals."

"What mean you?" said Vindex of Rome.

I explained my difficulties with Diognetos and the Artists' Guild, wringing all the pathos from my plight of which it was capable.

Kallias, the Phoenician architect, said: "In Arados such shameful injustice would never be allowed."

"It is a shame," said Nikolaos, the full citizen. "Some of us on the Council think that old Diognetos, however brilliant he may have been, has become too rigid. It is all very well to conserve the wisdom of our forebears, but one should not reject all new ideas merely because they are new."

Vindex added: "You should have heard him roar when I suggested that he try arches of stone or brick, as we do, instead of these costly and fragile solid architraves."

"I can well believe it," said Nikolaos. "It was all we could do to get him to build some catapults of the torsion type. He said the flexion catapult had served Dionysios and Philip well, so why rush into some short-lived fad?"

"What was his objection to the torsion type?" I asked.

Nikolaos: "Too complex and hard to maintain, he said."

Giskon put in: "Time flees, so we must pass on to the next victim. Zenon of Kition, arise. Berosos, question him."

The Babylonian began with the same question that Gobryas had asked me, namely: how did Zenon justify his existence?

The young Phoenician twisted his hands and feet and finally answered: "I—I really cannot justify it at all, my masters. Th-that is, in fact, the thing I most ardently seek."

"Mean you that you seek justification for existing?" said Berosos.

"Yes. That is it."

"Why?"

"B-because I am not happy about it. I must know, why am I here? How should I live? How can I protect myself against the bludgeonings of Fate?" Zenon gained courage and fluency. "I've read the legends of the Phoenicians and the Judaeans and the Hellenes, as far as my business allowed me, and none satisfies me. In fact, they seem childish. Imagine, immortal gods breaking one another's heads, tumbling one another's wives, and massacring harmless mortals with lightnings and floods!"

Giskon munched up a fistful of chick-peas, saying: "What's the use of being a god if you cannot amuse yourself as you like?"

"Disgusting!" said Zenon without cracking a smile. "What sort of gods are those? If they are as foolish and lustful as men, why should we appeal to them for help? Something more rational must rule the universe."

Nikolaos said: "Advanced thinkers say those tales are merely allegories to convey deeper truths to the initiated."

"That may be, but how does that help a simple trader like me? How do I know, when I set out with a cargo of purple or spices, that a storm will not send my ship to the bottom, or that I shan't be seized by pirates and sold as a slave? When I come ashore in a fair city like this, what assurance have I that I shan't awaken to find the roaring mercenaries of some, shameless warlord battering down the gates? How, in such a frightful world, can there be any relation between my virtue and my fate? How can I find a sound moral basis for my actions?"

"You might try the philosophers," said Nikolaos.

"I have never known a philosopher. Are there any in Rhodes?"

"There is Eudemos, who is editing the treatises of Aristoteles of Stageira. I believe, however, that he is in Miletos just now. You might arrange a trading voyage to Athens, where you will find more philosophers gathered than in any other city."

Giskon said: "Let's pass on to the last victim. I shall question Kallias of Arados myself. Tell us, O Kallias: How do you justify your existence?"

Kallias patted his hair into place, rose, and said: "First, my masters, let me thank you for a delightful banquet, far beyond my poor deserts.

"As to self-justification, I am, as you know, an architect, traveling in search of commissions. It is with some diffidence that I bring up the subject in the city of Rhodes, which has given such outstanding architects to the world. The great Deinokrates, for one, was born in Rhodes, albeit reared in Macedonia. Your present municipal architect, Diognetos, might well be numbered among the great architects. By comparison my achievements count for little.

"However, even the strongest cedar succumbs with time to age and rot. I am concerned whether this magnificent city be protected by the latest and most effective methods of siege warfare. We all know that in the last century siegecraft has been revolutionized. You may have heard of the invention of the movable suspended ram by my countryman, Pephrasmenos of Tyre; or of the inventions of Diades, who served the divine Alexander: his movable tower, his borer, his climbing machine, and his crane."

Zenon said: "If machines of war become any more frightful, people will insist on doing away with war altogether. This cannot go on."

"I sympathize with that idea," said Kallias, "but I fear that is easier said than done. To continue: Is Rhodes prepared to withstand assault by these and even more modern machines? Whilst I do not claim to read the minds of the warlords, it is known that the surest way to invite attack is to be unprepared for it."

"We have the friendship of Ptolemaios," said Nikolaos, "with all the wealth of Egypt behind him."

"Yes? And what will befall when the Antigonos and his all-daring son fight another round of their eternal war against Ptolemaios? Will not Rhodes' very alliance with Ptolemaios bring Antigonos upon you? Rich though the satrap of Egypt be, Antigonos is not poor either, and he is much closer to hand. Who knows the future?"

"The stars say—" began Berosos, but Kallias plunged on:

"Who knows but that the Antigonians and the Ptolemaians may destroy one another, leaving Kasandros or Lysimachos to pick up the remains? These are grim and ruthless men who will stick at nought to serve their ambition. If it suited them to pile the heads of every living being in Rhodes in the marketplace, be assured they would do it without a qualm. Are you ready for such an outcome? It is the municipal architect's duty to prepare the defense of the city. What has your Diognetos done?" Kallias ended with an impassioned gesture.

"I believe that our walls are in good condition," said Nikolaos. "We have an adequate artillery, with missiles, besides small arms and armor for all the men in the city."

"Think you that bows, slings, and catapults of the ordinary kinds will stop the great armored engines Demetrios could bring against you? Your artillery, I gather, is mostly of the solid-bow type. Modern torsion catapults will outrange and outshoot these and drive the defenders from the wall. You will be like a man fighting with a sword of lath and a shield of papyrus."

"Well, then, what would you?" said Nikolaos.

Kallias drew a long breath. "First, let me protest my unworthiness and lack of personal ambition. I would not meddle in Rhodian affairs, save that I love the beauty of Rhodes and hate to think of her going down to destruction, as did proud Tyre within the memory of many here. I have, however, given thought to the defense of the city. Here are some of my ideas."

Kallias picked up a roll of large sheets of papyrus and began unrolling them one by one and holding them up to our view.

"Here," he said, "is my sluing crane. Can you all see the drawing? When a hostile siege engine nears the wall, the crane swings on its pivot until its end is over the machine. Then it seizes the engine by means of these tongs. When the crew pulls on the ropes, the hostile machine is raised into the air, thus. Naturally, the enemies in the engine are shaken out, and most are slain by the fall. Then the crane rotates on its base, carrying the captured engine over the wall, and lowers it to the ground inside the city."

"*Euge! Euge!*" cried several of the Strangers.

"Thank you, sirs," said Kallias. He went on to explain the mechanical features of his turning crane. Knowing something of architectural engineering, I found his ideas most ingenious.

Other sheets illustrated other devices. There was an enormous hammer, mechanically operated so as to smash siege machines near the walls. There were catapults that worked on new principles, such as falling weights or the compression of air by a piston in a bronze cylinder. The turning crane, however, elicited the most admiration.

Nikolaos: "Your voice has the sound of Dodonian bronze, O Kallias. Could you repeat that lecture before the Council?"

"Oh, sir, you are much too kind! Of course I can, if you think my poor ideas worthy of their notice."

"I think we ought to go into this further. Diognetos' contract runs out soon, and there is a question of whether we ought to renew it. Tell me where I can reach you, and we shall see."

The party soon broke up. The last I saw of Berosos, he stood at a street corner, pointing up to the stars, which spangled the sky like daisies on a black meadow, and expounded his theories of astrology to Zenon of Kition.

The day after my dinner with the Seven Strangers, my father said:

"Genetor was here last night, Chares. He's pleased with you, despite your radicalism, and wants to know when the betrothal will be made formal."

"Oh, divinity! I haven't even seen the girl."

"That can be arranged."

I beat my head with my fists. "For Hera's sake, Father, put him off! I'm too confused to think clearly about such things. At the moment I don't even have a future in my chosen profession to offer."

My father sighed. "I'll try, but henceforth you must think up your own excuses."

Two days later, with Kavaros' help, I loaded fifty bronzen mirrors on an ass and took them across the town to the house of Glôs the engraver for finishing. Glôs said:

"Have you heard the news?"

"What news?"

"About Diognetos and the Council."

"No, what is it?"

"The Council has refused to renew his contract. Nay more, they'll recommend to the Assembly a new contract with this Phoenician wanderer, this Kallias of Arados. Do you know him?"

"I've met him."

"What is he like?"

"I was much impressed. He combined great charm with brilliant ideas."

Glôs: "Well, then, perhaps it won't be a disaster for our beautiful city after all. Of course the Council has long been at loggerheads with Diognetos because of his conservatism. Still, he is deemed one of the world's ablest municipal architects. And he can't be bribed."

"Diognetos did not impress me," I said. "At least, with Kallias I might have a chance to get some commissions."

When work slackened at the foundry, I amused myself by modeling a clay head of Kavaros in a corner. The Kelt said:

"To be sure, young master, if I did not know that this was me here and that was the statue there, I would be expecting to hear that thing talking with my own voice. If I ever need a spare head, I will know where to get one, like those three champions I fought in the battle with the Trokmoi."

"What's that?" I asked.

"Did I not tell you? We put our bravest fighters in the front rank; so, being the most valiant of my clan, I was foremost—"

"Except at climbing masts," I put in. On the *Galatea* we had amused and warmed ourselves by playing tag, until I found that I could always escape the Kelt by swarming up the rope ladder to the masthead, for he had a deathly fear of heights. Mere height has never bothered me, and I could have made a living as a sailor. Kavaros rejoined:

"I was trained as a warrior, sir, not a—what do you call these beasties the young gentlemen keep for pets, that look like ugly little men?"

"A monkey?"

"A monkey, that is it. Anyway, the Trokmoi had three champions, who fought side by side in their front rank, so I found myself fighting all three of them at once. It was real warm work for a while, until I struck a blow the like of which has never been seen, nor ever will be seen. Would you believe it, sir, it took off the heads of all three of those omadhauns at the same time? If you will come to the land of the Tektosages, I will show you the heads to prove it."

"Kavaros," I said, "why are slaves such liars?"

"Why, Master Chares! Everything I tell you is the perfect truth, and I can prove it."

"I didn't say you; I said slaves in general."

"Oh, well, now, that is different. If I may ask you one in return, sir, what other defense does a poor slave have? As we say, who has no shield must use his cloak; who has no sword must use his stick, only it sounds prettier in the Keltic.

"Now, as I was saying, one of these fellows I hit was Genthios, a famous fighter of the Trokmoi. And would you believe it? Such a fierce man was he that he fought on for hours before he discovered that the head of him was off. It was only when he put up his hand to wipe the sweat off his face that he found it out and fell down dead."

A few days after my talk with Glôs, the Assembly met. As a mere tribesman, I could not attend. In Rhodes we have about six thousand adult men classed as citizens in the broad sense of the word. However, the property qualification for full or voting citizenship is so high that less than a third of these can take part in the government. The rest are second-class or non-voting citizens, or, as I have called them here, tribesmen.

I was working on my father's contract when there came a noise from the street. From the door of the foundry I saw a crowd approaching. At the head was Kallias, flushed with triumph. Others crowded after him, showering him with praise and congratulations. He stopped at our door, grasped my hand, and pulled me into the street.

"Behold!" he said. "Here is the first of past injustices that I, as your new architect, shall right. This is the most brilliant of our young artists, just returned from study on the mainland and denied a chance to exercise his genius by the hidebound stupidity and malignant jealousy of his elders. O Chares, I, Kallias, say that you shall have a commission from the city ere the year be out."

The admirers cheered. I was delighted, if embarrassed at being hauled without warning into public view. Kallias continued:

"Can you show me an example of your work?"

I said: "If you will step in, I'll show you a piece I've been working on."

Kallias entered the foundry, hitching his cloak up daintily to avoid soiling it. I showed him the clay head of Kavaros.

"This is only a rough sketch, a mere bagatelle," I said. "You can see that I lack the space for serious work."

"It shows real talent, Chares," he said. "You will be a great sculptor if you persist. I shall certainly arrange for you to receive an opportunity to match your promise with performance. Rejoice!"

When several days passed without my hearing from Kallias, I went to his temporary office, which Giskon had allowed him to set up in one of the rooms of his house. Kallias was cordial but vague about the reason for my coming until I reminded him of his promise of a commission.

"Of course!" he said. "Forgive me, O best one, I have been so submerged in detail that things have slipped my memory. Yes, you shall have a commission. However, you must first give evidence of being a responsible contractor."

"What does that mean, sir?"

"You will have to have a proper workshop, and you must submit a sample of your work. A bronze casting of that head of the Kelt would do for the latter."

I explained about my difficulty in getting a studio. Kallias promised to speak to Nikolaos.

Again there came a delay of a ten-day. When I again went to Kallias' office and reminded him, he bestirred himself at once.

Nikolaos, it transpired, owned a tumbledown barn of a house on the slopes of the akropolis, on the outskirts of the city, which was now vacant. He agreed to let me rent it on credit until I could get started.

I had a quarrel with my father when he learned what I was up to. The poor man kept hoping against hope that I should settle down for good and all, to become a foundry manager.

"Very well, Chares," he said, "if you are so independent as all that, you can live in your new palace. Expect no more free food and lodging from me."

"All right, I won't," I said, and marched out in high dudgeon, Kavaros staggering after me with my baggage. At the new house we slept on moldy straw pallets and ate sitting on the floor for want of chairs.

It took some time to turn the house into a studio, especially as Kavaros and I had to build most of our equipment—ovens, furnaces, and the like—by ourselves. Before we had finished, I ran out of money. Kavaros and I got hungrier and hungrier until Sosias dropped in one day to say:

"Master Chares, this is not official. But your mother asked me to tell you that if you offered to help your father in the foundry from time to time, when there is a rush on, he is willing that you should eat at home."

"Thanks for the offer, Sosias. I will think about the matter and let them know," I said. When Sosias had gone, I turned on Kavaros. "You didn't tell Sosias we were starving so he could pass the word to my mother, who, you knew, would try to bring about a compromise between my father and me, now did you?"

"Why, sir, I do not know what you are talking about! But it is true that, unless I get some food to put between my belly and my backbone, I will be as weak as green wine, and so of no help to you. And you do not want that, now do you, master dear?"

"Dog-faced savage!" I growled. "But I suppose it would be defying Fate to refuse the offer."

So matters were again patched up between my father and myself. To complete my equipment, lay in some bronze stock, and pay my rent, I had to earn some quick money. This I undertook to do by making terra-cotta statuettes for household ornaments and votive offerings. To find outlets for these, I used my acquaintance with Genetor to get an introduction to his cousin Nereus, the high priest of Helios-Apollon.

I was actually making a few drachmai from my terra cottas when I had a visitor at the studio. This was Lykon, the older sculptor who had been so nasty at the meeting of the Artists' Guild.

"Be in good health, O Chares," he said. "What's this I hear about your breaking into the manufacture of terra cottas?"

"It's true enough. There are some waiting to be painted. Why?"

"Because I am Rhodes's maker of terra cottas. I have an established business, which I have built up by several years of effort. There is not enough demand to support two manufactories, and I will certainly not give up mine. So you had better find something else."

"Has Rhodes given you a legal monopoly of this business?"

"No, but custom has the force of law. I'm giving you a chance to withdraw gracefully."

"To the afterworld with you! I'll make what I please and sell it where I can."

"I'm giving you fair warning—"

"Get out!"

Lykon looked as if he were about to say: "Put me out if you can!" But then he caught sight of Kavaros, absently tapping his open palm with a heavy mallet. The sculptor went without further word.

"We seem to gather enemies as offal gathers flies," I said. "If I could only get a commission for something big: say, a colossal Alexander. Can't you imagine one standing down there?" I pointed down the hillside toward the harbor.

"I am after thinking about this fellow Alexander," said Kavaros. "You do talk about making a great statue of him, but belike that is not the best plan."

"Why not?"

"Well, for one thing, sir, Master Lysippos has made statues of Alexander—little statues and life-sized statues and gigantical statues—all over Hellas and the islands. I have seen some of them myself. So who will dance and sing for joy when you say you want to make one more? Then again, too, the fellow is dead. Perhaps he was the greatest general of all, or even the son of a god, but still, he is not here to pay for statues of himself. And they do be saying that all his children and kinsmen have been murthered; so there is no commission there, either. A dead corpse has no vanity. Why do you not take some living prince or general for your model? I do not rightly understand money, as a Keltic gentleman does things only for honor and friendship; but it seems to me that, if you need the stuff, that is the way to get it."

I gave the slave a hard look. "You may be a barbarian from the unexplored wilds of the trackless North, but at times you show a keen wit indeed. I'll think about your suggestion. Meanwhile let's get that head of you cast, to have something to show Kallias."

Three days later I arrived again at Giskon's house. Kavaros carried the bronze head, saying: "Indeed and it is a two-headed man that I am, like the giant that my great-grandfather fought in the Land of Mist. Why do you not make a double of me, master dear, and then you could let me go and keep the statue?"

Kallias greeted me with effusive charm. "A splendid work!" he cried. "So vital! One can almost hear it speaking with a Keltic accent.

Now to business. The most important project now in progress is the new theater. This will require statues, and I hope to number yours among them.

"However, there is an obstacle. The Artists' Guild, having gotten wind of my intentions, protested against my hiring a sculptor not of their membership. My reply was that Chares is perfectly willing to join but has been kept out because of the personal prejudice of some members, and that it were unjust to deprive a man of his livelihood on such grounds.

"Now, I daresay I could force the issue and defeat your detractors. But I would not begin my term of office by a quarrel with those with whom I must work. I have therefore arranged with Protogenes to decide the matter by a contest in which you shall have a chance to show off your new method of sculpture. If you win, you shall enter the Guild without further delay.

"In the marketplace stands a bronze bust of Homer. You and Lykon, who seems to be your principal foe, shall each make a copy of it. He shall use a clay copy and a sand or plaster mold, while you shall employ your lost-wax method. Both the fidelity of the copy and the speed with which it is made shall be considered in judging the results. The judges shall be Protogenes, Nikolaos, and myself. As your studio is short of facilities, you shall both use that of Lykon. Does that suit you?"

"Certainly, sir," I said. "When will this be?"

"Tomorrow. Now another matter. I find that, as municipal architect, I am also director of Rhodes's defenses and general of her artillery. In the arsenal are six new catapults built under my predecessor. While they are not of the latest and most efficient design, they are still a substantial addition to the city's defenses. And crews have not yet been assigned to them. Have you been enrolled in the armed forces?"

"No, sir."

"If a war scare arise, you will hear from the Board of Generals soon enough. However, let us consider your position. You cannot join the marines, because that branch is reserved for rich young citizens. Our cavalry is a joke, and anyway you own no horse. That leaves the infantry and the artillery. You are rather small to bear the panoply of a hoplites, but in the artillery your knowledge of engineering would stand you in good stead."

"What had you in mind, O Kallias?"

"With your education, you could be a double-pay man in command of a catapult. How say you?"

"That would be fine. Thank you, sir."

Lykon and I stood in Lykon's studio, with the bust of Homer before us and our materials around us. The audience comprised the three judges and most of the Artists' Guild.

When Protogenes said: "Go!" Lykon and I oiled our hands and sprang to our tasks. While our slaves cut slabs of clay to convenient size, we picked up these slabs and built up models on the armatures that rose from our workstands.

We worked in tense silence, save when we both tried to measure the original bust at the same time and got in each other's way. In a trice we were thrusting at each other with our calipers and shouting threats and curses. Lykon had dealt me a scratch in the forearm when Kallias and Nikolaos pulled us apart, and Protogenes admonished us.

"After this," he said, "he who gets to the bust first shall finish his measurements before the other may approach it. He who breaks this rule shall be disqualified."

I finished the core of my bust—a rough shape of sandy clay like the final head but a little smaller—while Lykon was still bringing his clay bust up to size; my revolving workstand gave me an advantage. Then Kavaros handed me a brush and a bucketful of melted red-tinted beeswax. The tedious task of painting on the wax let Lykon get ahead of me. Once I had built my wax to its final size, however, the process of paring it down, inscribing the surface detail, and adding the sprues and vents went faster than Lykon's finishing his clay bust. I had almost caught up with him when he began laying on the clay slip he was using for his one-piece mold.

Then I constructed my mold of oily sand held in place by a flask of reinforced clay laid on around it. When my mold was built out, I secured it to the core by driving long bronze nails into it.

When both molds had set, Lykon turned his mold on its side and began digging out the clay, while Kavaros kindled a fire in the brick oven that Lykon used for baking his terra cottas. Meanwhile I turned my mold over and nailed a board to its base. Then Kavaros and I used the board to maneuver the mold into the oven.

Lykon continued to scrape the clay out of his mold. When that task was done, he began to build up his core, even and anon thrusting it into the mold to see how it fitted. After a while my stare made him nervous, for he jerked around and said:

"Why aren't you working on your mold and core?"

"They're all done. In a few hours, when the wax has melted out and the mold has dried, I shall be ready to pour."

Lykon threw his tool to the floor. "What sort of Thessalian wit is this?" he shouted.

"Nothing but Lysippos' lost-wax process, man. I once tried to tell you about it, but you wouldn't listen."

"There's no use trying to compete with such trickery!"

Protogenes spoke: "O Lykon, you agreed to the terms of this contest, knowing that Chares had a new method. Do you wish to be known as a poor sport?"

"I'll show you!" said Lykon. Without bothering to build his core further, he put it, and his mold, in the oven to dry beside my mold.

"Let us lunch while waiting," said Kallias.

The slaves brought food. As we ate, the tension relaxed, although Lykon continued to grumble and brood. Afterward, over a jug of wine, we entertained one another with jokes and stories.

"This contest," said Kavaros, "reminds me of the time my great-grandfather contested with Agnoman the Ogre. This ogre was an unpleasant fellow, nine cubits tall, with long green hair all over and a pair of bat's wings growing out of his back, the which he could take off and hang up when they inconvenienced him. He lived in a cave on top of Mount Golameira, which is so high that if a young man fell off the top, he would be dead of old age before he got to the bottom.

"Now, this Agnoman flew far and wide over the lands of the Scythians and the Roxolanians and the Issedonians, raiding caravans and kidnaping princesses and having himself a rare old time. At last he kidnaped Nessia, the daughter of the king of the Tektosages. So the king called in my ancestor, as he always did when things got insurmountable. 'Gargantyos,' he said—for that was my forebear's name—'if you will rescue my darling Nessia, you shall have her and half my kingdom.'

"Well, my ancestor's first job was to get to the top of Mount Golameira. So he made himself a special chariot to be pulled by four-and-twenty eagles. He had a terrible time training the eagles, but at last, on a fine summer's evening, he took off and guided these birds over the plains of Getika and Scythia and the Rhiphaian Mountains until he came to Mount Golameira. So tall was it that my great-grandfather had to fly back and forth zigzag for hours to reach the top.

"My ancestor had been flying by moonlight, because, being a clever man, he had found out about the habits of Agnoman. The ogre did his hunting at night, returning to his cave at sunrise. So it was well before sunrise when my great-grandfather brought the eagles to a halt on the ledge outside the cave and went in.

"Agnoman must have been a Persian ogre, because he had most luxurious ideas. The cave was all fixed up with gold and jewels that the ogre had stolen, and there on a silken couch lay Nessia. Indeed and she was glad to see my ancestor, calling him her hero and savior and hugging and kissing him until the breath was fair squeezed out of him, and him a big strong warrior.

"'That is fine, my dear,' said he at last, 'but soon the sun will be up and Agnoman will be back on those horrid bat's wings. So let us be going!'

"Nessia agreed. But then the difficulty arose, of what she was to take with her. My great-grandfather would have gone without taking anything, except perhaps a handful of gold and jewels such as a man could snatch up in a hurry. But Nessia must try on gorgeous silken gowns, one after another, until she found the most becoming one. And she must try on the earrings and necklaces and other gew-gaws to see which went best with which gown, and all the time my ancestor getting more and more nervous; not that he was a timorous man, you understand, but it seemed like spitting in the faces of the immortal gods to fool around so.

"Sure enough, the sun arose and Agnoman came back while Nessia was still trying on goodly gowns and glittering jewels. The ogre understood right away what was going on, being intelligent as ogres go, and bared the big teeth of him to eat my ancestor. But my forebear, backing up against the wall and holding Agnoman off with his sword, said: 'If you have any Keltic blood in your veins, Agnoman my lad, it is sporting blood, and you will not decline a fair contest.'

"'What have ye in mind?' said Agnoman.

"'I will fight you with broadswords, fair and square,' said my great-grandfather, 'and if I win I take the maid and such of your wealth as I can carry, while if you win you may eat me without resistance.'

"The ogre said: 'I am thinking there is a catch to that offer, as I can eat you anyway. Howsomever, I do like the spirit of you; so let us not quibble but have at it.' And he hung his wings up on the wall and went for my ancestor with his sword.

"Indeed and that was a gigantical fight. For three days and three nights they fenced, and so loud was the clatter that the king of Persia, a thousand leagues away, ordered out his army, thinking he was invaded. At the end of that time the swords of both were worn down to the hilts, and neither had laid a scratch upon the other.

"'It is fools that we are,' said my great-grandfather. 'Since swords will get us nowhere, let us make a wrestle of it.'

"So for three days and three nights they wrestled. Such was the force with which they threw each other around that rocks as big as houses were shaken loose from the ceiling of the cave and fell down upon them, but so busy with their wrestle were they that they never noticed.

"Then Agnoman said: 'Wrestling is getting us nowhere either. But I will propose another contest. Do ye see my bathtub, there? Well, I will fill it, and we will put our heads under water, and the one who takes his head out first is the loser.'

"And so they did. My ancestor took a deep breath and plunged his head into the bathtub, which was big enough to sail a ship in. When he had held his head under water for three days and three nights, he found he was getting short of breath. Thinking he might as well be eaten as drowned, he took his head out. Then he nudged Agnoman, saying: 'Come on up, ogre darling; you win.' But never a bit did Agnoman move, having drowned himself dead rather than lose the contest. And the moral is, games are fine, but do not confuse them with serious business."

"What happened then?" I asked.

"Nothing much. Nessia insisted on loading the car with gold and jewels from the ogre's hoard. My ancestor objected that the eagles could not carry the weight, but the lady was determined, and as she was a king's daughter, he did not take so strong a line with her as he might have.

"Sure enough, when the four-and-twenty eagles took flight, they quickly lost height because of the extra weight. When they were over a lake in the Atmonian country, and losing height with every flap of their wings, a flock of ducks flew up from the lake. The four-and-twenty eagles, thinking that what they most needed was a duck dinner, twisted about and upset the chariot. The next thing my ancestor knew, he and the lady and the ogre's hoard were all dumped in a patch of soft black mud in a marsh in the middle of the lake.

"When my ancestor had dug the mud off the face of him, he saw it was a good ten or twelve furlongs' swim to the nearest land. So he said to the girl: 'Nessia, my dear, off with the clothes and into the water, for it is no warmer nor less hungry we will be, waiting around here until nightfall.'

"But the king's daughter cried and carried on because she would not give up the Persian queen's gown she was wearing, or the thirty pounds of gold and jewels she had on besides, which is unsuitable for to swim with. So my great-grandfather hit her a bit of a clip on the jaw and took the things off her himself. He swam to the mainland, holding her face above water with one arm; and there he stole clothes and food and horses from the Atmonians, and so they got home.

"But when the king wanted to give his daughter to my ancestor, he said: 'Thank you, sir, and I will be having the half of the kingdom, if you do not mind. But as for the wench, keep her. Honor is worth more nor life, but gold and jewels are not, and a woman who proves three times running that she values them so is too big a fool for me to wish to be related to her by marriage.'

"Becoming angry, the king would not give the half of the kingdom without the maid. So my ancestor went off by himself and met the Elf-king's daughter, but that is another story."

* * *

When the sun went down behind the akropolis, we lit the furnace and set our crucibles to heating. We withdrew our molds from the oven, wherein they had baked all day. The red beeswax in mine had melted and run down into the bowl we had set on the floor of the oven. Lykon assembled his core and mold, and we both placed our molds in the sand pit and packed them against upset.

Then, when our bronze had melted, we poured. I left the hoisting and tipping of my crucible to Kavaros; not that I was not strong enough, but that forty pounds of crucible and molten metal on the end of a long-handled tongs are more safely manipulated by a large man than by a small one.

Next morning we chiseled off our molds and dug out our cores. Anybody could see that the surface of my casting presented a far better texture than Lykon's. However, I still had the task of cutting off my sprues, rods, and nail ends. While Lykon ground and filed at the surface flaws in his bust, I filed down the stumps of the rods. At last I stopped work and said:

"There you are, gentlemen."

Lykon stopped, too, for his bust had so many surface flaws that he could have worked on them for days. After the judges had conferred in whispers, Protogenes said:

"The two busts were finished at about the same time. The two are of about equally good—or bad—workmanship. To tell the truth, neither looks much like the original; but that, I suppose, is the inevitable result of haste. Anyway, since nobody knows what Homer really looked like, one bust may be as much like him as the other.

"However, Chares' method allows a better control of surface texture, especially in giving smoothness where smoothness is desired. It also saves bronze, as his core follows the surface of the mold more closely. Hence his bust weighs less than half as much as Lykon's. Chares wins."

"*Euge!*" cried my friends among the audience.

Lykon glared at me and stalked out without another word. Feeling magnanimous, I should have been glad to be friends with him, but he had evidently made up his mind that I was the leading fly in his ointment. Now that I look back, I can see that Lykon was in many ways not a bad sort, with the usual assortment of human virtues and faults. Unfortunately his virtues did not include a liking for Chares the Lindian.

I sat in Kallias' office in Giskon's house while the architect talked of his plans for the new theater. Most of the stonework was already in place, but not the colonnades, the stage, and the ornamental statuary.

"One must think on a large scale," said Kallias. "Poor old Diognetos could think of no more than two statues to flank the seats. I shall have four: of Aischylos, Sophokles, Euripides, and Aristophanes."

I said: "When I was in Athens, a fellow named Menandros was making quite a reputation as a writer of comedies. Ought we to consider him?"

"No, it were safer to stick to those who are safely dead. Now, it should be possible to give you a contract for two of these and Lykon that for the other two. Would that suit you?"

Considering that I was still young and unknown, the offer was very flattering. "It pleases me greatly," I said.

Then we argued prices, with the usual hours of haggling. Kallias cited my youth and inexperience, while I brought forward the never-ending rise in the costs of materials, which could throw all one's calculations awry.

At length we agreed on a price of five hundred drachmai for each statue. This was more than I expected.

"Now," said Kallias, "there is the matter of the models to be used. By good luck, Protogenes made a set of sketches, years ago in Athens, of an authentic bust of Sophokles, said to have been made from life. These will, I think, enable us to make an adequate statue without going outside Rhodes.

"For the other three, however, we have nothing on Rhodes as to how they looked. I may be able to write to Athens, to have some sketches sent. But if you will get to work on the Sophokles, I will take care of the rest."

"I understand."

"Good. Now, there is one other matter, which I hope you will also understand." Kallias glanced toward the door. "You will admit, young man, that I have gone to a lot of trouble on your account. A ten-day ago you faced a life of bronze founding and the thwarting of all your high artistic hopes. Now you are a member of the Guild and have been offered a contract that would make many experienced sculptors envious. Think not that I am unaware that the terms are generous."

"True," I said.

"Furthermore, I have staked my own reputation on your turning out statues that shall do the city credit. Now, perhaps you think I have done all these things solely for admiration of your blazing young genius."

So self-conceited was I that I had thought that Kallias had favored me for just that reason. My guardian spirit, however, warned me not to say so.

"Having done much and risked much for you," he said, "I expect you to show equal generosity toward me, out of the money you will get for these statues. Let us say, about a hundred and fifty drachmai a statue."

I sat with my mouth open. Then I croaked: "I—I shall have to think this over, O Kallias. Give me until tomorrow."

"Oh, no! I know what you plan. You would go home and discuss the matter with your father or with some trusted friend. Thus our deal would become known. You must make up your mind here and now, or never hope to get a contract from me again."

I pondered the matter. I should have known what was coming. For an instant I even regretted that old Diognetos was not still the city's architect. He at least was not one of those who, as the saying goes, praises the good while pursuing his own profit at all costs.

Kallias put on his charm. "After all, my dear young man, have I not been your friend? And friends have all in common. Well, despite my fine new post, I am pinched for money. I face the cost of buying a house and moving my family hither from Arados. You would not starve your friend, would you?"

At length, eagerness to get a start and lust for fame overcame my scruples. I said: "I agree in principle, but you ask too much. Make it a hundred drachmai per statue."

Kallias laughed. "One could tell that you are part Phoenician. Make it a hundred and twenty-five, no less."

"Done," I said. "Now, if you will show me where the finished statues are to stand—"

Giskon burst in, his beard abristle. "Kallias!" he cried. "I've just come from the marketplace. Demetrios has sailed from Peiraieus, and the Board of Generals meets tonight in the Town Hall."

"Indeed?" said Kallias. "Very well, I shall be there. Chares, I fear we must drop this talk of statuary. Come with me to the arsenal and meet your new command. Wait! You must be identified."

Kallias brought out from his secretarial chest a disk of clay with a thong strung through a hole. With a stylus he scratched on the disk: "This is Chares Nikonos, auth. by Kallias."

He hung the disk about my neck, saying: "Do not take this tag off whilst you are on restricted ground unless you want a sentry's spear through your brisket. Come."

The arsenal and the dockyards form a mass of buildings that take up a good part of the shore of the Great Harbor. The whole is surrounded by a high brick wall with iron spikes along the top. It is constantly patrolled, even in peacetime. The sentries at the gate struck their spears against their shields in salute to Kallias.

We passed through the dockyard, where a new trireme was completing. Kallias said:

"I keep telling Superintendent Rhesos that we shall be destroyed if we build nought but these obsolete little craft when all the other powers are launching fivers, sixers, and so on up. Compared to them, our ships are like sardines to sharks. But"—he shrugged—"none heeds the prophet of new ideas until too late."

He led me into the arsenal. We passed long rows of spears, swords, cuirasses, helmets, and greaves, gleaming quietly in their racks, before we came to the section where the missile weapons were stored.

Here stood scores of bows, hundreds of sheaves of arrows, stacks of javelins, bundles of slings, and bags of sling bullets. There was also a rack of those small hand catapults called scorpions or belly bows. There were stacks of catapult darts of various lengths, and pyramids of catapult balls.

At last we reached the large catapults. Those most in evidence were four enormous stone throwers of the flexion type, twelve cubits long over all, with huge bows of horn and wood affixed to their muzzles by iron brackets. Kallias jerked a contemptuous thumb.

"This was my predecessor's idea of defending the city," he said. "As lately as five years ago he bought these from one Isidoros of Abydos, even though the flexion catapult is obsolete. Today one can get the same cast of the same weight of projectile, with half the over-all weight, by the use of the torsion principle. Now *these* are something else."

Kallias indicated the six new torsion catapults, smaller than those of Isidoros but still of imposing size, lined up on the main floor. They stood on rollers with their metal parts greased and their wood polished. The architect said:

"Thank the gods that Rhodes has one intelligent man: Bias the carpenter. Failing to convert Diognetos to the torsion principle, he carried his battle to the Council, which authorized these engines on an experimental basis. Take your pick."

I gasped with delighted astonishment, stammered my thanks, and went to the machines. I chose the one that seemed to have the stoutest and tautest torsion skeins.

"Know you how to work one?" asked Kallias.

"A little. I played around them as a child; I have read about them; and in Argos they let me load and shoot one at practice."

"Well, that puts you ahead of most recruits. If I be any prophet, crews will be assigned tomorrow. If there be anybody whom you wish for your crew, enlist him forthwith, or you will have to take whom fate allots."

Book II

DEMETRIOS

As I crossed the marketplace on the way to my studio, I came upon two swarthy acquaintances from the Seven Strangers: Onas the Egyptian and Berosos the Babylonian. The former proposed that we stop at a wine shop. We squeezed past the counter to a table, and Onas said:

"I trust that the local will suit. Evios stocks not the costly vintages of Chios."

"If Rhodian is good enough for export, it's good enough for me," I said. "I'm no exquisite who sniffs and sips and says, 'Ah, indeed it is good, but the Lesbian vintage of nine years ago was better.'"

"Anything for me," said Berosos, "so that it lighten my liver."

"What ails his liver?" I asked.

Said Onas: "Nought. He means he suffers the pangs of unrequited love. This time it is the daughter of Aratos the miller. Last month it was the wife of—"

"Must you blab my secrets?" said Berosos. "At least I do love those of the opposite sex, unlike many hereabouts. Hither, seeking Onas, I came—as, finding no hope for my suit in the stars, I sought his help in getting one of these Egyptian love potions."

"I told him I was a lapidary, not an apothecary," said Onas. "I seek a man who owes me for the carving of a carnelian, and who seems to possess an invisibility spell, for he vanishes whenever a creditor appears. What brings you hither, O Chares?"

I told them of the threat to the peace of Rhodes and of the rank that Kallias had offered me. "Now I seek squad mates. Would you two care to join?"

"I might," said Onas. "Fain would I take up again the sword of my forebears. Besides, I like Rhodes to dwell in, and if trouble come, the surest way of being clasped to the city's bosom is to serve in its forces. The marines are not open to foreigners, and rowing is dull work for anybody with the wit to walk around a puddle. How about you, Fatty?"

"Me!" squealed Berosos, terror starting from his bottomless black eyes. "Istar! What an idea!"

I said: "You told me you were doomed by the stars to become a soldier. If that be so, would you not rather fight at long range?"

"But—but we Babylonians have lost all aptitude for war, since King Xerxes disarmed us, nearly two hundred years ago!"

Onas touched his necklace of amulets. "If you would but buy one of these, you need not fear the spear in its thrust or the arrow in its flight."

"What could I do?" wailed Berosos. "I know not one end of a catapult from the other, and not strong enough to turn those great windlasses am I."

Said I: "Your eyesight is keener than that of most; you can see stars that others cannot. You shall be our aimer, who lines up the catapult with the target and guesses the distance."

A little more talk brought Berosos around, albeit with sighs and moans for the fate awaiting him. Onas said:

"I, too, will join, if my wife permit."

Berosos laughed. "That is the Egyptian for you!"

"Whatever uncivilized nations may do," said Onas, "*we* look upon marriage as a partnership." We paid and rose.

I asked: "Have you a wife, Berosos?"

The Babylonian sighed. "I had, ere my city was by the Macedonians ravaged. In the confusion she vanished, and though her with diligence I sought, no trace did I find. She may have been slain, or sold, or by some lustful soldier carried off."

"Or," said Onas, "she may have run away to escape your lectures. Here we are."

Onas led us into his shop. Instead of taking us straight to his dwelling, on the floor above, he insisted on showing us his stock. There were black onyxes and green chrysophrases and red sardonyxes, which the Egyptian was carving with his tiny drills and burrs for the rings of rich citizens. There were red carbuncles condensed from the urine of lynxes, a thunderstone that had fallen from the sky, and a lodestone from the land of the Hyperboreans.

"Watch," he said, and showed us how the lodestone would pick up an iron nail. Then he brought out a fine purple amethyst.

"Wear this and you need never fear drunkenness, such is its mystic power. And here is a piece of genuine amber from the fog-bound North. Watch."

He produced a small feather, rubbed the amber against his sleeve, and then picked up the feather with it as the lodestone had picked up the nail.

"There is more magic in gems than in all your stars," he said. In the dimness of the shop Onas seemed a different man from the bluff, soldierly fellow he was outside. His eyes seemed larger; they seemed to look through Berosos and me to some distant vision.

"Close your eyes," he said, "and face the corner, and I will show you my good stones."

We did as he bade us. We heard him moving and opening things, and then he said: "Turn!"

Onas held a tray, from which gems winked up like the eyes of unknown beasts in a forest night. He held up one pale, colorless stone.

"This," he said, "is the true diamond. It is less beautiful than most gems, because it is so hard that no tool can cut it. However, in magical potency it surpasses all other gems. It gives its wearer the qualities of resistance, stubbornness, unflinching determination, and virtual invulnerability. Comes it from the north of India, from mountains so high they are eternally covered with that—that—what call you it when rain falls frozen, not as hail, but in feathery flakes?"

"Snow?" I said.

"Aye, snow. On these mountains so intense is the cold that water, once frozen, can never be melted again; and this eternal ice we call the diamond."

He told us of his other fine gems—a ruby, an emerald, a fine pearl from the Arabian Sea—and then said: "As my friends, you two would be entitled to a great reduction of price. This green chrysolite, for instance, would make a fine ring gem, preventing fevers, madness, and nocturnal terrors. For you I would cut it for only—"

The spell broke. Berosos and I burst into protests of poverty; we could not think such extravagant baubles; we were young men, our fortunes unmade....

At last, with a sigh, Onas put away his gems. I said: "At least, old boy, with a stock like that, you're never in danger of starvation. That box you showed us contains a fair estate by itself."

"Say not so," he replied. "What of high interest rates, and the dangers of theft and loss, it is a chancy business. Lucky the year that I end not up in debt to Elavos the Syrian! Come."

He led us up the stairway to an apartment. Here he presented us to a small, slight, dark woman. "My wife, Nembto," he said. Then he spoke to her in his own tongue.

Nembto: "I pleased. You sit. I get lunch."

She hurled a crackling string of Egyptian syllables at Onas, who, though twice her size, quailed. Then she went out. Berosos asked:

"What said she? 'Just wait until I get you alone, you scoundrel'?"

"Not quite," said the Egyptian. "She did chide me a little for not giving her warning and thus letting guests see the house in disorder. Excuse me, friends."

He followed his wife to the kitchen, whence came sounds of spirited argument. When he returned, he said:

"It is all arranged about the soldiering. She balked at first but gave in when I told her that people are paid for this duty. Hold out your cups...."

The smallest crew to fight a catapult like ours is eight: four cockers, a loader, an aimer, a trigger man, and of course the commander. We also had four extra men to take the place of the fallen, relieve the cockers when they tired, and provide the thews for moving the engine, as it weighed a good fifteen talents.

The six catapults formed a battery under commands of Bias the carpenter. Bias was, like me, a tribesman, respectable but neither rich nor learned; a middle-aged man with the knobby hands and wrinkled neck of a lifelong artisan. The full citizens reserved most of the commissioned ranks to themselves; but, as no gentleman would dirty his hands on a mechanical contrivance like a catapult, they left this post to Bias, who knew more practical engineering than the whole lot of them together.

My squad picked the name *Talos* for our catapult, after the stone-throwing bronzen man whom the god Hephaistos made for King Minos. The other five engines of the battery became the *Eros*, *Helios*, *Herakles*, *Artemis*, and *Orion*.

Three mornings after my visit to the armory, a pair of mules pulled each of the six catapults out through the great gate in the South Wall. We rumbled through the suburbs under a clear blue sky and into the country. The crewmen tramped beside their catapults, with Bias at their head and their servants straggling behind.

We halted at a farm where several haystacks were dotted about a field. The mules were unhitched and led back to graze, while the catapults were levered up to take the rollers from under them.

"Men!" began Bias, squinting at a sheet of papyrus on which he had written notes. "The first rule of the artilleryman is: 'Never get in front of your own piece.' If you're not half-witted, like an artilleryman oughtn't to be, you can figure out why without me telling you.

"The second rule is: 'Never stand inside the radius of the throwing arms.' Sometimes a catapult goes off when you don't expect it, and one of those arms can send your head flying like a hockey ball.

"The third rule is: 'Inspect and adjust your piece before and after every use.' A catapult is as fickle as a woman. Unless you keep it in good humor by adjusting it all the time, it starts casting its missiles every which way, or it breaks down and won't shoot at all, or it flies to pieces and smashes its crew like bugs. The skeins get too tight or chafe against the stress bolts, and they break when the engine is cocked. Or they go slack and lose their tension. The tension changes with the weather; a damp day slackens them, while a dry one makes them taut. They have to be oiled every month to keep them from getting brittle.

"You've got to inspect your piece whether you think it needs it or not. In fact, inspect all the harder when you think it don't need it, on account of that's just when something goes wrong.

"Now, there's two general types of catapult: the flexion type, which has a big bow fastened to the frame, so we get our tension by bending the arms of the bow; and the torsion type, like these here, with two rigid throwing arms passed through torsion skeins. The flexion type we don't use much any more except for scorpions, or when we haven't got the materials or the engineering skill to build the torsion type.

"Catapults of each type can be built in different sizes. We generally call the big ones stone throwers, on account of they shoot balls of stone or brick weighing from ten pounds up to a talent, for distances up to twelve plethra.[4] In most stone throwers the trough is fixed in position at a slope to give the greatest range. So range can be varied only by pulling the string back different distances before discharge. . . ."

Bias went on to tell us about dart throwers, like ours, in which the range could also be varied by changing the slope of the trough. He pointed out all the parts of a catapult; the base, the pedestal, the ranging strut, the trough, the rack, and the recoiler with its cross-head, finger, trigger knob, and pawls; the windlass, the frame, the torsion skeins, the skein shackles, the throwing arms, and the string. He told us what each part did, and how to perform each step in the cycle of operations. He showed us how to aim a catapult by moving it with crowbars and ropes and how to level it with plumb bob and wedges.

"Now," said he when we had all aimed at a distant haystack, "we'll—*Ea!* Didn't I just tell you never to step in front of a catapult? Didn't I? Do you want your fool head knocked off?"

When the offending soldier seemed properly abashed, Bias continued: "Now we'll shoot one dart each. Cockers, cock your pieces."

The catapults groaned as the six recoilers crept back down their troughs. The cockers' muscles bulged as they turned their windlasses. The pawls clicked over the notches of the racks.

---

4 A plethron = 100 feet.

"Stop at notch ten, six short of maximum," said Bias. "See that the pawls of the recoiler are firmly engaged with the racks. Slack off the windlasses. Loaders, load your pieces."

Our missiles were six-pound darts three cubits long, with iron heads, wooden shafts, and bronzen vanes at their after ends. Pronax, the loader of my squad, placed our first dart in the groove on the upper side of the recoiler.

Bias: "Trigger men, stand by to strike your trigger knobs. The commander of each catapult will give the order to shoot, and then the trigger man will hit the trigger knob with his mallet. Remember: Don't hit the knob until you've been ordered to, and then hit it quickly and smartly. And don't get any part of you in the way of the string or of the throwing arms. If you do, we'll have to break in a new recruit, and that's a lot of trouble.

"Now, does everybody understand? I don't want nobody shooting out of turn. *Eros* shoots first. Shoot, *Eros*!"

"Hit it!" cried the double-pay man in command of *Eros*.

Eros' trigger man was so nervous that he missed his knob and smote the bronze rack instead, denting his mallet. The man quailed as Bias scowled. The carpenter, glaring, said:

"It looks like *Eros* is going to shoot last instead of first. Another thing to remember is to use the standard words of command. When you mean 'shoot,' say 'shoot,' not 'give the polluted bastards one in the guts.' In a battle, where you can hardly hear yourself think anyway, cute little speeches like that only confuse your men. All right now, *Talos*, shoot!"

"Shoot!" I repeated.

Onas muttered a magical spell and smote his knob one clean blow. With a crash, the throwing arms flew forward against the frame; the dart departed with a swish. Up, up it rose, then down. It flew over the haystack and disappeared.

"Of course we missed," said Pronax. "Egyptian spells don't work here where the gods of the Hellenes reign."

"I will be fetching it, master dear!" said Kavaros, starting to run toward the haystack.

"Come back!" I shouted. But the Kelt kept on.

Bias said: "*Helios*, shoot!"

"*Ē!*" I cried. "Not while my man—"

Helios' trigger man struck his knob; off went the dart. It flew over Kavaros' head. He halted at its screech, looked frantically about, and threw himself on the ground. The next time I called him, he came back readily, hanging his head at the laughter of the battery.

"That," said Bias, "gives you an idea of what happens to people who go running around a shooting range without orders. *Artemis*, shoot!"

Kavaros said: "Is it not a terrible thing the way war is being spoilt by all these dreadful machines? Bad cess to the man who invented them!"

When each piece had shot one dart, the slaves had gone to fetch the missiles, and all the recoilers had been pulled forward into the starting position again, Bias unrolled his papyrus and spoke:

"Your next task is to calibrate your pieces for range. There's sixteen notches in each rack. You'll have to shoot sixteen darts in succession, one from each setting. Then you pace off the distance from the catapult to each dart and write it down on one of these tablets. Then you repeat this with the strut in the intermediate position.

"Such a list of ranges is called a range table, and it's very useful to the new artillery officer. After you get more experience, you won't need it. You'll learn to make allowances for windage, dampness, fatigue of the skeins, and so forth. There's more to being an artilleryman than it looks like. The spearmen and archers have to practice, sure, but the artillery's where you've got to have real intelligence."

"To save confusion, write with charcoal the number of each dart on its shaft, so there won't be no question as to which dart was shot from which setting."

I asked: "Sir, wouldn't one range table do for all six pieces?"

"No. You see, artilleryman, no two engines work just the same way, even when they're built to the same plans."

Calibration took two days. Then we began target practice. The *Talos* shot as well as any in the battery, despite a good deal of bickering between me and my crew.

When, after the first day of target practice, we got back to the arsenal and were being paid off, Bias took me aside and said:

"One of the generals was out watching."

"I saw him," I said.

Bias smiled. "He asked: 'Who's that good-looking little fellow, with the curly black hair, who runs around like he's crazy and screams at his men?' I thought you'd like to know."

"Look here," I said, "am I in command of them or am I not? And if I am, are they not supposed to obey my commands instantly, without dispute? And to treat me respectfully?"

"Oh, you are, you are. At least for now."

"What do you mean by that?" I shouted.

"Look, sonny, a squad that hates its commander won't be an effective force, especially in a branch like the artillery, where intelligent co-operation is needed. So, when we higher-ups see a unit going to pieces because the men can't get along, we find another officer. And come to think of it, I'm your commander, too, and you're not speaking to me in no very respectful tone. I've known men to be flogged for less, see?"

I muttered a surly assent.

"Besides," Bias went on, "just remember that you've been given double-pay rank, not because you ever fought a battle, but because your old man is a successful businessman, and because they think your fancy education somehow qualifies you. Well, maybe it does and maybe it don't, but you'd be wise not to strut around like you was the divine Alexander until you've seen a little blood shed in anger. Do you understand me?"

I was so enraged I could hardly speak. I came near to telling Bias where he could put my position. But my guardian daimon checked my haughty spirit. (Years later it occurred to me that Bias must have found it as hard to control himself as I had.)

Swallowing my pride, I said: "Yes, sir. I'm sorry. What is it I do that seems to rub everybody the wrong way?"

Bias thought. "Put it this way. You're one of the touchiest people I ever saw when it comes to *your* feelings and *your* dignity. If anybody crosses or slights you the least bit, you want to fight him, horse, foot, and artillery. But you don't care a half-farthing whose toes *you* trample on. Their feelings and dignity don't mean a thing to you."

I made a wry face. "I don't try deliberately to quarrel with anybody. It is just—just—"

"Well?"

"Oh, I suppose I'm so wrapped up in whatever task I am trying to accomplish that I simply don't think about others."

"Maybe, but you'll sure make life hard for yourself that way. Even if you're as smart as you think you are, people won't put up with that sort of thing."

Well, I do not like to admit I am wrong any better than the next man. But I can smell dung when my nose is rubbed in it, and if my anger is quick to rise, it is equally quick to wane. Humbly I asked:

"What do you suggest, Bias?"

"For one thing, when a man makes some little mistake, don't shout in front of all the rest that he's a thick-skinned idiot. Take him aside and quietly point out what he's done wrong. Give him a chance to mend his ways before you yell at him like he was a criminal."

The third day went more smoothly, except that Onas arrived late for drill. I tried (though with some backsliding) to profit from Bias' advice. Thus, I did not scream at the Egyptian but chided him gently when we were alone.

I found keen pleasure in the creak of the skeins, the crash of the throwing arms, and the whistle of the darts. I might be only a little longer than our missiles myself, but with *Talos* I could overthrow the mightiest warrior—nay more, even Antigonos himself, who was said to be seven feet tall.

Furthermore, my military duties gave me an excuse once more to put off my family on the subject of my marriage to Io.

We were setting out on our fourth day of practice when a slave ran up and said: "Are you Chares Nikonos, sir?"

"Yes. What is it?"

"You are commanded to turn your catapult over to one of your men, sir, and come to the Council Chamber at once."

"Who wants me?" said I, nettled.

"The Council, sir."

"Oh. Very well. Onas, take over."

I found the Council and the generals, Kallias among them, awaiting me with grave faces. Kallias said:

"O Chares, events have caught up with us ere we were ready. Demetrios son of Antigonos is at Loryma, almost within sight of us, with a great force. He demands that Rhodes unite with him and Antigonos in their new war against Ptolemaios.

"I will not try to explain the politics of the matter; that is the affair of these gentlemen. I will only say that we cannot accede to Demetrios' demand, and that on the other hand we must gain time to prepare for his attack.

"An embassy will leave for Loryma tomorrow. While they strive to placate Demetrios, you will approach him, saying that the city has voted to build a statue of him, twice life size, at our own expense. You have been chosen as sculptor, and you are there to make models and sketches. Do you understand?"

"Y—yes, sir."

"Can you do it?"

"I think so."

"Very well. Have you any questions?"

"Yes, sir. How much shall I be paid?"

Kallias and President Damoteles traded smiles. Kallias said: "The Council has voted to pay you two thousand drachmai, besides the cost of the bronze."

This was a better commission than that for the statues for the theater. I said:

"I thank you, my masters. May I ask another question?"

"Speak," said President Damoteles.

"Why was I chosen? I know I have annoyed some by premature and youthful boasts, and I also know that I'm the youngest practicing sculptor in Rhodes, with little to show."

Damoteles: "You have impressed some here with the skill you have already shown. Moreover, your new method of casting promises to speed the task; and in this project we want speed, lest Demetrios decide we mock him and come against us anyway. Go home and gather your gear. The *Peripolos* sails at dawn."

I went home and told my parents. To Kavaros I said: "Pack our gear. We're going to Karia on a job. And do not think to run away. I've taken out a policy on you from Dolon and Magnes, the best slave catchers in the world."

Kavaros grinned slyly. "Sure now, master darling, what would a poor Kelt on the run do in those wild countries of Asia? If he could not bespeak the people, they would like as not eat him for dinner."

From Rhodes the Karian coast, a hundred furlongs off, looks like a solid wall of blue-green hills, rising steeply to the tableland of Asia Minor. As one nears it, it opens out into bays and headlands.

The *Peripolos*, the old sacred trireme of Rhodes, with the red rose of Rhodes aglow on her sail, entered the Kaunian Gulf. On our left Mount Phoinix, crowned with its citadel, rose from the promontory of Kynos-Sema.

The ships of Demetrios stitched the waters of the gulf before us, rowing back and forth at exercises. After we had passed Mount Phoinix, every good stretch of beach had ships drawn up. Tubby merchantmen also plied the waters, bringing supplies to Demetrios' army.

I stood on the forecastle deck with the embassy, looking keenly forward to seeing the great Demetrios, of whom many spoke as another Alexander. Would he make a suitable subject for my long-dreamt-of Colossus? Would he come up to my ideal of perfect manhood? I had seen him once, from afar, and had heard contradictory tales of his character. What was he really like?

On the deck Admiral Exekestos, a big bellowing potbellied man, argues with Rhesos, the Superintendent of Docks, about the design of ships.

"Look at that!" said the admiral, pointing to an enormous galley with a single bank of sweeps. A pair of light catapults sat on its forecastle deck, like grasshoppers crouched to spring; between them a statue of a Titan hurling a boulder rose from the stem post. The golden eagle of the Antigonians glowed from the sail.

"That," said the admiral, "is one of these seveners. Our spies tell us Demetrios has over thirty ships above fivers in rate. What should we ever do against *them*?"

"Our triremes and triemiolias, with their highly trained rowers, can always outmaneuver those clumsy things," said Rhesos.

"Much good that would do us! These battle transports do not try to maneuver and ram; they disorganize the foe by an artillery bombardment, then grapple and overwhelm him by boarding. With so broad a deck, they can carry many times as many marines as we. The conventional trireme is as obsolete as the bronzen sword."

Rhesos shrugged. "We beat Attalos with them. And how could our taxpayers ever support sixers and seveners, with their hordes of hungry rowers?"

"Their extra cost is not so great as the number of rowers implies; for, with several men on each oar of a single bank, we should need but one trained rower for each oar. The rest can be labor of the lowest class."

"But still, where should we find so many rowers? Such ships may be practical for Antigonos, with the manpower of his vast satrapy to draw upon, but they were absurd for Rhodes."

"Not so, my dear Rhesos. The mainland of Hellas is caught in the pinch of poverty. Let word spread that several hundred places on our benches are open, and they'll swim hither to enlist. And we must learn to mount catapults on our ships, to match Demetrios' devices. I tell you, the state that falls behind in technical improvements is lost—"

"Ahoy!" shouted a man on the forecastle deck of the sevener. "Who are you?"

Our captain shouted back: "The *Peripolos* of Rhodes, bearing an embassy to the General Demetrios."

"This is the *Devastator*, of the Imperial Macedonian Navy," said the other. "Follow us."

The sevener turned ponderously toward Loryma, showing the eagle of gilded wood on her stern. As Loryma came into sight, I could see, in the fields around the city, archers shooting at butts and companies of infantry marching to and fro with long Macedonian pikes. Rhesos said:

"Whatever befall, the folk of Loryma will have their crops sorely hurt by trampling."

The anchorage was crowded. Many of Demetrios' ships, like the sevener that guided us, were too heavy to beach without special machinery. We threaded our way through the swarm of great war galleys with much exchange of shouts and curses between the captain of the *Devastator* and those of the other ships.

When we arrived at Loryma's lone pier, it was already occupied by a fiver on one side and a sevener on the other. We had to anchor and sit in the harbor for hours until the fiver finished loading and pulled out.

The shore swarmed with soldiers, slaves bearing burdens, camp followers, and sutlers selling food and supplies to the troops. Most of the townsfolk of Loryma were not to be seen. They prudently kept out of sight, not wishing to have soldiers bully them, rob them, or, in a moment of pique, slice off their heads. Moreover, they had sent all the free women with any pretensions to virtue back into the hills.

Demetrios' officers were everywhere, inspecting and commanding. A group of them bustled over to our side of the pier, nodding their tall crests of red and green and blue. Exekestos told them who we were. The officers shouted commands in Macedonian, and the oars were shipped. The ship was pulled up to the pier and made fast.

We climbed down the ladder, followed by our slaves with the luggage. Exekestos introduced himself and the rest of the embassy to the Antigonian officers.

"And who is the youth?" asked the senior Macedonian.

"Chares son of Nikon, a sculptor," said Exekestos. "To commemorate your lord's liberation of Athens, we plan to rear a heroic statue of your lord in our city. We brought Chares along to make sketches and models."

"A shrewd move," said the officer. "Demetrios likes pretty boys."

He spoke to a youth who accompanied him and sent the lad racing up toward the town. In my younger days few things so enraged me as to be called a "pretty boy." But I had to learn not to make an issue of the matter on every occasion, lest I spend my life in quarrels and have no time left for art.

We made small talk with the Macedonians until the boy came back. After a whispered consultation between him and the senior officer, the latter said:

"The general cannot see the embassy until the day after tomorrow because of the press of business."

Beside me, Rhesos muttered: "By the! Does he deem himself a king already? One can get a sight of Pharnabazos sooner than of him."

"However," continued the officer, "we can let the sculptor start work at once. Go with the boy, what's-your-name."

I followed the youth with misgivings. On one hand, I am after all part Phoenician, and Phoenicians are not so free and easy toward homosexual love affairs as Hellenes. Moreover, I personally prefer women. On the other, I should find it hard to plead that I could not give in to the general's wishes because of a foreign prejudice. Some would even say it was my patriotic duty to yield.

Pondering gloomy thoughts, I followed the boy into the town's best house, from which Demetrios had evicted the owners.

I had seen Demetrios only once, when he entered Athens after taking Mounychia from Kasandros' men. He had marched through the Melitean Gate with a company of foot. The citizens, summoned to a special assembly, gathered at the Pnyx. Demetrios went past, tall and splendid in purple and gold. Some said that this was Alexander come again—nay more, that this was an improvement over the original Alexander. Demetrios was not only taller; he was also more humanly likable than the tense and fiery little Titan.

Inside, Demetrios had told the Athenians (who expected some crushing levy to pay their liberator's soldiers) that he had come to restore their ancient liberties; that their old constitution was again in force; and that his father would send them 150,000 medimnoi[5] of wheat and timber enough for a hundred triremes. It was, no doubt, their relief at not being squeezed by their latest overlord that led the Athenians to bestow all those preposterous honors upon Demetrios and Antigonos: that they should henceforth be known as Tutelary Gods and Saviors; that the month Mounychion should be renamed "Demetrion"; and much besides.

A hunchbacked usher led me into the andron. Here I found the general and three other men on the floor, poring over a diagram on a great sheet of papyrus, measuring four by six feet. The diagram showed a war galley. Around the room lay not only rolls of similar

5 A medimnos = 1½ bushels.

sheets but also wooden models of ships, siege towers, catapults, and other engines of war.

Demetrios spoke: "I think your niner would work, true enough. But tell me, what is the largest rate ever built?"

The man addressed said: "Let me think, my lord. The divine Alexander once built a tenner, and of course your father made ten of them for his attack on Tyre. Some are still in service."

"Has anybody ever built a ship with more than ten files of rowers on a side?"

"Not to my knowledge, my lord."

Demetrios grinned and slapped the man on the back. "Then we will build an elevener! Draw up the plans, with estimates of cost. Arrange the rowers in two banks, six-over-five." He looked up at me. "Rejoice! Are you the sculptor?"

"Yes, sir."

"What is your name?"

"Chares Nikonos, of Lindos. And this is my man."

"Very well, Chares, get to work. Do what you like, only do not bother me."

"Sir!" I said.

"What is it?"

"I may have to bother you later on, to do your statue justice. I shall need to make some measurements and perhaps a life mask."

"What is a life mask?"

"A mold of your face, in clay."

"It sounds uncomfortable. We shall see." Demetrios got up off the floor and shouted to the usher: "Send in Epimachos!"

While the naval architects rolled up their plan, an Athenian came in and began to talk about a monstrous belfry or movable siege tower which, I gathered, Demetrios hoped soon to build.

At first I thought he meant to use it against Rhodes. The thought so alarmed me that my hands shook as I sketched. Then Demetrios said:

"But what is the ground before Salamis like?"

I almost dropped my charcoal. There are two places called Salamis: one an island with a small city of the same name off the coast of Attika, in sight of Peiraieus; the other a city on the east coast of

Cyprus. Demetrios would hardly mean to attack the Attic Salamis, as he had just come from Athens, which was friendly to him. If, on the other hand, he was bound toward Cyprus, now held by the troops of Ptolemaios, this news would certainly interest my government.

I hid my excitement and bent my attention to my subject. Demetrios Antigonou was one of the handsomest men of his time. He was no more than five years older than I—that is to say, about thirty. His light brown hair curled to his nape in the kind of mane affected by the divine Alexander. Demetrios also resembled Alexander somewhat in feature, although Alexander had been a little man, whereas Demetrios was six feet tall and magnificently muscled.

The main difference lay in this: Demetrios kept, even in maturity, a certain childish or womanish softness and roundness of feature, which contrasted with his Heraklean body. He wore only shoes and a simple tunic, though this shirt was of the finest wool, with a broad border of true Tyrian purple.

I worked for hours. Demetrios was a restless model, always jumping up and moving about. A certain amount of this is helpful to the sculptor, as it shows him the play of light and shade on the subject's features. But Demetrios was never in the same position for three heartbeats. Now and then he cast a glance at me and struck a heroic attitude, with his chin up and shoulders drawn back; the next instant, oblivious of me, he would be absorbed in some new military problem. When Demetrios had finished with Epimachos and his belfry, he sent for his chief of artillery, Apollonios, who brought in a model of a catapult of new design. At last the general dismissed Apollonios and said:

"That is all for today, sculptor. How far along are you?"

"Another day and a half should finish it, sir."

"Good. I shall see you tomorrow then. Rejoice!" Out he swept.

The Rhodian embassy had quarters in tents on the edge of town. When I retired that night, the ambassadors had not yet come back from dinner with Demetrios. Next morning I arose to find Exekestos seated upon a stool in front of his tent with his head in his hands. I said:

"Good day, sir."

The admiral groaned and looked up at me with bloodshot eyes. "You are a kakodaimon sent to haunt me for my sins," he said. "Go away."

"Why, sir—"

"Oh, never mind. Dear Herakles! I am not without experience of the world, yet in trying to keep up with these Macedonians in the drinking of wine neat, I am but a babe. Beware the Macedonian, Chares, especially when he proffers hospitality."

"A wild party, sir?"

"So it seemed to us, though to Demetrios and his fawning parasites I daresay it was as tame as barley broth. Imagine, mature and respectable men like us dancing a Cretan fling! And the women those Corinthiasts had in—but then, I must not shock your young ears. How went the sculptural session?"

When I told of Demetrios' remark about Salamis, Exekestos said: "Aha! We may have time to prepare our defense after all. How far have you gone?"

"Two more days should finish the task. Tomorrow I shall make a sketch in clay, and the next day take measurements and perhaps a life mask."

"Go to it, and keep your ears open and your mouth shut."

The next day I spent in modeling a sketch of the general's head in the round. Demetrios conferred for hours with his officers about pay, promotion, food, and equipment for his men. Trying to listen to the talk in hope of picking up something of value slowed my work, so that I had not finished my model when Demetrios departed.

At the tents Exekestos again asked how nearly done I was. I told him: "I should be finished late tomorrow. When will the embassy complete its mission?"

"Our meeting with Demetrios is planned for tomorrow morning. If all go as I expect, we shall be ready to leave at the end of the meeting."

Next morning the hunchback ushered me into the andron that Demetrios used as his office. As I stepped into the room, there was a sharp sound. Something struck me a heavy blow on the forehead.

Demetrios and Apollonios crouched on the other side of the room behind the model of the latter's new catapult. The general was rocking and holding his sides with mirth, throwing back his head and opening wide his mouth to emit loud, braying laughs.

I had left a bucket of water clay in the room, with damp cloths over the bucket to keep the clay from drying out. Demetrios had scooped out a fistful of clay, molded it into a ball, and laid an ambush for me.

With the best grace I could muster, I peeled the flattened lump of clay off my face and got to work, while Demetrios dictated letters. Presently the hunchback appeared.

"My lord!" he said. "The Rhodians are here."

"Tell them to wait, Evagoras," said Demetrios. "I must dress to receive them."

The general went out. After a long interval he returned in his diplomatic robes. A gorgeous sight he was, from the headband spangled with gold down to the purple felt boots decorated with patterns in gold thread. He always had a weakness for fancy dress, and now he had outdone himself. While I quietly put the finishing touches on the model, the embassy was presented.

"Well, my good men," said Demetrios, "the reason I have summoned you is this. The bearing of Ptolemaios toward my father has become intolerable. He has invaded Kilikia by sea, and, although I drove his force from those parts, he committed much damage, which he refuses to pay for. He oppresses our friends, both Phoenician and Greek, in Cyprus, who bear the tyranny of his brother Menelaos. With the cruel Kasandros and the grim Lysimachos he plots our overthrow.

"We have sent him a final demand, which he has rejected. The sword being thus forced into our hand, honor demands that we sheathe it not until justice has been done. I am now on my way to do battle with Menelaos.

"Placed as you Rhodians are off the coast of Anatolia, you must know that your interests are closely linked with ours. What affects the satrapy of Antigonos affects you. It is therefore only right that you, who enjoy the security bought by our hard-fought victories, shall undertake your proper share of the toil and the risk. As the virtue, the courage, and the justice of Rhodians are known throughout the civilized world, I need not belabor the point. Nay more, your own sense of duty will point out to you the only path you can decently follow."

"And what is that, sir?" said Exekestos.

"Why, to join us in our war against the corrupt and decadent tyrant of the Delta—against him who sits, like a fat spider in the center of his web, safe in Egypt while sending forth his armies to fight and his agents to bribe and intrigue. How say you? Ten ships—the number you sent six years ago with my father to the first liberation of Hellas—would do."

Exekestos replied: "You forget, O Demetrios, that Rhodes has a treaty of amity with Ptolemaios, who has ever been our friend. The honor whereof you spoke forbids us to attack him. We shall be glad to have the friendship of the great Antigonos and his valiant son, but not at the cost of our ties with Egypt."

While they argued, I put the finishing touches on the sketch. They talked for an hour, sent for wine, and talked for another hour. They cited precedents and claims going back to the siege of Troy. As the discussion ground on, Demetrios ever became more demanding and haughty. When it transpired that the Rhodians would not retreat a digit from their stand, Demetrios stood up and said:

"Then go your ways, dog-faced little Rhodians. I have neither the time for fruitless haggling nor the meekness to beg for that which I may demand. But think not that your refusal will be forgotten."

The embassy bowed itself out. The general turned to me. "Are you done yet, little man?"

I said: "I have finished my clay sketch, sir. Now I must take measurements."

"So? Let us be at it then." Demetrios pulled off his robe and shirt and stood naked before us.

Kavaros and I began measuring him with tape and calipers while I noted the figures on my tablet. Certainly Demetrios was a splendidly developed man, though no god; neither golden thigh nor unwinking gaze had he, nor did he glide through the air instead of walking.

When we had finished, I stepped back to see if I had overlooked anything. Demetrios was staring at me with a significant look in his eye. He said to Kavaros:

"Leave us, slave."

The Kelt looked a question at me. I said: "You may go, Kavaros. Wait outside."

Kavaros went. Demetrios led me to a couch.

"Sit, Rhodian," he said, drawing me down. "How would you like to work for me? I can find a useful post for a beautiful youth like you, especially if he show true friendship toward his general."

"But, sir, my first loyalty must be to my city!"

"Oh, take it not so much to heart. The day of these little self-governing city-states is done, though they know it not. This is the age of empire, when an able man who fears not to risk all on one throw may win the rule of the world! Were it not well to be the friend of such a man?"

"But, my lord—"

"Besides, the high and mighty line that your city is taking may well result in its utter destruction, like that of Tyre. You would not go down to the shades with your stiff-necked fools of countrymen, now would you?"

As he spoke, Demetrios caressed me. Despite his faults, which were many and grave, there was something wonderfully attractive about him; he could radiate charm even when sitting perfectly still.

But I have explained my view of such liaisons, and I had no intention of being bullied into one of them, even by the world's greatest general, and even though he was twice my size. I said:

"But, sir, we haven't yet finished our work!"

"Forsooth? I thought the measurements concluded matters."

"No, I must make a life mask. As you won't be in Rhodes to pose, I shall need one faithfully to reproduce your face."

"Oh, let us first pleasure ourselves. One little kiss—"

"No, sir; no, sir! I could not possibly concentrate on my art after such an ecstasy. I'll tell you: Let me make the mask, and then you may do as you like."

"This mask sounds like a disagreeable ordeal," quoth Demetrios.

"It is not so bad if the subject doesn't panic, and only thus can I do justice to the beauty of your person."

"Do you really think me beautiful, dear Chares?"

"Your beauty outdazzles the sun's."

"I hope you really mean that. Of course my parasites say so, too, but they are a lot of wretched flatterers, with no more greatness of soul than the modern Athenians. They would praise an ass among apes for a meal." Demetrios sighed. "Verily, the great man finds gold and rubies more easily come by than true friendship."

"Yes, my lord, but let me show you how this mask works. You might even find a military application for the trick. They say you can find one for practically anything."

Thus by distracting the warlord I managed to wrench out of his grasp. "Kavaros!" I called.

"See that you keep your word, fair Chares," said Demetrios. "You shall never leave this dwelling otherwise."

"Never fear, sir. Kavaros, mix up a batch of soft clay for a life mask. Now, General, recline on your back. Let me put this cushion under your head. Are you comfortable? Next, I oil your face. That is so the clay shall easily come off.... Now I put these straws up your nostrils, so you can breathe through the clay. Hold them, please. Close your eyes. You must hold still for most of an hour, but you've had practice on the drill field."

I smeared the clay on his face. When he grunted, I said: "No, sir, don't try to talk or you will spoil the mask and perhaps get a mouthful of clay."

I built up the mold until there was nothing to be seen of Demetrios' face but a large blob of clay. I said:

"Now we must wait. It's tedious, but we must all suffer a little for art. The mask may seem to grow hot, but that will do no harm. If the straws collapse so you cannot breathe, wave your arms and I'll free you. There is no danger. We shall be right here, ready to help. I'll tell you when the clay is ready to be taken off. Clean up this mess, Kavaros. We mustn't leave the general's headquarters looking thus."

While talking, loudly enough to cover the sound of my movements, I tiptoed about and helped the Kelt to gather up my gear and the model of General Demetrios' head. We stole to the door. I cast a glance back at the couch on which Demetrios lay. Although his face was hidden, an observant man could still infer the tenor of his thoughts.

We sauntered boldly out of the house and down the street toward the waterfront. Said Kavaros:

"And what did himself want of you, young master? Is it what I am thinking?"

"You think correctly, old boy. I told him: after the making of the mask."

"You mean you walked off and left—oh, what an enormous sly fellow you are!" Kavaros began to laugh uncontrollably, though I told him to stop. He guffawed, gurgled, snorted, sputtered, and shook with mirth all the way to the ship.

"We had a king of the Tektosages like that to once," he said. "One of his young men stabbed him in a fit of jealousy, poor man. Loving women is risky enough."

"I can tell you one thing," I said. "This lecherous warlord is no ideal of mine, to be immortalized by a colossus in bronze. And say nothing to anyone of our little trick."

"Why, sir?"

"If we keep quiet, he may do so, too, rather than look like a fool. But if we boast of outwitting him, he may feel that honor compels him to make trouble for us."

I reported to Exekestos and said: "All done, sir." The rowers filed aboard, each bearing his personal cushion. The sailors pushed off with their poles. The coxswain gave the beat, and the flutist took it up. And away went the *Peripolos.*

Had I been less avid for glory and less urgently in need of money, I might have subcontracted part of my new task to Lykon and others and thus have finished sooner. However, I did not, thus confirming Lykon in his bitter dislike of me. Except for the pedestal, which task I gave to Makar, I did all the work myself, with the help of Kavaros and a few unskilled workmen hired from time to time.

A twelve-foot bronze cannot be cast in one piece. I therefore had to make, first, a small clay model, and then a full-sized model in clay, and take partial molds from the latter. Then I had to cast separate pieces—one for the trunk, one for each limb, and so forth—to be joined by riveting. To make the statue stable, I planned to cast the lower parts of thicker metals than the upper, a trick I learned from

Lysippos. Further to secure it, I planned to insert iron braces into holes in the pedestal, extending up inside the legs of the statue.

I was putting the finishing touches on the small model, showing Demetrios with spear, shield, helmet, and boots, but otherwise nude, when Kallias' ruddy, round face appeared at the door.

"Rejoice, dear Chares!" cried he, all smiles. "I would have come to see your work sooner, but I have been gathering material for my sluing crane. How is our Demetrios coming? Ah, splendid! Are you sure he prefers his clothes off?"

"That's what he told me," I said. "This is a conventional pose of the god Ares, which Demetrios wishes to affect."

"Well, he is the man to please. Not that I should care to see myself standing naked in the marketplace, but I am no Hellene. Here, Kavaros, leave off your work for a while. Take this and go buy yourself a drink. Your master and I would confer."

"I thank your lordship," said Kavaros. He trotted off down the path, whistling a wild Keltic tune.

"Now then," said Kallias, "since our contract for the Sophokles is in abeyance because of this war threat, I once more find myself pressed. I therefore expect you to observe the same terms with me on the contract for the Demetrios as we had planned on the Sophokles."

"Meaning?"

"Meaning a commission of one-fourth of the total, or five hundred drachmai. I do not ask for a share of your allowance for the cost of the bronze, but then I am not greedy."

I found myself liking Kallias less and less. "Look here," I said, "this contract was given me by the President himself, without any mention of a piece for you. I see no reason to make you a sharer in all my gains."

"Ah, but who arranged things so that you got the contract? I did. I would have made my terms clear before the job was formally offered, had I had a chance." He touched the model with a finger that bore a massy golden ring. "Now that I look closely, I am not sure that I like your execution. It has too much of this low modern realism, not enough idealistic inspiration. Would it not be a shame if you finished the statue and the Council, on my advice, refused it?"

I said: "Just for instance, what would happen if I bore tales to the President?"

He grinned. "Try it. It were my word against yours, and I think I know whose would prevail."

He was probably right. With his charm and glibness, even though a foreigner, he could talk the Council into belief that night was day, offal was gold, and Kallias of Arados was an honest man.

I tried to beat him down at least to the hundred and fifty drachmai agreed upon for the Sophokles, but to no avail. At last I said:

"Go walk! If you will hurry up the payment of my first installment, I'll give you what you ask."

"Good boy! As your Sophokles says, no word that brings a profit is wrong. Let me compliment you on the splendid showing of your catapult team. With such as you to defend her, the City of Roses needs fear no foreign foe."

"Save you," I said. He went off with a laugh and a wave.

When I got home for dinner, my father said: "Chares, Genetor will visit us this evening, bringing his wife and daughter, so that you can see the maid."

"But Father! I'm not ready..."

I argued in vain. My father said: "I want no more trouble, young man! It's enough that you're allowed to meet her. As long as I'm feeding you, I expect this much consideration at least."

I was too low in the mind to persist in the argument. The girl turned out to be small, slight, blue-eyed, and fair-haired; not at all ugly, but making no more impression upon me than as if she had been a sparrow on the roof tiles. She spoke in a timid little squeak:

"It is an honor to meet you, O Chares. I will try to do my wifely duty toward you in all things."

"Of course she will; she is a good girl!" said Genetor. He beckoned his slave. "I brought a jug of real Chian—it cost me a pretty obolos, too—in which we can pledge the union of our families. Let us pray to the Bright One to give these young people a healthy, wholesome life together and send them strong sons."

I drank the precious golden stuff silently, thinking that I now knew how a fly feels in a spider's web while the spider swathes him in gossamer the better to devour him. I thought, if ever I did wed,

I should prefer a wife with more sparkle and drive than this poor frightened child. The kind of woman I thought I wanted was said to occur in foreign lands—in Egypt, say, or Persia. While Io no doubt had many of what Hellenes consider wifely virtues, I was sure she would bore me to death in a month.

I continued to drill my catapult crew, though now we met but once a ten-day. We wore light steel caps and leather jacks of uniform pattern, so that we looked a little more like soldiers. There had been but one bad accident, when *Eros'* loader strayed into the path of one of his own engine's throwing arms and had his shoulder broken. The unfortunate man never did recover the full use of his arm.

After these drills, Onas and Berosos and I would sit in Evios' tavern for an hour over a cup of wine, recounting stories and advising one another about life's problems. Onas had many tales to tell of the wonders and mysteries of his ancient land. While his purpose seemed to be to impress us with the magical might of Egyptian wizardry, the things that fascinated me the most were the architectural and sculptural wonders of the country: the pyramids, the temples, and the colossal statues.

Boedromion came, and with it bands of small boys begging from door to door, singing:

"The swallow has come, has come!
Fair weather she brings; and fair seasons.
White is her breast; and black
Is her hair. O man! Of your plenty
Some pressed fruit fetch, a cup
Of wine, and a tray of cheeses...."

We were into Pyanepsion; the first rain of the season had fallen. I worked on the large model while Makar chiseled away at the pedestal. One day Glôs the engraver came into the studio, puffing from haste and wild with excitement.

"Antigonos has sent a fleet to attack us!" he cried. "Look!"

Out in the blue was a squadron of ships. I peered and said: "That's no invasion fleet. I see but five galleys."

"Then what do you mean to do?"

"We shall see."

The ships rowed slowly past the harbor, the sun sparkling on their deck fighters' armor. They moved on down the coast toward Lindos, then slowly turned about and came back.

A merchantman came into sight around the North Point, sailing before Zephyros. The five galleys closed in upon it. There was no fight, but presently two galleys set out toward Loryma with the merchantman in tow.

"It's a blockade," said Glôs.

Now the old *Peripolos* put out from the Great Harbor. Although she was plainly coming to parley, the Antigonian ships bore down upon her in such a menacing manner that she hastily backed into the harbor, not daring to turn for fear of exposing her side to their rams.

Trumpets blasted down in the harbor, and the sun winked on moving metal. I said: "Perhaps we had better go down to see if they want us."

At the entrance to the dockyards I found the rest of my catapult squad and some of our officers in a fine state of confusion. First, Bias told us to drag *Talos* out of the arsenal. When we had done so, the battalion leader bade us take the catapult back into the shed. Then Kallias told us to wait. After we had waited for hours, and the sun was sinking, he appeared again.

"Which catapult of the *Eros* type has a full crew here?" he said. "Call the roll, Bias."

It turned out that *Talos* was the only one whose entire squad was present. Even Onas, usually late to everything, was there.

Kallias said:

"The Board of Generals has decided to give battle on the morrow. To face the *Myraina*, the sevener out there, we must have at least one catapult on our ships. As an experiment we shall mount *Talos* on the bow of our newest trireme, the *Halia*. Get that engine down to the quays, quickly."

"What about our dinner?" wailed Berosos.

"Dinner!" shouted Kallias. "The man's city is attacked and he talks of dinner!"

We hauled the *Talos* to where the *Halia* lay. Bias was already on the forecastle arguing with the shipwrights. He insisted that the figurehead of Halia riding a dolphin must be sawn down so that the catapult could be centered, while they wanted the catapult mounted off the centerline and the ship left as it was.

"Won't it make your boat tip over sidewise?" said Bias.

The head shipwright laughed. "Listen to the landlubber! Look here, mate, this little dinghy takes a hundred and eighty rowers, besides sailors and marines. Your little spring-trap don't weigh no more than six strong men, so the list will be so small you couldn't even see it. Besides, we'll pile the darts on the other side to balance."

The shipwright won. We worked far into the night, installing clamps and cleats to hold the catapult to the deck. We also built a rack for the darts and low wicker screens around the forecastle, like the spray lattices of an undecked ship, to protect the crew from missiles. At last we hauled the engine up the plank to the deck.

Half the Rhodian navy was in its home port, while the other half patrolled the coasts of the Aegean for pirates.

At Rhodes itself we had six ships that day, four of them standard triremes and two of the new triemiolias. This is a modified trireme, with its oars and rigging specially arranged to facilitate the pursuit of pirates.

Facing us was the Antigonian squadron, with three ships on duty and more at Loryma, awaiting their turn to relieve the blockading squadron.

The *Halia*'s coxswain set the stroke with his call of: "*Rhyppapai! Papai! Rhyppapai! Papai!*" The flutist took up the beat with his mournful toot as we rowed out of the Great Harbor in single file. As we cleared the moles, the ships began to roll and pitch. The wind tumbled gray-and-white clouds across the sky like masses of windblown weed; the sun blinked on and off. There was confusion among the rowers, with oars clattering and coxswains shouting.

I had a nervous knot in the midriff—less, I think, fear of the coming battle than fear that I should, in my first action, play the coward or the fool before my comrades.

"Sick already am I," moaned Berosos, looking green under his swarthiness.

Every time our ram dipped into the water, the splash sent spray whipping over the forecastle. We crouched behind our screens with the six archers. The file of marines, rich youths in splendid armor, occupied the quarterdeck, the wind whipping their scarlet cloaks and many-hued horsehair plumes.

The Antigonians, who had been up around North Point, headed toward us. Their sailors hastily furled their small battle sails and lowered the light boat masts.

Captain Damophilos hurried forward, saying: "We shall divide into two squadrons, one consisting of this ship and the triemiolias. It will be our honor to attack the *Myraina*."

From their faces, my squad would have been happy to leave that honor to others. Berosos said:

"But, Captain, two catapults has the big ship. What will she be doing with them?"

"You do not think to fight a battle without risk, do you?"

"No, but it were well if one could," said the Babylonian, raising a wan smile from his squad mates.

Damophilos said: "Do not try to be funny; it is the wrong time. If it will hearten you, know that Demetrios' shipboard artillery is made up of three-span dart throwers, which we easily outrange. Three notes on the trumpet, thus"—he whistled—"mean 'shoot at will.' Four notes, like this—mean 'cease shooting.'"

I asked: "What if the trumpeter be slain?"

"If there be too much noise for my commands to be heard, I will send messengers."

"How shall we aim the ship, since the catapult is solidly fixed to the deck?"

"Leave that to me. I will sight from the stern past the bow post and command the helmsman. You worry about range. Does everybody understand?"

When he had satisfied himself, Damophilos hastened back to the quarterdeck. Onas said:

"Great gods of Egypt, they are almost upon us!"

The Antigonian ships were closing fast. Pronax, the loader, said:

"Herakles! It's too bad we didn't have some target practice afloat before this battle. How shall we ever hit anything with the catapult leaping like a kid in the spring?"

I said: "What range do you make, Berosos?"

Berosos shaded his eyes. "Twenty plethra—perhaps nineteen."

Because of her size, the *Myraina* could not quickly stop or turn. Nevertheless, she was much faster than any other ship present, having two hundred and eighty rowers. She pulled ahead of the two Antigonian triremes. The other Rhodian squadron, having drawn off to one side, aimed to cut in behind the *Myraina* and separate her from her companions.

Captain Damophilos shouted a command. Our rowers dug in their oars and braked to a stop, while the two triemiolias, the *Euryalê* and the *Active*, raced ahead.

Berosos said: "In the name of Mardoukos, Chares, let us load. In range are we."

"Cockers, cock your piece," I said. I had held off loading because if a catapult is left cocked too long, the skeins lose some of their power. "What range, Berosos?"

"Fourteen plethra."

"Pawls in the sixteenth notch," I said, trying to read the range table from the fluttering sheet of papyrus. "Load your piece."

"May we shoot?" said Onas, nervously hefting his mallet.

"Hold your tongue! Stand by."

I looked back and caught the eye of Damophilos, who nudged the trumpeter, who blew three notes.

Onas at once struck the trigger knob. *Talos* crashed. As *Halia*'s bow was digging into the waves at the end of a down-roll, the dart plunged into the water far short of the *Myraina*.

"Zeus ruin you, you god-detested fool!" I shouted. "You're not to shoot until I command!"

"We ought to shoot when the ship is level," said Berosos.

"No," said a cocker, "we ought to shoot when the ship is at the end of a roll, and standing still, and make allowances for the slant of the deck."

"Be quiet, all of you," I said. "Pull up your recoiler. Cock your piece. Fourteenth—no, thirteenth notch. Load your piece—"

There came across the water the sound of a catapult's discharge. A three-span dart whistled past with an unnerving sound and splashed into the water astern of the *Halia*. My crew leaped and ducked like chickens at whom a hawk has stooped.

"Get back!" I screamed. I waited for one more pitch of the ship. Then, as it neared a level position on its up-roll, I cried: "Shoot!"

Onas had been reciting a spell; hence he was slow with his mallet. As a result, the deck was slanted up as he smote, and the dart flew high above the *Myraina*.

A second sound of discharge came from the sevener, and a dart whizzed toward us and struck with a thud, a few feet away. Berosos shrieked with fear and covered his eyes.

"So much for your Egyptian spells!" said Pronax, pulling the missile out of the planking. "At least we shall have an extra dart when ours give out."

"Pull up your recoiler. Cock your piece," I said. "What's the range?"

"Nine plethra," said Berosos.

"Tenth notch...Load your piece."

Meanwhile the *Euryalê* and the *Active* drove forward, converging to take the *Myraina*'s oars from either side. A strident yelling arose as the triemiolias dug in to get up speed and then shipped their oars on the side toward the sevener. Their quarry could not follow suit, because a sevener's long sweeps cannot be quickly withdrawn through the oarlocks.

Missiles flew from the deck of the *Myraina* to the triemiolias and back again: arrows, javelins, and sling bullets. The *Myraina*'s oarsmen laid their oars back flat against the sides of their ship. The triemiolias struck glancing blows against these compacted masses of oars. There was a groaning and cracking of timbers.

A grapnel on the end of a rope flew from the *Myraina* to one of the smaller ships, but somebody caught it and threw it overboard before it could catch in the woodwork. Then the ships were past one another and rowing again.

Berosos said: "If they once grapple us, lost are we. They must have a hundred marines aboard that thing."

I was about to give the word to shoot when I realized that the *Halia* no longer faced her target. The flutist's pipe resounded again; the trireme's oars drove her on a curving course to take her out of the path of the *Myraina*. Belatedly the trumpet sounded to cease shooting.

The sevener altered her course to keep headed toward us. The *Myraina*'s catapults crashed again, and the darts whizzed past our stern, causing the gleaming marines to duck.

Still the *Myraina* strained on her starboard oars to catch us on her ram. Closer and closer came the great bronze beak, green with patina and spotted white with sea growths, lifting out of the water in cascades of foam and plunging back in. Above it reared the figurehead of the sea monster for which the ship was named.

Now did Rhodian seamanship show itself. The *Halia*'s rowers, in perfect time, strained at their oars until they bent, to give us that extra little barleycorn of needed speed. We plunged through the heaving green seas and away.

The double-pay man in command of the archers said: "Get out of the way, mechanics, so we can fight!"

He and his archers aimed their bows over the wicker screen. The bows twanged; the airborne arrows hissed away. Arrows from the *Myraina* whistled past us. Two stuck quivering in the forecastle deck. Back in the waist, a sailor screamed with an arrow through his body. The *Myraina* rowed across our stern so close that it is a wonder her oars did not strike us. Thick catheads, projecting from her sides above the waterline, shielded her from ramming by smaller ships. From her deck, crowded with yelling archers and marines, came a shower of missiles.

A sling bullet bounced off the deck and glanced from my ribs, fetching a grunt from me and leaving a three-day bruise. On the quarterdeck our marines cast javelins.

The ships drew apart. Damophilos shouted: "Port rowers, drag your oars! Steersmen, steer hard to port!"

The *Halia* turned in a short circle, so as to bring up facing the stern of the receding *Myraina*. Meanwhile the triemiolias followed a wider circle in the other direction.

I glanced toward the other squadron, maneuvering with the two Antigonian triremes. Shouts and crashes floated across the heaving waters, but all five ships were still in action.

Damophilos brought us around, into the wake of the sevener, and gave the signal to shoot. When Onas tried to put another spell on a dart, Pronax said:

"Forget this nonsense! Pray to the Bright One and see what happens." He clasped his hands. "Heavenly ancestor, far-casting Apollon, god of the sun and of Rhodes, aid thy children in their need. . . ."

Talos crashed. The dart rose, skimmed over the stern of *Myraina*, and plunged into her waist. We yelled with delight as Pronax, grinning, picked up the next dart.

We all prayed this time; even I. I might not believe in gods, but a battle was no time for testing philosophical theories. We made another hit.

The triemiolias rowed parallel to the *Myraina* on her left. They were not fast enough to get ahead of her, and if they turned toward her, she would escape them before they could close.

This time, however, the sevener saved her foes from a stern chase by wheeling toward them. We followed, shooting dart after dart.

Closer came the *Myraina* to the smaller ships. As before, the latter converged upon her in hope of breaking her oars.

At the last moment, like some great African beast in a rage, the *Myraina* lurched to one side. With a terrible crash her ram stuck the *Active*'s bow just aft of the base of the latter's ram.

Then followed one of the most extraordinary scenes of instant destruction that I have ever beheld. In a twinkling the *Active* fell all to pieces. Men and parts of the ship poured into the water. One moment, there rowed a stout triemiolia; the next, nothing could be seen but a tangle of boards, spars, oars, ropes, and splashing, struggling men, screaming thinly over the whistle of wind and the roar of battle. Ropes were tangled around the *Myraina*'s ram, from which splintered boards slid off into the foaming water.

A second crash followed, as the *Euryalê* struck the starboard side of the *Myraina*. Although the catheads warded the larger ship from the ram of the smaller, the triemiolia broke several of the *Myraina*'s oars.

The *Halia* now neared the stern of the *Myraina*, which, slowed by her collision with the *Active*, was barely moving. Debris tangled the sevener's oars and trailed from her ram, further retarding her movement.

On the quarterdeck of the *Myraina* stood a clump of officers, wrapped in wind-whipped scarlet cloaks. As my ship approached, I picked out the Antigonian admiral by his gilded armor and by the shield bearers huddled about him.

As we closed, our archers began to shoot. The shield bearers brought up their shields, so that the arrows aimed at the admiral struck harmlessly against them; the other officers ducked out of the way. A squad of Antigonian archers began shooting back, though the wind blew their shafts every which way.

"Cock your piece," I said, "third notch. Load your piece. We'll try to pick off that popinjay."

"Range two and a half," said Berosos. "Range two plethra, Range..."

I said a short but fervent prayer to Helios-Apollon; then, when our bow stopped heaving for an instant: "Shoot!"

Onas struck his knob. Away went the dart. I felt a pang of disappointment when I saw that the missile was going to miss. Then, at the last minute, like a puff of breath from the lips of the god, a blast of wind swerved it. It plunged into the group on the *Myraina*'s quarterdeck.

The group flew apart in a whirl of limbs and a flutter of garments. There was shouting and scurrying on the deck of the sevener. All on the *Halia* howled with joy.

I would have loaded again, but Damophilos sounded the signal to cease shooting. With his hands cupped around his mouth, he bellowed:

"You up forward, hold fast! We are about to ram!"

The chant of the coxswain came faster as the *Halia* picked up speed. The *Euryalê* lay off to the right of the *Myraina* like a wounded sea beast, hardly moving.

Now, however, the *Myraina* also speeded up. She plowed through the tangle that remained of the *Active* and headed for the Asiatic shore. With a final exchange of arrows, she raised her boat mast, hoisted her boat sail, and drew out of range.

I saw that the other fight had also ended. Although no ships seemed to have been sunk, the two Antigonian triremes were also rowing in the direction of Kynos-Sema. They were low in the water and sluggish, laboring like crippled centipedes with many oars broken or lost. Our three other triremes seemed in no better case.

The *Halia* stopped at the mass of wreckage and began hauling swimmers out of the water, by rope and oar and clutching hand, to cough and retch on the deck. Most of the *Active*'s crew were still alive, clinging to oars and timbers. All but one of the marines, however, had been drowned by the weight of their armor; the lucky man had happened to seize the yard as the ship broke up.

While we hauled the dripping survivors out of the wrack, the Antigonian ships receded. Berosos shouted:

"Behold, one of them sinks!"

It was true; one of the Antigonian triremes was almost awash. Her oars had stopped. As we watched, the *Myraina* came alongside to take off her people. These were still clambering up the sevener's sweeps and sides when the trireme rolled quietly over and lay bottom up, like a wallowing whale, with waves breaking against her keel.

By the time we had rescued all of the *Active*'s crew who were still afloat, the *Myraina* and her remaining consort were small in the distance. The high, bright sun lit up the golden eagles on their sterns. As they dipped and bobbed off into the blue distance toward Asia Minor, our five ships clustered, and the captains conferred in shouts. Bits of wreckage from the *Active* drifted past.

Our officers soon gave up the idea of chasing the Antigonians. Except for the *Halia*, every one of our surviving ships had taken under-water damage. Sailors bailed and pumped furiously; pailfuls of water, glittering like showers of gems, flew up and over their sides. So our squadron limped back into the Great Harbor.

The moles and rooftops were covered with Rhodians, who cheered us lustily even though our victory had been, not an overwhelming triumph, but a barely achieved repulse of a mighty foe who would surely return for further reckoning. We marched out the shipyard gate through cheering crowds and returned to our homes. And so ended the bloody business of the day.

Two days later a messenger summoned me from my studio to a special meeting of the Assembly. Wondering whether I was to be commended or condemned, I followed him. I was keenly interested in the Assembly meeting, as I had never seen one.

The full citizens were spread around the seats of the old theater, wrapped in cloaks of many colors, for even in balmy Rhodes it sometimes waxes cool in late autumn. The Councilmen and the magistrates occupied a reserved section. I was hustled to a seat in the front row, where sat a number of those who had fought in the sea battle. Here were Admiral Exekestos and the ships' captains, the sun flashing on their best parade armor. After a long wait for late arrivals, President Damoteles made a speech praising our heroism.

Rhodians have a tendency to carry eloquence to the point where it becomes a vice. Listening to the wordy and windy declamations of our public men, I have sometimes wished to be back in the Peloponnesos, hearing the Spartans' curt one-word replies.

However, even Damoteles' rhetoric flagged at last. He said: "Chares Nikonos, stand forth."

With pounding heart and flushing face, I obeyed, Damoteles said:

"O Chares, for slaying the Antigonian admiral, thus putting the mighty foe to flight, the city of Rhodes confers upon you this medal."

He hung around my neck a golden sun disk, four digits wide from tip to tip of the spreading rays and suspended from a purple ribbon. Then others were called up, the highest in rank coming last. Some received sun disks on ribbons like mine. The captains got larger sun disks on golden chains, while Admiral Exekestos was honored with a Rhodian naval crown: a thin diadem of gold with a sun disk in front, over his brow, and roses and tridents at sides and back. Solon the goldsmith must have labored far into the night to finish these gleaming baubles in time for presentation.

Proud as I was of my medal, I could not help thinking that, had I been a full citizen, I might have obtained a better one—say, one with a chain. I looked about the Assembly and set my jaw, vowing by Helios-Apollon and all the gods to sit there as a voter someday.

Python of Kallithea, who had captained the *Euryalê*, invited all the decorated ones to his house to dine. The feast turned into an immoderate revel, for Captain Python was a lavish host.

Python was one of a group of sea-loving Rhodian magnates who take their trierarchies so seriously that, instead of merely paying their assessments for the maintenance of a ship and leaving its actual command to a hired vice-captain, they insist upon running the vessel themselves. Sometimes this works out well, and from this group most of Rhodes's admirals are chosen. Sometimes, however, the amateur captain has faults such that it were better for him to stay ashore, collect his rents, and leave the command of the ship to the working-class professional.

Although I later came to know Python better, I paid him little heed on this occasion save to note that he was a tall, fair-haired man who laughed a great deal. The spirit of Dionysos had its way with me, so that my memory for the latter part of the repast is clouded. When my head cleared again, I was sitting in a waterfront tavern, arm in arm with friends and strangers and bawling naughty songs in chorus. Our harmony was hampered by the lusty bellows of Onas. The Egyptian was one of those who cannot carry a tune but always insists on trying, in a voice to slay the night raven itself.

As my wits returned to their post of command, I perceived Berosos the Babylonian expounding his astrological doctrines to a middle-aged stranger by drawing diagrams in wine with his finger on the table top.

"Thus a planet in its ascendant," said he, "has a positive effect—"

"Oh, rubbish!" I said. "One might as well say the Persian Magi rule the world by their spells and cantrips. The skeptical Pyrron—"

"But they *do*!" shouted Gobryas from the other table. "Were it not for the Magians' benign incantations, the universe would vanish in a puff of smoke, thus!" He blew out one of the lamps, plunging the room into gloom.

"Very interesting, very interesting," said the stranger. "I must make a note of that." He peered at my medal. "What does that betoken, young sir?" His speech was that of a traveled and educated Rhodian.

"For killing the Antigonian admiral," I said in my broadest Lindian. "I shot him right between the eyes, I did, with my little catapult, as he stood on the stern of his ship. There was this abandoned sodomite, see, sneering at us from his quarterdeck, in his gilded armor and all, see; and here were we, see, aiming the good old *Talos*—"

The stranger smiled. "I don't wish to belittle your achievement, my young friend, but something is erroneous here."

"What do you mean, good sir?"

"Only that the Antigonian admiral was not killed. At least he was alive when I saw him yesterday."

"You saw him yesterday?" I said, half sobered at once.

"Certainly."

"How? Where?"

"In Loryma. My ship put in there temporarily on its way from Miletos. Let me present myself. My name is Eudemos."

"The philosopher?"

"I endeavor to be one."

Gobryas leaned over and pointed at me. "O Eudemos!" he bawled. "That modest little violet is the world's greatest sculptor. He himself has said it, so it must be true."

"Indeed?" said Eudemos. "Well, master sculptor or master catapultist, it transpires that this missile of yours only grazed the admiral's helmet and stunned him."

"Oh, plague! Does that mean they'll take my medal from me?"

"I think not, for this temporary indisposition of the admiral effected our victory."

"How?"

"It disorganized the Antigonian squadron for the nonce. The captain of the *Myraina* did not know what to do next. When he saw the two Antigonian triremes withdrawing, he did likewise, not realizing the extent of the damages to the Rhodian ships. The admiral didn't recover consciousness until they were picking up the crew of the *Kirkê* less than a furlong from Kynos-Sema—"

"Did the other trireme sink, too?"

"Yes, didn't you know? Anyway, the admiral was much incensed. He asserted that, with most of the Rhodian ships crippled, the *Myraina* could have turned about and plowed through the lot, sinking them one after another. And, in truth, the *Halia* could not have done much to prevent her.

"The admiral still possessed two triremes in reserve at Loryma, and he might have essayed another attack. But he did not know how long the repairs on the Rhodian ships would require, and the spirit of his squadron was depressed by the loss of two ships. While they didn't confide their true reasons to me, the fact is that yesterday they departed eastward."

I said: "It's lucky the fight was so near our own harbor. Had it been near Loryma, things would have turned out differently."

"Thank the Unmoved Mover for that," replied Eudemos.

"Thank the what?"

"That is a term of my master Aristoteles for God. Of course, there is a question of the propriety of thanking God for any particular event among human beings. It is easy to demonstrate by logic that there must be a God, but it is something else to prove that this God reacts to events on our mundane plane in the emotional and sympathetic manner of a mortal man, as the many assume that he does. If, as I think has been proved, the universe operates on a basis of pure reason, it were inconsistent for this God capriciously to intervene...."

Eudemos launched on a theological argument, which made me regret that Zenon of Kition was absent. The Phoenician had a taste for this kind of speculation, but he had long since sailed from Rhodes.

As for me, I was confused. I had thought myself a good, solid atheist, along with Evemeros and Theodoros, but the answer of Apollon to our prayers during the battle had shaken my unfaith. On the other hand, I have never been so profound a thinker as to follow the arguments of Peripatetics like Eudemos. It did seem to me that his God was more of a mathematical theorem than a living god like Helios-Apollon, whom one could worship with some hope of getting what one wanted in return. This Unmoved Mover, from a practical point of view, was hardly better than no god at all.

However, I had too much wine aboard to argue intelligently. I caught the eye of Doris the flute girl and, by a few simple maneuvers, ended the evening in her bed, in one of the two small rooms she occupied at the back of her owner's house. Truly is wine called the milk of Aphroditê.

A jolly evening it was, but I lived to regret it. The next day I got up with four heads instead of one, as the saying is. It took half a cabbage to cure my headache.

Moreover, my parents let me know, without actually saying so, that their feelings had been hurt by my going off to this party without first coming home to let them share my pride in the medal. Such a thought had never entered my selfish young head. I never realized how often I wounded them by my actions until my own children began treating me in the same heedless way. How hard it is to see one's own faults!

With my contract for the statue of Demetrios Antigonou confirmed, I should have felt prosperous and, for one of my years, successful. But the graft that Kallias extorted from me left no margin on which to relax. I still had to work day and night, to squeeze every obolos, and to sponge on my parents for food. I barely took time to shave, let alone to oil myself decently or take proper workouts in the gymnasium. My lunches were loaves of Rhodian lentil bread, hastily washed down with cheap wine between bouts of work.

Moreover, I ran into difficulties in casting the parts of the statue. One of my casts cracked because I stripped off the mold too quickly. Another came out with a hole in it because I had not allowed for an adequate thickness of metal between the mold and the core. Still another was ruined by my failure thoroughly to dry out the core, so that the steam caused a small explosion when the bronze was poured, spattering Kavaros, the studio, and me with molten bronze. Luckily we sustained only a few small superficial burns. As a result of all these mishaps, everything took longer than planned.

I was tempted to sound out the other artists and artisans who had received contracts through Kallias—Bias the carpenter, for instance, who was beginning the construction of Kallias' sluing crane. But I never worked up the courage, fearing to expose my own guilt to somebody who would use the knowledge against me. My father asked:

"What in Herakles' name do you do with all your earnings, Chares? Bury them in the ground, like a squirrel preparing for winter?"

I muttered something about the ever-rising price of materials.

"Oh, don't give me that!" said my father. "I know the price of copper and bronze better than you do. Is it that flute girl again? It's all right for a young man to have a mistress of that class before he weds; it keeps him from bothering decent women. But the girl shouldn't soak up all his substance as a sponge takes water!"

Not wishing to reveal my corrupt relations with Kallias, I did not tell the real reason for my penury. I said: "I have to slave and scrimp to get far enough ahead of my creditors."

"You could accomplish the same end far more easily if you would work full time for me in the foundry."

"And give up my goal in life? You should know me better than that, sir."

My father sighed. "I suppose it's that wretched colossal statue you talk about. The way you're going, you'll never be able to buy the bronze for its little toe, let alone the whole thing."

So things went until the month of Poseideon. One day, wrapped in my heaviest cloak against the driving rain, I slopped and skidded down the muddy slopes of the akropolis to the Town Hall, in answer to a summons from the Council. When I arrived, President Damoteles said:

"O Chares, how far along is the statue of Demetrios?"

"All but the head has been cast, sir, and I expect to pour that soon."

"How long will it take to finish?"

"Weather permitting, we should have it up in a month. Why, sir? Long though it has taken, it is but a fraction of the time that a marble statue of that size would require."

"It is not that, Master Chares. The Council has decided to send an embassy to Antigonos in Syria, for word has reached us that he took ill our driving off his blockaders and swears vengeance upon us. The Kyklops is a rough, tough old man, not lightly to be flouted.

"Therefore, our ambassadors, of which I shall be one, will try to soften his ire, in hope at least of gaining time. Further to melt him down, we plan to do with him as we did with his son: to take you along as official sculptor, to make what measurements and sketches you need to construct a heroic statue of him. Terms will be as before. Do you agree?"

Perhaps in the father, if not in the son, was my ideal to be found. Of course, Antigonos was old and one-eyed now, but a colossal statue could show him as he was in his younger and more heroic years.

"Certainly, sir," said I, sincerely. "I am honored!"

"Then be ready to sail at dawn the day after tomorrow."

Book III

ANTIGONOS

The sacred trireme *Peripolos*, mended after the action off Rhodes, crept eastward through curtains of rain along the southern coast of Asia Minor. Through the shifting gray sheets could be glimpsed the olive-green rampart of the Lykian hills. Kavaros, with his cloak pulled over his head, leaned on the rail and wept into his red mustache.

"Why weep?" I asked. "Isn't there enough water without your tears?"

"*Ara!* The sight of all this water is making me think of my lost freedom. If you could see your way to promise me, sir, that after a certain time I will be going home—"

Touched, I was tempted to offer him another chance to earn his freedom. But I hardened my heart. I still had my mission. For great works of art to be created, the artist must be freed from the myriad chores of everyday living, and this can be done only by a slave. Is not immortal art more important, I asked myself, than the mortal happiness of one barbarous foreigner?

"You should see my country," he went on. "The blue-eyed lassies watching the sheep; the white-robed priests in their sacred groves; some of the boys coming back from a bit of a raid, with maybe some heads from the neighboring tribe to hang over the gate...Ah, indeed and it is a beautiful sight. If I could only see it again before I die—"

"That's as the gods decide," I said.

He chuckled. "Calling on the gods, and you a terrible atheist? Few favors for you would they do, I am thinking."

Like all galleys, we had to stop at every port along the coast to sleep our rowers. We passed Mount Kragos, where Bellerophon slew the Chimaera, and stopped at Patara and Myra and other coastal towns. At Korakesion, perched on a crag as dizzy as that of my native Lindos, begins the land called Rough Kilikia, which has a bad repute for piracy. No indubitable pirates did we see—aside from some stares and muttering at a tavern in Kelenderis—but then, no pirate in his senses would attack a well-armed trireme.

We did see several thirty- and forty-oared rowing craft tied up at seaside villages. They were too small for warships and called for too large a crew for merchantmen. Had we not had a more pressing mission, we might have cruised about, lurking behind promontories in hope of catching one of these dubious craft in a predacious swoop on some fat-bellied trader; for we look upon the suppression of piracy as the special duty, honor, and glory of Rhodes. But, as things were, our captain held straight on.

At Soloi, Rough Kilikia flattens out into the fertile plain of Flat Kilikia. It is said that Soloi was settled by colonists from my own Lindos. However, when I sought to test this legend by speaking with the Solians, no trace of the Lindian dialect did I find. Instead, the Solians spoke the strangest and most corrupt Greek I have ever heard.

We rounded the Gulf of Issos and, at the end of the month of Poseideon, reached the mouth of the Syrian Orontes. This is a shallow stream, navigable only a few furlongs from its mouth. The banks were lined with Antigonos' docks and shipyards, although but few warships were present. The rest had joined Demetrios in Cyprus.

We anchored at the head of navigation and went ashore under the watchful scowls of Antigonos' Macedonian officers. After a delay while President Damoteles made himself known to the Antigonian commander, we bedded down in a tavern in the village and fought the vermin—and without catapults, too—throughout the night.

Next morning the commanding officer appeared with a file of cavalry, a string of mules, and one spirited black stallion that bared its teeth and rolled its eyes as the grooms dragged it forward. The officer said with a grin:

"I suppose the president of a free Hellenic city would like something more dignified than a mule, eh? Here you are, O President."

Damoteles looked at the horse and said: "We Rhodians are famous for our seamanship, for our oratory, and for the high plane of our public life. But no Pindaros will ever write panegyrics in praise of our horsemanship. Take it away and give me a mule, if you please."

The officer turned to me. "How about the sculptor? Here, young fellow, show us backwoodsmen how a horse should be ridden!"

I gave Damoteles a stricken glance, but no help did I get from that quarter. While I had been on a horse perhaps three times in my life, to decline would not inspire respect for us either.

"Well—" I said.

The soldiers jeered.

"All right," I said. "Give me a leg-up,"

The next thing I knew, I had been hoisted up to the pad and the reins put into my hand. The grooms released the animal, which at once put down its head and bucked. At the second buck I lost my knee grip and went sprawling into the dirt. My head struck a stone with force enough to make me see the goddess Selenê riding the starry night. The soldiers guffawed.

"Would you like to try again?" said the officer.

Kavaros murmured: "I could gentle the beast down for you, master darling, if I could give him a bit of a ride."

The Kelt had often boasted of his skill as a rider, driver, and all-around horseman. Now, I thought, he should be put to the test. I said to the officer:

"May I do as I like with the beast, provided I don't harm him, as long as we're in Syria?"

"Aye, you may."

"Take him, Kavaros," I said.

Kavaros took three steps and vaulted on the horse. The stallion bucked as before, but Kavaros stuck like a burr, yelling hideous Keltic war cries and slapping the beast with the loose end of the reins. After a few bucks the animal gave up and suffered himself to be guided about as tamely as any other horse. Perhaps the Kelt's weight, half again as great as mine, helped to quiet the beast.

Kavaros leaped lightly down and handed the reins to me. "Try him now, sir," he said, clasping his hands for me to mount.

"You!" he barked as the horse began to roll his eyes again. "Mind your manners or it will be the worse for you!"

The horse obeyed. Thereafter I rode the horse but took care to keep close to Kavaros, in case I needed his help again.

"It is all in knowing how to handle the beast," he explained while giving me pointers in riding. "Like the time my great-grandfather Gargantyos and his friend Leonnorios had to handle the dragon."

"What was that?" said I, as he knew I should.

"It was when they were hunting in the foothills of the Rhiphaians to once. Seeing that night was about to overtake them, they camped at the mouth of a cave in the side of a hill, not knowing that a dragon had slept the winter in that cave and was getting ready to wake up.

"So my great-grandfather and his friend built a bit of a fire at the entrance to this cave, and soon the dragon was thawed out and came roaring out to eat them. Well, naturally, my ancestor and Leonnorios were surprised, and they started to run around the hill, and the dragon after them. But the dragon was so long that when its head was snapping at them from behind, they were treading on the end of its tail in front, because it went nearly the whole way around the hill. So when they had run around the hill fifty times, neither gaining nor losing, my great-grandfather said: 'Leonnorios darling, it is out of breath I soon will be unless we think of some way to whop this gigantical worm. Let you catch the tail of it, which wriggles on ahead of us, and that will stop the monster from chasing us round this hill, the scenery of which becomes less beautiful every time I pass it. I will take care of the head.'

"So Leonnorios caught the tail and braced his feet and pulled. This stopped the dragon. And my great-grandfather caught hold of the nose, holding the muzzle in both hands so it could not open its mouth. And they pulled and pulled until they stretched that dragon out so thin that they cut it up into short lengths to make harp strings. And the harp that was strung with the strings from the dragon had so sweet a tone that no maiden who heard my ancestor sing to the tune of it could resist him, which is how the clan is after having so many strong warriors."

We rode up the north bank of the river, escorted by the file under a double-pay man. For a hundred and sixty furlongs we followed the river. At that point it cuts through a tremendous vale between the Lebanon Mountains to the south and the Taurus to the north. The mountains descend to the river in terraces and tawny cliffs, spotted with groves of oak and sycamore and with plantings of olives, figs, and vines. We turned up a tributary of the Orontes and presently came to Antigonos' new capital.

Had it ever been completed, Antigoneia would have been as large a city as Rhodes. The clink of masons' hammers resounded from the hillsides as an army of workmen swarmed over the great empty space. While most of the vegetation had been removed from this area, no houses had yet been completed, save huts for workers and for a few Phoenicians and Syrians who had moved in to be among the first citizens.

The artisans worked on a theater, a town hall, a splendid temple of Zeus, a stadium, and a palace. Everywhere were blocks of marble on ox-drawn carts and sleds, architects waving scrolls of papyrus and shouting at foremen, and workmen trotting about with baskets of earth and buckets of mortar and plaster.

There were also the tents of an army camp, with soldiers drilling. Among these tents rose one of great magnificence, with a gilded wooden eagle perched atop its central pole. Off to one side there stood an enormous funeral pyre. I asked Damoteles:

"The satrap hasn't just died on us, has he?"

"Hush!" said the President. "No such luck."

Our double-pay man galloped ahead to tell of our coming. As we picked our way through the embryonic city, the man rode back and led us to the half-built palace.

Here we found a group of Antigonian notables, both soldiers and civilians, looking on at the sweating workmen. It was easy to pick out Antigonos son of Philippos, satrap of Syria and Anatolia.

Antigonos was not seven feet tall—I measured him—but he was almost six and a half, and with the towering crest on his helmet of gilded bronze he looked his nickname of "Kyklops." In his younger days Antigonos had been outstanding for physical might even among Alexander's Companions, who included such monsters of brawn as Lysimachos and Seleukos. Now, nearing eighty, he had become paunchy and unwieldy, leaning heavily on a walking stick. A shortcut beard of snowy white covered his heavy jowls. One cold blue eye looked out of a somber face bronzed with sun, wrinkled with age, and seamed with the scars of old battles. A black patch covered the empty socket on the other side.

His voice was like the mutter of distant thunder. "What wants Rhodes of me?" he growled. "You have seen my son."

"Yes, sir," said President Damoteles. "That is what we have come to consult you about."

"Why?"

Damoteles was an experienced politician, not easily put out of countenance, but the glare of that terrible eye made him falter.

"Why? Well, sir—well, we were unable to come to an agreement with Demetrios—"

"I know that."

"So we thought that could we but confer in person with you, O Antigonos, these misunderstandings—"

"By the gods and spirits!" roared Antigonos. "My son has full power to act in my name. He and I understand each other perfectly. If you wish an agreement with us, seek it with him. I have matters to think of other than the impudence of one little offshore island."

He turned and began to totter off on his shrunken shanks. Damoteles, not moving from where he stood, raised his voice in the manner of a trained orator. He said:

"Then, O Antigonos, are we dismissed? You will not receive the representatives of holy Rhodes?"

Antigonos turned back. He gave us a slight, mocking bow. "I forget. You are a free Hellenic republic and as such entitled to deference, even from me. Naughty old Antigonos forgets his manners." He snorted. "I have just lost my younger son, and his funeral will occupy me for some days. Apply to my ushers in another ten-day, and we shall see whether you mean business or wish merely to break wind by the mouth. Athenaios, see that they are quartered."

The bodyguard to whom Antigonos spoke, a stout, black-browed fellow in a gilded canvas corselet, found us tents. That night we messed in a large tent with a multitude of Antigonos' officers and officials and other envoys from afar. Athenaios, the bodyguard in charge of us, pointed out a group of trousered, bearded men at a neighboring table, with curious caps that came low over their necks and were gathered into bunches in front.

"Behold the fornicating Armenians!" shouted Athenaios, who like many of the Macedonians was noisy from heavy draughts of wine before the meal. He was eating like a Thessalian and drinking like a Byzantine.

"What are they here for?" I asked.

"The old dispute. Their king helped Ariarathes to seize our province of Kappadokia whilst we were busy fighting Seleukos. We demand that the Armenian withdraw support from this usurper, so that we can corner Ariarathes and mete him the same medicine that Eumenes dealt his scoundrelly father, ha!" The Macedonian drew a finger across his throat.

On the other side of me a bearded, middle-aged man in civilian dress spoke up: "The trouble is, you have no Eumenes to perform the task for you."

"Say you so?" barked Athenaios. "If the satrap would give me a good division, I would sweep Kappadokia clear in a month."

"You were not so successful against the Arabs of Nabataea," said the other.

"Harken to him who speaks! How about your great asphalt raid?"

"What is all this?" I asked. "I fear I don't follow."

Said Athenaios: "This so-called scholar"—he jerked a greasy thumb at the graybeard—"is Hieronymos of Kardia. He followed Eumenes until Antigonos caught them both and put an end to Eumenes. Since, with the death of his fellow Kardian, Hieronymos was out of work, and as the satrap decided he was harmless and perhaps even useful, he joined our merry band.

"Well, later the young Demetrios and I led forays against the Nabataeans, without much success, because of the wildness of the land and the numbers and mobility of the barbarians. When we returned, Hieronymos taunted us and boasted how easily he, Hieronymos the Great, would rout these cowardly Arabs. So Antigonos gave him command of a force to gather asphalt from the Asphalt Lake—or, as some call it, the Dead Sea—a lake of brine set amid dry and dreary hills on the margins of Judaea.

"Hieronymos gathered a fleet of boats and embarked his men, resolute to do their task, ha! But the Arabs who make their living from this asphalt came out in swarms on rafts of reeds. They showered our scholar-hero's force with such a storm of arrows that most of those in the boats were slain. Hieronymos escaped with the remnant, though with his repute as universal genius somewhat tattered. Be that not true, my learned historian?"

"At least," snapped Hieronymos, "I wasn't surprised asleep without proper watches, as you were."

"Why you god-detested temple thief—" cried Athenaios, fumbling ominously at his belt.

"Please, gentlemen!" I said. "You're both bigger than I, and if you fight in here, I shall be crushed between you like an insect. The moral would seem to be that Arabs are bad people to meddle with, ashore or afloat."

At least, I distracted Athenaios' anger for the moment. Shaking his finger under my nose like a schoolmaster, he rasped at me: "It is all a matter of adapting one's force to the task, young fellow. A properly outfitted force of light cavalry, with no foot to slow it down, could easily sweep away those lying, thieving, murdering savages."

An elderly man, who had been eating quietly, spoke up: "If the Arabs are thieves when they defend their asphalt pond, then what are you when you try to take it from them?"

"That is entirely different," said Athenaios, striking the table with his fist. "We serve the divine Alexander's empire; we therefore represent civilization. It is right and natural that we should rule the less cultured peoples, for their own good as well as for ours. If all these Arabs and Armenians and such-like scum would only submit quietly, they would find themselves the gainers in the long run. But then, one cannot expect you artists to understand matters of war and statecraft. You had better stick to your painting."

The Macedonian belched heavily and began exploring his mouth for a piece of roast that was stuck between his teeth.

"No doubt, no doubt," said the elderly one, with a faint smile. He turned to me. "Young man, I am Apelles of Kôs. May I have the pleasure Of your acquaintance?"

A little awed—for I had heard much of this painter—I gave my name. He said: "You must be with the Rhodians, then. What is your position in the embassy?"

I told Apelles of the plans for the statue of Antigonos.

"A sculptor?" he said. "Then you must know my old friend Protogenes."

"Certainly, he's president of our Artists' Guild."

"You must remember me to him. I haven't seen him for years, though I was the one who gave him his start. When will you begin the statue of the satrap?"

"I don't know. Antigonos told us not to trouble him for another ten-day, and nobody else will listen to us. I should like to get started soon. I intend to employ the new methods of my master Lysippos."

Apelles chuckled. "So you studied under Lysippos? Didn't you find him a somewhat thorny character?"

"At times, though I should prefer a difficult teacher of the first rank to an amiable mediocrity. Why, do you know him, too?"

"I used to, years ago, when we were both pursuing the wild young Alexander over hill and dale in Asia Minor and trying to make him hold still long enough to paint and model his portrait. Lysippos used to criticize me for painting Alexander hurling a thunderbolt."

"Why, sir?"

"Thunderbolts, he said, were meet only for gods; I should have depicted Alexander with a spear, as he had done. This was before Alexander officially became a god, you see. But I did not mind. Lysippos is a great sculptor for all his crabbed ways." Apelles paused and gave me a meaningful look. "Let me have a word with you after dinner."

Athenaios, who had overheard, gave a shout of laughter. "Watch yourself, youngster! You know what these Ionians do with pretty boys."

Apelles said: "At my age? You flatter me, Athenaios. And anyway, Koans are of Dorian origin."

After dinner I met Apelles on the parade ground. He spat.

"Macedonians!" he snapped. "I don't see how Hieronymos stands their Triballian swinishness, for he is a man of real intellect.

"However, that's not what I asked you here for. I am just finishing a portrait of the satrap and should like to depart, but merchantmen are few at this time of year. I should also like to see Protogenes again. If you can work things to get me passage back on your sacred ship, I will arrange with the satrap to have him pose for both of us at once."

That suited me. When I broached the matter to Damoteles, he shrugged. "We can always find room for so distinguished a passenger as Apelles, though the gods only know when we shall sail. It might not be for months."

Four days later, after the funeral games for Antigonos' son Philippos (who had died of a sickness), I found myself in an otherwise almost empty tent with Apelles, awaiting our subject. At one side of the tent stood Apelles' easel and, on a table, his other painting gear. At the other side stood a curious object: a length of log, carven in the shape of a horse's back, with four short wooden legs to support it and a saddle pad strapped upon it. Beside it stood a folding camp chair.

While Kavaros set up my equipment, I asked: "May I see the portrait?"

"Surely." Apelles pulled the cover off the painting. It was a breathtaking piece of work, showing Antigonos marching beside his horse, in the attitude of one commanding his troops. The most striking thing about it was that the satrap was shown partly from the side, instead of from the front as in all the other portraits I had ever seen. Apelles explained:

"That's to hide his blind eye. The old fellow is sensitive about it. We argued for days about his pose before we hit upon this one."

Kavaros said: "And how will you be getting a horse in here, sir, for a model of the horse in the picture?"

"That is his charger," said Apelles, pointing to the wooden thing. "My original plan was to paint him mounted, using that wooden horse. But hoisting the old man on and off his oaken steed proved such a difficult business that we gave the idea up."

Kavaros gave an unslavelike roar of laughter. "Master darling, we need some of those for the Rhodian cavalry, I am thinking. Even they could sit on them without falling off on their heads."

"Hush!" said Apelles. "He comes."

The aged giant tottered in on his stick, wearing gilded parade armor and accompanied by two of his bodyguards. He settled with a grunt into the camp chair.

"Never grow old, Apelles," he said. "Would that Demetrios were a decade older, so I could die knowing our realm was in responsible hands. Well, go ahead, go ahead. You, too, young what's-your-name. And think not to get me to change my policies toward Rhodes by erecting statues to me. Antigonos is too old a fox to be caught by such dog-faced flatteries."

Apelles and I got to work. People kept coming in with messages to deliver or papers for the satrap to sign, but between these interruptions he held still long enough for our purposes. After sketching the restless and active Demetrios, this task was not difficult.

Now that I had a closer look at Antigonos, I saw that Apelles had lopped at least twenty years from his age in the portrait. This, however, did not seem a tactful thing to mention in the satrap's presence.

During the next month I came to know Apelles better. He had a quality that struck me because it is so rare. That was the ability to criticize his own work and compare it, in a perfectly detached and cold-blooded way, with that of his rivals, as if he were another man altogether.

"Certainly I am a good painter," he said. "Possibly one of the best. But others surpass me in this or that respect. Melanthios is better than I at grouping, while I have never attained the nicety of measurement of Asklepiodotos. From what I remember of the work of Protogenes, he is as good as or better than I in most respects, but in one virtue I am his master. I know when to stop work on a picture, while he will go on fussing with it long after it's really finished. I am keen to see his work, to determine whether he has overcome this fault."

As I had never known any artist who could take such an objective view of his own achievements, I was vastly impressed. I even sought to imitate Apelles in this regard, though I fear without immediate success; for I have always been something of a passionate, hot-blooded partisan by nature, not at all objective.

The wind and rain abated, the atmosphere warmed, and our lady Persephonê painted the hillsides with the scarlet of anemones, the gold of serpents' milk, the blue of hyacinths, and the purple of rhododendron. My task went slowly, for one thing because Antigonos flatly refused to have a life mask made.

I had much idle time when the satrap was not available for posing. This I spent in playing hockey, in pursuit of intrigues with the camp-following women, and in fending off amorous advances from soldiers. Truth to tell, the real Macedonians bothered me less in this matter than the motley horde of southern Greek mercenaries who had enlisted in the Antigonian forces.

The satrap grunted and snorted at our work and, when in a good mood, cracked jokes of an earthy humor. He was an engaging old tyrant, with a rough natural majesty about him. I began to see why, though his rivals dreaded his craft and ferocity, his subjects liked and admired him.

Apelles was cleaning up his gear after finishing the portrait, and our model had stumped off with his guards. Apelles asked:

"How soon will your embassy have its interview? There's nothing to keep me here now, and I should like to get back to Kôs."

"I don't know. The word is still: no appointments. These Macedonians seem to be waiting for something they won't tell us about."

Said Apelles: "Probably for news of Demetrios' fate on Cyprus. If the boy wonder beats the Ptolemaians, I should expect Antigonos to take a tougher line with Rhodes."

"Why?"

"Because he'll be able to afford to. At the same time, there is something more than that coming up. There's whispering in corners and sly half-finished sentences. My slave tells me they are preparing a festival of some sort."

I still had a little work to do on the clay head I was making of Antigonos, and the satrap had promised to give me one more sitting the next day. We had agreed to cope with the problem of his empty eye socket by letting a lock of his hair fall down over the missing eye, as if it had escaped from under his helmet. I found him sitting in his camp chair.

"I had that polluted wooden horse taken to the cavalry tents," he said, "to teach the recruits how to vault into the saddle. It reminds me of one time when I was campaigning against Ariarathes of Kappadokia—the father of the present Ariarathes—what is it?"

A messenger came in, breathing hard. "My lord!" he cried. "A ship has arrived from Cyprus bearing news."

"What news?" asked the satrap.

"I do not know, my lord. Your son's friend, Aristodemos of Miletos, came ashore alone. He is now on his way up the river to Antigoneia."

"Did anybody question him?"

"Yes, sir, but he refused to give his news to anybody but you."

"Get out, fool!" roared Antigonos, heaving himself out of his chair. "Go back to meet this Aristodemos. Tell him I demand to know at once the fate of my son. Then return to me forthwith."

"Aye, my lord." The messenger scuttled out, and Antigonos started to follow him with his bodyguards.

I said: "But, sir, if you will only stay a little while, I shall have finished—"

"To the crows with you and your clay! I have more important matters."

Off he stumped. Kavaros said: "Ah, well, if himself does not care if the statue looks like him, why should we be fretting over it either?"

As there was nothing more to do until I recaptured my model, we cleaned up and waited. After lunch Antigonos appeared in front of his tent. I hovered nearby, hoping for a chance to speak to the satrap and make another appointment.

Down the tributary almost to its confluence with the Orontes, small in the distance, a man on a mule came in sight. Several others clustered about him. As he drew near, I could see that they were hurling questions at him while he rode in silence.

Reaching the edge of the cleared space, Aristodemos dismounted, handed the reins to one of his questioners, and walked slowly across the area toward the satrap. His face was grave and composed. The questioners fell back.

When he was within a quarter-plethron, Aristodemos halted, raised his hands, and cried: "Rejoice, King Antigonos! We have defeated Ptolemaios by sea and have taken Cyprus and sixteen thousand eight hundred prisoners, including a son and a brother of Ptolemaios!"

The old man swayed. There was a scurry among his guards to find a chair for him, but the satrap waved them back.

I started at the word "king," and so, I fancy, did others who were not in on the plot. The Macedonian officers, however, set up a cry of "Hail, King Antigonos! Hail, King Antigonos!" The soldiers took it up, too, until the hillsides rang with roars of "Hail, King Antigonos!"

We non-Macedonians exchanged looks of surprise, alarm, and displeasure. But, like most of the others, I joined in the acclamations.

Two officers stepped up to Antigonos with a slender golden diadem, which they set on his bald head. The satrap made motions to show how much all this astonished him. The noise died down.

Antigonos took off the diadem and held it in his fingers, turning it this way and that. He spoke:

"I thank you, Macedonians. For too long has the empire of the divine Alexander drifted without a proper king at its head. As the house of Philip son of Amyntas has, alas, come to an end, the Macedonian army is the only body in the world that can choose a successor to fill this void. Perhaps I fill it a little too fully"—he grinned and slapped his paunch—"but I swear by Zeus and all the gods and goddesses to do my duty by you and by the empire; I, and my son Demetrios, who by your leave shall be co-ruler with me. For, as any fool can see, I am not so young as once I was, and I need his help. To him I shall send a diadem like this one, as token of his royal rank. Now there shall be feasting and fun for three days, no more drill during that time, and an extra month's pay for everybody. Rejoice, one and all!"

The soldiers cheered again. Aristodemos stepped up with a crafty smile. One could see that he was looking for a handsome tip for having brought the news; his fingers practically twitched. He said:

"I hailed you first, Great King."

"So you did," said Antigonos, grinning. "You are welcome, O Aristodemos. But as you saw fit to torture me with so long a wait for your good news, you may wait a while yourself for the reward of it."

Aristodemos' face fell before they were swallowed up in the cheering crowd. I did no more work on my portrait head that day.

At the feast that night I sat between Apelles and Hieronymos of Kardia. While Apelles was his serene old self, Hieronymos was in a dour and dismal mood, staring listlessly at his food and drinking wine in great gulps, not with Hellenic moderation.

"What ails you, my friend?" I asked him, leaning close to be heard above the uproar of the drunken Macedonians. "This is supposed to be a celebration."

"What have I to celebrate?" snarled the historian.

"The accession of your great king."

"Stupid ox! It is I who was supposed to hail old One-eye as king. But that ready-for-aught Aristodemos got wind of the plan and forestalled me. The king would have rewarded me. Now he must recompense Aristodemos to make the event appear spontaneous."

"Do you mean the whole thing was planned?"

"Are you so simple as to believe otherwise? We rehearsed it carefully. Antigonos himself selected me as the one to hail him."

Apelles leaned around me and asked: "Why should the satr—the king have chosen one who is not a Macedonian?"

"Because," said Hieronymos, "had he elected one of his Macedonian officers, that would have incited one more murderous feud among them. Those not picked would have cherished a grudge against the fortunate man."

Apelles smiled. "Nice people. Aren't you ashamed, as a citizen of a free republican city, to promote one more oriental tyranny?"

"Don't prate to me of freedom!" snapped Hieronymos. "Kardia has been under Lysimachos' thumb for years, with no more freedom than he allows us. This free-city ideal is but a transitory phase, anyway. Soon they will all be swallowed up in the great kingdoms and empires that are forming."

"Not Rhodes!" I cried, smiting the table.

"Yes, pretty little Rhodes as well. What does this freedom of yours signify, anyway, but the freedom of your ruling class to amass more and more wealth by dealings with Ptolemaios? Naturally *they* do not wish their produce cart upset. But the remainder of you would be better off under Antigonos. Now, there is a real king for you! If you don't think so, inquire of the countrymen hereabouts how they like his rule."

"Never! We will resist to the last man, as the Tyrians did against Alexander."

"Go ahead and see how much good it does you. When your corpses have been decently interred, the conqueror will bring in people from other regions of his realm to take your places."

Apelles: "O Hieronymos, it is all very well to hail Antigonos as ruler of Alexander's empire, but there is much of it that he doesn't rule and isn't likely to. What will the other satraps do? I cannot imagine their acquiescing to my lord's claim without a murmur."

Hieronymos shrugged. "I suppose they, too, will assume the title of king and fight it out as they have long been doing. At any rate, there should be ample employment in the foreseeable future for men possessing special skills in war and politics. Among whom I—ahem—dare count myself. The thought quite cheers me up."

The historian attacked his plate with gusto, whilst I sat dourly, saying little and thinking much.

While I put the finishing touches on the clay head of Antigonos, the king gave ear with ill-concealed impatience to a long and high-minded speech from President Damoteles on peace, justice, and international friendship. At last Antigonos struck the ground with his stick.

"Enough!" he growled. "You speak of peace, but the only folk who have ever had peace for the asking are those so strong that none dares molest them. You speak of justice, but there is no justice as between states, nor has there ever been. Justice means laws and courts and punishments, and where are the laws that rule states, the courts that try them, and the punishments inflicted on them? The gods, you may say, but if so they have been remiss. Otherwise, relations among states are governed by nought but force and guile. Our friendship you may have, but on our terms—namely, that you join us against the satrap of Egypt, who rebels against our lawful authority as ruler of Alexander's empire, duly elected by the one body with the right and power to do so: the Macedonian army."

It occurred to me that Antigonos' talk of the "Macedonian army" was but pretense to give a veneer of legality to his assumption of the kingship. He did not have the whole Macedonian army. He had but a fraction of it, padded out with native levies and Greek mercenaries, as did each of the other Successors. As there was no way of assembling the whole Macedonian army, there was no legal way of choosing a true and lawful successor to the divine Alexander—if the rule of such a conqueror be considered legal in the first place. The king continued:

"Well, gentlemen, there it is. How say you? Yes or no?"

"Great King," began Damoteles, "let me explain our position—"

"To the afterworld with you!" bellowed Antigonos. "You mean 'no,' but you hope by wrapping your refusal in a cocoon of sophistical quibbles to talk me round. Well, it is too hot for such games. 'No' it is, and 'no' it shall be, and you may go home to await the reward of your defiance. You are the authors of an unjust war between us, and so your blood shall be on your own heads. Get out of my sight, all of you!" He turned his terrible eye on me. "Are you done yet, boy? Good! Get along with your countrymen. When I have taken your city, I shall look for the statue. If it turn out well, I shall order that you be spared."

On the voyage home Apelles made me promise, when we got to Rhodes, to take him at once to Protogenes' studio.

Accordingly, when we arrived, I sent Kavaros home with the baggage and walked Apelles out to the suburb, south of the wall. Finding Protogenes' door open and the place deserted, we went in. There was a neat vegetable garden in which Protogenes raised most of his own food, for he was a man of solitary and abstemious habits. We went on into the studio and halted before the great picture of Ialysos.

This painting occupied an entire wall of the room, being about eight by sixteen feet. A common joke in Rhodes was to ask Protogenes what he expected to do with the picture when it was finished, as the frame was too large to go through the door. Protogenes simply said that when he was offered enough for it to be worthwhile, he would knock down the wall and then brick it up again.

The painting showed the legend of Ialysos, the eldest of the three sons of Kerkaphos and Kyrbê, who was a granddaughter of Helios-Apollon. These three founded the cities of Ialysos, Lindos, and Kameiros, named for their respective founders. In Protogenes' picture Ialysos was trying to defend the people of his city against the plague of huge serpents, which infested the land and slew many, including the three heroes.

Long stood Apelles silently before the painting. At last he roused himself.

"A great labor and a wonderful success," he said. "It is true that some of my own works surpass it in charm, but one cannot have everything on the same panel." He bent forward to look at a detail. "How in Hera's name did Protogenes ever get so lifelike an effect? Look at the foam on that dog's jaws!" He pointed to Ialysos' faithful hound, which was helping the hero to fight the serpents.

"I know the tale of that," I said. "Protogenes kept trying and trying to get that effect, and wiping the paint off and starting over. At last, in a fit of temper, he hurled his sponge at the painting. It struck right on the mouth of the dog and gave the effect that you see."

"It takes quick wit to seize upon a stroke of luck when it comes," said Apelles. "I only hope he won't give in to his old vice of working and reworking the details. Did you ever hear how I gave him his start?"

"No, sir."

Apelles' eyes saw back over the decades. "It was about twenty years ago, when Protogenes was not much older than you are now. At that time I was already established. He, however, had come hither from Kaunos a few years before and was trying to work up a clientele. To live, he even painted ships in the dockyards as a common laborer.

"While I was visiting here, one of the local magnates said to me: 'Apelles, have you ever seen the work of our man Protogenes?'

"'No,' said I. 'Who is he?'

"'Nobody of importance,' said the moneybag. 'Just a local boy from the mainland who, some think, shows promise. I would not mention him in the same breath as you, of course. Do not disturb yourself on his account.'

"This made me curious, so I sought out Protogenes. I found him living in a shack on barley porridge and beans, with a pile of unsold paintings. As soon as I saw them in a good light, I knew that here was a master. When I praised the paintings, Protogenes looked at me in astonishment.

"'Why, sir,' he said, 'do you really mean you think them *good*? You're not jesting at the expense of a poor ship's painter, I hope?'

"'I'll show you who is jesting,' I said. 'How much for the lot?'

"He began totting up his prices—five drachmai for this, ten for that, and he'd throw in this poor one free, and so forth. When I saw that the total would be absurdly small, I said: 'Here, man, I can't take all day. I will give you fifty pounds for the stack.' Remember, the drachma was worth more in those days.

""His eyes bulged out like those of a lobster, and he sat down on his stool. 'Five—thousand—drachmai!' he whispered. 'Are you feeling all right, sir?'

"'I have never felt better,' I said, and called for my slave and counted out the money. Then I made arrangements to take away the paintings, leaving Protogenes fanning himself with his hat and mumbling."

I said: "I can understand his astonishment."

"Oh, I wasn't being so rash as this story sounds. For, when I got the paintings to my quarters, I spread a rumor about the town that I had bought them to sell as my own. Of course that started a vogue for Protogenes' pictures, and I was readily able to sell my purchases to the Rhodians at a profit. Thereafter Protogenes had no difficulty—"

There was a shuffling sound; the old woman who kept house for Protogenes stood in the doorway.

"Rejoice, Demo," I said. "Where's the master? Here's a visitor to see him."

"He's in town, sir. I don't know when a will be back. Who shall I say called with you, O Chares?"

I was about to speak when Apelles touched my arm. "Wait," he said.

He went to Protogenes' painting supplies, mixed up a little red paint, pointed a brush, and approached a blank panel that stood on an easel. He stood back for an instant; then, with one firm stroke, painted a red line across the panel, no more than a barleycorn in width and as straight as if he had ruled it with a straightedge.

I had seen him perform such feats before. He had insisted on doing a little painting on the *Peripolos* every day, rain or shine, to keep his hand in. But I never ceased to wonder that a man who must have been nearly seventy should keep so keen an eye and so steady a hand.

"Tell your master, this one," he said to Demo, indicating the line. "We shall be back after lunch."

I guided Apelles around the town, introducing him proudly to some of my friends. Then I took him home for lunch; a little nervously, for I was snobbish enough to worry lest a rich and famous artist sneer at the establishment of a mere bronze founder. I need not have concerned myself; Apelles fitted in perfectly.

Afterward we returned to Protogenes' house. Demo cackled:

"The master came in, gentlemen, and looked at the line on the board and said a knew the lion by its claw. That there line, quotha, could only have been painted by Apelles of Kôs. Be you he?"

Apelles smiled and wagged his head affirmatively.

"Well, then," continued Demo, "a took a brush, a did, and—but look at it yourself."

Apelles peered at the stripe on the blank panel. "Herakles!"

Protogenes had mixed some black paint and drawn, on top of the red line, a still finer black line, so that the red could be seen on either side of the black.

Apelles now mixed up some more red paint. He hunted down Protogenes' smallest brush, dipped it, pointed it to the fineness of a needle, and slowly, squinting and pursing his lips, drew another red line atop the black—a line no thicker than a horsehair.

"*Phy!*" he said. "Now let's see him put another one on top of *that*!"

For now the original red line had become five adjacent lines: red, black, red, black, and red. By no mortal hand could another line have been added atop of those already there, yet leaving the edges of the previous lines still showing.

"The master begs your pardon, gentlemen," said Demo, "but a had to go out to deliver a picture. A said a'd be back in an hour."

"Tell him we shall be in Evios' tavern," I said.

Thus it was that an hour later Protogenes found Apelles conversing with Berosos and me in the tavern. The two great painters hailed and embraced each other with an affection heartening to behold.

They soon forgot us younger men in their eager talk of things that happened before Theognis was born (as they say), and Berosos and I reluctantly excused ourselves.

Protogenes later presented the panel with the three superimposed lines on it to the city, as a memorial of his extraordinary contest with Apelles. It hangs today in the temple of Apollon on the akropolis, attracting more attention by its narrow lines on a blank surface than any of the other paintings there.

I succeeded in avoiding Kallias until the head of the statue of Demetrios was cast and the finished statue riveted together on the edge of the marketplace, at the beginning of the third year of the 118th Olympiad.

When the last rivet was in place, Kavaros and I climbed down the ladder amid the cheers of the onlookers. I sent Kavaros to Kallias' house with news of the completion of the work. The Kelt came back to say that the official viewing would be the next morning, and would I please be there?

This time there was an official party. Kallias prowled around the statue, peering at it from all angles as if he had not long before made up his mind to accept it. At last, with judicious frowns and nods, he said:

"I find this statue a very creditable work and recommend that the city accept it."

President Damoteles said to the assembled Council: "You have heard our architect, gentlemen. How say you?"

All the Councilors voted "aye." Damoteles spoke in praise of the statue and motioned a slave, who handed him a bag of coins. He presented this to me amid more cheers. Then he invited me to dinner.

I went, so excited that I was sure I could never eat a bite. The meal disillusioned me a little, for the talk among Damoteles and his friends was almost entirely either of finance or of local politics, two subjects that have always bored me to the screaming point. The few younger men talked of sports, which from my point of view was but little improvement. When I could, I hid my work-roughened hands, feeling ashamed of their contrast with those of the other diners, soft and smooth and rosy.

Nonetheless, I was happy; for, I thought, I had at last arrived. I would make these rich and important men respect me at all costs, no matter what trials I had to undergo.

The next day was the one day in ten that the crew of the catapult *Talos* devoted to drill. Now that all the crews of Bias' battery (save that of unhappy *Eros*, which continued to fumble) had attained a fair accuracy, Bias was training us to speed our loading.

"If you can shoot twice as fast as the enemy," he said, "it's the same as having twice as many catapults. Now, cockers, put your backs into it this time. We'll start loading when I blow this whistle and see who gets off his dart first."

Talos barely beat *Artemis*, our rival for first place in the battery, commanded by Phaon of Astyra. When the drill was over and the battery rumbling back through the suburbs, I asked Bias if I might speak to him privately.

"Sure," he said. "What's on your mind, Chares? I'd say you was coming along pretty good, though you've still got a ways to go. When you started with us, I wouldn't have bet on you to last a month."

"It isn't that," I said, "but another thing. Can I trust your confidence?"

"Ever hear of me doing different from what I said?"

In a low voice I told Bias of my relations with Kallias. "It's driving me mad," I said. "He'll be around tomorrow to collect a quarter of my fee for the Demetrios, leaving me with nothing to show for my work. Moreover, he will probably want a similar commission on the next statue, the Antigonos. What can I do? I would not spend my life working solely to enrich Kallias. Have you had trouble of that sort with him?"

Bias tramped a while in silence. Then he spat. "That temple-robbing sodomite! Yes, he tried the same thing on me. First it was just a little gift, which I didn't mind; but he's greedier than a purple shell, and it got to be a big bite out of my gross fees. I finally told him to go jump in the harbor."

"But didn't he—ah—"

"Threaten to bar me from future contracts? Oh, sure. But, you see, I've been doing contract work for the full citizens for thirty years, and they know I don't fool around. So he don't scare me. You, being a beginner, wasn't in such a good position."

We neared the Great Gate. One of the two towers flanking it was half hidden in scaffolding, the beginnings of the great sluing crane that Kallias proposed to erect.

Bias gestured. "Take that damned thing. I keep building it like he says to, but I know it won't work. This bastard has some real bright ideas, see, but no practical engineering experience. When I heard he was a torsion man, I thought he was going to be pretty good, but it turns out he can't add two and two. So nothing comes out like he expects.

"I try to tell him that, with his design, his crane will lift maybe ten or twenty talents; but talking about lifting a belfry or a tortoise, weighing thousands of talents, is drivel. So he looks wise and says: 'I shall consider your point, my good man, and make such modifications in my design as seem indicated.' Next day he says: 'We shall add cross bracing here, and use a rope of heavier gage there, with more men on the crew.' So now he's got a crane that can lift maybe thirty talents. But as for hoisting a belfry, it's like trying to spit on the moon. And every time he changes the design, the part that's already built has got to be taken down."

I said: "It's too bad the city's time and money should be wasted, with war and invasion impending. Would it do any good to complain to the Council?"

"Ah, they're all in it together. What do you suppose this rise in prices is, but some smart scheme to make the stinking-rich richer and us poorer? I might make trouble for Kallias, but it wouldn't do me no good. They'd say I was a subversive element."

"But what shall *I* do about Kallias?"

"Well, son, in dealing with friends of the rich, it don't pay to hoist the red flag if you don't have to. They stick together, right or wrong. And since you promised Kallias a cut on the Demetrios, you might as well give it to him as make a mortal enemy of him by refusing. But at the same time, like they say, putting up with old wrongs is asking for new ones. If I was you, I'd turn him down on any more commissions. Now the first statue's up, you've got a reputation to trade on, see? If the Antigonos turns out as good as the Demetrios, it wouldn't be easy for Kallias to say to the Council: 'This second statue's a piece of junk;

turn it down.' You might even tell him you've compared notes with his other contractors, and if he wants to fight you'll have friends on your side. No names, though."

When he had secured the catapults in the armory, I set out for home with Kavaros. At the marketplace I stopped to admire my Demetrios. There was a waterfront loafer named Aktis, who made a little money by guiding parties of travelers about the city, pointing out the monuments, the quays, and the temples.

Now Aktis was haranguing a dozen about my statue. To hear him talk, one would think that the great Chares had already surpassed the achievements of Pheidias, Bryaxis, and Lysippos put together. While I knew that this was not true (however self-conceited I may have been), it braced my self-confidence to hear it.

And none too soon. When I reached my studio, intending to take advantage of the long summer day, I found the fleshy form of Kallias already there, lolling in my chair and smiling sweetly.

"Rejoice!" he said. "How is the eagle-eyed artilleryman?"

"Well enough, O Kallias. What brings you here?"

"You know, my dear colleague. Dismiss your slave, and we will talk."

When I had sent Kavaros away, Kallias said: "Now, my commission on the Demetrios, please."

I silently counted out the money.

"Many thanks," he said, letting the glittering stream of coins pour into his wallet. "There will, of course, be the same arrangement on the Antigonos."

"No, there won't," I said.

"What? Do not tell me that you would raise my commission!" He smiled, but in the way of a man who tries to make a joke of something that he does not think funny at all.

"No, sir." I mean that the money I've just given you is the last cut out of my fees that you can expect. I'm through."

"You mean you will not build the Antigonos?"

"Not at all. I mean I will keep all the money."

"Do not be absurd. I can cut you off from future contracts like *that*." He snapped his fingers.

"I'll take the chance. The Demetrios has turned out well; everybody praises it, even you. The Antigonos should be no worse, and if you try to get the Council to reject it, I'll take the whole story to them."

Kallias laughed unpleasantly. "The mouse would beard the lion! Silly boy, know you not that I hold the Council in the hollow of my hand? Guess whom they will believe, if it come to that."

"I have considered that. In fact, I've been around to your other contractors, comparing stories. Know that I shall have friends on my side if it comes to a fight."

Kallias jumped up, face flushed, fists clenched, and murder in his eyes. For an instant I thought he would attack me. As he took a step forward, grasping his heavy walking stick in both hands, I sprang to my workbench and snatched up my mason's mallet.

The sight of the mallet halted him. "Ungrateful young fool!" he spat. "Would you throw away a promising career for simple selfish unwillingness to share your good fortune? Why should I go out of my way to help you for nothing? Your contumacy may inconvenience me, but you cannot possibly improve your own prospects."

"What prospects?" I said. "After I've paid you off, there is nothing left over for me above the cost of materials and labor. I still have to sponge on my parents, and I'm tired of it."

Kallias put on a sympathetic smile, like an actor donning a comic mask. He glided close and patted my arm with a pudgy hand. "Well, if you are that badly pressed, I could adjust my commission."

"No. I'm through with commissions."

"I will ask only one-eighth." His voice changed again, from wheedling to threatening. "But that I must have or you shall do no more work for Rhodes."

"Go ahead and ask. I'll leave Rhodes before I will pay an obolos more. If you don't like the new arrangement, pay me back the money I just gave you."

"Pay you back—why, you insolent—"

"Then leave me alone, please. I have work to do."

Kallias struck the earth with his stick. "People who cross me often have occasion to regret it. Forget it not. When you are in a more reasonable mood, I shall be willing to talk of these matters further." Then he was gone.

Although I tried to be even more careful of details, to furnish Kallias with no valid excuse for rejecting the finished statue, the Antigonos went faster than had the Demetrios, because I avoided many of my earlier blunders. As all young men must, I was learning the painful lesson that there is no substitute for experience.

Through the summer, rumors came to Rhodes of King Antigonos' expedition into Egypt. At the time of our embassy to Antigoneia the troops of Ptolemaios, the satrap of Egypt, held Cyprus under the command of Ptolemaios' brother Menelaos. Demetrios Antigonou landed and besieged Menelaos in Salamis. Demetrios also built the monstrous belfry whose design I had heard him discuss. When the tower attacked the city, however, the defenders burnt it.

Then Ptolemaios himself led a vast fleet, of over three hundred ships, to his brother's relief. Demetrios, however, won an overwhelming victory in a great sea battle off Salamis.

When Ptolemaios fled back to Egypt, the island surrendered. Demetrios, leaving his own garrisons in Cyprus, rejoined his father at Antigoneia. With a huge force the two self-proclaimed kings moved down the coasts of Syria and Palestine toward Egypt.

For a while Rhodes heard nothing but faint and contradictory rumors: that Antigonos had conquered Egypt and slain Ptolemaios; that Ptolemaios had killed both Antigonos and his son; that Antigonos and Ptolemaios had agreed to divide the world between them. The agitation in Rhodes died down. Genetor pressed my father to set a date for my wedding to Io, and my father in turn pressed me.

"To the crows with the lot!" I said. "Tell Genetor I lost my shirt gambling, if you like, and it will take a year to straighten out my finances."

"Now, Chares," said my father, "we all know that's not true. You must be doing better or you wouldn't be able to help with the household expenses. When Genetor was made a full citizen, I feared he would back out; but no, he assures me his intentions are still firm."

"Well, I won't commit myself to any dates until this statue is done. Kallias has soured on me, and if he persuaded the Council to reject the Antigonos, you can see what a hole that would leave me in."

We got no solid news of the Antigonian invasion of Egypt until the end of Pyanepsion. Then Giskon invited me to another dinner of the Seven Strangers. Knowing that I was too inept to make many friends myself, while neither my father's small circle of cronies nor the Artists' Guild with its narrowly professional interests provided me with the range of human contacts I needed, he had taken pity on me.

Giskon's other guest was a Phoenician, Abibalos of Arados. When the clubmen learnt that Abibalos had just come from Antigoneia, they showered him with questions: Where was Antigonos? Where was Demetrios? What had befallen Egypt?

"As for the kings," said Abibalos, "I saw them a bare ten-day ago, in Antigoneia. Antigonos seemed weary, but his son was as full of health and high spirits as ever."

"What about the invasion?" cried Sarpedon.

"It failed."

"Was there a great battle?" asked Gobryas.

"Not so. The land forces had a difficult march through the wilderness separating Gaza from the mouths of the Nile—"

"That is the land of Sos," said Onas, "or Sinai, as the Judaeans call it. It is the shield of Egypt. For days one sees nought but baking, tumbled rocks to the south, a harborless sea to the north, and between them a strip of treacherous salt marsh and quicksand."

"Antigonos made careful preparations," continued Abibalos, "with great stocks of food and water carried on camels. But they suffered for all of that: Antigonos not least, for he is too old and unwieldly for desert marches. Meanwhile the fleet, under Demetrios, met blustering onshore winds, so that several ships were driven aground and lost.

"The army advanced to within sight of the Pelusiac mouth of the Nile and encamped. At this point I arrived with a cargo of Syrian wheat and wine for the soldiers. I saw the end of the campaign; I, Abibalos of Arados, saw it with my own eyes.

"While Antigonos made ready to force the crossing of the river, Ptolemaios came up with his army and occupied the far side, which he had already fortified. Then he sent men in small boats to row near the eastern shore and call out to Antigonos' men, offering them princely bribes to desert to him.

"As the army's pay was in arrears, many did desert in the manner suggested, until Antigonos drew up a line of trusted guards along the shore and drove off the boats with missiles. He also caught some deserters and had them put to death by horrible tortures. *Oi!* The screams, the blood, the smell of burning flesh! I still dream of them, though I am no newly hatched chick and know much of man's villainy to man. Antigonos Kyklops is an amusing old scoundrel, but when his blood is up, he becomes a monster of cruelty.

"However, neither threats nor tortures nor promises could halt the wane of the army's spirit. I knew this sooner than did the king; I, Abibalos of Arados, knew it. For when an army begins to crumble, the soldiers begin to plunder and abuse the merchants and sutlers—a thing the officers never allow when all goes well. When my fellow trader, Magon of Berytos, was foully tortured and slain by a file of cavalrymen, and none was punished for the deed, I knew what was toward.

"I would have sailed at once but that onshore winds held me pinned to the Pelusiac mouth. In three days it became plain to Antigonos that he could not cross the river because of high water and the foe's strong position. He could not outflank Ptolemaios by marching upstream, because the ground is too cut up by lakes and marshes for the movement of so large a force. He could not outflank his opponent by sea because of the shape of the coast and the adverse winds, which continued to wreck his ships. If he stayed where he was, his army would melt away by desertion or would mutiny and slay him, as did the men of the regent Perdikkas.

"So Antigonos ordered retreat. Now he's back home but, as you can imagine, in no very pleasant humor. His men start and go pale when he roars at them."

Shocked by this account, I said: "Did Antigonos himself really order those tortures?"

"Order them? He stood over the executioners, harkening them on and making ingenious suggestions. 'That fellow has a pair of fine blue eyes; just hand them to me,' he'd say."

"I can hardly believe it," I said. "When I met him in Antigoneia, he seemed a man of truly kingly quality."

Nikolaos, the full citizen, said: "If by kingly quality you mean cold-blooded treachery and murder, then Antigonos is your man. Do you know the tale of Kleopatra, the divine Alexander's sister?"

"No, sir. Tell me."

"Thrice a widow, she dwelt in Sardeis, where all the Successors sought her hand as a means to the kingship. Two years ago she decided to cast her lot with Ptolemaios. But when she tried to leave Sardeis, the governor, acting on Antigonos' orders, imprisoned her and hired certain women to kill her.

"Antigonos, not wishing the odium of the murder, had her buried with royal rites and the women publicly beheaded. I believe he had first had their tongues cut out, so they could not cry out to accuse him at the end. Oh, well, the tale can be matched from the history of any of the other Successors." He turned back to Abibalos. "What of the king's plans?"

"Who knows," said the Phoenician. "Antigonos has always been one for keeping his own counsel and then pouncing like a lion. There are rumors that he will attack this or that Successor—Kasandros, or Lysimachos, or Seleukos, who has lately established his rule over the eastern lands as far as India."

Said Vindex of Rome thoughtfully: "Suppose Antigonos decides to take up his unfinished business with Rhodes?"

"That is what concerns me," said Nikolaos. "Last year, when Antigonos sent those ships to blockade us, everybody was full of patriotic fervor, rushing about and preparing for war. Now this peaceful interval has sapped our spirit. Even my colleagues on the Council insist that all will be well, so let us have business as usual."

"I know," I said. "Last year the Council placed a huge order for bronze shield facings with my father. He laid in a supply of ingot bronze, and then the Council canceled the order, leaving him with enough bronze to take care of his ordinary business for years."

"Tell your father not to sell his stock of bronze," said Nikolaos. "There's a good chance that we shall soon need those shield facings after all. That is, if our politicians can rouse themselves from their game of profits and mutual praises before it be too late."

"This government by elected politicians is simply not practical," said Gobryas the Persian. "I have watched it in action for some time now, and though it be heresy to you, I say you need a king to tell you what to do."

Vindex spoke up: "Do not be hasty to abandon republican government, whatever its shortcomings. We Romans threw out our kings two hundred years ago and have never regretted it. I have read a little history, and for every folly committed by an elective government I can match it with two greater follies done by kings."

"What you mean, my friend," said Nikolaos, "is that most men are fools, and no change in form of government will alter that basic fact."

Later somebody mentioned Kallias of Arados. Abibalos asked: "Is that a man of about my age, rather stout and ruddy, with good Greek and ingratiating manner?"

When told that it was indeed Kallias, who had supplanted the city's municipal architect, the Phoenician burst out laughing but refused to tell why.

"No, gentlemen," he said. "I mind my own business. Who stirs up a hornets' nest can expect to be stung."

But we pressed him. When he had been assured that not even the sun should hear of what he told us, he said:

"The Phoenician name of this Kallias is Iaphê ben-Motgen, and he was all but run out of Arados. He built us a new Town Hall—you know how he can worm his way into any job—incorporating, he assured us, the latest improvements. Alas! the new building fell down during the dedication, killing half our Council.

"When brought to trial, the man averred that an imperceptible earthquake at that moment shook down the structure. Although nobody else had felt the quake, he cast enough doubt on the prosecution's case so that the court let him go with a warning. But as no one would hire him, he set out to make his fortune elsewhere. Although

I knew that he had sent for his family to join him, I had not heard whither he went."

"Oh, come," said Nikolaos. "Surely he is not so bad as that. He has given every satisfaction here."

"Why—the—" I began, meaning to burst out with the true tale of Kallias' graft and incompetence. But again my guardian spirit checked me.

No more than a stone that has left the hand can one stop a word that has left the tongue. Nikolaos, I thought, would be a difficult person to turn against Kallias, because he had introduced the man to the Council and so was partly responsible for the city's putting its trust in him.

"Let us hope he continues to give satisfaction," said Abibalos. "I will only say that I should hate to see the defense of *my* city entrusted to him. Who said: 'The best equipment for life is effrontery'? That, my masters, is the motto of Iaphê ben-Motgen, alias Kallias."

When I got to the studio next morning, I brooded over the clay model for the head of the Antigonos. What I had learnt of the satrap demolished this ideal, also. On an impulse I hurled the model to the floor.

Kavaros ran in at the crash. He cried: "Oh, master darling! What a dreadful thing? Broken in fifty pieces it is, and how will we ever get it back together?"

"We shan't. I must make another. Pick up the pieces. We'll glue them together to give us something to work from."

"How did it ever happen, sir?"

"Sheer stupidity, Kavaros."

Second thoughts had made me regret my outburst. After all, I still had a contract with the city to fulfill, and to default upon it would cost me what small progress I had made toward my goal.

As winter came on, people asked me with increasing frequency how long it would take me to finish the Antigonos. I told them that I had run into unexpected technical difficulties, having to do with the statue's weapons and armor. The Antigonos would not be nude, like the Demetrios, but clad in the panoply of a modern general.

The truth is, however, that I was deliberately dallying. I feared that, once the statue was finished, Kallias would reject it and I should have to force the issue with him. While I have not lacked courage for physical combat, the thought of a prolonged public quarrel with this cunning adventurer, as slippery as a Phaselite, filled me with dread.

Once I passed Kallias in the marketplace. He said nothing but glanced at the half-finished statue of Antigonos and back to me with a sly and sinister smile.

Now my father, my friends, and even some of the city's officials began to pester me to know what was holding up the work. At length I shut myself up in my studio and refused to see anybody, living a life of morose misanthropy like that of Herakleitos the philosopher. I rejected all invitations until Kavaros said:

"A bad thing it is, master, for a young fellow to shut himself up like a dead corpse, and you so handsome and all."

In a rage I fell upon the Kelt with a lath and beat him until he ran out of the studio. Then, feeling utterly ashamed of myself, I sat for hours looking out over the city, which lay under a gray, wet, windy sky. Feeling pressed from all directions—by Kallias, by Genetor, by the Antigonian threat to my city, and by my own lofty ambitions—I felt that, as the saying goes, it is best not to be born, but if one be born, the next best thing is to die forthwith.

At length my guardian spirit—or was it the Bright One himself?—said to me: Come, boy, the deathless gods love not stupidity. So you are in a predicament? That is nought new. Most mortals are, most of the time. As fast as you get out of one, you will fall into another. What of it? That is the difference between being alive and being dead. Only the dead have no problems, and the shades have a dull time of it. That time will come upon you soon enough; therefore, gather your forces and return to the fray!

So I went back to work on the statue, determined to finish it and let Kallias do his worst. When I heard a stealthy step, I called:

"Kavaros!"

"Yes, sir."

"There's a Persian custom of giving gifts to a man on his birthday. I don't know when your last one was, but here is a tetradrachmon for it."

Kavaros turned the massive coin over and handed it back, saying: "Thank you, master, but if you do not mind I will not be taking it."

"What? Are you crazy?"

"No, sir. It is a matter of honor."

"Honor? You?"

"I do not know if I can make you understand, sir. I know I am just a slave, and if you beat me I have to bear it, lest something worse happen to me—like being sold to a mining contractor, say. But at home I was a gentleman, and a gentleman would not hire himself out to be beaten for money."

I found this quiet rebuke so crushing that for a long time I stood silent. At last I said:

"Well, slave or gentleman, you've been a good friend to me. I know you want to be free, so you shall be—as soon as my great statue is done."

"Is it this one that you mean?" he said, eagerly indicating the half-finished Antigonos.

"No. I mean my colossus; the one I dream of."

"Oh. Well, sir, I will be looking forward to it someday, anyway. And now do we work some more on the one-eyed fellow?"

We pitched in, and in a few ten-days had the Antigonos all up and in place except for the arms and head. I found the work distasteful, as the subject had become revolting to me; but soonest begun, soonest done.

In Anthesterion, during the heaviest rain of the winter, somebody knocked on the outer door of the studio. Although I pretended not to hear, the knocking kept on until I ordered Kavaros to open the door. As the visitor came in, I burst out:

"By the Dog of Egypt! How can a creative artist work if he is constantly interrupted by this fiendish racket?" Then I saw that it was Onas.

"I have orders from Bias to fetch you," said the Egyptian. "We are wanted at the armory. Demetrios is back at Loryma."

* * *

In the armory Bias explained the plans of the Board of Generals. New catapults of all sizes would be ordered. Until they were finished, we must be prepared to rush our battery either to the moles, to repel attack by sea, or to the South Wall, to repulse assault by land.

As I was leaving the armory, who should come puffing up to me but Kallias, with an umbrella hat on his head.

"Chares!" he said. "Get the rest of that statue up, forthwith!"

"Oh?"

"Do not 'oh' me, young man. I know you can finish it in a few days if you wish. And fear not that I shall reject it. The Assembly is about to vote some fancy honors to the kings, and it would not look well to leave their statues unfinished."

Two days later Kavaros and I drove the last rivet holding the statue's head to its trunk, and the Antigonos was complete. When the municipal treasurer paid me off, he said:

"It is good that you finished that statue, Chares. You took so long that there was a move afoot to cancel your contract. The Council might have done it, too, had it not been for your servant."

"Kavaros? Why, what did he do?"

"He came to us and told us the real reason for the delay: how he had gotten drunk and broken your molds."

I turned away to hide a tear, resolving that the good Kavaros should be freed as soon as I could afford to buy a replacement for him, colossus or no colossus.

Thereafter I had little time for sculpture. My father got a new contract for shield facings, and I put in long hours in the foundry. When not casting and hammering the thin bronze disks or punching the letter *rho* (for Rhodes) into them, I was drilling with the crew of the *Talos*. Day and night the streets of beautiful Rhodes resounded to the tramp of infantry marching to drill and back, or of reservists hastening to a practice muster.

I heard that another embassy had been sent to Loryma; then that it had returned without an agreement. I got the true story of the embassy from Damophilos, who, with some other friends of my father, attended a dinner at our house.

"I sometimes think the royalists are right," Damophilos said. "From the craven conduct of our embassy one would indeed infer that democracy has no future."

"What did they do?" asked my father. "I know they refused the king's demands, which doesn't sound cowardly to me. After all, there are men in Rhodes who remember when Queen Artemisia took the city and stacked the heads of Councilmen in the theater like a pile of catapult balls."

Damophilos blew his nose, for he had caught cold on the rainy voyage. "At first they refused the king's demands. Then, when Demetrios threatened utterly to destroy the city, they hastily agreed—that is, to join him against Ptolemaios.

"But who is given too much wants yet more. Becoming haughty and insulting, Demetrios asked for a hundred of the noblest citizens as hostages and for the right to bring his fleet into our harbors. All our statues and other honors have not softened these royal robbers in the least.

"Once we let him into the harbors, he could do as he liked—raze the city and slay us all if it suited him. In fact, I suspect him of just such a plan. His soldiers grumble because their pay is in arrears. It would be just like him, having failed to loot Egypt, to promise them the sack of Rhodes to soothe them.

"But what really spilt the perfume into the soup was the demand for noble hostages. These would include all the members of the embassy, who, naturally, were not eager to be carried off as pledges for the good behavior of Rhodes, and have their throats cut if some hothead started a patriotic riot at home. So they finally said 'no.'"

"If we must fight, we must," said my father. "When we grow too soft to defend ourselves, we no longer merit our liberty."

"*Euge!*" said Damophilos. "Though the sight of Demetrios' vast armament at Loryma might dampen that noble sentiment. But there, I should be harkening you on, not sapping your spirit by ill-timed cynicisms." He turned to me. "By the way, the king asked after you."

"How so?" I asked with a hollow feeling.

"'Where is that pretty young sculptor, whatever his name was?' he said, adding that he wanted you among the hostages. What about it, Chares?"

None would have blamed me much if I had confessed to being Demetrios' catamite. However, I told the true tale of my escape.

"If he want me now," I said, "it is not to make love to me but to kill me."

Damophilos laughed with the rest, albeit grimly. "Had Chares been less finical, it might have been better for Rhodes. But I like the lad's spirit. If all our flabby, money-grubbing, pleasure-loving citizens show the like, Rhodes may—just may—have a chance."

Early in Elaphebolion, Demetrios sailed from Loryma. I was down on the South Mole, in helmet and leather jack, commanding *Talos*. What I saw was enough to terrify a demigod.

The entire sea between Rhodes and the mainland seemed filled with purple-hulled ships. In the van came a long rank of Demetrios' great battle transports, sixers and seveners and some of even higher rates. In the center rowed a ship that was larger than any, flying an admiral's purple sails: Demetrios' new elevener. It had a feature unheard of in those days: two full-sized masts, each bearing a sail. On the sterns of hundreds of ships gleamed the golden eagles of the empire, while the same device was painted or embroidered upon their sails.

Behind the battle transports came hundreds of other ships. There were great blocks of fivers and smaller galleys, towing transports for men and horses. Behind these came still other hundreds of vessels: low, lean, thirty- and forty-oared craft with blue-gray hulls—Demetrios' piratical allies. There must have been at least a thousand ships belonging to pirates and slavers. Everybody knew that Rhodes had not been plundered for years, and news of Demetrios' attack had brought out all the pirates of Crete and the Anatolian coasts, like vultures to a dying beef.

News of the gathering of the pirates firmed our spirits as nothing else could have done. We knew that, even if Demetrios was inclined to leniency if the city fell, he could never protect us from his evil allies, who hated Rhodes for her long campaigns against them. The streets would run with blood, heads would be piled in the squares, and those who lived would do so as slaves in Carthage of Italy or other distant lands.

Behind us, on shore, the women wept as in the time of Nannakos, and the old men prayed. The murmur of it came across the water.

Closer and closer crept the great fleet. As the ships of the first rank neared, the following ranks became visible. Never had so vast a fleet, in all of history, been gathered under one man.

Bias, still looking the artisan despite his crested helmet, said: "It looks like he's going to stand straight into the harbor, sails up and all, to see if we'll let him in without a fight. Cock and load your pieces, but don't nobody shoot till I give the word."

On came the swarm, the elevener pulling to the front. Capacious though our two harbors were, they could never have held all the ships arrayed against us. I said:

"Give the range, Berosos."

"Twenty-two plethra," he said.

We waited in taut silence.

"Twenty plethra."

"Eighteen plethra."

"Cockers, cock your piece," I said. "Sixteenth notch. Train to the left. A little more; good. Load your piece."

All up and down the mole, torsion skeins creaked and pawls clicked over their racks.

"Sixteen plethra," said Berosos.

A little white wave curled over the ram of the elevener as it wallowed toward us through the deep blue sea. Gulls circled and mewed. The sun glittered on the helmets of the marines who crowded Demetrios' decks. Sailors scurried to furl the sails of the leading ships. Up in folds went the painted golden eagles.

"Fifteen plethra," said Berosos.

"Shoot at will!" cried Bias, and the cry was taken up by the other battery commanders.

"Shoot!" I said.

Onas struck his knob. With a rattling crash the catapults up and down the mole let fly. The darts arose in long arcs with a simultaneous shriek.

"Pull up your recoiler," I said. "Cock your piece; fourteenth notch. Load your piece. Hurry, curse you! Train to the right; that big fellow. Shoot! Pull up your recoiler—"

An answering chorus of thumps and crashes came from the leading ships, and darts streaked toward us. I soon found the difference between shooting afloat and ashore. While the defenders scored many hits, the tossing of the ships caused nearly all the enemy's missiles to fly wild.

The air was full of missiles, coming and going. Three-span darts whistled about us like rain. We shot and shot, flinching a little as a dart came close, but always coming back to shoot again. After one bad shot I said:

"Your ranging is off, Berosos. You're giving them too short."

"Not I!" he said. "Our skeins are weakening, instead."

Whichever was true, I began adding a notch or two to the pull-back of the recoiler, and soon we were hitting again. Closer came the great ships, with darts sticking from their woodwork like spines from a hedgehog. Although their decks were too high for us to see our hits on Demetrios' men, we knew we had scored heavily.

The scorpion men cocked their weapons, raised them, and set their butt braces against their breasts. Archers nocked their shafts; slingers fitted bullets into their pouches. The yells of the men on the ships and the shore became one long howl, as of a myriad of wolves. Several of our men lay in their blood on the mole, and none could spare the time to help them. Bolts, bullets, and arrows whizzed off to rain upon the ships, where the gilded soldiery now crouched behind their shields. Even the heavy old flexion catapults built by Isidoros, moved by tremendous exertions to the moles, discharged their one-talent balls with booming crashes.

Onas muttered: "At least there will be no doubt in the king's mind of his welcome."

The elevener swung off to our right, southward toward Lindos. Like a platoon of phalangites doing a column-left, the vast mass of ships followed, most of them turning while out of range.

"Cease shooting!" commanded Bias.

While our wounded and slain were carried off, the fleet crept south with thousands of oars rising and falling until it had passed the end of the city wall. Here is a kind of third harbor—a natural one, formed by a sandspit, the Southeast Peninsula, that runs out toward the Chatar Rocks. This South Harbor, as it is called, has not been developed, because the other two have sufficed for commerce and naval craft; it was used by fishermen only.

Now, Demetrios could not use the near side of the South Harbor, because it could be reached by our engines. So the fleet entered the harbor on the far side and lined up along the Southeast Peninsula. Other ships, for which room was wanting in South Harbor, passed around the rocks and came to rest on the indented coast beyond.

As the sun went down behind the akropolis, throwing the temple of Helios-Apollon into black relief, the king's ships, with much shouting, splashing, and trumpet braying, found their berths. The smaller ones were drawn up on the strand while the larger rode at anchor.

We stood to our arms until after sunset. When the stars had come out, a shooting star flashed across the sky. Berosos said:

"Right through the Virgin! Blood and doom and disaster dire shall there be—"

"Hold your tongue!" I said. "We have a short way with fortunetellers who predict disaster in wartime."

Bias bustled up. "Chares! Did you have trouble with falling range?"

"Yes, a little."

"Then take your piece back to the shed. We'll adjust the skeins tonight."

Groaning with weariness, we levered *Talos* up on its rollers and hauled it along the mole. *Artemis* and the ever-unlucky *Eros* came with us, for they, too, had had troubles.

In the armory Bias struck the skeins of *Talos* with a mallet, thrust an awl between them and moved it this way and that, and finally said:

"I don't think we'll unwind and restring her. We'll shim up those shackles by driving wedges under the shackle rings."

After commanding one of the mechanics to deal with this, he passed on to the other engines.

Whereas *Eros* had the same trouble as *Talos*, the trigger mechanism of *Artemis* had been giving difficulty. While Bias and his mechanics worked on the latter fault, the mechanics set stepladders against *Talos* and *Eros*, climbed up, and began adding tension to our skeins by wedging up the shackles. Now and then they paused to hammer the skeins and listen to their tones, to make sure that the tension was equal on both sides. On *Talos* all went well, but from *Eros* came a loud crack and a groan of tortured carpentry.

"Oh, plague!" cried Bias. "Broke the polluted stress bolt, it did. If that smith has made us flawed bolts, I'll tear him to pieces."

As a result of this mishap, both skeins had to be unwound from the catapult frame and laid out on the armory floor. The frame had to be checked for warping and other damage. Where Bias thought it a little strained, he drove in extra nails.

When a new stress bolt had been laid in the notches of the shackle ring, we restrung the skeins by means of an enormous iron needle, passing it up and down. As each skein was over two hundred cubits long, this was a laborious business. When the skein was all laid, the strongest men in the battery pulled on the loose end with tongs until the strands were equally tensioned, after which the free end was secured to a cleat. Then the throwing arms were inserted, the string was made fast, and the catapult was ready.

By the time we finished, dawn approached. Our officers did not let us go home for fear that, once asleep at home, it would take an army to round us up again. We caught what winks we could on piles of rope and then shambled out into the dawn.

Book IV

BIAS

Several days later we were standing to arms on the waterfront while the Assembly met in the old theater. Outside the walls, Demetrios built his camp. The sound of his axes resounded over the city as his men felled trees on the slopes as far as the Vale of Butterflies. The sound spurred our determination, for Rhodes cut its trees with care, so that the supply of timber for ships and export should never fall.

Life had become grim. Nightly the sky glowed red with the flames of burning villages. Demetrios' horse and bands of pirates ranged the isle, slaying, plundering, and enslaving. Of the islanders not caught by Demetrios' ravagers, some fled to the mainland in boats while others drove their stock up into the wildest parts of the interior.

On the day that we repelled Demetrios' fleet from the Great Harbor, thousands of refugees from nearby towns had hastened in through the South Gate. So crowded was the city that the commanders of the recruits now had to drive cattle and sheep off the athletic field before their men could drill upon it.

I gave up my lease on the studio, moved what equipment I could to my parents' house, and spent my off-duty time assisting my father in the foundry. Orders poured in upon him: for helmets, cuirasses, greaves, shield facings, arrowheads, caltrops, and other warlike gear. If my father and I bickered now, it was only over such questions as how to turn out more castings each day. I do not think we had ever before looked upon each other as friends; to me he had always been a hard, pushing, scolding taskmaster, while to him I suppose I was a peculiarly willful, contrary, and disagreeable boy.

On the day of which I write, as there seemed but little likelihood of attack, Bias let us go into town for lunch. We of the *Talos* crushed into Evios' tavern for something wherewith to wash down our victuals. The crew of *Artemis* crowded in after us, filling the place. There was much chaff and shouting:

"Look at these tyros who grab the best seats! They couldn't hit Mount Atabyrios at ten paces!"

To which my crew rejoined: "Oh, is that so? They're going to put you duffers in the infantry, lest you shoot backwards and slay our own generals!"

Phaon, the double-pay man in command of *Artemis*, had attended the Assembly that morning. He was a full citizen, being of pure Hellenic blood and having inherited land around Astyra. Now he appeared, gleaming like a god, to rejoin his crew. In reply to our questions, he said:

"By the Earth, I should never have believed that our garrulous Assembly could so bestir itself!"

"What have they done?" I asked.

Phaon ticked off the new laws on his fingers. "All resident aliens and slaves may join the armed forces, while foreigners who will neither fight nor make arms shall be expelled. This will save provisions and guard us against treachery."

Onas interrupted: "Are you not glad that we talked you into enlisting, Berosos? Else you were one of those cast out."

Phaon continued: "Slaves who prove themselves brave in battle shall be bought from their masters after the war, freed, and offered enrollment as tribesmen.

"Those who fall in battle shall be buried at public expense; their parents and children shall be maintained from the public treasury. Their sons, on reaching manhood, shall be crowned in the theater at the Dionysia and given a full suit of armor, while their daughters shall be given dowries from the treasury."

Berosos said: "Almost a pleasure to be slain in this war they will make it. However, having no children, to live I should prefer."

Phaon went on: "You should have seen how the richer citizens poured out their treasure! Never have I witnessed such enthusiasm. Then we decided to send another embassy to Demetrios, to beg him to do nothing to the city that he might regret."

Said somebody: "I thought an embassy was sent yesterday."

"So it was, but Demetrios, with a rude gesture, told them he was too busy with his fortifications to talk. All he would agree to was an arrangement for ransoming prisoners on either side."

I said: "We shan't get far with this self-conceited popinjay by talk."

"We realize that," said Phaon. "Therefore, we shall also dispatch envoys to Ptolemaios, Kasandros, and Lysimachos, asking for help. We hope to convince them that it's to their advantage that such a great trading center, halfway between Hellas and the ports of Phoenicia and Egypt, shall remain free and open to all."

Just then another man, in old but serviceable armor, pushed his way into the tavern, squeezed between the tables, and hailed me. Between the dimness and the disguising effect of the helmet I did not recognize him until I got a look at his sweeping red mustache. There could be but one such adornment in Rhodes.

"Kavaros!" I cried. "By Zeus the Savior, what are you doing here in that rig?"

"It is a soldier I am now, sir," he said. "When I heard that the Assembly had voted to enroll all able-bodied slaves, I got in at the head of the line."

"Sit with us, fellow soldier," I said. "What will they put you in, the infantry?"

"That they have, and I am after drilling on the athletic field all morning. Though, to be sure, I do not like your Greek ways of fighting."

"What's wrong with them?"

"Oh, it is this business of standing in line, with your shields in front of you like the tiles on a roof, and everybody stepping forward at the same time and giving a poke with the spear at the same time, as if worked by strings they were. Now, in my country it is different. We strip ourselves naked and rush upon the enemy in one grand charge, shouting and yelling as if to wake a dead corpse. Indeed and a beautiful sight it is, with the long swords waving and the plumes in the helmets nodding! But still, this kind of fighting is better than no fighting at all."

When we got back to the mole, Bias hailed me. "Walk this way," he said.

When we were out of earshot of the catapults, he spoke: "I've been having lunch with the Council, me and the other contractors. Your father was there."

"Yes?" I said.

"As you might expect, they want us to do enough work to keep us busy for years, and have it finished by the day before yesterday." He spat. "Stupid oxen! They think their money will even turn time backwards. If they'd passed out these orders a few months ago, we'd have something accomplished. And we're supposed to do miracles at cost, too."

"You mean with no profit?"

"Sure. They say: 'We're giving our money, the soldiers are giving their lives, so the least you craftsmen can do is to give your skill.' First they wanted us to work for nothing at all. I had to point out that in the first place we couldn't do that unless they could get us supplies and materials free, and, second, that we had to eat."

"What are we going to do?"

"Well, it don't look like Demetrios will attack us without a lot of preparation. So we're going to cut down these catapult crews to skeletons and put the rest of the men to work."

"On what?" I asked.

"There's plenty, with all these new contracts. I got two big ones: to make another battery of catapults and to build a penthouse on this mole to protect the crews and lengthen our range."

"What about Kallias' great sluing crane?"

Bias smiled, creasing his face into a mass of wrinkles. "Kallias is hopping around like he was dancing the kordax, trying to get it done. But I know it won't work, so I'll see that he don't use none of my good men on it."

"Have you spoken to the Council about the crane?"

"Sure. I brought it up today, with a sheet of figures to prove my point. All it got me was that Kallias blew up and practically had 'em convinced that I was a traitor. I can't fight him before the Council, on account of I don't have a tongue loose at both ends like him. But now I think he's going to hang himself. Do you know what his latest idea is?"

"No, what?"

"Torsion scorpions. I've shown him figures to prove the torsion principle's not practical in such small sizes. But no, he says: if it works on a big machine, it'll work on a small one. So he's got one of my competitors building one."

"What do you want me to do, Bias?"

He laid his hairy, freckled hand on my arm. "You're a pretty good little fellow in spite of that sassy manner, and I need your help."

"Thanks, but how?"

"Helping to oversee some of my contracts. The trouble with Rhodes is, it's got too many orators and not enough engineers. We can't blow Demetrios' army away by talk, though you might think so to hear some of our politicians speechify. You may not be an experienced engineer, but you have at least studied the theory and aren't too much of a gentleman to use your hands."

I said: "That's kind of you, but my father needs me in the foundry."

"Oh, I've spoken to Nikon. He would like you, but he admits the work you'd do would be that of any competent bronzesmith, while you can use your engineering to better advantage working for me. So I'll lend him one of my men in your place."

"Oh. Perhaps you could also use Berosos, my Babylonian aimer. He knows mathematics."

"Sure."

"And if there's such a shortage of engineering talent, what is our former municipal architect doing?"

"Diognetos is kind of retired, I guess. He's never forgiven the city for throwing him out."

"Perhaps we could ask him to forget the past. If the city perish, it will be his throat along with the rest."

"All right, let's." Bias started briskly back along the mole to the waterfront.

When Diognetos' porter announced us, the architect appeared, leaning upon a stick. His beard seemed longer than ever and his general aspect just as forbidding. He frowned.

"Let me see," he said. "You are Bias Gorgou, the torsion-catapult enthusiast. And you—*tsk*, *tsk*, I cannot quite place you, young man."

"Chares Nikonos, sir," I said. "I—"

"Oh! Now I know. You are one of those who plotted to deprive me of my architect's post and turn it over to that Phoenician swindler. What do you here?"

I began: "O Diognetos, whatever be the truth about Kallias—and I, too, have suffered at his hands—our beloved city lies in deadly peril."

"What is the fate of this race of drunkards and fornicators to me?" said Diognetos. "I am a Rhodian in name only. My city has spurned me and cast me out."

"Ah, but you are in the city. If it fall, you will suffer with the rest."

"What would you have me do?" said Diognetos. "I am past the age for wielding a spear."

Bias spoke: "Sure, sir, but you're a technical man, and we need every one we can find, to boss the building of defenses and engines. Now, I'm no politician, but I know enough men on the Council so that I could maybe get them to offer you a good job, in spite of what Kallias might say—"

Diognetos struck the ground with his stick. "May you not live out the year!" he roared. "Has Rhodes the dog-faced insolence first to cast me out and humiliate me, and then, as soon as she is in trouble, to send emissaries to ask me to forgive and forget? Ordure! Diognetos is not so careless of his honor. Your talk of the city's fall frightens me not a whit. I am soon to die anyway, and how could I die more happily than seeing this ungrateful city going down in ruin? Begone or I will set the dog upon you!"

We left Diognetos muttering about "this accursed tribe of adulterers and rattlepates." As we walked back to the waterfront, Bias said:

"It looks like we'll have to do without the old vulture's help."

We walked to the marketplace in silence, where towered the heroic statues of our assailant and his father. Their bronze still glowed a ruddy brown, the patina of age not having yet greened them over. Bias jerked his thumb, saying:

"It seems kind of funny, don't it, to have statues of these jacklegs standing there when we're at war with them? All that good bronze would be better used for armor."

"I hope not!" I said. "Those are my masterpieces."

"Forget your own glory for once, Chares, and think of your city."

"I am thinking of it," said I, casting about for some unselfish reason for preserving the statues. "Look: Either we shall win or we shall lose. If we win, and keep the statues, people will say: 'What greatness of soul the Rhodians have, to preserve their art even when it immortalizes their foes!' While, if we lose, the fact that we spared the statues might incline Demetrios to mercy."

"That's clever but it don't convince me," said Bias. "Metal is metal, no matter what it's used for."

At the waterfront we passed Makar the stonecutter, bossing a gang of workmen who were heightening the harbor wall.

"Rejoice, Makar!" I said. "Where did you get all that fine stone?"

"It arrived but a ten-day ago for the new theater," said Makar. "Kallias didn't much like my taking it for this work, since the theater is a pet project of his. But I faced him down before the Council."

"Good for you!" I said. "When you run out of theater stones, round up all those marble sundials that Berosos has sold the people. They will give you one more course for your wall."

Bias: "That gives me an idea, Chares. You said the Babylonian was an expert at calculating, didn't you? Well, run out on the mole and fetch him; then meet me in the armory."

Berosos and I found Bias in the armory with a scroll spread out on a table. Around him dust swirled as workmen carried dull-gleaming weapons and armor hither and yon. The great building rang with the sound of hammer and whetstone as the city's fighting gear was readied.

Bias coughed and raised his voice. "This is Diades' book, *On the Construction of Engines of War*. Diades invented the belfry for the divine Alexander, and—"

"I crave your pardon, sir," said Berosos, "but never did this Diades invent the movable siege tower. My people did."

"Oh?"

"Aye, sir. In Babylonia reliefs hundreds of years old I can show you, depicting Babylonians attacking cities by means of belfries on wheels, with rams—"

Berosos would have no doubt given us a history of siegecraft from the Flood on down, but the blunt Bias cut him off. "All right, all right, let's get back to business. We've got to build some new catapults, and I'd like to try for a greater range than anybody has obtained so far."

"How?" I said.

"Look. Diades gives the standard formula for dart throwers: the length of the dart should be nine times the diameter of the skeins. Then he gives all these other proportions.

"All right so far, but I don't see how we can ever get beyond the present ranges with these same proportions; we can only change the size of the missile. What I propose is to use the same frame as in the *Eros* class, but with a longer trough, a longer recoiler, longer throwing arms, and a dart only two cubits long or less. That's still heavy enough to go through the best armor at extreme ranges...."

We passed the afternoon in designing the new machines and calculating weights and proportions. Out on the mole Phaon, commanding the skeleton crews in Bias' absence, kept watch toward the south. But Demetrios made no move.

Another ten-day passed. With the departure of winter, anemones again bloomed scarlet on the slopes of the akropolis. Demetrios' huge triple palisade of timber crept around his camp. Everywhere, in Rhodes and in the Antigonian camp, sounded the buzz and clangor of the tools of the mason, the carpenter, and the smith, the clatter of weapons, and the shouts of drillmasters. Even my father, who was in the inactive reserve, turned out for drill with the other middle-aged tribesmen.

Nor were the unseen powers neglected. The altars of the gods ran red with the blood of sacrificed animals. The official soothsayers studied the omens and pronounced Rhodes unconquerable.

Meanwhile, despite new laws against their activities, our host of wizards and witches and necromancers sought clues to the future of individuals in the cracks of a burnt shoulder blade, or in the ripples of water in a basin, or by the squeaks of spirits summoned from the lands of the dead. I suspected Berosos of doing a thriving business of this sort.

Amazing rumors ran the rounds. The most extravagant was that Demetrios was building an engine of war the like of which had never been seen. It was as big as Souphis' pyramid, it ran either on land or in the water, and it was propelled by some magical source of power furnished by an Egyptian wizard who sat in an armored control chamber and muttered mystical spells.

I trotted to and fro between the armory and Bias' shop while his workmen sawed and planed the structural members of the first of the new catapults. Once, on my way to the foundry with a sack of wooden patterns from which to cast the bronze fittings for the dart thrower, I was stopped by a mournful procession. Here went several hundred men, women, and children, many in rich oriental robes, prodded along by Rhodian spears. They were the aliens who would neither fight nor make arms, together with their families.

I played truant long enough to watch the outcome. South through the winding streets filed the sad parade until it reached the wall. Up the steps it went. At the top, rope ladders dangled from the crenelations of the parapet.

Before me lay the suburb, from which a pall of dust arose as Demetrios' men demolished the houses. Now and then a rumble and a crash told of the fall of another dwelling. A few idle Antigonian soldiers stood beyond bowshot and shouted taunts at the city.

At the sight of the ladders, the shirkers wailed and tore their hair and beards, beseeching the Rhodians to have pity. Indeed, the spectacle brought tears to the eyes of many onlookers. But these foreigners, mostly Phoenician, Syrian, and Anatolian tradesmen who had become too fat and soft for anything strenuous, had had their chance and failed it. At spear point they lowered themselves, over the parapet, crying that they would fall and be dashed to pieces. All, however, safely made the descent.

For a while they huddled in a moaning mass at the foot of the wall. When our officers threatened to drop stones upon them, they straggled off. Demetrios' soldiers pounced upon them as soon as they were out of bowshot, and led them off to the slavers. Those too old for such disposal they sworded to death on the spot.

Seeing Glôs the engraver nearby, I hailed him. Some misguided recruiting officer had assigned him to the infantry. As no cuirass in town would fit his girth, he was wearing one much too small, with wide gaps showing at the sides between its back and breastplates.

I pointed toward the section of the suburb where lay Protogenes' house. "What has become of the president of our guild?" I asked. "I haven't seen him since the siege began. I hope he is not so mad as to stay outside the wall."

"That's exactly what he has done," replied Glôs.

"Dear Herakles! Why?"

"When Demetrios' fleet appeared, and somebody shouted to Protogenes to snatch up his valuables and run for the gate, he pointed to the painting of Ialysos and asked: 'How could anybody snatch up that?' He was, he said, nearly finished with it, and he would not abandon his life's masterpiece to the caprices of a naughty boy with delusions of being a king."

"Has he been killed?"

"No. The embassy that made the agreement on prisoners also asked Demetrios to protect Protogenes and his paintings, as, whoever won the war, the king would not wish to be known as a wanton destroyer of art. Demetrios replied that he would rather burn the portrait that Apelles made of Antigonos than harm Protogenes' masterpiece. He posted a guard over the house to make sure that nobody molested the painter."

When I reached the foundry, I found my father grimy from toil and red-eyed from long hours. We talked in a businesslike way of the casting of the parts for the new engine. Then he cleared his throat in embarrassment.

"Er—Chares," he said, "I've been talking with my friend Genetor again."

"Yes?" said I, my scalp prickling with apprehension. Of all times, I thought, to put pressure on me to wed!

"He hopes you will not be too put out if he asks that your wedding be postponed."

"Oh?" Hope sprang to life anew in my breast.

"The reason is this new sumptuary legislation, forbidding all big displays and entertainments as long as the siege shall last. This includes weddings. Of course we could make our sacrifices, get the blessing of a priest, and sign our contracts before a magistrate, and you would be legally wed. But Genetor and I consider that our social position demands a proper wedding with a feast and procession. We hope you will understand—"

I repressed a grin. "Tell him I understand perfectly, Father."

My father looked at me with a faint smile of his own. "I will. And don't think I do not understand you, too, you rascal!"

The pilot model of the new catapult began to take shape. Once I asked Bias:

"Why make just one? Why not a dozen? This seems to me a waste of time."

"Son," he said, "when you've had more experience, you'll know that no machine works like you think it will. By making just one, we can correct the mistakes in the design in the rest of the lot. But if we made the whole dozen at the beginning and they all had the same bad fault, we'd be in a fix."

Then Captain Damophilos bustled into the armory. "O Bias!" he cried. "I want the *Talos* and her crew aboard the *Halia* by sunset."

Bias cursed. "I need these boys! Go take another engine."

"No. They served with me before, and I know them. Besides, they are the straightest shooters in your whole battery."

"What do you want them for?"

"We shall raid Demetrios' anchorages south of his camp. Hundreds of small ships are drawn up there, and we can burn and wreck scores before the heavy warships can sally out to stop us."

A long and stubborn argument resulted in the calling in, first of our battalion commander, then of Kallias, and finally of Admiral Exekestos. Damophilos won.

"O Chares," he said at the close of the interview, "see that the metal fittings of your engine are clean and polished before you bring it aboard. There shall be no dirty gear on *my* ship!"

Scudding clouds hid the full moon as the *Halia*, with slow strokes, pulled out of the Great Harbor. Behind her came two triemiolias: the *Euryalê*, which had fought in the action off Rhodes the previous year, and the *Agile*, a new ship of the same class as the ill-fated *Active*. All was dark save for a faint pearly radiance from the thick clouds above.

I stood on the forecastle of the *Halia* with my crew and the archers, peering into the dark. On the bow and the quarterdeck of each ship stood a sailor with a hooded lantern to warn off consorts and thus avert collisions. We carried double the usual number of lookouts.

Nothing stirred ashore. Except for the armory and the bobbing lanterns of the night watch, no lights showed from the dark mass of the city, as the Assembly had forbidden night lights lest traitors signal the foe. South of the wall a few fires flickered in Demetrios' camp. Otherwise nobody would have thought that thousands of men were preparing for mortal combat. We had about seven thousand—six thousand Rhodians and a thousand aliens—plus whatever force we could raise by arming slaves. Demetrios had nearly forty thousand, not counting his piratical allies—a force as great as that wherewith Alexander had overthrown the mighty Persian Empire.

We swung wide of the Chatar Rocks. Demetrios had joined these rocks to the Southwest Peninsular by a mole. His entire army had built this mole in one day, trotting back and forth with stones and baskets of earth.

There was a step behind me, and Captain Damophilos came up. He touched Berosos' arm, pointed, and spoke low:

"Do you see anything off that way?"

"Nay, sir. It is too dark."

"Demetrios is building something new in these coves. He keeps soldiers in the hills back of the shore and warships patrolling the waters, so that our spies have not been able to get near. Keep watch, in case the moon should break through."

We crept silently south, our vision gaining strength as our eyes became used to the darkness. The coast between Rhodes and the resort village of Kallithea, thirty furlongs away, is deeply embayed. In these bays were drawn up hundreds of smaller craft—sailing ships and thirty- and forty-oared galleys—belonging to the pirates and slavers who had followed Demetrios to the island. Damophilos said:

"Now hear this. The *Agile* will stand guard to signal us when the great galleys come out, whilst we and the *Euryalê* go into these coves and clean out as many pirate craft as we can. We shall use the ram and the catapult, and we have a fire pot burning in the storeroom under this deck for lighting incendiary missiles. You archers will be given arrows wrapped in tow, and a man will light them with a torch as you shoot them into the ships. Remember: a flaming arrow must be shot from a half-drawn bow lest its speed through the air blow out the flame.

"Chares, set your catapult for horizontal shooting. You may not get a decent shot, but let fly when you are aimed at a crowd of the enemy. All of you, obey your officers, keep quiet, do not get excited, come back to your ship quickly when signaled, and do not slaughter all your prisoners. Try to capture the better-dressed ones alive, so that we can wring information from them before selling them back to Demetrios."

Then he was gone. Eons parsed as we crept south.

At last we found a bay that suited Damophilos. While the *Agile* dropped astern, the *Halia* turned shoreward. The *Euryalê* turned also, but separately, into another bay. She was presently hidden from us, by a dark point of land.

The clouds began to thin out; now and then Selenê cast a dart of moonlight upon the earth. One of these shafts brushed the bay, showing ship after ship. While most were drawn up on the beach, several rode at anchor. Most were hemiolias—biremes modified for piratical purposes.

Halia swung her snout toward the rounded stern of one of these craft. We speeded up a little. A fast walk is enough to drive a ram through the thin sides of a ship; greater speed is likely to damage the rammer as well as the rammed.

We were within a ship's length of our quarry when a sleepy hail came from the deck of the hemiolia. *Halia* kept on.

Yellow lights flickered as our sailors kindled torches and brought them flaming up to the forecastle deck. From the anchored ship came shouts of alarm. There was a clank of weapons as men scurried to muster on the quarterdeck.

"Keep off! Keep off!" screamed a voice, evidently hoping that we were a friendly craft coming in to anchor.

Berosos said: "We are aimed squarely into that crowd, Chares."

"Shoot!" I said.

Onas struck the trigger; *Talos* crashed. The group on the quarterdeck, mustering with spears and swords, scattered. As the moonlight waxed, I saw a man writhing on the deck.

"We got one!" I cried—foolishly, for an attack such as ours calls for silence except for the necessary commands.

Our ram crunched through the stern planking of the ship at the waterline. The jar threw me forward against the catapult, so that I sustained a nasty knock and cut my lip against the rack.

Our archers aimed their fire arrows over the rail while a couple of sailors with torches passed from one to the next, lighting the balls of tow wrapped around the arrows. Soon a shower of fire arrows whizzed into the waist of the hostile ship, lighting it up.

From the rest of the bay came a chorus of shouts and trumpet calls and the rattle of accoutrements.

With a yell our file of marines pushed past us and scrambled over the bow to the quarterdeck of the victim. There was a brief clang of weapons, a few death screams, and the splash of many pirates diving over the side. *Halia*'s trumpet sounded the recall. The marines came back, waving paltry bits of loot and dragging a prisoner.

Damophilos gave the command to back, as the stricken ship was settling and dragging our bow down with her. Our oarsmen pushed on their looms; the ram slid out with a crackle and a crunch. The archers loosed another flight of fire arrows.

Halia turned her bow toward another ship at anchor. The crew of this ship dropped their anchor cable, put out a few oars, and tried to run for it. They had not made more than three strokes when the *Halia*'s ram found their side. Crash!

This time I had the sense to clutch the rail. I had little else to do, because at such a short range the pirate's deck was too low to reach with our catapult. Again we poured in fire arrows, swept the deck, and withdrew just as the moon winked out once more and the dark closed in upon us.

One other ship remained at anchor, seemingly deserted. We punched our ram into her side; then the marines went aboard and kindled a fire under the quarterdeck.

That left the ships drawn up on shore. Many were too far up on the strand to reach with our ram.

Trumpets blasted away to the north, in Demetrios' camp, and there was a half-seen scuttling on shore, as when one steps into an abandoned building and the mice run for cover. As we swung again toward the shore, a group of men appeared in the light of a campfire. Somebody harangued them. From the adjacent bay came sounds of crash and clash as the *Euryalê* struck her first victim.

"Range!" I called.

"Eight and a half plethra, if the dark deceive me not," said Berosos.

"Cock your piece; twelfth notch."

"Eight plethra."

"Load your piece."

"Seven plethra."

"Shoot!"

The dart whistled into the mass about the fire, skewering a man. The pirates scattered with cries of dismay. When our bow gently touched the sand, and marines and sailors scrambled down off the bow and waded ashore, they found the beach deserted. I would have gone ashore with them, but a bark from Damophilos brought me back. Our landing party went along the line of ships, throwing torches and bundles of flaming tow into them, or building fires under their bilges.

Damophilos came up to the forecastle deck. "O Berosos!" he said. "Yours are the keenest eyes here. Tell me what you see."

Berosos held up his hands to shade his eyes from the blazes. "Methinks men muster on yonder hill. The gleam of firelight on breastplates I see; these must be some of Demetrios' regulars."

"Sound the recall!" cried Damophilos to the trumpeter.

"Captain!" said the boatswain. "The *Agile* signals us."

"Sound the recall again," said Damophilos. "Archers, we will fire the remaining ships with arrows; stand by. Why in the name of the Dog don't those men hurry?"

Our landing party straggled back. Damophilos cupped his hands and shouted: "Last man shall be left ashore!"

This brought them on the run. When all were aboard, the *Halia* backed water and turned parallel to the shore. A dozen ships were ablaze, yellow flames glancing from the waters and lighting the bellies of billowing clouds of smoke. Several more vessels began to catch.

We rowed along the shore, past the four ships to which fire had not yet been applied. Our archers showered them with fire and set at least one alight.

Now, however, a crowd of men appeared in the firelight: a mixed multitude of pirates and soldiers. Demetrios' officers directed them. Some shouted threats and taunts across the dark waters; others, more practically, rushed to the ships and fought the fires. They threw helmetfuls of water on the blazes, pulled fire arrows out of the woodwork, beat and kicked at the smaller fires, or threw sand into the flames. Many ships, however, had blazed too high to be saved.

"Speed up the beat! Raise the boat sail!" came Damophilos' voice from the quarterdeck.

The sound of the flutist's notes came faster. *Halia* began to roll in the swells outside the bay. The fires receded, merging with distance into a single blaze. A dark shape appeared ahead; Damophilos and his executive officer agreed that it must be the *Euryalê*. From another dark shape came frantic lantern signals.

We rowed briskly north, our battle sail adding to our speed. Then two more shapes came into view, growing larger by the heartbeat. It was plain that these were two of Demetrios' heavy warships, put out to intercept us. In the dark they looked twice the size of any ship I had seen.

The two triemiolias had drawn ahead of the *Halia*. Now they swung out to sea. One of the Antigonians followed. To my ears came the distant sound of hails and responses.

The other ship bore down upon us. Damophilos held to his course, though it would bring us almost within spitting distance of the Antigonian.

"Ahoy!" came a hail out of the dark. "Who are you?"

"The *'Ektor* of Miletos!" cried Damophilos, dropping his h's like an Ionian. "Come to join King Demetrios. Are you Rhodian or Antigonian?"

"Antigonian! Heave to for inspection!"

"You are a dirty Rhodian and I will not stop!" shouted Damophilos. "Follow me into the 'arbor if you wish to speak me."

"Stop, I tell you, or I'll ram!"

"Get out of my way, and you may send an officer aboard. Careful, you stupid ox, or you'll 'ave us both sunk!"

The two ships passed on opposite courses, just far enough apart to keep their oars from clashing. At Damophilos' orders our rowers lifted their oars and rested on them, as if he really meant to stop. The Antigonian ship did likewise. Then, as the natural drift of the ships began to carry them apart, Damophilos cried:

"Forward! Flank speed!"

Our rowers dug in their oars and strained at the looms. The *Halia* leaped like a living thing. Cries of rage came from the Antigonian's deck. A few arrows whistled past us or stuck in the woodwork. Iros, one of my cockers, suddenly choked, staggered, waved his arms wildly, and fell with an arrow through his throat. He died before we could do anything.

Pronax, our loader, said: "It'll take that big thing time to turn around; but, once she does, she can overtake us."

The Antigonian almost disappeared astern; the triemiolias were out of sight to seaward. We pulled to the north at a steady stroke. There was little sound but the swish of our bow through the waves, the thump of the oars against the thole pins, and the peep of the flutist's pipe. Formless dark shapes of bay and headland drifted past us to port.

A rent appeared in the overcast, through which the moon blazed down in full silvery glory. After we had groped so long beneath a canopy of clouds, the moonlight seemed as bright as day. It lit up a bay in which strange machines were building.

Damophilos hastened forward. "Berosos! Look yonder and tell me what you see."

Berosos peered. "A pair of ships conjoined together I see, with a platform erected over them on which some sort of tower is a-building. Two—three—four such pairs I see. Then, over that way, a whole mass of ships I see—"

"What else?"

"Not far enough advanced are the works, except on the second pair of ships yonder. The thing upon them seems to be a catapult of the largest size."

We all strained our eyes, trying to pick out further details, though none could see more than Berosos had described. Then a sailor called:

"Captain! The Antigonian is coming up astern!"

The moon showed the ship that had challenged us about two furlongs astern and closing the gap.

"Row harder!" cried Damophilos. "Put your backs into it. Raise the beat, coxswain. Flank speed, if you would see your homes again!"

The *Halia* speeded up a little, but not much, as our rowers had been pulling hard for a quarter-hour and were tiring. Closer came the Antigonian. Off to starboard the two triemiolias appeared, with the other large ship in pursuit. Astern two more great black shapes crawled out from shore.

Our pursuer gained until we could again hear the hail of its captain. Then came the thump of catapults. Missiles whispered past us.

"*Rhyppapai! Papai!*" called our coxswain.

Damophilos: "Archers, come aft! The rest of you on the forecastle, take cover."

While the archers filed back to take up the arrow fight, the crew of the *Talos* went below to the storeroom beneath the forecastle deck. We crowded around the door, peering out until a three-span dart whizzed through the opening, passing within a few digits of my head, and buried itself in the planking. Thereafter we were less eager spectators.

As we neared the moles of our harbor, our trumpeter sounded the alarm. Answering flourishes came from the shore. Through the storeroom door I glimpsed the yellow blink of torchlight as men manned the batteries on the South Mole.

The *Euryalê* and the *Agile* passed into the harbor ahead of us. As we came around the end of the South Mole, our catapults on the mole awoke with thumps and crashes. We came out on deck to see our pursuers sheer off. We were safe.

A few days later, a team of mules hauled Bias' new catapult down to the waterfront. I came with Bias and several of his workmen and the crew of the *Talos*, which had been given the honor of proving the new weapon.

We rumbled out the sea gate in the harbor wall, which Makar was still valiantly raising. Outside the wall lay a broad strip of paving ordinarily crowded with cargoes awaiting transshipment but now almost bare. Along the edge of this waterfront ran the quays and piers and the walled-off section that housed the arsenal and the dockyards. The four moles jutted out from shore like the tentacles of some sea creature, embracing the two harbors.

Two of Bias' penthouses stood on the mole, for the Council had ordered a second. Each was a stout shed with thick timbers on the seaward side, whence hostile missiles might come. The first story provided quarters for the crews and space for ammunition. A battery of catapults, hauled up wooden ramps, lined the roof, which was surrounded by a low wall of heavy timber to shield the crews.

The four Isisdorian stone throwers occupied the penthouse at the far end of the mole, while the six dart throwers of Bias' own battery stood on the other penthouse, between the mole's end and the base.

We could not mount similar works on the other moles for lack of space. Therefore, battery platforms were being erected on three large merchant ships moored in the Great Harbor, on each of which would be placed another battery.

Bias said: "We'll ground her at the base of the mole. Ah, there's one of the temple thieves now!"

Bias referred to one of the light Antigonian galleys—perhaps of piratical origin—on whose bow Demetrios had built a small penthouse. This structure had a single three-span dart thrower inside and an iron shutter in front to protect the crew. Demetrios had outfitted several ships in this manner, and others with light towers for archers forward. Every day one or more appeared off the harbor to harass the workmen strengthening our defenses.

At first the workmen scattered like quail before a hawk when the missiles whizzed over. In time they became used to them, discovering that shots from a bobbing platform at single scattered individuals make few hits indeed. Now the clatter of hammers and the snore of saws hardly paused as the missiles arrived.

At the base of the mole we levered the new catapult off its rollers and set it up. I asked:

"Do you want maximum range?"

"Not the first time. Try the tenth notch. Somebody tell them people on the mole to stop shooting so we can fix our range."

We cocked our new engine. It was a beautiful piece of construction, light and graceful but strong, with five trough positions and twenty notches in its racks. The handlers trained the trough on the target with rope and crowbar. I gave the word:

"Shoot!"

The first dart rose high and fell just short of the two catapult ships. On the next shot I gave the crosshead one more notch and scored a clean hit.

We whooped and danced. The ships, aware of us now, turned their bows toward us and let fly. One three-span dart plunked into the water nearby, while another struck the paving and clattered end over end till it struck the harbor wall.

"Again," said Bias.

Again we made a hit. The third shot missed by a small margin, but the fourth struck home. Our target turned and rowed off, with some confusion among its rowers where men in the undecked waist had been struck. We continued to send darts after it until maximum range had been reached. The catapult sang like a bird in spring.

Berosos said: "By the gods, O Bias, methinks your engine can shoot seventeen or eighteen plethra!"

I said: "That must be a world's record. A cheer for Bias, boys!"

"*Iai!*" they cried.

Bias gave us a wrinkled, leathery grin. "Thanks, fellows, but let's wait and see how she turns out in endurance and ease of maintenance. A practical engineer don't make promises until he knows from experience."

The new catapult proved a great success, save that the complicated skein shackles (which had built-in wedges for tautening the skeins) made the process of restringing it more laborious than with those of the older kinds. We named the class after aspects of the weather; thus the pilot model became *Lightning*.

As I assisted Bias with the building of eleven more of this model, I came to know the carpenter better and to respect him more: "wise to resolve, and patient to perform." Bias had his faults, as who does not? Besides the crudity of his speech and manners, he was filled with rancorous resentment toward the full citizens, who were richer and more powerful than he. On the other hand, he despised slaves and unskilled workmen as lazy, worthless half-wits and bullied them when he commanded them.

At the same time Bias was one of those rarities: an utterly honest and truthful man. If he said a thing was so, you could be sure it was. And he knew more about building things than anybody I have known, including some of the world's outstanding architects and engineers.

The third year of the 118th Olympiad drew to a close. So absorbed was I in soldiering and catapult building that summer stole upon me unawares, and I almost forgot the other pleasures that our lovely city still afforded. When outraged nature drove me at last to visit my friend the flute girl, I found Berosos there before me. As I opened the door, something jangled.

The Babylonian had been sitting on a couch beside Doris, with an astrological chart spread out upon his knees. I suppose he had been telling her that the stars compelled her to be intimate with him—a novel approach, though not one that I should care to use. On the table stood cups and two small jars of wine.

Berosos jumped up, dropping his chart and spilling his wine. "Oh, dear Chares, how sorry am I! I meant not to intrude. I merely stopped for a talk. Doris and I have known each other for long—"

"Save your excuses, old boy," I said.

I looked into the wine jars. Sure enough, a small red mullet floated belly-up in one. It is said that wine in which such a fish has been drowned will infallibly prevent a woman from conceiving. In fact, Theseus the fishmonger kept a supply of live red mullets in a tub for the convenience of the pleasure women of the town.

I laughed at the flustered Babylonian. "You came for the same thing I did. Well and good, I shall withdraw and come back later."

"You mean you two won't quarrel over me?" said Doris in a disappointed voice.

"No, my dear. I'm much too busy these days. By the way, Berosos, how are all the great love affairs coming?"

"I know not wh-what you mean," he said. I daresay he blushed, though his skin was too swarthy to mark it easily.

"Never mind, I was only teasing." I looked more closely at the door. "Ah, I see. You have a bell that rings every time somebody opens the door. What's the purpose of that, Doris?"

"My master, the old stinkpot, put that up," she said. "That's so he can keep track of the number of friends I entertain and collect his share of my earnings."

"Do you know, Berosos, I think we could put this knavish device out of action. A little lump of beeswax—"

"Oh, no!" said Doris. "If old Theron doesn't hear the bell at all, he'll know something has been done to it. Then he will not only beat me but also bore a hole through the wall or something, the better to spy upon me."

Berosos peered at the bell. "Methinks we could invent a means that would enable Doris to turn the bell on or off as she lists."

He and I fell into a lively discussion of possible methods of activating and silencing the bell, until Doris burst out: "Why in the name of Zeus the King did I ever become friends with a couple of engineers? I expect you, when you visit me, to tell me the things a woman likes to hear: how beautiful and charming I am, and how you adore me. Instead, Berosos gives me lectures in astronomy while Chares always wants to make technical improvements in my poor little apartment!"

"I'm going now, anyway," I said. "Farewell, and have a good—ah—talk."

* * *

The next day a trumpet blast brought me in haste to the South Mole, to take command of *Talos*. Out at sea lay a number of Demetrios' great ships, flinging darts and even stones from their catapults. Although the morning had been fair, as I reached my post the sky clouded over and a moaning wind sprang up. The galleys, great and small, wallowed and tossed until they had to pull in their lower oars and block the ports, and their missiles flew wilder than ever.

A ten-pound ball, however, struck the frame of *Artemis* with a crash. One of the uprights was cracked, so that the tension of the skein on that side pulled the whole frame out of true.

Bias popped up from the ammunition room. "Woe and misfortune!" he cried. "She'll have to go back to the shop. Phaon, get the mules and the tackle for letting her down the ramp."

The desultory missile fight went on as we lowered the crippled engine. As the day wore on, however, and the water waxed rougher, the Antigonians gave up. One by one the ships turned and rowed away.

Unseasonable rain pattered down that night and continued the next day. I said to Bias:

"Sir, we now have one full battery of the new engines ready to mount. Why don't we bring in the remaining pieces of the old battery, so that when the weather clears, we can run the new ones up into position at once? I don't think Demetrios will attack while this sea keeps up."

"Maybe," grunted the carpenter. "We got word from a spy that the boy wonder was all set to bring out his new seagoing engines for a full assault yesterday, but Poseidon had other ideas. All right, let's round up the boys and get to it."

All but two of the catapults of the *Eros* class had been dismounted. *Orion* rested on the mole near its landward end, waiting to be hauled to the armory, while *Eros* stood on the mainland at the base of the mole. The rain—most unusual in Skirophorion on our lovely island—had thinned to a drizzle; darkness had fallen; a fog had come down upon us. The sea subsided.

We worked far into the evening. Torchlight was reflected in yellow ripples from the puddles on the pavement; at a distance each torch appeared as a weird glowing ball of orange in the fog. Phaon remarked:

"Would not this be a fine time for Demetrios to make a surprise attack?"

"You have too much imagination," I said. "Tell Simon to slack off on that rope before he pitches us all over the edge."

Faintly through the fog came the calls of the sentries, announcing midnight. We maneuvered *Herakles*, the last but one of the battery, toward the head of the ramp. Here we had to fasten ropes to the ends of the rollers lest they get loose from the frame and go rolling down the ramp on their own. With crowbars we teased the catapult over the top of the ramp.

"Watch out below!" Bias called down. "Chares, get some more men on those ropes or she'll get away from us."

"Grab it, Pronax," I said. "You, too, and you, whatever your name is. *Ea*, Onas! We need your thews!"

The men's shoes skidded on the wet wood of the top of the penthouse. Seeing that the engine was likely to pull loose after all, I seized the rope myself. Down went *Herakles*, a digit at a time. The catapult had been lowered halfway down the ramp when there came a sound from the dark.

"What's that?" I said. "Listen!"

"Come on!" came Bias' voice from the head of the ramp. "We don't want to be here all night. Stand clear, Kriton!"

The sound waxed until there was no doubt of what it was: the splash and thump of the oars of light rowing craft.

"Battery leader!" I called. "Something is coming—"

Even as I spoke, the bark of commands and the clatter of weapons came from the seaward end of the mole. The sound was repeated, closer to hand: against the mole where stood our penthouse. Lanterns bobbed in the dark.

Somebody shouted: "The Macedonians come!"

There was a rush of feet around the base of the penthouse, Almost as one man, those holding the *Herakles*' ropes let go and dashed for the ladder to the ammunition room, or to the ramp, or lowered themselves over the edge of the penthouse roof and jumped. Most of the torchbearers dropped their torches and links, which sputtered and went out.

I found myself the only man holding my rope. The weight of the engine dragged me at ever-mounting speed toward the ramp until I let go just in time.

The *Herakles* rumbled down the ramp, struck the paving of the mole with a bang, and continued on its course. With a crash it rammed the *Orion*. There was a frightful shriek from the darkness; one of the men of the battery was caught between the two engines and had his legs crushed.

Other artillerymen slid or scrambled down the ramp. I followed. Except for myself and a few others who wore swords, we were all unarmed save for daggers.

I reached the foot of the ramp at the tail of the fleeing crowd. Beside me an Antigonian, looking a plethron tall in his crested helmet, loomed out of the darkness. His stabbing-spear jabbed out; the point transpierced an artilleryman, who fell with a scream.

I had my hand on the hilt of the short sword that had been issued to me. Hardly knowing what I did, I swept out the blade and aimed a cut at the spearman's arm. The blade bit through; the spear clattered to the pavement.

I stepped in, slashing and thrusting before the man could bring his shield around to ward me off. Somehow my point found his groin, below the edge of his corselet. It went through the straps of his kilt, and down he went with a groan.

My most urgent need was for a shield. Not a man in the battery bore one, and without shields there was no hope of stopping the Antigonian spears. With my free hand I tugged the fallen man's shield from his arm. It was of Macedonian pattern: a small buckler of wood and leather, without a bronze facing, made to be thrust up the left arm to free the hand for managing the long Macedonian pike, for which there is but little use in a siege.

When I got the shield on my arm, I found Antigonians all around me. If none speared me, it must have been that in the darkness they were unsure of who I was. They clattered shoreward in pursuit of the artillerymen. I ran with them, gaining because of my lighter gear and my familiarity with the site.

A few steps brought me to where the two catapults stood: *Orion*, previously lowered from the penthouse, and *Herakles*, which had smashed into *Orion* when the men had released the ropes. The man who had been crushed lay still, wedged into the space between the engines.

Although the two catapults blocked most of the mole, around one side a passage still existed. Here a little crowd was gathering: Antigonians trying to force their way past, and Rhodians striving to stop them.

I took two running steps toward an Antigonian who stood with his back to me while he jabbed at the Rhodians before him. I swung my sword up for a cut at his neck—and stumbled over a body. My shield struck the back of his corselet and gave him a violent push. He shouted something, doubled up, and fell to hands and knees.

I almost fell on top of the man, recovered my footing, and got my shield up just in time to block the swing of a sword. Such was the force of the blow that I thought my arm had been broken.

"Temple-robbing sodomite!" gasped the Rhodian, swinging his blade up again.

"Bias!" I cried. "It's I! Chares!"

"Chares? Well, don't stand there! Get in line with us!"

I stepped over the body of the man whom I had pushed and Bias had slain, and crowded into line. The carpenter had somehow obtained a shield and stood in the middle of our little group, blocking spear thrusts and dealing out sword blows at the nearest Antigonians. Behind the mass of foes, an officer shouted:

"Push on, men! They are but a handful! Push on!"

The Antigonians continued to jab. While we could parry or block their thrusts to some degree, we could not effectively fight back, because the reach of their spears was much greater than that of our swords.

I blocked and parried with the rest, panting: "Hasn't anybody gone for help?"

"The way they was running," snarled Bias, "they won't stop short of Kameiros."

The pressure from behind forced the foremost Antigonians forward. They were pushed upon us willy-nilly, thrusting furiously with their spears. One of our men went down with a scream and a gurgle. The next instant a spear point, darting out of the dark like a serpent's tongue, pierced my right leg below the knee. Feeling the sting of the steel, I struck at the man who had speared me and missed. As I put my weight on the wounded leg, it folded under me.

Down I went. A spear point glanced off my helmet; another was stopped by my leathern corselet. There was a confusion of legs all around me. I seemed to be alone in a forest of bronze-greaved Antigonian limbs, all tramping past me.

Then came a great yelling. The greaved legs stumbled back toward the penthouse. A tall figure loomed into the feeble lantern light, swinging a sword twice the length of mine and uttering hideous cries in the gargling Keltic tongue. I did not have to see the red mustache to recognize my former slave. The long sword flashed in the lantern light; an Antigonian cried out and fell off the mole with a splash. Others followed Kavaros.

Somebody caught my ankles and pulled me out of the press. At the base of the mole they hauled me to my feet.

"Are you still alive?" someone asked.

"I hope so," I said.

"Good. You don't look it, with that blood all over you."

They had fetched back the bodies of several more who had fallen in the fight for the mole, but I seemed the only one still living. Rhodian soldiers, summoned by trumpet blasts, were streaming out the harbor gate and hastening to the base of the mole, where *Eros* stood. Officers strove to get them into order.

The group that had rushed the Antigonians now fell back to the base of the mole. Some began gathering stones and timbers and building a barricade across the mole, a few paces out from its base.

The Antigonians, meanwhile, held off. They now held nine-tenths of the mole, including the two penthouses. For a while they stood in a bristling line across the mole, shields and spears at ready. Then the line broke and retreated. Behind them other Antigonians had also been erecting a barricade, using the benches and other simple furniture that we had placed in the penthouses, and stones pried up from the paving of the mole.

Darkness overhung the two groups of men, lightened fitfully by torches and lanterns. There was a buzz of talk, the grunting and panting of men moving heavy weights, and the thump of stones and timbers dropped into place.

Bias found me and looked at the wound in my leg. He said: "Here, Onas! Help Chares back and tie him up; then report to me."

With one arm about the stalwart Egyptian's neck, I hobbled back to his house in downtown Rhodes. His wife, Nembto, cleansed my wound with healing herbs and bound it up. Despite the ache that soon set in, I caught a little sleep before dawn—sleep, however, in which I dreamt that a shark was slowly chewing off my leg, all the while making love to me in King Demetrios' voice.

The fog was turning to pearl when I was awakened. Onas was there with Berosos and two others of the crew to carry me home on a litter made of spear shafts. We had not yet reached home when trumpets blew from all quarters. My friends did the last block to my house at a trot, summoned my parents, stammered hasty explanations, and ran off to take up their duties.

My mother almost fainted when she saw me, for my clothes and I had been drenched with Antigonian blood and I had washed off but little of it at Onas' house. Both parents made a great fuss over me. I realized that, in their own ways, they really loved me more than my cross-grained nature deserved from them.

Now the fog was lifting. I said: "Dear ones, please get me to the roof, where I can see!"

"Don't be silly, son," they exclaimed in the same breath. Despite my protests, my father and Sosias bore me off to bed and propped me up with pillows. My father said:

"Stop fidgeting like a fresh-caught fish, Chares! If you're not careful, you'll start your wound bleeding again. I will personally go up to the roof from time to time and bring you a report on the battle."

I ate a little and slept a little, in spite of the fact that, by straining an ear, I could plainly hear the cries and crashes of the growing battle. When my father came in again, he said:

"Several hundred of Demetrios' men hold the mole and the catapults on it, which they have turned about to face the shore. They've also moored to the mole two engines, each made up of a pair of ships lashed together and a wooden platform, bearing several powerful catapults. With these engines they have driven our men back from the waterfront. Now I must see to the foundry. I'll tell you more later."

It would take more than a mere battle to distract my father for long from the careful and efficient operation of his establishment. Later in the day he resumed his account:

"Demetrios' whole fleet is attacking the harbor. Herakles, but the man has ingenious ideas! First comes a pair of triremes pushing a boom of logs studded with spikes, to protect his ships from a sudden sortie by our little fleet. Then come two more sea engines, each of which is a tower mounted on a pair of hulls. Lastly come a swarm of small craft bearing troops and more catapults."

"Ye gods, could I only be there to strike one blow for my city!" I cried, twisting on my bed. "How are we doing?"

"It's too early to tell. When I came down, missiles were flying like raindrops from both sides."

"Father!" I said. 'Tell Mother to put up some lunches and have the slaves take them down to the harbor and give them to Onas. This will be a long day and my crew will be hungry.

"Aye-aye, sir!" said my father with a twinkle. "We're hampered by having only one man slave, Sosias, and he is out looking for a physician for you. But I'll see that your crew is fed."

"I don't need a physician for this scratch," I said. "And what's become of the other servants?"

"Kion and Daos have enlisted, and Pontikos has disappeared. Now lie quietly. As long as you're wounded, I'm your commanding officer."

I lay unhappily while my mother read to me to take my mind off the ache in my leg and the distant uproar. But even the duel between fleet Achilleus and noble Hektor seemed petty and amateurish compared to the mighty struggle now raging.

My father came in before dinner, wearing his old cuirass and looking haggard. He explained:

"Word was sent for the reservists to stand by, though happily we weren't needed. By the gods and spirits, though, for a time I thought we were done for! Demetrios' sea towers were pushed up to the waterfront by triremes. Then his archers in the towers drove our men from the harbor wall, which they overtopped."

"What saved us?"

"Incendiary darts from our catapults. We got a nice little fire blazing on one of the towers, and both were pulled back. Now Demetrios has settled down to a heavy bombardment of the harbor wall with his stone throwers. That's the booming you hear."

My mother felt my forehead. "He has a fever, Nikon. We simply must get Doctor Heron."

"Sosias has been looking for him for hours," said my father. "But all the physicians are busy at the walls. We shall have to depend on prayer and common sense."

There came a knocking on the outer door. It was Kavaros, with dents in his helmet, a bandage around his left arm, and a glow in his eyes.

"Ah, young sir, it is living again that I am," he said. "Was it not you that was pulled out by the feet, this morning in that shindy on the mole?"

"Yes. Where did you get that whopping great barbarian sword?"

Kavaros pulled out the blade. "Indeed and a better tool for fighting it is than these little choppers you use, which do be good only for cutting up a piece of meat into hash for the old people who have no teeth left. One of my officers, who picked it up in Illyria, gave it to me. But not so well made is it as those of the Tektosages, which have more spring to the blade. Now, let me think, I came here for some reason. Oh, Battery-leader Bias wants Master Chares at the armory to help him sort the arrows and sling bullets and things they are picking up."

"He cannot go tonight," said my father. "He's wounded and feverish."

"I can too go," I said, beginning to rise.

My parents flew at me with protests. As we struggled, I to rise and they to force me back upon the bed, everything began to whirl, and I swooned away.

"How do you feel, my darling?" asked my mother.

"As weak as a new puppy," I said. "How long was I out of my mind?"

"Two days. You raved about wishing to fight Demetrios single-handed, and many times you tried to leave your bed."

"How goes the battle?"

"Your father will tell you when he comes in. Now drink some broth, like a good boy."

Boom! A distant concussion sounded, much louder than anything I had heard from the battle yet.

"Zeus! What's that, Mother?" I asked.

"Some horrid new engine. Now, take another spoonful—"

When he came, my father said: "The day before yesterday Demetrios attacked again with his sea towers. This time the towers were covered with green hides, so that our flaming darts had no effect. But Superintendent Rhesos had prepared some jugs of incendiary mixture—naphtha laced with sulphur—and our stone throwers hurled these at the towers. When the towers had been well splashed, a single incendiary dart set a fine blaze on one, and both were pulled out again."

Boom! "What is that thing, Father?"

"I'm coming to that. Yesterday Demetrios' men ran two big merchantmen up to the South Mole and unloaded great masses of timber and fittings, which they began to assemble despite a harassing bombardment from our wall. This morning the sun disclosed two new catapults larger than any I ever heard of. They cast three-talent balls, more than a foot in diameter. With these and his other stone throwers, Demetrios seeks to batter down our harbor wall while with long-range dart throwers he hampers Makar's efforts to strengthen it. The gods only know what the outcome will be."

Book V

PYTHON

When I rejoined my crew, limping on a stick, the first thing I saw in the dim light before dawn was their crop of beards. (I let mine grow for a while, too, but alas! it was no success, being sparse and straggly, with bare patches. Since then I have kept my face well shaven, in accordance with modern fashions.)

The *Lightning* was mounted atop the harbor wall, midway between the arsenal and the base of the East Mole. Pronax, the loader, was missing; a man named Mys had taken his place. Berosos had a bandage around his neck where an arrow had grazed him.

Of the battery as a whole, the ill-fated *Eros* was gone for good. It had been smashed by a ball in the waterfront fighting, the day after Demetrios had seized the South Mole.

As for the wall itself, the pounding from Demetrios' stone throwers had opened cracks in the towers and curtain walls into which a man could thrust his hand. Other balls had knocked gaps in the parapet, so that it gaped like a row of broken teeth.

Even before dawn the ugly little brown figure of Makar dashed about, ordering his men to the repair and reinforcement of the wall. But he seemed to be losing ground.

Out on the South Mole stood Demetrios' two new giant stone throwers. The frames of these catapults towered twenty-five feet into the air, and their throwing arms alone were over ten feet long. There was a familiarity about them that nagged me until I realized that they were the full-sized versions of the model that I had seen the engineer Apollonios demonstrate.

Smaller catapults, including those captured from us, stood on the penthouses. Two of Demetrios' sea engines lay moored to the mole, one bearing three stone throwers on its platform and the other four dart throwers.

The waterfront was littered with broken stone and with cracked and broken catapult balls. The unbroken three-talent balls from the heavy engines had not been collected, because we had nothing to shoot them with.

My comrades told me of our unsuccessful attack on Demetrios' fleet with lifeboats the night after the capture of the mole; of infantry attacks with ladders against the wall; of how Pronax was slain by a dart.

As the sun, glowing like molten bronze in a crucible, rose behind them, little black figures moved about the mole. Nearby, Bias passed the command:

"Shoot at will!"

"We are laid for the right-hand one of the big fellows," said Onas.

"Cock your piece," I said.

Apollonios' great engines took a long time to cock. When the recoiler of the right-hand one was at last pulled back, the loaders rolled one of the balls up on a kind of stretcher or litter: a long wooden frame with a handle at each corner. Then four men raised the frame shoulder high and decanted the ball into its place in the trough.

Another wait, and the stone thrower went off with a tremendous crash. The three-talent ball sped high into the air, whispered down upon us so that we all flinched, and struck the wall with a thunderous *boom.* The impact shook the entire wall; I could feel the structure rock beneath my feet. The ball, rebounding, rolled back across the waterfront almost to the water's edge and stopped, spinning slowly for a few turns before it lay still.

Then the other engine discharged. *Boom!*

We cranked and shot, shading our eyes against the rising sun and making tiny adjustments to try to drop our darts amid the laboring crews of the heavy stone throwers. Demetrios' other catapults on the mole and on the moored sea engines opened up also.

As the sun, now a golden disk, sprang clear of the blue horizon, a mass of hostile ships appeared at the entrance to the Great Harbor, with masts lowered and oars rising and falling. Two triremes rowed into the harbor, as far apart as the width of the entrance allowed. Each held the end of a boom of floating logs, chained together and studded with iron spikes. The triremes pushed this boom out of sight around the arsenal to face the Rhodian fleet, which lay, fully manned, prepared to sally forth.

Following the boom, several light missile ships took stations in the harbor and added their barrage of three-span darts to those whistling up from the mole.

Toward noon the *Lightning* fell still. Bias called up from the ground outside the wall:

"O Chares! Why don't you shoot?"

"We're down to our last six darts, sir. I am saving those for an assault. When can we get some more?"

"Plague! The god-detested smiths promised a hundred for the battery by noon, but I doubt if they'll get them done. I've sent Phaon to pick some from the salvage pile. Meanwhile, eat."

While we ate, we grumbled over the conditions imposed by the siege. Mys, our new loader, said: "All this talk of keeping prices down is a lot of ordure. Do you know what happened to me last night?"

"What?" I said.

"I went into Evios' tavern for a drop, and the abandoned rascal had the impudence to say he was out of Rhodian, though he had some rare Chian and Lesbian at twice the fixed price! I drank a cup, but it was the same old local wine. This is Evios' way of getting around price control."

"The joy girls have put up their prices, too," said one of the cockers. "They claim the Assembly's decrees don't apply to them."

"If they go much higher," said another, "I may have to become a boy-lover after all."

"And a water-drinker as well," said Mys.

Said another: "But that's unhealthy!"

"Which is?"

"Why, water-drinking—"

Boom! went a three-talent ball. With a rumble and roar a section of the wall slid into ruin. When the cloud of dust had cleared, the wall looked as if some Titan had taken a huge bite out of it. From a height of twenty feet it swooped down to a mere ten, then up again. Below the broken section lay a heap of shattered stone and mortar, providing attackers with a ready-made ramp.

Trumpets blasted. Demetrios pulled his men together for an assault, while our officers shouted orders to repair the break and to mass to repel the attack.

Makar and his men, heedless of missiles, swarmed into the gap and began building it up again, stone by stone. Others brought timber balks and some of the three-talent balls that Demetrios had been shooting at us, to build into the wall. Rhodian infantry gathered around the break.

I said: "Boys, to cover the base of the wall at the break, we must move our piece so it hangs out over the waterfront."

"How shall we do that?" said Onas.

"Do you see yonder break in the parapet? We'll slide old *Lightning* down there and push the right-hand strut of the base out through the gap."

Berosos: "Take care that you overbalance the engine not, lest it topple from the wall."

With rope and crowbar we did what I had said. Now, by shooting with the trough horizontal, I could make our darts skim the top of the parapet at a narrow angle and drop down where I expected the foe to swarm.

The Antigonians advanced again. First came the two sea towers and the sea engine bearing the dart throwers. With them came the troopships. Ahead flew clouds of missiles, skipping and bouncing from the masonry; an arrow stood quivering in *Lightning*'s outer upright.

Two troopships rowed up between the sea towers and put out gangplanks. The soldiers tumbled ashore and clattered across the pavement, crying: "*Eleleu!*" Some carried ladders. A standard-bearer, holding aloft a golden eagle on a pole, led each company. Their officers harkened them on with shouts.

They rushed toward the break in the wall, their horsehair crests nodding. The sunlight, flashing on their bronze cuirasses, made them look like a swarm of glossy beetles. The cry arose from the defenders:

"Ladder! Ladder!"

Two other troopships, seeking places to put their men ashore, struck hidden rocks. As they settled, their men screamed for help; some cast off their armor to swim.

Those who had rushed to the break in the wall placed their ladders against the pile of debris and climbed, holding high their small Macedonian shields to ward off missiles.

"Shoot!" I cried.

A dart from *Lightning* plunged into the crowd. As nobody else had turned his catapult at such an angle as mine, *Lightning* was the only heavy weapon that, at the moment, bore upon the attackers.

The Rhodians on the wall shot arrows and hurled twirl spears down upon the Antigonians, who swarmed like ants up the pile of tailings. As the Antigonians neared the top of the pile, they became jammed together, for the pile tapered to the top. *Lightning* struck again and again, but for every man who fell, two took his place. Presently an Antigonian hoisted himself into the gap; then another.

We shot the last of our six darts. Every one was a fair hit, but when they were gone there was nothing for us to do.

"Where's the polluted Phaon?" I cried.

As the Antigonians began to climb down the inner side of the gap in the wall, missile troops on the ground inside let fly such a storm of arrows, scorpion bolts, and bullets that several of the invaders were slain, tumbling head over heels to the ground inside. The rest shrank back.

Other Antigonians sought to climb up the sides of the break to reach the top of the wall. Our soldiers jabbed down at them with spears.

"Chares!" screamed Mys. "Ladder!"

The loader was reaching over the parapet and slashing at an Antigonian on a ladder, not three cubits away. Sweat ran down the mercenary's red face from under his crested helm. He caught Mys's blows on his shield, raised himself to the level of the parapet, shifted his spear from his left to his right hand, and prepared to spring.

I snatched a crowbar and rushed at the man. The point took him in the chest. As he started to topple, he caught the top of the ladder. I pushed; man and ladder fell over backwards.

"Did somebody call me?" said Phaon.

He and another man appeared, each bearing a bundle of darts on his shoulder. Phaon dropped his bundle at my feet and ran off, followed by his companion, while more Rhodians ran up to tip baskets of stones over the parapet on the heads of the attackers below.

"Resume shooting!" I cried. "Cock your piece..."

We renewed our bombardment. Some darts, assembled in haste, were the wrong size. We shot them anyway, making what allowances we could for differences of weight.

On the far side of the gap several ladders were raised against the wall. Some were thrown down; but the Antigonians gained the tops of others, because our men were too few there. A din arose: shouts and screams, and the clatter of steel against steel and bronze. I raised our range and began dropping darts among the crowd around the feet of these ladders.

Then help came. Several of the merchant ships on which we had erected catapults, by paying out and hauling in their mooring ropes, had turned themselves around so that their catapults bore upon the attackers on the waterfront. Darts began streaking in from several directions. They scarcely could miss. Missiles plowed through the mass, sometimes striking down two or three men at once.

Rhodian archers pushed through the crowd atop the wall toward the break, to ply their bows. I glimpsed Gobryas, wearing the garb of a Rhodian archer over his trousers, bending his powerful Persian bow toward the foe. Soon the Antigonians who had crowded into the gap in the wall began to tumble out of it and to slide and stumble down the pile of debris.

An officer bawled in my ear: "Shoot faster! They break!"

The Antigonians on the waterfront milled uncertainly, stumbling over the bodies and catapult balls which littered the pavement. Some straggled back to their ships despite the shouts and blows of their officers.

The gate opened; our infantry sallied. The Antigonians scuttled for their ships. Those who had gained the top of the wall were cut off and soon those who survived gave up. Demetrios' attacking force withdrew once more, leaving the waterfront carpeted with bronze-clad bodies and puddled with crimson pools.

The Rhodians pried the bronze beaks off the wrecked Antigonian ships for trophies and burnt the wrecks, lest Demetrios' people tow them away and repair them.

Seven days passed; the fourth year of the 118th Olympiad began. Demetrios repaired his engines and ships while Rhodes busied herself with rebuilding her defenses.

Despite the continuing bombardment from Demetrios' stone throwers, Makar and his men, sweating like horses in the heat of Hekatombaion, labored on the gap in the wall. It was hard to get much done during the day, especially after one of the men was mashed flat by a three-talent ball. Instead, they worked all night, by torchlight, when the catapult crews could not see to correct their ranges.

Makar's crew not only filled the gap in the harbor wall with well-fitted stones; they also raised the entire wall and its parapet by six feet. Running short of stone of the proper sizes, they dismantled the half-built temple of Aphroditê, with apologies to the goddess and promises of a better temple when the siege should be won. Mys asked Bias:

"Aren't you afraid the goddess will smite us with impotence?"

The carpenter gave him a wry smile. "When you get to my age, son, it don't make enough difference to matter."

Then, on the morn of the eighth day after his last retreat, Demetrios' fleet again appeared before the Great Harbor. The heavy artillery opened up, pounding the harbor wall.

Beside me on the wall, Berosos called off the ranges: "Fifteen plethra—fourteen and a half plethra—fourteen plethra—"

"Shoot!" I cried.

Onas struck his knob, and the game was on. We cranked and shot and trained the dart thrower right and left and shot again.

Demetrios had learnt from his last defeat. His men could not press their attack on the wall under cross-bombardment from the catapults on our merchantmen. His sea engines therefore moved toward these craft. Streaks of fire laced the air as fire arrows and fire darts flew toward our catapult ships. Soon the ships were covered with missiles, sticking in the planking with their balls of tow ablaze. Here and there a plume of blue smoke arose from a ship as the fire caught.

While the archers on the merchantmen crouched behind their screens, shooting fast at the attackers, the marines fought the fires. They wrenched out the missiles and threw them overboard; they beat at the flames and dashed water upon them.

The din rose and rose. Again the sea towers shouldered up to the breakwater. Jugs of incendiary compound flew from our stone throwers. Our counter-bombardment was weaker than it had been; Bias' battery, for example, was down to three catapults.

The troopships rowed shoreward. This time a man stood in the bow of each with a long pole. This he thrust into the water ahead of the ship to guard against hidden rocks. As the crews of our catapult ships were busy fighting fires, they could not shoot at the assaulting Antigonian infantry.

The first troopship pushed out its gangplank; the infantry swarmed ashore, its armor blazing in the sun.

"Train left!" I said. "All the way round!"

"The stars boded evil—" began Berosos.

I shook him. "Shut up and bear a hand!"

We sent a dart plunging into the first wave of attackers. Near us, two men appeared on the wall, leaning over the parapet. One was a scorpion man; the other, looking very martial in gold-chased armor, was Kallias.

The weapon that the scorpion man bore was unusual. Instead of a bow affixed to its muzzle, it had a frame, like that of a torsion catapult but smaller. This frame held a pair of torsion skeins and throwing arms. The whole contraption was so heavy and awkward that Kallias had to lend a hand to cock it and then to raise it so that it lay across the parapet. The scorpion man placed a bolt in the groove.

"O Chares!" said Kallias. "Move your men aside for an instant, to give me a clear shot."

The scorpion man raised the butt plate to his chest and squinted along his trough. As he depressed the muzzle to aim at the Antigonians, the bolt began to slide down the grove, faster and faster, until it fell off the end and dropped to the waterfront below.

"*Baalim!*" shouted Kallias. "How do you make these things stick in their groove?"

"There's several ways, sir, but this one isn't designed for shooting down."

"What can we do with this one, now?"

"I suppose a drop of pitch or honey, sir, or anything sticky—"

"Well, where is it? Where is it?"

"I haven't any, sir. I tried to tell you, but you hustled me up here before—"

"Liar! Traitor!" screamed Kallias, hitting the man in the face.

"I am not!" the man shouted back. "If you would only listen—"

"Resume shooting, men," I said.

We sped more missiles into the thick of the Antigonians, leaving Kallias and his unfortunate arbalester to argue. A cry rang along the wall:

"The ships are coming out! The fleet is coming!"

From our post we could not yet see our ships putting out of the dockyard, because the roof of the armory blocked our vision. Three of our heaviest triremes, however, had already burst through the spiked boom. Now, around the end of the armory, our yellow-hulled ships appeared, the water foaming over their beaks.

The first to receive their attack was a light missile ship. A Rhodian trireme took her amidships. With a tremendous crackling and splintering the missile ship broke up. The trireme plowed on through the wreckage.

"Keep your minds on your shooting!" I said. For it was all we could do not to stand idly gauping at the sea fight that developed in the Great Harbor.

One of our triremes bore down upon the nearer of the sea towers. The tower was meant to be towed, not rowed, though it had a few oars for emergencies. The trireme that pushed it into place had withdrawn out into the harbor. Men on the sea tower rushed about, putting oars in the ports and trying to get the machine under way. But their oar power was so feeble, in proportion to the mass of the engine, that the thing had hardly moved when the ram of the Rhodian crunched through its side.

Farther out another trireme sank another missile ship.

The ship that had rammed the sea tower withdrew. A huge hole had opened in the port hull of the pair on which the tower stood. Water poured into the rent, so that the pierced hull settled lower in the water. As the other hull did not settle, the tower leaned more and more. The more it leaned, the more it pressed the damaged hull down into the water.

Men screamed, dashed about the engine in confusion, and jumped or fell over the side. A couple of unlucky archers fell from the top of the tower.

Then the structure gave way. With a terrible groaning, crashing, and splintering, the whole mass of timber and hide collapsed, hurling spouts of white water into the air. The pile of junk drifted out into the harbor while the survivors among its crew waved frantically for rescue.

Another Rhodian trireme, out in the harbor, dueled with an Antigonian trireme, each backing and filling to try to get her ram into the other's side. Two Antigonian triremes picked up lines from the remaining sea tower and began to tow it away, while the smaller craft—the missile ships and troopships—hastily rowed out to sea.

The third Rhodian trireme rowed toward the remaining tower. The engine, towed at a slow walk, was a helpless target. Although darts and arrows rained on the Rhodian, our ship held on until her beak plowed into one of the tower's hulls.

When the attacker withdrew, this tower, in turn, began to lean. Over it went, farther and faster, until the tower struck the water with a splendid splash. The engine floated on its side with one supporting hull under water and the other in the air.

Cheers arose from the Rhodians along the shore, and screams of rage from the Antigonians. For, without the protection of the towers, the men who had landed on the waterfront had little hope of scaling the harbor wall.

Now a trumpet blew retreat. The Antigonians hurried back to the troopship that had put them ashore. The landing party left its dead, its wounded, and its ladder littering the pavement. The ship pushed off and rowed for the open sea, following the other troopships.

The Rhodian triremes converged upon the remaining Antigonian sea engine, the one bearing the dart throwers. But three Antigonian ships had taken the engine in tow and were pulling it swiftly out of the harbor.

Meanwhile the larger Antigonian warships pushed in between the fugitives and entered the harbor. A confused contention arose, with ships ramming and backing and ramming again, while flights of arrows arched overhead and deck fighters thrust at one another with long pikes. We of the *Lightning* did not dare to shoot, because our ships were too closely entangled with those of the foe.

Presently two of our galleys backed out of the fight, low in the water and with many oars broken or unmanned. I could see cracks and rents in their sides where Antigonian rams and catapult balls had struck home, but by arduous efforts their rowers got them back to the dockyard before they settled. We groaned as we saw the Antigonians board the third yellow-hulled ship and sweep her decks, though most of her people leaped overboard and struck out for shore. A Rhodian who cannot swim is like an Athenian who cannot argue.

In the end Demetrios called off his force. We hauled ashore the loose timbers from the wrecked sea towers and burnt the rest.

The next day, after a ten-day of bright clear weather, was overcast. We manned the *Lighting* again, but for a time nothing happened.

By noon the tale went round of how Admiral Exekestos, on the leading ship of the three that made the sortie, had been wounded and captured, along with the captain of the trireme. We sagely wagged our heads, agreeing that such rash tactics were justified only in such an emergency. Without his sea towers Demetrios would think twice before assailing our harbor again.

"Unless," said Mys, "that supertower we hear of really exists."

"I wouldn't give much credit to that," I said. "You know how rumors exaggerate everything."

Berosos: "I know I saw something the night of the raid down the coast. It could well be the engine of the rumors, as tall as the star towers that once rose over mighty Babylon."

"Oh, stuff!" I said. "The rumors also say that this engine will walk right up out of the water and crush our city flat. Where would Demetrios get the power to do that?"

"The gods grant that you be right," said the Babylonian. "But—*ari!* Look out yonder! That is the thing whereof we speak! Istar preserve us!"

"No!" I cried. "By Earth and the gods, it is!"

The "thing" was the rumored floating supertower, towed by a whole squadron of warships. Our trumpets called the men to their posts. As the engine came closer, I saw that it was mounted, not on two ships, but on six, side by side. Reckoning from the size of the ships, I estimated the tower's height as over seventy feet from the water.

Behind this new monster came all the rest of the fleet. Demetrios never gave up. Repulsed, he always thought up some new scheme or device and tried again. He was, in his way, a great commander—almost as great as the divine Alexander. I should have appreciated his genius more, however, had he not chosen my beautiful little city to demonstrate it on.

Where is Onas?" I said.

Then I saw him. He knelt a few paces away before a little copper statuette. In front of it he had started a small blaze of tinder and shavings, and he was muttering some spell or prayer.

With the ominously slow approach of this amazing engine, prayers no longer seemed foolish. As the tower neared, I could see that catapults were mounted around its base, while its vast height was pocked with arrow slits. In my mind's eye, I could follow the tragic course of the battle. The monster would be pushed up to shore, where its enormous missile power would drive our men from the wall. The troopships would swarm up all at once; ladders would rise everywhere along the harbor wall....

Just then a clear, beautiful ray of the sun broke through the clouds. I thought: O Bright One, I may not have believed in you, or indeed in any of the gods of my fathers. But if you do exist, forgive this sin of the least of your children. Save Rhodes, the city that worships you, and whose ancestor and patron you are. Save Rhodes, and I shall never doubt you again; nay more, I will devote my life to making a statue to you, the like of which has never been seen....

I opened my eyes. The beam of sunlight swept over the Rhodian waterfront. Half dazzled, I raised my glance. Skeptical philosophers may say that what happened then was but wish-begotten illusion, but I know what I saw.

On a cloud stood Helios-Apollon himself, nude, with a crown of spiky golden rays on his brow. His right hand shaded his eyes as he looked down from his height upon Rhodes.

Somebody nudged me. "*Ea*, Chares! They seem to be having trouble with that thing!"

The divine vision faded; I brought my gaze back down to the sea. An easy breeze had been blowing from the south, wafting the monstrous engine gently along. Now this wind freshened. The galleys labored heavily, their bows digging into the seas.

The five triremes towing the giant sea tower slowly dragged their burden level with the mouth of the Great Harbor, past the end of the South Mole. Then they turned shoreward and began rowing toward us. To us, the five ships in line seemed to be standing still, oars rising and falling without progress.

Still Notos freshened. The sky darkened, and the swell from the south increased. The tower, instead of docilely following the galleys into the harbor, developed a will of its own. It drifted northward, away from the harbor mouth, sluing around the galleys that towed it, Soon the whole mass of equipment was turned completely about, facing south. The galleys still strove to reach the harbor mouth, but ever the tower drifted northward.

Said Berosos: "Meseems, O Chares, that this tower presents to the wind an area equal to that of many sails."

"No wonder," I said, "that, when the wind blows adversely, the tow ships can't make head against it."

The waves rose higher. Across the water I thought I could hear the groan of timbers and the creak of ropes as the tower's structure was strained.

The tow ships angled in toward shore but could not bring the tower squarely in front of the harbor mouth. Nor did they dare to come too close to the moles of the Little Harbor lest their engine run aground.

A confused shouting came from the galleys, thin in the distance, as the officers strove to incite their rowers to greater efforts. The other ships of the invasion fleet hovered about their prized machine.

Now the wind whipped the cloaks of the Rhodian officers on the wall and fluttered the crimson crests of their helmets. The sea tower, slowly swaying, drifted farther north as if pushed by a giant unseen hand.

We watched in fascination. The swell rose until the triremes towing the tower had trouble in handling their oars. In the rest of the fleet, some ships took in their lower oars and closed the ports.

The sea tower swayed like a drunken man. The cries and commands from the tower and from its tow ships merged into a continuous high screaming. A larger, single-banked galley—a fiver or sixer—backed cautiously toward the mass of ships as if to help tow. The five triremes tossed in the swell and fouled one another's oars.

And even the wind rose and rose.

At last the sea tower swayed over, over, over—and did not recover. It leaned slowly, farther and farther, until, with a terrible crunching, crackling, groaning, crashing, and roaring, the structure settled down upon its side, throwing spray and broken timbers high into the air. One of the ships that formed its base was lifted clear of the water before it broke loose and fell back with another mighty splash.

Then there was only a huge mass of wreckage: timbers, ropes, hides, and bobbing heads. The five tow ships cast loose at once and circled to pick up survivors. One of these galleys, however, was soon in trouble herself. She had shipped so much water through her oar ports that she settled. While she was signaling for help, she suddenly capsized and floated bottom-up, surrounded by struggling men.

The other ships wheeled and rowed back into the teeth of the waves. Silently, one by one, they slipped out of sight. On our walls, officers and men cast upon the whistling gale a lengthy sigh of relief and nameless gratitude.

As for me, I thought: I need no mortal model for my colossus. It shall depict the far-casting Apollon himself, ancestor and savior of Rhodes. What a fool I have been to think that any mere human being could be worthy of such a labor! Nor need I fear wounds and death, because the god will protect me until the task be done.

An hour later we were earing in Evios' tavern when Bias entered. "Men!" he said. "Finish up and come back to your posts."

We uttered simultaneous groans, of which mine was not the softest. "But, Commander!" I said. "Surely Demetrios won't try another attack today, what of the weather and the loss of his tower."

"That's the point," said Bias. "We're going to retake the South Mole. The gods have given us this chance, and we'd be fools not to use it. While this storm lasts, they can't put fresh troops on the mole, but we can attack them in relays and wear them down, see? Hurry up; I want a continuous barrage."

Thus we spent two hours dragging *Lightning* along the wall to a point near the base of the mole. We faced the engine along the axis of the mole to rake the hostile positions. Other catapults were crowded up against ours on the wall or were set up on the waterfront.

"Begin shooting!" commanded Bias.

We wound up and let fly. So did the others; so did the engines on the catapult ships.

Although the wind threw our aim awry, we loaded and shot again and again. Then infantry marched out the gate and massed at the base of the mole. A standard-bearer raised the golden sun disk on a pole, the trumpet spoke, and the men charged.

The Antigonians massed to repel them. Arrows sang; ladders were placed against the foe's defensive wall, thrown down, and replaced. The din of sword and spear on shield and cuirass arose. Back and forth over the wall the fighting surged, while the catapults dropped darts and stones all over the mole.

The struggle went on until darkness made it impossible to tell whither our shots were going. That, however, did not end the attack. As fast as one battalion of infantry tired, it was pulled back and another was sent in, while small boats with archers in the bows prowled up and down the mole, shooting at close range.

Toward dawn a light ship succeeded in putting a Rhodian platoon ashore on the tip of the mole before they were discovered. These men held the end of the mole while reinforcements poured in. When day came, the Antigonians found themselves attacked from both ends of the mole. A rush from the base of the mole carried the defensive wall and swept the Antigonians back from around the penthouses. Staggering with weariness—for they had fought all night, against troops that were ever fresh—the survivors of the four hundred Antigonians surrendered.

We manned the *Lightning* again that morning but had nothing more to do. The Antigonians, in good order but without their arms, marched in single file off the mole, to the internment center that we had set up in the old theater to wait until their ransom should be arranged. After the whole men, hobbled the wounded. Because of the excellence of their armor, the infantry had suffered only moderate losses, though many had minor wounds. The artillerymen, less well protected, had suffered worse from our missiles. The exact number of casualties was hard to tell, as the Antigonians, lacking means for honorable burial or cremation, had thrown the corpses into the sea.

By this victory we not only augmented our store of small arms and armor but also captured several of Demetrios' catapults. These included the two great three-talent stone throwers on the mole and the smaller stone throwers on the sea engine moored to the mole.

The god-sent wind continued brisk. During the night it had swung around and now came from the northeast.

After dark a squadron of ships appeared from the direction of Asia Minor. They grew larger and turned into a group of merchant sailing craft. These stood into our harbor and made signals of recognition. A pair of Demetrios' battleships rowed out to intercept them, but too late; the ships were safe behind the South Mole before the Antigonians cleared their own harbors.

The newcomers furled their sails and pulled up to the breakwater by means of their sweeps. A hundred and fifty little dark light-armed soldiers scrambled ashore; their officers embraced ours, gabbling in the Cretan dialect.

These were men of Knossos. We had a treaty with the Knossians, by which they promised to abstain from piracy and to help us suppress the piracy of the other city-states of Crete. The Knossians did not like to give up piracy themselves; in fact, many of their young men went elsewhere to enlist in piratical crews. However, they loved an excuse to meddle in the other cities' affairs; for, next to robbery on the high seas, cutting their neighbors' throats is the greatest joy of the Cretans. Now they reinforced us in our hour of need.

The next day another group of ships appeared. After some anxious moments of speculation, we made out the scarlet lion of Ptolemaios on their sails. Some were merchantmen and some triremes, but the latter had their oar ports blocked and moved under sail alone in the brisk breeze.

The Egyptian ships filed into the harbor. They brought five hundred men from the forces of the satrap of Egypt, bedight in richly decorated armor, that of the officers glittering with gold inlay. As the soldiers marched ashore, cries of recognition went up from the watching Rhodians, for among these soldiers were many men of Rhodes who had gone to Egypt to seek service as mercenaries. Ptolemaios had shrewdly chosen these as the soldiers most willing to go to Rhodes and most likely to put up a stout fight when they got there.

The heat of high summer declined. As days passed without further attacks from the sea, spies brought word that Demetrios was preparing a huge assault by land. To this end he was gathering material wherewith to build unheard-of engines of war.

Again the sound of ax blows rang from the hills, and the remaining houses in the suburb, all but Protogenes' studio, were pulled down. Soon men began to pile timbers, three or four furlongs from the South Wall.

In Rhodes food grew so scarce that a well-padded paunch became a thing of reproach. Now and then a blockade runner, attracted by the bonuses offered for foodstuffs by our government, would slip into the Little Harbor at night. But still our food stores shrank and shrank.

Boys were sent around in bands to collect scrap metal for melting up to make weapons. A full citizen was brought to trial for trying to engross the supply of onions. When he was let off with a nominal fine, it was whispered that strings had been pulled by the other magnates, who were up to the same tricks and feared exposure in their turn.

Wild rumors circulated of the life, death, or dramatic moves of Antigonos and the other Successors of Alexander. A condemned criminal was sacrificed to Kronos inside the Great Gate. This was as near as we could get to the temple of Artemis Aristoboulê, outside the South Wall, where such sacrifices were traditionally observed.

Under Bias' direction we moved the dart throwers of the *Lightning* class from the waterfront to the South Wall. The wall itself was strengthened by Makar and his masons. When they had used all the stone intended for the new theater, they dismantled the old one. One of their tasks was to erect a wall against the inner side of the South Gate. Any serious attack would probably try to batter down the gate, and the best counter to this was to wall it up in advance.

Bias was promoted to battalion commander, and Phaon was moved up to take Bias' place as battery commander.

On my way to the armory, one morning in Boedromion, I got a surprise. Our entire active fleet at Rhodes—all nine ships—was gone from the dockyards. Nothing was left but two ships under repair and two new ones a-building.

I hastened into the armory building and found Bias. "What has happened?" I cried.

Bias grinned. "They've gone off on a raid. We figured it wouldn't do no good to tell everybody ahead of time."

I was amused to note that, since his promotion, the carpenter had come around to referring to the high command as "we." Theretofore it had always been "they," usually with a scornful tone and a sneer.

Later I persuaded Bias to give me the details. "You see, son, as long as it looked like the boy wonder was going to attack us by sea, we needed the fleet to take care of his engines. But now he's committed to a land attack, we thought the ships would be put to best use by raiding Demetrios' bases. All his big warships are gathered here, which leaves his staging points as bare as a newborn baby. And who would expect us, shut up here, to attack his rear? We'll give him a prod in the arse he'll remember!"

Half a ten-day later the ships came back, a squadron at a time, slipping past Demetrios' patrols at night when the wind favored them. Their hulls had been painted a piratical blue-gray before they set out, to make them less visible; even the gilded statues of Helios-Apollon on their sterns, which identified them as Rhodian, had been coated with this drab color. We gave them a whooping reception.

Damophilos' three triremes had sailed to Karpathos, halfway to Crete. There they had destroyed many of Demetrios' ships, while from the crews Damophilos impressed the best men into the Rhodian forces and sold the rest.

Menedemos, commanding three triemiolias, went to Patara in Lykia. Here he found an Antigonian trireme at anchor while its crew took its ease on shore. Menedemos burnt the trireme and captured several merchantmen. As he was preparing to return to Rhodes with his booty, an unsuspecting Antigonian quadrireme rowed into the river mouth. With a leonine pounce, Menedemos captured this powerful warship also, before its many deck fighters could get into their armor.

The quadrireme had come from Kilikia, bearing letters and money for Demetrios. It also carried a personal gift: a set of royal garments which the oldest of Demetrios' several wives, the lady Phila, had prepared for him with her own hands. There was also furniture decked with gold and ivory, and letters from Phila to her husband.

These robes were borne into the city in triumph. I recall a lively argument about them in Evios' tavern. Gobryas the Persian said:

"If it were up to me, I would publicly burn them. Thus should I show my contempt for the foe and gain great honor."

"They're too pretty for that," I said. "And if Demetrios spares our art, I am not inclined to destroy his. I would hang them in a temple—say, the temple of Helios-Apollon."

"Oh, you and your art!" said Phaon. "Let's set up a scarecrow on the South Wall and hang these robes upon it. That would infuriate this proud popinjay!"

"That is the trouble," said Berosos. "Wroth already with us he is, so why make him angrier? Fain would I give him the garments back with a polite letter of apology."

We all hooted at this suggestion, though looking back I can see that it had much sense. Giskon, now a platoon leader in the Foreign Regiment, said: "At least we should sell these gauds back to him, to get something for our trouble in capturing them."

"Harken to the moneygrubbing Phoenician!" cried Onas. "Were I a true Egyptian wizard and not a mere lapidary, I could work a powerful spell on these garments, to bring down Demetrios with thirty-six fevers, itches, and other ills."

And so it went. Somebody wanted to auction off the garments; somebody else, to offer them as a prize to the bravest Rhodian soldier. The Council, which had custody of the raiment, said nothing.

Our third squadron, under Amyntas, had cruised along the Ionian islands. Here they sank many ships bringing materials to Demetrios and captured many others. Our harbors, from which most traders had long since fled, grew crowded again as in peacetime.

This last sortie affected my work. Reporting to Bias one day, I found him in talk with a small man of about his own age.

"O Chares," said Bias, "this is Polemon of Athens, one of the engineers captured by Amyntas. He's your new assistant."

"Oh?" said I.

"Yes. He is said to be famous as a catapult designer, but we'll see. You watch him to see he don't bugger our designs to get even."

The Athenian gave me a mocking smile. "I am sure, my dear fellow, that a technician as experienced as yourself would have no trouble in detecting my knavish tricks."

I flushed. Bias said: "Don't let him scare you, son. He knows his only chance of getting free again is to do right by us."

So I went to work with Polemon. In truth, I found it far less difficult than I had feared. Polemon really cared little about my youth, or about my inexperience, or even about which side he fought on. He was as devoted to his art of military ordnance as I was to sculpture. He would argue passionately for hours as to whether the trough of a catapult should be a digit longer or shorter, or whether there should be sixteen or eighteen notches in the rack. How fortunate for Rhodes that Amyntas had captured not only Polemon but also ten other engineers, equally famous and dedicated, on their way to join Demetrios!

Early in Pyanepsion, one morning, I was summoned to the Town Hall. Here I found a meeting of notables. These included President Damoteles; the Council; Kallias, municipal architect and general of artillery; Damophilos, now admiral in Exekestos' place; and Captain Python. Bias, too, had been summoned.

"Rejoice, O Chares!" said Admiral Damophilos. "We have decided to give Demetrios' fancy robes to Ptolemaios, in hope of persuading him to send us more help. We wonder if we should put you and your catapult crew aboard the *Halia*, which will bear this gift."

I gave a broad grin of delight. Here was a chance not only to get away from the grind of the siege but also to see the wonders of Egypt—especially those in the fields of sculpture and architecture—of which Onas had told me.

Bias, however, was of another mind. He rasped: "Look, gentlemen, I slave to make these men into artillerymen. Out of Phaon's whole battery, half are half-wits and fumble-fingers. A couple of pieces have got pretty good crews, thanks to me beating them over the head for two years. Finally I get one real crew that can hit the side of a mountain two tries out of three—and then, by Herakles, you send 'em off on some chase after gryphon's eggs, just when they're most needed here! It don't make sense."

President Damoteles: "O Bias, we appreciate your work. But today nearly all of Demetrios' large warships carry catapults. With our small fleet we dare not give the foe any advantage. We could be wiped out in an hour's engagement, whereas Demetrios can lose a score of ships and never feel it."

"But a couple of this crew are engineers, too," said Bias. "Are you trying to cripple our war production?"

Captain Python broke in: "Excuse me, but as I shall command the ship for this voyage, I know what I need. With all our newly captured engineers, you can spare a couple of Rhodians."

"But why this particular team?" persisted Bias. "I've got a couple of others you could have, and welcome."

"This crew has special virtues, my good Bias," said Python.

Python of Kallithea had captained the *Euryalê* in the previous actions; in fact, there had been criticism of his handling of the triemiolia in the nocturnal raid down the coast. His critics said that as a result of his hesitation to close with the pirates, his ship had not done the half of the damage wrought by the *Halia*. Now, with the *Euryalê* laid up for repairs and the *Halia* masterless since the promotion of Damophilos, Python had been given the latter ship. He was a tall, light-haired man with a long, narrow face, a bulging forehead, jutting ears, and a tremendous nose. Whatever his ability as a naval tactician, he was the most affable of all our ship's captains.

Python continued: "Berosos the Babylonian is a keen-eyed astronomer who can help with navigation, for we shall have to cross the open sea. Onas can interpret, should we make a landfall where no Greek is spoken. Chares is a sculptor, and Ptolemaios has a weakness for artists and intellectuals."

Bias screwed up his wrinkled, mottled face. "I don't know about them foreigners. How do you know they won't desert as soon as they touch Egypt?"

Damoteles looked at me. "What say you, O Chares?"

I said: "Onas I am sure of, sir. His wife and child remain here, and he is a devoted family man. Berosos I am less certain of, though I believe he is in love with a local girl—let me see—I think it's the younger daughter of Thales the cobbler."

Said Bias: "Don't put too much faith in that. Berosos is in love with a new girl every month."

"We must take some chances," said the President. He turned to the Council. "Now that you have heard all sides, gentlemen, how do you vote?"

The *Halia* nosed southward over a bright blue sea. To ready the trireme for her voyage, the shipwrights had completely blocked the oar ports of the lower or thalamite and the upper or thranite bank, leaving a single bank of intermediate or zygite oars. For these, the workmen had rearranged the benches so that the oars could be pulled either by one or by two men. Then we embarked two-thirds of the normal complement of rowers, for use when the wind was foul.

During the first day we had a hazy sky and a gentle southerly breeze, bothersome only in that it made the rowers, pulling in hourly shifts, sweat to make head against it. There was a light fall of dust on the decks, a condition that we recognized as the blowing of sand from the African deserts.

The sun set without reddening; it sank into the dusty haze, fading to a grayish-yellow ball which simply disappeared long before it reached the horizon. A long, glassy swell from the west made us roll uncomfortably, and compelled our rowers to use a short stroke with a high recovery. Captain Python kept his soothsayer busy reading omens.

During the night the ship continued to roll. Polaris was invisible in the murk, but Berosos showed Captain Python where it would be by sighting on two stars of the Bear. The captain came up to the forecastle deck, where we lay rolled in our cloaks, around the old *Talos*. (The *Lightning* had been taken over by a new crew in Rhodes.)

"How are you doing, fellows?" he said.

"Very well, sir," I said.

"Good. Let me know if anything is amiss."

"I never knew a sea captain so friendly and democratic," murmured Mys, the loader.

"That is all very well," muttered Onas, "but the main matter is, will he give us the right commands in time of danger and doubt?"

The roll increased; the ship's timbers groaned. Toward dawn the stars were blotted out; the wind shifted; rain pattered down.

Rain continued through the morning. Then the rain ceased; azure holes appeared in the tattered clouds. As a strong west wind set in, the ship rolled more than ever. Many were seasick.

Captain Python, on his quarterdeck, conferred at length with his executive officer, his boatswain, and his soothsayer. At last he had the oars pulled in and the covers lashed to the oar ports. At the same time the sailors raised the sail. The wind was now westerly enough so that by bracing the sail around, we could run due south.

All day we sailed while the rowers took their ease. The ship heeled ominously with every swell, so that we on the forecastle deck looked down into blue-black depths. Captain Python slouched about with tight-pressed lips and a nervous, uncertain air. After Damophilos' perfectionism, Python's discipline seemed lax.

The wind continued through the night. The trireme leaked, for the shipwrights had done a hasty job of repairing her after the battle in the Great Harbor, and the rough weather had loosened her seams again. Rowers and sailors bailed with buckets and pumps.

We on deck were cold and soaked. During the night Berosos was often awakened to try to find a star through the tumbling clouds. Some of Python's geniality had gone by the board, for I could hear him over the sounds of wind and sea, shouting:

"Stupid ox! Lying barbarian!"

When Berosos came back, he settled down in his corner, grumbling: "He thinks I can see a mouse through a millstone."

With dawn the sun appeared through the clouds to set us on the right path again. The wind swung round to the north and became the normal etesian trade.

Dawn of our fourth day showed us a long, slim line of yellow beach, topped by a band of green, between sea and sky. Python strode up to the bow.

"Onas!" he said. "What part of the African coast is that?"

The Egyptian, who had been glum and despondent as a result of being parted from his wife, roused himself. "I know not, sir. From the Pelusiac mouth to Cyrene the coast of Egypt looks much the same."

"Berosos, do you know where we are?" said Python.

The Babylonian spread his hands. "I should guess, sir, that the strong west winds of the last two days have eastward borne us."

"East of Alexandria?"

"Who but the gods should know? But I do think so."

"Then would you sail westward until you came to a town where we can ask?"

"Aye, sir."

"How about you, Onas? Do you agree?"

"Aye, sir, but I would also take soundings, as the water along this coast is shoal."

Python: "Have you any ideas, Chares?"

"Nothing to add to what these men have said, sir."

Python looked around uncertainly, then went away, issuing his commands.

As we neared the coast, the *Halia* put about and headed westward. Presently a sailor came up to the bow with a sounding lead, which he whirled by its cord and threw ahead of the ship from time to time.

My first impression of Egypt, whereof so many romantic tales are told, was of flat, dreary monotony. Ever stretched the beach, and beyond it the low sky-lining mass of palms and reeds. After a while the sameness was broken by a fishing village. Python turned inshore to question the villagers. As we approached, however, the Egyptians fled.

"They think us slavers," explained Onas.

The lookout in the bow called: "It's shoaling!"

The next instant the *Halia* grounded with a creak of timbers. The mast swayed like a reed in the wind; men who had not braced themselves were sent staggering.

"What in the name of the Dog?" yelled Python. "I will flay that lookout alive!"

The officers rushed forward, shouting at the lookout as he reeled his lead in. The terrified sailor said:

"But I did call out, sir; indeed I did, sir; these men heard me, but the ship kept on, sir—"

"Your pardon, sirs," said Onas, "but were it not well to get off soon? The folk in these parts live by brigandage, and if they see us stranded, they will swarm out to assail us."

"Oh," said Captain Python. "Come aft, everybody. Coxswain, put the full crew on the oars."

We went aft to raise the bow by shifting our weight. The rowers braced themselves, two to each oar, and backed water with all their might. After they had made several strokes without moving us, Python called a halt.

"We dare not wear them out," he said. "Who has an idea?"

The executive officer said: "If the rowers make their strokes alternately, first on one side and then on the other, we may wriggle off."

"Good," said Python, and commanded the coxswain.

This time the men pushed first on one side, so that the ship swung about its bow as about a pivot; then on the other side, so that it swung back. After a few strokes somebody shouted:

"She moves!"

The *Halia* backed off the shoal, turned, and continued along the coast, while the first lieutenant went below to look for new leaks. The catapult crew returned to its post.

"Does this go on forever?" I asked Onas.

"Forsooth, not much is Egypt to see from the sea. All our great cities and monuments lie inland."

What lies back of that shore?"

"A land we call the Pasture, being nought but reed-bordered lakes and lagoons, inhabited by thieves and pirates." He broke off staring ahead. "Berosos, look and tell me if we near not that whereof I spoke."

The Babylonian shaded his eyes from the glare. Ahead, but closer to the beach, lay a ship, her mast rising at an angle. Berosos said:

"A merchantman I see—a large one, methinks—with smaller craft about it. Nought else can I see."

"Beshrew me," said Onas, becoming cheerfully animated again at the prospect of a fight, "if the merchantman have not grounded and if those small craft be not the pirates of the Pasture!"

I went aft to tell Python. He came forward at once and watched as the grounded merchantman slowly grew to our gaze. Soon we could all see the big roundship, heeled over, with the small craft of the Egyptians circling about it. The sun blinked on pinpoints of metal.

"Right you are, Onas," said Berosos. "There are ten or twelve boats. Some stand back and shoot arrows at those on the merchantman, while others close with it and strive to clamber up the sides. Archers in the basket at the merchantman's masthead shoot down at the attackers."

A faint sound of shouting came to our ears. I asked Python: "Shall I prepare the catapult for action, sir?"

"Oh?" he said. "Do you think we should try to rescue them?"

"Why, could Rhodians do otherwise?"

"I do not know. I have a mission to carry out and must not risk it. We leak, and another grounding would finish us. But—Berosos, what would you do?"

"The less fighting I see, the happier I am," said the Babylonian with a lugubrious countenance.

Python chewed a fingernail. Then he went aft. I could see him asking his other officers their opinions while the soothsayer scanned the empty sky for birds and the placid sea for fish. Then Python commanded the sail to be furled and the oars to be put out, but took so long that at last I went aft and spoke boldly:

"Captain, if we don't aid that ship soon, they will be beyond help."

Python gave a kind of shudder. "Prepare the catapult."

This time Python posted two lookouts on the bow. We brought up our darts from the storeroom.

With short, gentle strokes we nosed inshore. We had an advantage over the merchantman, for a big roundship fully laden has more draft than a trireme.

Berosos called ranges: "Fifteen plethra—Fourteen plethra—"

I trotted back and forth along the deck, pointing out targets to Python. At last we were lined up and at the right distance.

"Shoot!"

The dart struck one of the attacking craft. As one man, the Egyptians leaped into the water and began swimming ashore, though the boat, being made of tarred bundles of reeds, did not seem fatally damaged.

We crept closer, dropping dart after dart among the attackers. Some became panicky and began to swim or paddle shoreward. Others were made of stouter stuff. Several boats paddled toward us while men in their waists shot arrows of reed at us. They were tall dark men with long black hair, naked but for strips of dirty linen about their loins, and they yammered and gabbled and screeched like a cageful of monkeys.

Python swung our bow and headed into the cluster of boats from which the arrows came. Most of them scuttled out of the way, like water beetles when one steps into a pool, but one we caught on our ram. The boat was tossed on its back, and its screaming occupants were thrown into the water. They struck out for shore while our archers picked them off.

The boats that had remained around the merchantman now drew off, also. At first they stood off at a bowshot's distance, but a few darts sent them scuttling out of range of the catapult. There they remained in a sullen line, bobbing on the gentle swells, in water too shallow for us to pursue them.

We pulled alongside the merchantman. Python called down: "This is the *Halia*, of Rhodes. I am Python of Kallithea, commanding. Who are you?"

A stout, broad-shouldered ox of a man with a long black beard, a dented helmet, and a bloody sword, called back: "Thank the gods for beautiful Rhodes! I am Sapher of Sidon, master of the *Anath*. Can you pull us off?"

A group of men crowded up behind the Sidonian: six sailors and eight passengers, most of them wounded but all armed with swords, spears, and improvised clubs. Three men lay dead on the bloodstained deck: a passenger, a sailor, and a pirate, the last still clutching his copper-bladed hatchet. Two sailors with bows clambered down the mast from the fighting top.

"I will look at your ship first," said Python.

He climbed down the ladder to the deck of the *Anath*. He and Sapher walked about the slanting deck, talking in animated undertones. Then they vanished into the hold, from which a straggle of women, children, and slaves emerged. When the two captains reappeared, they had plainly come to a private agreement.

We made lines fast to the *Anath*. But though our rowers strained at their oars and stirred the clear, shallow water into muddy foam, they could not budge the merchantman. They pulled straight, and they pulled from side to side. After an hour of this they became too fatigued to pull strongly.

"We cannot get you off, my friend," Python called over the water.

"Then I am ruined!" The Phoenician burst into tears and pleaded. Python agreed to one more try, but this did no good either.

At last Sapher called: "Can you then take off my people and goods?"

"We shall see. I am coming aboard," said Python.

We backed up to the *Anath*, and again our captain went aboard the trader. I suppose they struck another bargain, for soon Sapher's sailors began passing cargo up to our deck: jars of Byblian wine, sacks of Syrian wool, and bars of Kilikian iron. The largest element in his cargo, a shipment of Lebanese timber, he had to abandon, because the *Halia* lacked room for anything so bulky.

The passengers climbed up another ladder, while our boatswain waited at the top to collect passage money from them. One, an elderly Hellene with a bloody bandage around his head, seemed familiar. When his eye lighted upon me with a look of recognition, I cried:

"Apelles!"

For it was indeed the great painter. We embraced.

"I didn't know you with that rag on your face," I said. "What do you mean, a man of your age, getting involved in brawls with vulgar brigands?"

"Chares, when a man comes at you with an ax to dash your brains out, you hit him with whatever you have. How come you here?"

When I had seen Apelles settled in a corner of the forecastle deck, I told him of our mission. He said: "I have heard of Demetrios' attack on Rhodes; a pity. As for me, having painted all the notables in my part of the world, I thought I would have a try at Alexandria, whither many eminent persons have removed in recent years."

"Why not paint Ptolemaios himself?"

"I shall do better to keep out of his way. He and I fell out many years ago."

"Oh? Tell me, sir!"

Said Apelles: "Well—ah—it is not exactly the kind of thing one talks about. However, it was while the divine Alexander was campaigning in Asia Minor and I was painting his portrait. Ptolemaios was one of Alexander's Companions. Also, there was a young lady named Pankaspê, a victim of war's upheavals, who had found favor with the king. When I finished his portrait, Alexander liked it so well that he sent Pankaspê to me with orders to paint her nude.

"Enter Eros. Word came to the ears of the king that his painter had fallen madly in love with the lady, and, in truth, I trembled so at the sight of her glorious form that I could scarcely hold a brush steady. Alexander called me in and asked if this tale were true. Not knowing whether he would have my head for it, I stammered an assent.

"'Then take her, friend,' quoth he. 'It will make you happy, and in the long run she, too, will be happier than with me. I have no time to cultivate the art of pleasing women. Now be off with you. I am preparing to march.'

"So Pankaspê and I have dwelt together in harmony ever since. She was the model for my 'Aphroditê Rising from the Sea' and for many other paintings. I even wedded her legally a few years back."

"How does Ptolemaios come into it?"

"Ah, you see, he had had his eye on this same lady, but naturally he couldn't go to the king and say: 'Give me your favorite mistress, sire.' I was told that he was in a great rage when he heard of the king's gift and swore to cook my heart in a stewpan someday. I doubt, however, that he would go out of his way to molest me after all these years, and that is how I come to be here. A good thing it is that you people came when you did. But what took you so long once you saw us? We wondered for a while if you were in league with the pirates."

I lowered my voice. "Our captain is an amiable fellow and a good enough officer as long as he has a higher officer to tell him what to do. But he goes to pieces when he's forced to act on his own. How came you to be stranded?"

"Becoming impatient, Sapher tried to sail from Gaza before he was assured of fair winds. Hence we ran aground in a sandstorm, and the north wind that followed pushed us up on shore so that nothing could pull us off save a battleship."

A tall, lean, bald, bushy-browed man, younger than Apelles, spoke in a mixed Italiot accent: "It is too bad that this grounding was not on the shores of the ocean. There, the water rises and falls several cubits each day, so that if grounded at low tide, you will float off later."

Apelles: "Allow me to present some of my fellow passengers, O Chares. This"—he indicated the lean man who had just spoken—"is the learned Dikaiarchos of Messana, a geographer on his way to Egypt on behalf of Kasandros, to obtain information about the country and its commercial needs. This is Theodoros of Cyrene, a philosopher."

"Rejoice!" I said. "O Theodoros, I heard you lecture in Athens several years ago."

"You did?" said Theodoros, a lively little graybeard. "Which lecture was it? The one on the folly of supernaturalism?"

"Yes, sir. You certainly smote the demon superstition with might and main."

"He smote it once too often," said Dikaiarchos. "He preached on the absurdity of all supernatural belief, and the Athenians turned him out of Attika."

"Proving my point," said Theodoros.

"How?" asked Apelles.

"If the gods do not exist, as I maintain, there is nought to fear from my lecturing. If they do, they might well be wroth with me; but in that case they would smite me as an individual, and the Athenians need not fear for themselves. Therefore, only superstitious people would expel a lecturer for expressing opinions such as mine; hence, the Athenians are superstitious, which was to have been demonstrated."

"The gods might aim a thunderbolt at you and miss," said Apelles.

"If they be such poor shots, they are no gods."

I spoke up: "You are no doubt wiser than I, O Theodoros, but I wouldn't joke about the gods. With my own eyes I saw the far-casting Apollon save Rhodes in answer to our prayers."

"Eh? What is this?" said Theodoros.

I told the story of the overthrow of Demetrios' giant sea tower by the providential windstorm. "And if that isn't evidence," I said, "I don't know what is."

Theodoros cackled. "It is evidence that you, young sir, were in a wrought-up state from excitement and lack of proper sleep and victuals, and so liable to see anything. And how about all the cities that have fallen despite the prayers of their people? Where is your logic?"

"I don't know about other cities—" I began with, heat, but Dikaiarchos cut me off.

"Pay him no heed, Master Chares," said he. "Theodoros will argue on any side of any subject, for sheer love of disputation. I prefer to assemble good, substantial facts and let others play intellectual games with them."

The last of Sapher's cargo was moved to the *Halia*, where it was stowed here, there, and everywhere. We cast off and pulled away from the *Anath*. Captain Sapher stood with his elbows on the rail, weeping into his beard.

"I grieve with you," I said.

"Twenty years," he said. "For twenty years I slave and scrimp, from common sailor to master mariner, until I can own my own ship. And then, on my third voyage—"

"Could you get a battleship to pull your vessel off?"

"Nay. The bribes to Ptolemaios' officials would eat up most of her value, and by the time the galley got here, the natives would have plundered her of what cargo remains and burnt the rest. Or else the first strong north wind will break her up. Forsooth, the gods have requited me hardly for my sins."

"Indeed, they are not to be trifled with," I said. "May we all keep on their good sides from now on."

Crowded as was the forecastle deck already, several more rescued travelers squeezed in with us. There was a young Hellene on his way to enlist in the Ptolemaic army as a mercenary, a couple of traders, and three whom I came to know better. One was Azarias ben-Moses (or, as we should say, Azarias Moseôs) a Judaean weaver of Bousiris: a subdued, round-shouldered, bearded little man who said little because he knew but a few words of Greek. I discovered, however, that with some difficulty and repetition I could speak to him, using my limited Phoenician, because the Judaeans speak a dialect of that language.

"I was visiting Jerusalem in connection with an inheritance," he said, "and was on my way home when this disaster struck. By the one god Iao, I thought we were all dead men, when your ship sailed into sight! Though I am but a poor man, I would do aught that lay in my power for any of you, should you ask a favor of me."

"Just where are we?" I said.

"I think we are a little east of the Phatnitic mouth. Soon we shall reach Tamiathis,[6] where I leave you to ascend the river to my home. These two go with me, or rather, I go with them as far as Bousiris."

One of the two indicated, a big blond man, spoke Greek with a strong Kilikian accent. "I am Alexis of Tarsos, sir, and this is my partner, Semken of Koptos." He indicated a small dark man with a scar on his chin. "What does a Rhodian ship so far from Rhodes, with a war on?"

6 Modern Damietta or Dumyât

I told the tale of the capture of Demetrios' royal robes, and of our present mission.

"Could one see these robes?" queried Semken.

"You would have to ask Captain Python. He keeps them locked up, I suppose. How do you make your living?"

Alexis and Semken pointed to a huge leathern bag they had brought aboard. "Here is our stock," said Alexis. "We are bookdealers. We export rolls of raw papyrus from Egypt to the Greek lands, where we sell them and buy completed manuscripts to bring back to Egypt. Such books find a ready market among Ptolemaios' Greek officials."

"It sounds interesting," I said. "Is it profitable?"

"It is a living," said Alexis, "save that there is too cursed much governmental interference in trade. The latest rumor has it that Ptolemaios plans to nationalize the papyrus industry."

"If that be true, we are ruined," said Semken. "At least I am. As a Hellene, Alexis can no doubt get a job in some governmental office; but, as an Egyptian, I cannot rise even in my own land, all the good posts being reserved for Hellenes. Is that not an outrage?"

"I had rather find some other commodity to trade in," said Alexis. "Long ago I swore never to do as Semken suggests: become a governmental clerk and sit all day in an office, squeezing bribes from the people and intriguing against my fellow bureaucrats. No, give me a life of travel and adventure."

Onas said: "Has either of you ever seen the terrible *Book of Thôth*?"

The bookdealers looked at one another. Semken spoke: "Once in my life have I seen it. In a shadowy crypt beneath the pyramid of an ancient king it was, in the hands of an aged wizard. For years this warlock had sought the book, to master the mighty spells that should enable him to stop the sun in the sky and to raise and lower the Nile at his will. At last he found it in the bony hands of the withered mummy of this king of olden times.

"Quickly the wizard tore the book from the hands of the mummy, which crumbled into dust as he did so. Hastily he unrolled the book and began to recite its cantrips. Our rushlights flickered, and the darkness deepened. A sense of gloom and horror descended upon me. And then—oh, my masters, what a memory is this!—there came upon us some presence from the nighted gulfs beyond the grave. A living darkness folded the wizard in its batlike wings; he screamed and was no more. How I escaped the demon's claws I know not; they found me wandering in the desert, screaming mad. Even now, years later, I fear to sleep lest I dream of this awful event."

I shuddered with the rest. If a liar, Semken was a most artistic one.

As the sun set redly before us, Python ordered the anchors dropped lest we run aground in the darkness. I spent the pleasantest night since the start of our voyage, since the air was mild and the ship barely moved.

The next morning I observed Alexis in converse with Captain Python. They walked the deck together; the Tarsian seemed to be wheedling the captain, who long frowned and tossed his head in the negative. But at last Alexis' grin showed that Python had yielded.

Itching to know what went forward, I fell in with them. "Sir," I said, "we used almost half our darts in yesterday's fight. Ought we not to obtain some more at Alexandria?"

"Yes, yes, I suppose so," said Python. "Remind me of it when we get there."

"When will that be, sir?"

"We shall reach Tamiathis by noon, and there we shall lay up for repairs. I do not care to have this leaky old basket sink under me in the middle of Alexandria's harbor."

"And then, sir?"

"We shall be several days in Tamiathis. Then, if the omens let us sail at once, Alexandria is less than two days' sail, with reasonable winds."

Alexis of Tarsos said: "Pray then, Captain, may we see that of which we spoke now, before we reach port and leave you?"

"Oh, very well. Fetch your comrade."

"What's this?" I said.

The guileless Python spoke: "This man has talked me into showing him the royal robes."

"If he, a stranger, may see them, then surely I may also."

"Well—ah—I do not know. I cannot admit everybody—"

"Not all at once, sir, but surely common justice entitles your own warriors..."

In the end Python gave in once more. I fetched the catapult crew aft to Python's cabin. As soon as the other passengers, the archers, the marines, and the sailors saw that something was afoot, they hastened aft also. Soon there was a jostling crowd on the deck, which pushed and shouted until the marine officer and I beat and cursed them into line, filing into the cabin and out again.

When most of the crew had been through the cabin, I fell into line behind Azarias. When the Judaean saw the garments, he uttered a guttural exclamation and reached out as if to try the goods with his fingers.

"Hands off, fellow!" snapped Python.

"What, sir?" said the weaver, but in his native tongue. I translated; Azarias had wished to determine if the quality of the robe was as fine as it seemed, as he was in the business.

The suit consisted of a white linen shirt with a purple stripe, a silken, sleeved robe of Persian cut, a purple felt hat, and high felt boots. All were bright with gold. The robe was pale blue, with a purple border and astronomical symbols worked in golden thread and spangles. The hat had a band in the form of a golden laurel wreath. Certainly Demetrios would have presented a godlike spectacle in this ornate array.

We killed time as the ship plodded westward. While Onas taught Egyptian checkers to Dikaiarchos the geographer, and others engaged in other pastimes, Azarias attached himself to me. He seemed a nice little man, and I was glad to practice my rusty Phoenician. When I told him of my art and of my plans for the world's finest colossus, he said:

"*Ouai*, young sir, how sad for you! How I grieve!"

"By the gods, why?"

"Because the only true god, the lord Iao, has forbidden the making of graven images. I fear it will go hard with you in the next world."

"He may have forbidden you, but I have heard nothing of this. Anyway, what makes you think that your god is the only one?"

"He himself has said so, through his holy books and the mouths of his prophets."

"Well, the god I worship has approved my plan for his statue and will guard and guide me to its completion, for the glory of the god and of beautiful Rhodes. It's too bad that you and Theodoros have no language in common, for there would be hot theological argument."

"Why, what is his view of sacred matters?"

"Whereas you believe in no gods but Iao, he carries this skepticism to its logical conclusion and believes in no gods at all. The difference seems slight to me."

"Mock not the lord Iao. I had an uncle..." Azarias went into a long tale of the calamities that befell this uncle as a result of flouting the singular rules of eating that the Judaean religion imposes upon its followers. The uncle's wife had run off with a Nabataean smuggler; his daughter had become a belly dancer in an Egyptian tavern in Gaza; and sickness and poverty dogged his path.

In the afternoon we reached the Phatnitic mouth of the Nile and turned into its broad stream. We passed two of Ptolemaios' black-hulled triremes, anchored in the shallows with gilded wooden statues of Alexander shining on their sterns. Then, twenty or more furlongs from the mouth, we came to Tamiathis, standing in a sandy waste on the eastern shore of the river.

Tamiathis lies on a narrow neck of land, with the Nile in front and the reedy borders of Lake Tanis behind. Basically a fishing village, it has grown to something more because of Ptolemaios' building a small naval station with a slip for minor repairs. Furthermore, here travelers for Memphis and points south leave the coastal ships and take to river boats.

Three fat-bellied merchantmen were tied up to the crumbling quay. Fishing smacks and river boats clustered along the waterfront. Loafers slept in the sunshine; mangy dogs fought over scraps of offal; a barber shaved the scalp of a customer.

The *Halia* pulled up to one end of the quay. Using Onas as interpreter, Python shouted orders and threats at the masters of the light craft until they made space for the trireme. We drew in our oars and tied up.

A gleaming Ptolemaic officer and two Greek civilians climbed aboard and went to Python. "I am Tauros, commandant of the port," said the officer, "and these are Chief Customs Inspector Pelias and his assistant. Pray assemble your crew and passengers."

The trumpeter blew; the rowers, smelling strongly of sweat, filed up on deck. Commandant Tauros raised his voice:

"O strangers! You are entering the domains of Ptolemaios son of Lagos, king of Egypt and the surrounding lands!"

King? I thought. Ptolemaios must have heard of Antigonos' assumption of royal rank and done likewise.

"Before you go ashore," continued the commandant, "you must show your baggage to the assistant customs inspector and pay the import tax that he levies. When you go ashore, behave as a guest in the house of another."

"He means," put in Python, "that if we catch any of you abandoned rascals fighting with the natives, we will hang you from the yardarm."

"Another thing," said Tauros. "Do not kill any animals while you are in Egypt. Many animals are sacred to the Egyptians, different ones in different parts of the land. The cat, the dog, the bull, the hawk, and the ibis are sacred everywhere. Be particularly careful not to harm a cat—not, that is, unless you wish to be torn to bits by a frenzied mob. Also, Egyptians deem it extremely uncouth to relieve oneself in the street, so it is better not to do so."

The commandant and the chief customs inspector turned aside to plunge into a wrangle with Python and Sapher. My crew and I went ashore to trudge the dusty streets with sand in our shoes and to sit in a tavern, drink beer, and scratch fleabites.

Dikaiarchos, who happened by, kept treating us—"Because," he said, "I wish to test the dictum of Aristoteles, that men who are drunk on wine fall prone, while those who are drunk on beer fall supine."

Before this philosophical point could be settled, however, Azarias of Bousiris pushed into the tavern and came over to me, asking:

"Have you seen Alexis and Semken, sir?"

"Not I. Why?"

"I had arranged to take a river boat with them, to share the expense. Now they have disappeared, and I fear they have gone without me. I know not how they got their baggage through customs so quickly. They must have bribed the inspectors."

I felt a pricking of unease, as if my guardian spirit were trying to warn me, but I brushed it aside. "What will you do?"

"I must needs wait until another party is bound upriver. I cannot afford to hire a boat all to myself."

"You might as well sit with us and drink, then."

"I thank you, but—*avoi!*—the rules of my religion forbid. I shall see you back at the ship."

As the team and I were heartily tired of cold meals eaten on deck, we arranged with the taverner for a proper dinner that night. Onas, knowing the Egyptian language, went to buy materials for this feast. I strolled back to the waterfront to watch the unloading of Sapher's cargo. Captain Sapher, standing on the quay and directing his men, said:

"There may be hope yet. I have arranged with the Royal Navy to try to pull off the *Anath* tomorrow, if the brigands have not destroyed her."

The last of the salvaged cargo came shore. The *Halia* pushed off into the stream, turned, and backed up to the slip. When it was made fast, the rowers let themselves down over the stern. With hawsers they pulled the ship up on the slip, on rollers. When the *Halia* was secured, Captain Python prowled around the hull, giving commands:

"Scrape those barnacles—Drive an extra peg here—Recalk that seam—Oh, rejoice, Chares. It looks as though three days' work should see us through, if the omens let us sail then."

"Could the crew of the *Talos* feast you at the tavern tonight, sir?"

"Thank you, but I am entertaining the commandant on the ship."

"While she lies on the slip?"

"Surely. Nothing could go wrong, unless some joker cut the cables and let us roll back into the river, and the marines will guard against that. Have a good dinner."

Our feast, served on bean leaves for plates, went off splendidly, despite the absence of our genial captain. The taverner brought in a dancer, one of the class peculiar to Egypt and known as belly dancers. Her specialty was to stand rigid while her hips and breasts quivered and jiggled and rotated in small circles.

The crew roared its approval, and even Berosos and Dikaiarchos ceased their argument, as to whether the moon in its courses faces constantly toward the sun or toward the earth, to watch. As she was going out, I stopped her and asked if I might see her later.

"I have one more dance. I meet you in hour outside," she said.

Having time to work up my anticipation, I bethought me that I was not presenting my most seductive appearance. Although I had bathed and shaved, I wore my hard-used artilleryman's corselet, kilt, and hobnailed shoes. If I went back to the ship, I could get out my best soft shoes, shirt, and cloak, comb my curly hair, oil my skin, and borrow some scent from a shipmate.

Like the other men of the *Talos*, I had engaged a bed in the dormitory of the tavern, for even the most bug-ridden bed seemed like luxury after four nights on a pine deck. That, however, could wait.

On her rollers, the *Halia* loomed up as a huge black towering mass in the moonlight. I identified myself to the marine sentries and climbed the ladder. Snores from rowers and others who were sleeping aboard rumbled up from the oar deck, while light and snatches of song came from the captain's cabin under the quarterdeck. Python, I thought, was having quite a party.

I was finishing my toilette on the forecastle deck when the noise from the captain's cabin was broken by a cry of rage and anguish. There was a moment of silence, then a yammer of voices. The door to the cabin flew open. Out rushed Captain Python, shouting:

"Leonidas! Damon! Chares! Where is everybody? Something terrible has befallen!"

Some of the rowers roused themselves to grunt questions from the oar deck, but the first officer, the boatswain, and the marine officer had all gone into the town. I said:

"Here I am, sir. What is it?"

As I reached the main deck, Python ran forward, waving his fists above his head. He tried to speak, but only an inarticulate stammer came forth. Never had I seen our usually easygoing captain so excited. Behind him, Commandant Tauros emerged from the cabin, together with two scantily clad girls.

"The—the robe is gone!" shouted Python at last.

"Demetrios' royal robe?"

"What—what did you think I meant? Somebody has stolen it! Who took it? Where is it?" Python grabbed me by the shoulders and shook me.

"Please, Captain!" I said. "I haven't seen this precious robe. Is it just the robe that is missing, or all of Demetrios' regalia?"

"Only the robe. I—I opened the chest to show these garments to my guests just now, and—but who could have done it?"

I said: "How about those so-called bookdealers, Semken and Alexis? Azarias the Judaean says they left in haste without him, early this afternoon."

"Herakles! I think you have it. It was the Hellene, Alexis, who was so eager to see the garments, was it not?"

"Yes, he it was who persuaded you to open the chest."

"Do not try to blame me, you young scoundrel! It was you who told him about these things in the first place. Therefore it is you who have ruined us and perhaps our city as well! I ought to hang you—"

With a snarl Python aimed a blow at my head. Luckily I saw it coming in time to duck.

"Captain!" I cried, dancing back out of reach of the frantic man's fists. "Pull yourself together! You'll never recover the robe by beating me."

"He speaks sense, man," said the commandant. "The main thing is to get your bauble back."

"What can you do, Tauros? What can anybody do?" moaned Python. "I am ruined! I should have paid more heed to the omens."

I said: "I remember now that a couple of years ago, when I returned to Rhodes from my apprenticeship, I was told of a daring theft of all the books in our public library. Suspected were a pair of bookdealers who had visited the island and whose descriptions are answered by Alexis and Semken. So I have no doubt that they are the thieves."

"Why did you not think of that sooner?" said Python.

"Call it stupidity, sir. The next thing, however, is to find out whither they went. Their plan was to go up the Phatnitic branch, taking Azarias as far as Bousiris. So they must be bound for some hideout south of that city."

"Sailing up the river, eh?" said Python. "Then why do we not launch the ship and go after them? With our oars we could easily catch them."

Commandant Tauros said: "You have never sailed a trireme on the Nile. This branch writhes like a serpent in pain. Hence you must go slowly, with a native pilot to show you the channel, lest you ground on a sand bar. These river craft, which can sail on a heavy dew, need not be so careful, and thus you lose your advantage of speed. Moreover—did you say these fellows fled in the afternoon?"

"Yes," I said, "or so Azarias told me."

"Then they are already halfway to Bousiris, with this brisk breeze. And with the calking out of your planks and your girding cables off, your ship could not pursue them anyway."

"Could you not go after the thieves in one of your ships?"

"My dear Python," said Tauros, "I should love to oblige you. But my orders are to watch for hostile fleets and protect the coastal shipping. It would cost me my commission to go haring off after a pair of petty sneak thieves. Why do you not present the king with the remaining garments and say nothing about the theft of the robe?"

"He would find out, fear not. And the robe is the most important item in this wardrobe. I could present the robe without the hat, shirt, and shoes, but not the other things without the robe. Besides, the omens are bad."

I thought, Ptolemaios would certainly find out about it after Python had shouted the news of the theft in a voice that must have carried all over Tamiathis.

"Very well, then," said Tauros. "Let us gather our wits and take counsel as to how to retrieve your loss."

When we were gathered in the cabin under the wavering yellow light of a lamp, Commandant Tauros explained: "You will find many things strange in Egypt. For instance, many native Egyptians so lack appreciation of Greek civilization"—he cast an ironic glance at Onas—"that they plot to throw us out of the land. They form secret societies of liberation, and all that nonsense."

Onas said: "We had practice under the Persians, sir. It even worked for a time." He referred to the revolt of the Egyptians from the rule of the Persian king, Artaxerxes Memnon, whereby they achieved an independence which they precariously maintained for sixty years.

Said Tauros: "Well, let us not get into political argument. As I was about to say, many thieves and brigands take advantage of this situation. They cover their robberies by calling themselves liberators of the downtrodden Egyptian race. Believing this, the ordinary Egyptians will not inform on these rascals. Some thieves have formed virtual criminal kingdoms—invisible but covering great tracts of Egypt. Some, I suspect, have seized control of genuinely patriotic movements. They fight private wars, draw up treaties, and allot territories as if they were legitimate governments."

"Amazing!" said Python.

"Not so amazing, sir," said Onas, "when you consider how much longer we have been civilized than—ahem—than some other folk. However, Captain, I can tell you that Semken is no Koptian. I know a Memphite accent when I hear one." He turned to me. "Chares, ask Azarias whither these men said they were bound."

I repeated the question in Punic. Azarias replied: "Now that I think, they did not say. They were to drop me at Bousiris and go on—whither, I know not"

When this had been translated, I said: "You see, sir, the man Semken claims to be of Koptos but speaks the speech of Memphis, and avoids telling where he is going. I should guess that his hideout were in Memphis. That's a large city, is it not, Onas?"

"One of the world's greatest," said the Egyptian.

"Very well," said Python. "You, O Chares, are hereby charged with the recovery of Demetrios' robe. Pick the men to go with you—not too many—and make all arrangements. But do not come back without that garment."

"I will find it, sir," I said. "I shall need money, though."

"You shall have enough for your needs." Python smiled a weak, conciliatory smile. "I am sorry I lost my temper just now. Do not be angry with me. But we must have that robe back at all costs. The fate of our city depends upon it."

Book VI

MANETHÔS

When Onas and I put the proposal to him, Berosos showed an unflattering reluctance to come on our robe hunt.

"Why ask you me?" he said. We stood on the quay of Tamiathis, yawning from lack of sleep, early the morning after the fatal discovery. "No catchpole, I. In this cloudless clime you can find the North Star as well as I. Useless at either running or fighting am I, and I speak not the speech of the land. I should be of no use save for crocodile bait. Ask Mys instead."

Said I: "We asked you because we like you; you are our friend. But if the journey really affrights you—"

"Wait," said Onas. "Berosos, do you remember my speaking of my cousin Manethôs?"

"The one who knows the names of all the old kings?"

"Aye. Well, this is what we shall do. We shall stop at Sebennytos and ask my cousin, who is a priest of Thôth there, for help in tracking down our quarry. Far more than this Greek government, the Egyptian priesthoods know what goes on in the land. Thus shall you have an opportunity to learn the ancient lore of my people: their kings and gods, their myths and magic."

Berosos' expression of distaste had changed. He said: "Oh, that is different. When shall we start?"

Dikaiarchos of Messana strode up with a broad-brimmed hat on his head, exclaiming: "O Chares! What is this about your going to Memphis whilst the ship lies here out of water?"

I told the geographer of our mission.

"Indeed?" he said. "May I accompany you?"

"You, sir? Why?"

"To see the country. That's what I came to Egypt for."

"Well—ah—the chase may be rugged for one of your years, sir, and the quarry may bite when cornered, like the mouse in the story of King Agesilaos."

"Ha! Do you fear my senility?" Dikaiarchos seized me around the waist between his two large knobby hands and hoisted me into the air. Then he dropped me, saying:

"When you can do that to me, my fair young friend, it will be time to twit me on my age. As for the thieves' resisting—" He suddenly brought forth a long, gleaming, horseman's sword from under his cloak. "I can use this paring knife, also. In fact, I pinked some pirates with it yesterday."

"You are of course welcome to come," I said.

I spent the morning in rushing about for gear and supplies, and obtained an audience with Tauros while the barber shaved his jowls. The commandant said:

"If you will but wait an hour, Master Chares, I will find a map and write a letter to the strategoi through whose provinces you will pass. Meanwhile, have you bought mosquito nets?"

"What are they, sir?"

"The Egyptians, when they sleep, first rig little tents of linen gauze above themselves to keep off the mosquitoes, which are a terrible pest in the Delta."

"That I have discovered," said I, scratching. "I shall be back at noon, then."

When next I saw Tauros, he was studying a map spread out on a table in his study. He said: "Each nomos or province has a Macedonian strategos, in charge of military matters, and a monarch, usually an Egyptian, commanding civil ones. You will normally work through the strategos. We are in the Diospolite Nomos, or the Province of the Sanctuary, as the Egyptians call it. The strategos is a good friend of mine, but as Little Diospolis lies out of your way, you are not likely to meet him.

"You will go up the Phatnitic branch, thus, until you reach this fork. Let me see. The capitals of the Hermopolite and Mendesian provinces lie far from the Phatnitic branch. However, you should find the strategos of the Sebennytan Province in Sebennytos. His name is Neon; a good enough sort.

"At Bousiris you will find the strategos Thorax, whom I do not know. The capital of the next province on your left lies far to the east, but you can find a minor official in Leontopolis in case of need. Then you will come to Athribis, but I do not know who is the strategos of the Athribite Province. After Athribis, the next provincial capital you will pass is Memphis itself. The strategos is Alkman of Beroia, a famous warrior and a Macedonian of Macedonians."

"What is he like?"

"I have not seen him for many years. He it was who stood by Ptolemaios when Perdikkas' elephants overthrew the wall at the Fort of Camels, and all the other Ptolemaians fled, and Ptolemaios himself speared the first elephant as it lumbered through the breach."

Besides Onas, Berosos, Dikaiarchos, and myself, two other persons set forth with us: Dikaiarchos' slave Sambas, and Azarias, who merely wished a ride as far as his home.

What with one thing and another, we did not get off until midafternoon. Whenever I had all my voyagers assembled, somebody would think of one more article that we needed; then, when I had collected all the supplies for the journey, I found that one or another of my passengers had wandered off. After Onas did this twice, I forgot my good resolutions and berated him before all.

At last Horos, our boatman, and his son Zazamanx pushed our boat out into the stream. She was a twenty-cubit craft of small sycamore planks sewn together, with places for four oarsmen and a small cabin.

The boatmen stepped the mast and hoisted the sail. Zazamanx took his place on the broad, flat, duckbill-shaped overhang at the bow, peering down into the water, while Horos carried a paddle aft, thrust it into a notch in the high, recurved transom, and steered with it.

Horos was a stooped, gnarled, gap-toothed man, active as a monkey despite his evident age. His son was a big, solidly built, silent youth.

Horos knew a little Greek from doing business with the Hellenes of the naval station. He grinned at me, patted the boat's planks, and said:

"Fine boat, no?"

"It looks good to me. What do you call it?"

"*Hathor*. Best boat on river. You give me more money for riding in such fine boat. Much money."

I turned to Onas. "You made the arrangements for this voyage. Tell this knave he shall have what we agreed upon and not more."

There ensued a crackle of Egyptian dialogue, punctuated by hearty laughter. I gathered that the two were trading jocular insults.

Zazamanx called, "*Seka!*" from the bow. He picked up a rusty spear and poised it, staring down into the dark waters.

"Crocodile," said Horos to my question.

"Istar!" said Berosos. "Mean you that we bathed in the river with *those* things yesterday?"

"You were not devoured, were you?" said Onas.

Dikaiarchos: "I thought animals were sacred, yet Zazamanx would have taken a spear to this reptile."

"Crocodiles are sacred only in the Province of the Lower Palm Tree," explained Onas. "Elsewhere we slay them when we can."

"I could never live in Egypt," said I. "I could never remember what beast may be killed in which region."

I watched the boatmen's management of their craft with keen interest. The brisk etesian wind wafted us southward. Horos kept near the banks to avoid the swifter current of midstream, swerving out when Zazamanx called to beware of a shoal, and sometimes angling across the broad flood to take advantage of slack water on the far side.

Like the other branches of the lower Nile, the Phatnitic branch pursues a serpentine course. Now and then the river twisted about until, no matter how far around the sail was braced, it no longer served us. Then Horos and Zazamanx lowered it, put out two of the oars, and pulled with low grunts until the bend was passed.

The first time that he resumed his seat in the stern after one of these bouts, Horos said: "Hard work. Hot day. You pay me for whole trip now, yes?"

"Oh, be quiet!" I said.

The old man chuckled as if my rebuff were an excellent joke.

The banks of the Nile wafted slowly past: a reedy marsh, a palm grove, a village, then another marsh. Flocks of birds rose whirring from the marshes or winged, crying, overhead on their way south. The annual flood of the Nile was receding, though some low-lying fields still lay under sheets of water.

In fields which the falling water had laid bare, sturdy nut-brown peasants waded up to their calves in black mud, sowing this year's wheat. Women, stripped like the men to loin cloths or altogether naked, wielded heavy hoes. Now and then we passed a field in which naked boys chased animals back and forth with switches: now a flock of sheep, then a drove of pigs.

"Why are they doing that?" I asked Onas. "They'll run all the meat off their beasts."

"The animals tread the seed into the earth. In this soft mud such a scheme is easier than plowing."

All day we wound around bend after bend. Betimes we passed another duckbill-stemmed boat, whose occupants traded gossip with our boatmen in shouts across the water. When night came, we tied up near a village, ate our frugal meal, rigged our tents of gauze, and slept.

Next morning the marshes became fewer. Now and then a canal opened into the river on one side or the other. During the afternoon we reached Iseion, on the west bank. I should like to have studied the architecture of the majestic temple of Isis that rose against the skyline, but the urgency of my mission forbade. We pushed on to Sebennytos.

Onas' city came into view on our right, larger than Iseion, its walls of mud brick showing black against the red of the setting sun. Onas and I walked up the slope from the river to the gate. There lounged a single guard, wearing a helmet of crocodile skin. His huge wicker shield and bronze-pointed spear reposed against the wall.

We passed on into the city, a place of narrow dark streets and strong smells. I found General Neon in a crumbling mud-brick palace that had belonged to some forgotten governor of Persian times.

The strategos, a little round man, read the letter from Tauros, telling who we were and urging Ptolemaios' officials to give us every possible aid and succor.

"Wait," said Neon. He stepped into another room, whence came the buzz of speech. Soon he came back.

"I should be glad to help, my good sir," he said. "But I have just spoken to my spy, and he has seen no such folk as you describe in his rounds of the taverns. I imagine they stopped at Iseion, where the police are more lax, and passed by here without halting. Better luck upriver, perhaps."

Next Onas led me to the open place where stood the temple of Thôth. The lotus-topped capitals of its propylon rose black against the western sky, which was darkening from gold to apple-green to deep blue, while in the east the first stars shone like gems on a blue-black cloth. On either hand stone sphinxes brooded, and a bat wheeled and dipped overhead. To a Hellene the sight of an Egyptian temple speaks of ancient lore and occult wisdom, of mysterious rites and knowledge of forbidden things. Onas said:

"In the olden days you as a Hellene had not been admitted into the sacred precinct, let alone into the temple itself. However, things have changed."

He spoke to the man at the entrance, who walked off with leisurely strides. Soon another man appeared, looking ghostly in his white linen robe in the dusk. So quietly did he glide up that I started at the sight of him.

"*Ha*, Manethôs!" said Onas.

The other replied in kind, and the two touched noses, There was a swift exchange of speech. The white-robed man said to me in fluent though strongly accented Greek:

"Rejoice, O Chares! May the gods of Egypt ever watch over the friend of my kinsman." He made a ritualistic gesture. "Fain would I entertain you in proper fashion, but my house and I are in mourning. Still, will you step this way? First, however, must I ask you to leave your cloak with the porter, as wool may not be brought into the temple."

Manethôs led us into a small anteroom of the temple opening on the court. It was lit by lamps of curious shape that gave off a rancid smell of castor oil. Manethôs clapped his hands; a man brought small cups of wine for Onas and me. Manethôs did not drink. Now that I had a better look at him, I saw that he was a little younger than Onas and myself—that is, in his early twenties—and as tall as Onas though more slender of form. Manethôs' youthful appearance, however, conflicted with an extreme gravity of manner, suitable for a man of twice his age. His entire head, including his eyebrows, was shaven.

"What is the cause of your bereavement, sir?" I asked. "Why, our cat has died."

I almost burst into a raucous laugh. But my guardian spirit, together with a warning frown from Onas, caused me to clap a hand to my mouth. However, enough of the laugh had started on its way to cause Manethôs to give me a cold, hard look, like that of a cobra rearing to strike at a mouse.

"Something I ate," I said. "Pray accept my condolences." The priest grunted and turned to Onas. The two conversed in Egyptian while I sipped my wine and prowled about the chamber, scrutinizing the painted reliefs of gods and men and beasts, and combinations thereof, on the wall. After an hour of this I was becoming bored when Manethôs spoke:

"The ibis-headed man, O Chares, is Thôth, the god of wisdom, whom I serve. Some of your Greek priests identify him with their Hermes." "Indeed?" I said.

Onas spoke: "Excuse us for ignoring you, old fellow, but Manethôs has been telling me all that has befallen Uncle Sethos and Aunt Meritra and Cousin Tetephren and so on. My parents, thanks to the gods, still live, and I am fain to visit them on the morrow. Dwell they in a village, an hour's ride to the west."

"Herakles! You can't do that!" I exclaimed. "The trail of the thieves would grow cold while we waited."

Onas frowned. "Would you, after a long absence from Rhodes, fail to visit your parents if you touched there on a voyage? I cannot believe that you would be so wicked."

"No, but we must put first things first. We cannot risk our entire mission for a familial reunion."

"I shall not be gone above half a day, and I will go, whether you give me leave or not."

"As your superior officer, I forbid it!"

"Stop me if you can!"

"By the Dog, I will!"

We were both on our feet, and our shouts echoed through the silences of the temple. I had never before quarreled with the easygoing Onas, but this I deemed a matter of principle.

"Allow me to speak," said Manethôs. "You do, forsooth, have cause to push on in haste to Memphis. There will you either recover your stolen raiment or you will not. In either case you will then return down the river, in less haste than you went up it. Why not on your return stop long enough for Onas to make his visit? A day more or less will not matter then."

Shamefaced, Onas and I agreed to this plan. Manethôs resumed: "My cousin has told me of your quest and besought my aid in tracking down the thieves. Meseems the best way to do that were to go with you to Memphis, where I have connections among the priesthoods."

"That is too good of you, sir."

"Not entirely. I, too, have a mission, which your journey will enable me to accomplish. I wish to take the mummy of our cat to Memphis for burial in the holy cemetery of the cats there."

"Agreed with pleasure," I said. "When will you be ready?"

"Tomorrow morning. I must arrange with the high priest, my uncle, for leave from my duties. I will also pray to the wise Thôth to set our feet on the veritable path to success. Perhaps he will advise me in a dream."

Onas and Manethôs came aboard the *Hathor* at noon the next day. Manethôs wore a linen robe and headcloth, and shoes of papyrus. He carried a copper statue of a cat, twice life-size and weighing, I judged, five to ten pounds. I said:

"Have I misunderstood you, sir? I thought you were to bring the mummy of your cat on the journey."

"The mummy is in this," he said, tapping the ruddy copper.

"How did you get it into the statue?"

"Through the hole in the bottom, ere the base was riveted on." Manethôs set the statue in the corner of the cabin, whence it stared at us with a supercilious expression. The statue even included a pair of earrings in the cat's ears as I have seen on living cats in Egypt.

After the Sebennytan cousins came a free servant from the temple of Thôth, staggering under Manethôs' baggage. The servant, Phiôps, settled down on the boat to stay. These additions crowded the *Hathor* and brought expostulations from Horos. I was not sorry, however, to have another pair of strong hands aboard, as Dikaiarchos had made it plain that he did not wish others than himself to give orders to his slave.

Manethôs nodded gravely to Berosos and Dikaiarchos as I presented them. When I added, "And this is Azarias of Bousiris," however, something curious happened. Manethôs, his face blank, said:

"A Judaean?"

"Why, yes."

"Oh," said the priest, and turned away to see to the stowage of his gear.

Azarias, likewise, had failed to acknowledge the introduction. He glared with tight lips at the priest, as at a mortal foe.

"Do you know him?" I said to Azarias in Phoenician.

"*Ouph*, nay! Nor do I wish to," said the weaver. "But let us speak of another matter. We shall reach my city within the hour. I pray you, in the name of the lord Iao, to let me feast you and your fellow soldiers, the Egyptian and the Babylonian, at my house. It is the least I can do for your saving my life."

"I thank you, but I fear we have lost so much time in Sebennytos that we must press on...."

However, the little man pleaded so earnestly that I gave in. Then another thought struck me. I asked:

"How will you guest a group of foreigners, not of your religion, without violating your complex rules of eating?"

"*Na*, fear not. It is not the company that our laws restrict, but the manner of preparing the victuals."

Between Sebennytos and Bousiris, Azarias and Manethôs ignored each other in a way that not even the dullest could fail to mark.

We reached Bousiris while the afternoon sun still shone with Egyptian splendor.

First I sought out Thorax, the strategos of the Province of the Protector. His clerk said, "Wait," and went into the adjoining room, whence came the sound of snores. The snores ceased, and soon the clerk beckoned.

"What do *you* want?" growled Thorax, sitting on the edge of a couch and rubbing reddened eyes.

I showed Tauros' letter and spoke my piece.

"Oh, ordure!" muttered the strategos, glancing over the letter. "I know nothing of any such malefactors. If people cannot keep better watch over their property, they deserve to lose it. Try the deputy strategos at Leontopolis, or Hybrias at Athribis. Now leave me, my good man, for I am exceedingly busy."

Nettled, I went out, not doubting that the snores resumed as soon as I had gone. After I rejoined my comrades, Azarias led us to his house, whence came the clatter of looms.

As we entered, the noise of the looms desisted and a swarm of Judaeans flung themselves upon my fellow traveler. So swiftly flew the talk that, what of the peculiar accent wherewith these folk speak Phoenician, I could no longer follow. Azarias, arms flying, told of the attack on the *Anath* and of his subsequent rescue. His family burst into tears and wails when he told of his danger and screamed with joy at his deliverance. When he identified us as his saviors, they threw themselves upon us and kissed our hands, to my no small embarrassment.

Azarias' household included his wife, a short dumpy woman; three daughters and two sons, ranging in age from about five to fifteen; an apprentice; and several free servants. He showed us about, explaining the technical details of his looms. He had three of these for linen, two for wool, and one for silk. I suppose his family had developed the habit of shouting at one another to be heard over the clatter that arose when all these machines were in use at once. Pointing to the loom for silk, he said:

"This is a new thing, and not sure am I that it will gain me a profit. Any fool can weave wool, but for silk new ways are needed. We must tune the tension of our warp threads with utmost care, for silken threads yield less than those of wool. I learnt the art from a cousin in Jerusalem, who learnt it from a weaver in Sidon, who learnt it from a silk weaver of Kôs."

"Not Tryphon?"

"His father Anax, I believe. Why, know you Tryphon? A shrewd competitor, by all accounts."

Later, over Azarias' sweet Judaean wine, I asked: "Why did you and the priest so plainly dislike each other if you had never met?"

"Those wicked animal worshipers!" said the weaver with vehemence. "They hate us because we will not bow down to their false gods. Since we bring no offerings to their bestial demons, they strive to turn the people against us, to seduce away our youth to their abominable rites, to infect them with their barbarous superstitions, and to persecute and abuse us in every way they can. They hope to drive us back to Judaea. But we are not primitive tribesmen to be herded hither and yon at will. We are a holy race of ancient lineage, to whom the lord Iao has given the one true religion. If any would profit from knowing us, let him learn righteousness from our teachers and our sacred books. We are here lawfully, by invitation of the king, and by the rod of Moses here we will stay!"

His attitude seemed to me self-conceited, especially as everyone knows that the Hellenes alone have developed civilization to its highest form. But as Azarias was my host, it would not have been seemly to dispute him. Instead, I asked:

"How did you come to settle in Bousiris?"

"Fifteen years ago, Ptolemaios overran Judaea and captured our holy city of Jerusalem. Many of our people were carried off by his soldiers. One of these was my brother Ioudas. After these captives had slaved miserably for a time, an embassy of our leading men persuaded Ptolemaios that these were a people worth befriending: stout warriors, diligent workers, and virtuous citizens, not tricky traders or dissolute weaklings like some other folk.

"Accordingly, Ptolemaios bought up all the Judaean slaves in Egypt and freed them. He also invited more to settle in this land, to increase its wealth by their industry and its moral tone by their example. My brother wrote, urging me to remove hither, as my father's family was large and his business could not support all of us. Now there are over thirty Judaean families in Sebennytos."

"How do you get along with the Egyptians?"

"Not ill, save when those devils in the beast temples stir them up against us by their lies and calumnies."

Whatever the curious laws that govern the preparation of Judaean food and drink, I must say that the dinner was good. Even I, who normally care but little for my food, stuffed myself to the ears and sat groaning afterward, while Azarias bantered with Onas in Egyptian and with Berosos in Syrian. As we were leaving, the Judaean reiterated:

"Forget not: If I can do aught to help you in time of need, call upon me forthwith. Azarias ben-Moses spurns not his benefactors."

We found Manethôs and Dikaiarchos lounging in the *Hathor* over a jug of beer and talking learnedly of eras and dynasties. The next morning, when we had hoisted sail and breasted the flood to southward, I asked Manethôs:

"What lies between you and the Judaean weaver, that you should hate each other before you had exchanged a word?"

"Judaeans!" Manethôs spat over the side of the boat. "You know not what we Egyptians have suffered from these pestilent sand dwellers. Twice have they overrun us; twice have we driven them out; and now your Greek king is bringing them in for a third time."

"What's that? I have never heard of the Judaeans as conquerors."

Said Manethôs: "I will tell you. First, when Toutimaios was king of Egypt, a horde of these godless Asiatics invaded the land, calling themselves *Hyksôs* or 'Shepherds.' After a cruel and unrighteous rule of five hundred years these nomads were driven out by King Amosis. For four centuries thereafter all went well.

"Then King Amenophthis was advised by a seer that he should please the gods by cleansing the temples of the horde of cripples, blind men, and lepers that swarmed about them, begging for alms. The king accordingly gathered all these unfortunates and put them to forced labor. This, however, accomplished little, most of them being too feeble for heavy work.

"Amenophthis therefore sent them to the city of Avaris, which the Shepherds had built during their rule and which now stood empty. Here a renegade Egyptian priest named Osarseph obtained the leadership of the beggars. This Osarseph changed his name to Moses and intrigued with the Shepherds in Syria. At his urging, the latter again swept over the land, committing outrages and abominations like the burning of cities and the slaughter of sacred animals.

"King Amenophthis withdrew to Ethiopia without fighting, as he had been warned by the same seer that these polluted foreigners would rule the land for thirteen years. When the time was up, returned the king from the Southland and drove out both the Shepherds and the beggars. And from the Shepherds and the Egyptian beggars the Judaeans of today are descended. I can show you the passages in our ancient records where these things are set forth.

"Now Ptolemaios would bring these people back in. I will not speak of Greek rule over our holy land, for it is plain that the gods desire the Egyptians to be ruled—for a time—by barbarians. But I will speak about bringing in whole tribes of foreigners to do things that Egyptians can do just as well. If the king want soldiers, why brings he in Hellenes and Syrians and the like when we have a class of sturdy warriors, like Onas here, rusting away in idleness? If he want workers in wool and leather and metal, why import Judaeans when, for thousands of years Egypt has led the world in artistic taste and delicacy of workmanship?"

I shrugged, for it was a difficult argument to answer. "Perhaps he doesn't trust the Egyptians, knowing what happened to the Shepherd kings. Anyway, this Azarias seemed personally harmless."

"About Azarias' personal qualities I neither know nor care," said Manethôs. "He is in the vanguard of another invasion, the most deadly of all. Hellenes and Phoenicians and Babylonians we can put up with, but Judaeans threaten our very existence."

"How?"

"The other people of whom I spoke worship their gods and suffer us to worship ours undisturbed. But Judaeans openly sneer at our ancient religion; they even have the insolence to say that our gods exist not. Should such an atheistic heresy become widespread, the gods might turn off the Ior—that is, the Nile—in their anger and destroy us as punishment."

"What's that about the Nile?" said Dikaiarchos. "A favorite sport among learned Hellenes is to argue the cause of the rise and fall of this river. Is it true that in Ethiopia are two bottomless fountains, rising from the tops of conical mountains, one of which flows north to become the Nile while the other flows south into the lands of the headless men and the goat-pans?"

Manethôs allowed himself a rare smile. "I fear that some naughty compatriot of mine made up that tale to befool foreigners. The best opinion among our learned priests is that beyond Ethiopia to the south lies a lofty land of mountains and lakes, swarming with pygmies and elephants, where rain falls in summer only. The streams from these rains, coming together, form the Nile."

"Rain in summer?" said Dikaiarchos. "I have heard of such a thing in the far northern lands, but it seems almost too bizarre for belief."

"No stranger is it than the statements of you foreigners that in your lands rivers flow, east, west, and south as well as northward. To us, north is the only direction in which a proper river can flow."

Dikaiarchos laughed. "Well, if you will believe in my south-flowing streams, I'll believe in your summer rains."

I said: "O Manethôs, has your bird-headed god revealed anything to help us in our search?"

"Nay, not yet. True, he did visit me last night, but only to counsel me on personal matters."

Onas grinned. "Not in peace with his wife does Manethôs dwell. That is why he was so eager to come with us."

"May Seth shrivel you!" said the priest angrily. "I will thank you not to discuss my private affairs with outsiders. A sorry wight is he who exposes his kin."

"He's done you a favor, old boy," I said. "His words assure me that you are truly a human being like the rest of us. I had begun to wonder."

Manethôs grunted and withdrew into haughty silence. Being regarded as a common mortal was evidently not to his taste.

The banks of the Nile swept grandly past. Now the river ran straight for many furlongs; again, it wound in sharp bends, so that

Horos and Zazamanx had to break out the oars. Palm trees nodded upon the banks; camels swayed against the skyline. The camel moaned, the falcon screamed overhead in the fathomless blue, and the swape creaked as naked, chanting peasants worked its long boom up and down to raise water to their irrigation ditches.

Canals, large and small, opened into the Nile on either hand. Village after mud-walled village floated past, until I began to understand how so huge a population is credited by the geographers to Egypt. By comparison Hellas is a wild uninhabited waste.

At Leontopolis I was told that the deputy strategos for the Province of the Heseb Bull was away inspecting canals, and nobody else knew anything of my thieves. I began to feel that I had embarked on a fool's errand, plunging farther and farther southward into this mysterious land without even the faintest spoor of my game to guide me.

As the sun set, a red ball behind the western palms, Berosos drew geometrical figures in the wax of a writing tablet. Manethôs asked:

"What do you, Babylonian?"

"I prepare to cast our horoscope for the journey," replied Berosos.

"I have heard of this Babylonian system of divination by the stars. Forsooth, our Egyptian vaticinatory methods are of greater antiquity and wisdom than those of other nations; but still, I would fain have your scheme explained to me—as soon as I have completed my evening prayers." Manethôs spoke to the boat at large. "Allow me to suggest, gentlemen, that those of you who have gods do pray to them now."

When Manethôs had finished his own prayers, he spoke again to Berosos: "Very well, sir, will you set forth your science now?"

"Surely, my friend." Berosos plunged into his lecture. As he spoke, the stars came out, one by one, as if in obedience to his summons. He said:

"From preliminary indications, high hopes have I of a favorable premonstration."

I said: "Any time Berosos tells you that the stars assure you good luck, that's the time to beware."

"Heed him not, Manethôs," said Berosos. "These scoffing Hellenes are wont to parade their skepticism, not because they understand the higher truths but to magnify themselves by tearing others down."

"That's not true at all!" boomed Dikaiarchos. "For thousands of years, ever since your ancient civilizations arose, men have believed whatever their priests and kings told them, nine-tenths of it self-serving falsehood."

"How know you it was false?" said Manethôs.

"Because all these ancient myths and doctrines contradict one another. As my master, the great Aristoteles, so irrefutably demonstrated, if two statements are contradictory, both cannot possibly be true at once. So it is high time a little skepticism were applied to such matters, to winnow the wheat from the chaff."

"I can show you cases where the event fell out exactly as the stars foretold," said Berosos.

"No doubt, but that proves nothing unless you can also show two other things: that no predictions ever turned out badly, and that the events foretold would not have come to fruition in any case. For example, I can prophesy that the sun will rise tomorrow. Does that make me a prophet?"

Berosos replied: "If you come to Babylon, I will show you our ancient archives, dealing with the very points you raise."

"That may be," said Dikaiarchos, "but never yet have I seen a form of divination that would stand up under logical analysis."

Manethôs: "Believe you not that man can ever know the future?"

"I wouldn't go so far. While I will not accept any other form of divination, I think there may be something to prophetic dreams."

"Mean you, my learned friend, as when the wise Thôth warns me of the future in slumber?" said Manethôs.

"Essentially, yes."

"Then you do accept the gods?"

"Let's not jump to conclusions," said Dikaiarchos. "I have never seen a god and so know nothing of them. Furthermore, it may be better for us not to know the future; for, if we knew our fate in detail, who would strive to better his lot?"

"As to gods," I began, "I have seen—"

But Manethôs cut me off. "That depends on whether one's vision of the future be absolute or contingent. But if you discredit the gods, how then do you explain prescience in dreams?"

"It may be that in sleep or in hysterical frenzy the spirit loses its intimate connection with the body and is thus enabled to see through the barriers of time and space that normally hem us in. One might call it extrasensory perception. If, as Parmenides taught, all events—past, present, and future—coexist in an eternal now—"

"Then you do believe in the soul?" said Manethôs.

"That there exists a life principle that distinguishes the living from the dead, I concede. But as for the common concept that this spirit goes wandering off by itself, or survives the death of the body—*phy!* I'll believe that when I see it."

"I can enlighten you," said Manethôs gravely. "There exist not one but three souls in each body. The first, the *ba*, is immortal and divine and leaves the body at death. The second, the *chou* or intelligence, and the third, the *ka* or double, remain with the body. In time, if the body has been properly mummified, these three souls unite to revivify it.

"However, it is but just to say that the Osirians have a rival theory, according to which the *ka* is a divine emanation—"

"Gentlemen!" I said. "We have reached Athribis. You may stay aboard and dine on talk of the different kinds of soul, but I'm for town."

Again I sought the office of the strategos of the Province of the Great Black Bull. The results were even less satisfactory than the last time. A clerk said to me:

"No, whatever-your-name-is, you may not see General Hybrias. The strategos will see nobody, because he is computing the tax rolls with the nomarch. Come back next month, and then perhaps he will see you. No, you may not see the nomarch, who is helping the strategos with the tax rolls."

It struck me that the farther I got from Tamiathis, the less cooperation I got from Ptolemaios' officials. Such a state of affairs boded ill for my prospects of success in Memphis.

Above Athribis the river took several sharp bends. River traffic became thicker as we neared Memphis. The scenery changed, to remind us that we were about to leave the Delta, the broad flat land of wet black earth and thickly sown villages, shaped like the letter whose name it bears, and enter that part of Egypt where the Nile flows for thousands of furlongs through a narrow green valley between two vast bare deserts.

Already we had caught glimpses of these deserts. Rocky hills and sandy dunes marched in upon us from east and west. The farther south we went, the closer they came: yellow-brown hills from the Libyan Desert, on our right, and gray-brown hills from the Arabian Desert, on our left.

We reached the fork where the Nile divides into its two main branches: the Phatnitic, up which we had come, and the Bolbitinic, which empties into the sea farther west. Here we anchored for the night between two small islands, one of which shielded us from the wind and the other from the current.

The next day we sailed to southward again. Above the fork the river is divided by a multitude of islands, great and small. On the smaller isles reeds and long grasses waved in the steady etesian breeze, while Egyptian families picnicked by the waterside. The larger isles bore farms and villas.

Afternoon came, and ever we wound among the islands. Ever the desert came closer: especially a group of frowning hills that encroached from the east. The sun was low again when I cried out:

"The pyramids!"

There they were, three of them, tiny with distance and black against the reddening sky, rising from vast inclosures on a hill far back from the western bank. Dikaiarchos and Berosos hastened to look, shading their eyes. Onas and Manethôs, engrossed in a game of checkers, merely glanced up and back again to their game. They had seen these strange edifices before.

Manethôs said: "Here is something of interest to Master Berosos. On your left you see the town of Babylon, whose dwellers came aforetime from his land."

The town stood on the riverbank at the base of a rugged hill. Berosos was at once full of questions. Manethôs explained:

"King Sesostris of the Twelfth Dynasty conquered an empire as wide as that of Alexander and brought home thousands of captives, whom he compelled to labor at building temples. Now, the captives brought from Babylonia revolted and seized yon hill. They fortified this eminence, ravaged the country round about, and defeated all efforts to subdue them. At last the king offered them a treaty, by which they should be allowed to dwell in that place and manage their own affairs if they would be loyal subjects and give up their brigandage. So it was agreed, and they live there yet."

Berosos sighed. "Ah me! Once we, too, were a race of warriors and conquerors."

"Be thankful you are no longer," said Dikaiarchos. "These kings reap a bit of glory, but what do they accomplish besides burning cities, killing and enslaving multitudes, and destroying the accumulated wealth and wisdom of the ages to aggrandize their own mediocre selves? He who ascertains a new law of nature or invents a new device is greater than all your conquerors, and in the long run has more influence."

"You can afford to be philosophical, Hellene," said Manethôs. "You need not take orders from foreigners; you need not skip out of the way when a drunken foreign soldier swaggers down the street. You have no horde of foreign officials meddling in the affairs of your temple and selling the high-priesthood to the highest bidder."

"No doubt, but it does not alter my argument. I have written a book, proving that all the natural causes of human calamity—fire, flood, famine, plague, and wild beasts—have together slain fewer people than man himself by his wars and revolutions."

"I should rejoice to read it," said Manethôs. "Meanwhile I suggest that we stop for the night at Babylon and go on in the morning, as Memphis is another forty furlongs."

In Babylon-in-Egypt we entered another world. Here were the hooked noses, the flowing beards, the long curled hair, the knitted caps with dangling tails, and the guttural speech of Old Babylon. Berosos was delighted to discover that the people yet spoke the old Babylonian tongue.

"Outside of the rituals of the temples, scarcely ever is the old speech heard in Babylonia any more," he said. "We all speak Syrian in our everyday affairs."

During the evening I became separated from my companions; or rather, I separated myself, for what seemed a good reason. I succeeded in cajoling the reason into a compliant mood, despite the fact that neither of us understood a word of what the other said. Alas! At that point her husband came in, and I had to drop from a balcony and scurry around a few corners to preserve my gore for beautiful Rhodes.

Back at the boat, I found Onas and Dikaiarchos but not Berosos or the Egyptian priest. Fearing that they had met with foul play, I started out to look for them, when they appeared, singing. That is, each was singing a song in his native tongue and paying no heed to the song of the other. They had their arms about each other's necks, although Manethôs was usually careful, for religious reasons, not to touch foreigners. They reeled aboard and sat down with a force that strained the *Hathor*'s flimsy planks. Berosos' plump face was wreathed in smiles, and so was the normally solemn visage of Manethôs.

"Ye gods!" I said to the latter. "Aren't you violating a hundred rules of your temple, man?"

The priest waved a finger at me. "Nought that a few ritual puff—purifications will not cure. It would be different were I higher in the hierarchy. Know you what Berosos and I have done?"

"What?"

"We have taken a solemn oath. We have made a compact. Tell him, Berosos."

The Babylonian said: "Nay, the hiccups have I. You tell him."

"I will try. We have sworn, by Thôth and Osiris and Ammon, and by Nebos and some other Babylonian gods whose names escape me, that—that—what swore we, Berosos?"

"To—to write a book, each of us," said Berosos, "in Greek, setting forth the true histories of our great and glorious peoples. The history of Babylonia will I compose, while Manethôs shall write that of Egypt. We shall draw upon the ancient records of our nations, which you poor benighted Hellenes cannot even read. Thus shall you learn what a privilege it is to know us."

"Let alone," said Manethôs, "let alone make a cruise on the Nile with us. We shall—we shall—what was I going to say, Berosos? *Ech!* The lazy rascal sleeps."

Manethôs slumped down and joined his comrade in slumber.

Many have heard of the pyramids of Egypt, but not many Hellenes know that the three across the river from Babylon are not the only ones. There are many more, albeit smaller than the great ones of King Souphis and his successors. They stretch for leagues up the western bank of the Nile. In stately procession they filed past us, rising on the skyline beyond the palms and plowed fields and villas, until we came unto Memphis.

Memphis was by far the largest city that I had ever seen. A colossal wall of pearly limestone incloses the city proper, which stretches back from the waterfront across a spacious plain for thirty furlongs and along the river for sixty. Within the wall, many temples rise from the enormous spread of brown brick houses, and around them tower the upper parts of an army of gigantic statues.

When I remarked on the stunning size of the wall, Berosos said: "Vaster by far are the walls of Babylon, though now into decay they have fallen."

Horos guided the *Hathor* to a mooring place on the waterfront. Manethôs pointed toward the southeastern part of the city, saying:

"You will wish to find quarters for your company, O Chares. Yonder lies the foreign quarter, around the temple of Hathor, where inns of the Greek type are to be found."

"Show me thither, pray," I said.

The foreign quarter of Memphis is noisily colorful. Here one is jostled by men in Hellenic cloaks, men in sleeved robes, men in leather jackets, and men with naked upper bodies. Legs in kilts, and legs in trousers, and bare legs stride past; the blue eyes and lank pale hair of the Kelt mingle with the shiny black skin and tribal scars of the Ethiop. Atop the hurrying figures bob Libyan ostrich plumes, tall spiral Syrian hats, Arabian headcloths, Persian felt caps, and Indian turbans.

Here a liquid-eyed Iberian with black side whiskers under his little black woolen bonnet tries to make an assignation with a slender Indian girl in gauzy muslins and jingling silver gimcracks; there a curly-haired, scar-faced Etruscan quarrels with a booted, bearded, bowlegged Scythian; they shout insults with hands on knives until a Greek soldier from the garrison parts them with a threatening growl. A stocky, turbaned Kordian orders his horoscope read by a curly-bearded Babylonian; a slim, hawk-faced Nabataean and a fat Phoenician goldsmith haggle over a bracelet, with much waving of arms, invocation of strange gods, and crashing of gutturals.

Manethôs found us an inn. When we had eaten, he said: "You will, I suppose, wait upon the commandant whilst I seek my colleagues in the temple of Thôth. Ere I do that, I must have my head shaved and buy me new footgear, for the boat's bilge water has destroyed all the shoon I brought with me."

"Papyrus doesn't strike me as a practical material for shoes," I said.

"Belike not, but the rules of my religion compel it."

We left our comrades at the inn. Having helped Manethôs to buy a pair of paper shoes, I parted from him and bent my steps in the direction he had indicated, toward a flat-topped hill in the center of the city. On this akropolis stood the camp of the garrison and the palace of King Apries of former times. Manethôs told me that the hill on which the citadel rests is all man-made.

The palace, dating back before the Persian rule, is one of those rambling old edifices of which nearly every part has been demolished and rebuilt at one time or another, so that a chaos of architectural plans and styles results. Next to the room where I waited, workmen were noisily knocking down a wall. Lizards, fleeing the destruction of their homes, darted out of cracks in the wall of the waiting room and scuttled across the floor, pausing only to snap at a passing fly.

The receptionist was a rabbity little clerk named Thespis, who glanced fearfully from time to time toward the door to Alkman's office. When a man came out, Thespis put his head cautiously around the corner of the door. Then he beckoned to me.

"O General!" he said. "This is Chares of Lindos, an officer in the armed forces of Rhodes."

Alkman of Beroia glowered up at me from behind a papyrus-littered table. The strategos was an enormous man: nearly six feet tall, but so broad that he seemed squat. His arms were like the skeins of heavy stone throwers; his legs, like the trunks of gnarled old oaks. Against the fashion, he wore a bristling brown beard. Close-set pale-blue eyes looked out under bushy brows on either side of a nose that some weapon had smashed into a shapeless blob. He wore the undress tunic and kilt of the Ptolemaic army, and his voice was like thunder in the distant hills. One could easily imagine his facing Perdikkas' war elephant with nothing but a spear.

"What do you want?"

I presented my letter and spoke my speech. When I finished, there was silence. Alkman breathed heavily; I almost expected to see flame come from his nostrils.

"Oh, plague! As if I had not enough troubles," he growled, "with the fornicating Egyptians rioting, and taxes below estimates, and the remodeling of the polluted palace, Tauros has to send me a simpering little catamite on the maddest errand since Herakles went after Queen Hippolyta's belt—"

"Sir!" I said, feeling my face flush. "It may seem mad to you, but I'm only trying to carry out my orders as a soldier should—"

"*You* a soldier? Ha!"

"I am a double-pay man in command of a catapult, and we've fought for more than half a year—"

"Call you that cowardly long-range stuff fighting?"

"I don't care what you call it, General. But I represent a free Hellenic city on a legitimate errand. When I make a civil request, the least a fat-arsed bureaucrat like you can do is to give me a civil answer—"

"Get out, you stinking little he-whore!" roared Alkman in a voice that almost shook the plaster of the walls. With a wrench of his huge hairy hands he tore the letter from Tauros in two.

"Give me that!" I screamed, and dived for the papyrus.

It seems to me that I planted a punch on Alkman's misshapen nose. Then he picked me up with one hand while with the other he hit me a blow on the side of the head that nearly stunned me. I was dimly aware of being borne out through the anteroom to the front door of the palace, of being swung round and round as a quoit is whirled by an athlete, and of being hurled far out into space.

I alighted on the flagstones before the palace with a shattering impact. For an instant I lay, too dazed and pained to move. There was a burst of laughter from the sentries in front of the palace, and a remark about the strategos' having set a new Olympic record. Then I was aware of somebody's helping me up.

"Are any bones broken?" said Thespis in a low, hurried voice.

"I think not," I muttered, trying my joints and choking back tears of futile rage.

"Thank the gods for that! You must excuse the strategos. The Egyptians rioted a ten-day past, with three slain and much property destroyed, and it makes him touchy. None dares speak to him as you did; you are lucky he didn't kill you." Thespis raised his voice, winking at me: "No, get along, fellow! We have no time for such as you!"

"Are the Egyptians in revolt?"

"No, it was a religious affray. Some men of the Province of the Sistrum killed a crocodile and carried it through the streets, and the men of the Crocodilopolite Province resented this flaunting of the slaughter of their sacred beast. But the general has suffered from a headache, and what with one thing and another he has become the most choleric man in Egypt. Go now, my friend, and do not blame the rest of us." Then, in a changed voice: "No, I will not! The strategos has spoken, and that ends the matter!"

"Thanks," I murmured, and limped off.

When I got back to the inn, Dikaiarchos said: "By Zeus the King! What happened to you, Chares?"

I told of my treatment by General Alkman. My comrades clucked and nodded wisely but did not utter any helpful advice.

"You should learn to keep your temper, no matter what the provocation," said Dikaiarchos.

"Easier to say than to do," I said. "The whipworthy rogue would not have used me so foully had he not outweighed me by two to one."

The geographer shrugged. "It is your fate to be small, just as it is mine to be bald and Berosos' to be fat. One must learn to live with these—oh, here is Manethôs. Rejoice, O learned priest! What news?"

"What news indeed? By the triple phallus of Osiris, what ails our commander? Did you get caught in a riot?"

I repeated my tale.

"I like it not," said Manethôs.

"Neither did I."

"That is not what I meant. Tell me exactly what was said, as nearly as you can recall it."

When I had done so, Manethôs pursed his lips. "Forsooth, the strategos is a man of formidable repute, but nought said you at first to incite him to such insult and outrage. Now will I tell you what I have learned. No word of the robe has come to my colleagues, but I have heard somewhat of the state of things in Memphis.

"Ever since Alkman became strategos, organized crime in Memphis has flourished as never before. This is odd, because the strategos, a man of great force and vigor, could stamp out these iniquities as well as any man. One might speculate that these robbers flourish because he suffers them to, and that he suffers them to because it is profitable to him. But this, as I say, is mere surmise.

"Last month, on the tenth of Paophi, was a man named Mathotphes found floating in the Nile with his throat well cut. This Mathotphes was, it seems, the archthief of the entire Province of the White Wall, ruling the robbers, ruffians, burglars, kidnappers, cutpurses, smugglers, forgers, counterfeiters, assassins, and the like, even as General Alkman and the nomarch rule the honest folk. Ever since this event has the Memphite underworld been scuttling about in agitated fashion as do the insects when one overturns a flat stone, all wondering who will take Mathotphes' place. No sooner would the imps of rumor name one for this perilous post than the rapscallion would be found stabbed, poisoned or otherwise disposed of. It would seem that no successor has yet fought his way to the top of this dangerous dung heap.

"Since my colleagues in the temple of Thôth could tell me nought of the robe, they gave me introductions to priests in other temples. If it suits you, O Chares, I will start the rounds of these on the morrow."

Next morning all in our party wished to see the sights of Memphis. We therefore followed Manethôs through the narrow, winding, dusty streets, past block after block of blank brown walls. Striding ahead with an ivory-handled walking stick, he led us first to the small temple of Hathor in the foreign quarter. He pushed through the crowd of beggars—many blind, for blindness is a common affliction in Egypt—at the entrance to the sacred precinct. He left us in the courtyard (naturally, as we were not purified initiates) and disappeared into the temple proper. Soon he came out again, his visage glum.

"No luck," he said. "Next we shall try the great temple of Phtha."

This is the largest temple in Memphis, standing amid green groves in a spacious temenos in the midst of the city, south of the citadel where I had met with misfortune. About the main entrance, on the south side of the precinct, stand six colossal statues, two of them thirty cubits high and four of them twenty. I have been told that they represent either King Sesostris or the second King Rhameses, surnamed Osymandyas, and his family. In addition, there is an enormous statue, nearly thirty cubits long, lying on its back.

I burnt to examine these statues closely, to see what I could learn about the construction and erection of colossi. However, as soon as we appeared at the principal gate of the temenos, we were set upon not only by beggars but also by a swarm of would-be guides, who clamored:

"You want see sights, yes? Come with me! You want guide? Show you temple, pyramid, tomb? Ride camel? Me clever guide, know all secrets of ancient Memphis! Speak all languages! See dancing girl? Buy jewelry? Need passionate woman? See, here medicine for virility, made from black Ethiopian lotus! Make you good for ten stands a night! Want pretty boy? I get you rare drug, make you dream of heaven! Have fortune told? Come see orgy of Seth-worshipers! Buy antiquities from tombs of old kings? Come with me, I show you good time! See best belly dancer in Egypt, and lie with her afterward! Come, see rare curios in my shop..."

I asked Manethôs: "How do you say 'no' in Egyptian?"

"Say, *even*. If they persist, add *rhou-ek*, which means 'run away!'"

I said *even* and *rhou-ek* until our tormentors gave up and assailed other visitors, such as a lordly Persian couple behind us. For folk from many nations travel to Memphis to see its wondrous sights, and a class of Memphites has grown up to guide, guard, entertain, exploit, and prey upon these travelers.

We followed Manethôs into the temenos of Phtha, who to the Egyptians is the creator, the god of property and stability, and the tutelary deity of Memphis. Inside the temenos a swarm of concessionaires sold religious goods, such as little copper statues of Phtha to bury at the corner of one's lot to keep away evil spirits.

Again Manethôs left us in front of the temple while he went inside. This time he came out with a more cheerful expression.

"There is a rumor in the marketplace," he said, "of a daring theft downriver by a brace of local bullies. But nought can I learn of where the thieves and their plunder are now. Let us go on to the temple of Apis."

We trailed off southward to the temple of Apis, where dwells the sacred bull in a chamber. This chamber opens on a court surrounded by a colonnade whose columns are twelve-cubit statues. Then we marched northwest to the temple of Ammon. Gaining no advantage there, we went on to northward, along a wide asphalt-paved avenue, past the two great statues at the western gate of the temenos of Phtha, and past the sacred lake of Phtha. Here, in a park on the borders of the lake, was a space inclosed by a towering fence of thick bronze bars, with soldiers standing guard and a crowd of sight-seers jostling.

When we had wormed our way up to the bars, I saw that inside the inclosure stood the funeral car and casket of the divine Alexander himself. A breath-taking sight it was. The coffin rested on an enormous four-wheeled carriage of the Persian type, with gilded spokes and iron tires, and hubs in the form of lions' heads, each head holding a golden spear in its teeth. Stretched out from the front axle were four huge jointed poles, each having four quadruple yokes, for the vehicle was made to be drawn by sixty-four mules.

Around the sides of the wagon ran a colonnade upholding a roof of golden scales inlaid with precious stones, with a cornice from which projected golden heads of goat-stags. From the cornice hung four long painted panels showing Alexander and his bodyguards, his elephants, his cavalry, and his ships. At each corner of the roof stood a golden statue of Victory, and there were bells, golden wreaths, and other ornaments too numerous to list.

Between the columns of the colonnade I would see the huge golden sarcophagus of Alexander, on which lay a gold-embroidered purple robe and the armor and weapons of the great king. Over all floated a vasty purple banner with an olive wreath embroidered in golden thread. The bright Egyptian sun blazed on the gold and flashed on the precious stones until it made one's eyes ache.

When we had looked our fill, we continued northward to the temple of the goddess Neïth, where Manethôs made further inquiries. These, however, added nothing to what we had already heard. We crossed a canal and climbed the slopes to the west of the city, to the temple of Anoubis, the dog-headed judge of the dead. This temple stands on the edge of the desert, where a stride takes one from green field to golden-yellow sandy waste.

Thence we trudged, under the scorching Egyptian sun, west along a road lined with brooding sphinxes, where buff-brown pyramids, great and small, rise from inclosures on either hand, and graveyards spread far into the shimmering distance. Despite the heat, I shivered a little at the thought of all the centuries that had passed while kings and commoners were buried here. Hellas is such a new country by comparison!

I asked Onas about an enormous pyramid that rose in six diminishing stages, like giant's steps, on our left. He said:

"The wizard Imouthes built that structure as a tomb for King Sosorthos, who lived but a little time after the reigns of the gods and the demigods."

"What engineers those old fellows must have been!" I exclaimed.

Onas: "That was done, not by your materialistic technics, but by Imouthes' mighty magic."

Manethôs turned his head. "Rubbish, my dear cousin! The only magic used was that of organization and discipline. They quarried the stones with hammer stones and wooden chisels, dressed them with copper saws, hauled them up earthen ramps on sleds, and levered them into place with copper crowbars. My people are many and muscular, and—more to the point—they can work together for a common objective, a virtue for which the Hellenes have never been noted." He cast me a wry smile.

Footsore and weary, we came to the temple of Osiris. Here the clamor of bustling Memphis is heard no more. There is nothing to see but blue sky, golden sand, and this vast complex of sacred buildings; no sound but the murmur of hymns from the temple and the gentle hiss of blowing sand. Inside the temenos stood a great ithyphallic statue of Osiris, draped in a flame-colored robe and symbolizing the generative powers of the sun, the moon, and the Nile.

We sat listlessly in the shade of huge square columns while Manethôs conferred with the priests. Onas said:

"Beneath us lie great chambers wherein rest the mummies of the Apis bulls, each in its own sarcophagus."

Dikaiarchos roused himself. "Can the public see these divine bull coffins?"

"That depends. On certain feast days are the people admitted to services in the tunnels; although, as the entrances to the burial chambers are bricked up, not much is there to see. When an Apis dies and is embalmed, however, the whole city turns out to haul the sarcophagus along the sacred road from Memphis."

Manethôs came out of the temple. "I have not found your robe, my friends, but I may have discovered a means of recovering it. First, suffer me to explain that in Egypt it is an ancient custom for the owners of stolen goods to take them back from thieves on the payment of a small ransom—a fraction of the thing's true value—no questions being asked. For such deals to be consummated, certain men—traders in used wares—must act as intermediaries."

"You mean," said Dikaiarchos, "that you have a class of tolerated fences for stolen goods."

Manethôs shrugged. "That is how things are done. Now, in Memphis, the leading agent of this kind is Tis of Hanes, the dealer in antiquities. He must have done a brisk business for many a year, for he dwells in a costly villa not far from here. Let us, then, proceed to the house of Tis."

Manethôs led his drooping column back along the avenue of sphinxes and then by a path that wound by devious ways among cliffs and cemeteries. Turning a corner, we came upon a fair estate spread out on the side of a hill overlooking the gardens and palm groves of the outskirts of Memphis. A small blue lake glimmered before us, and the shadows of the western hills crept eastward over the city as the sun declined. The sharp chill of the desert night began to succeed the dry, sweat-devouring heat of the day.

A massive wall, to which many cities would not be ashamed to entrust their defense, inclosed the house and grounds. At the gate a peephole opened in answer to Manethôs' knock. The priest spoke into the hole. After a long wait, while a scarlet sun sank out of sight behind the cliffs, the gate swung open and an enormous Negro—a man seven feet tall, of lean and storklike build—admitted us.

Inside were palms and flowers and pools, two loinclothed gardeners working with trowel and watering pot, and a brace of armed watchmen. A man in white came toward us, calling out in good Greek:

"Welcome, friends! May Thôth grant that Tis of Hanes can aid you in finding your royal raiment. Which of you is which?"

Manethôs cast me a curious, slit-eyed glance, then presented us to Tis. The trader was a dark-skinned man of medium height, rather stout, with a large round head, bald at the top, and closecut graying hair. He had a turned-up nose and a long upper lip over a wide, drooping mouth. Though he was not impressive to look at, his manners were excellent, combining dignity without pomposity, courtesy without servility, and friendliness without vulgar familiarity.

"You are weary and fain to wash before dinner," he said. "You shall, of course, treat my house as your own during your stay. Allow me to show you to your apartments."

The house of Tis was large, with several courts and wings. Tis led us into the main hall.

Here I was struck by the extraordinary display of curious objects: exotic weapons hanging from the walls, strangely wrought vessels on stands, and curious statues in niches. There were things carved in wood and stone and crystal, or cast in bronze and silver and gold. Their value for the rare materials alone must have been great, and for their artistic curiosity, immense. Some of the statues suggested the mysteries of India or the dark menace of the lands beyond Ethiopia; others displayed affinity with the art of no race or nation I had ever heard of. Some were beautiful in an outlandish way, more were grotesque or obscene.

"I must show you my curios, O Chares," said Tis. "But, methinks, a warm bath were more to the point."

I joined Manethôs before we returned to the hall, saying: "Why did you look at me so curiously when Tis came to meet us?"

The priest replied: "Nought had I said to the Nubian porter of our mission, only that I craved audience with the master on a matter in his line of business. No one can know what is in another's heart, but this dealer in secondhand goods is both too rich and too knowing to suit me."

Then Tis took charge of us, presenting us to his wives. These were two, wearing long tight transparent dresses. The older, Amenardis, was a little taller than I, handsome in a bold angular way, with a full, richly curved body, like a black-haired Hera. As the Poet said, she moved a goddess and she looked a queen.

The younger, Thoueris, was a real little beauty, albeit plainly pregnant. She held a lotus, at which she sniffed from time to time.

Tis showed us about his house while smells of cookery pursued us. His greatest enthusiasm was reserved for the curios in the great hall.

"This," he said, "is the very sword that Alexander wielded at Issos."

"No offense intended, sir," I said, "but how can you be sure of the origin of such a keepsake?"

"A good question, O Chares. It were easy for some dealer to palm off any old blade on me with such a tale, think you? Well, I have traced the ownership of this sword back through former owners, and my agents have questioned those who still live, so there is little chance of my being fooled. Now this"—he held up a hideous little skull-faced figure carved in ivory of a curious hue, mottled with brown as if it had been aged in the ground for centuries—"is Tarn, the goddess of death of the Hyperboreans. This is the wand of a Hyrkanian sorcerer who rashly conjured up an invisible monster, which devoured him on the spot. His apprentice was so upset by the sight that he abandoned sorcery and sold the tools of his late master's trade, and thus this rod of power came into my hands." Tis handed me a shiny black stick with a golden gryphon on its head. "Have a care at whom you point that."

I said: "If I saw my master perish in such a manner, I doubt if 'upset' would be a strong enough word to describe my feeling."

Tis laughed. "Blame my imperfect Greek, best one. This cup is said—but this I assert not, for want of proof—to have come from the secret Arabian city of Oukar, where dwells a cult of such surpassing wickedness that its votaries have given up all the more usual sins as too respectable. This vessel, it is said, was used to catch the blood in some of their less abominable rites."

Onas had been following this catalogue of Bergaean wonders with bulging eyes. Now he said: "Master Tis, have you a copy of the terrible *Book of Thôth*?"

Tis smiled. "While I do not often confess it, I do possess a copy. However, I keep it safely locked up. Were I to show it to any chance visitor, he might, as many are wont to do, begin reading its spells aloud—you know, whispering or at least moving his lips—and then the gods only know what might happen. The less perilous rolls of my library are in here."

Tis led us into his library. All the walls, save for the door and window, were covered from floor to ceiling with bookcases. Most of the pigeonholes held scrolls, from the ends of which hung tags bearing the titles. Tis explained:

"This side comprises works in Egyptian; that side holds books in Greek; yonder section contains works in other tongues. Know, that I have devised an ingenious scheme to make it easier to find a book. In the Greek section all the authors whose names begin with *alpha* are placed here at the beginning of the section; then all those beginning with *beta*, and so on through the alpha-beta. I have done the same thing for my Egyptian collection, though of course the characters differ."

"By the!" I said. "I wish that some libraries, in which I've spent hours hunting for one title, had been arranged thus."

"I am rather proud of it myself," said Tis. "In fact, I wonder why nobody has thought of it before."

I asked: "Are all these books and rarities that you have shown us things that you mean to keep, or do you deal in them?"

Tis said: "I am a dealer in antiquities, curios, and used goods. My agents travel far and wide, seeking objects suitable for my trade." His wide mouth curled into a smile. "When I buy a thing, it is but a bit of time-worn trash, but when I come to sell, lo! that selfsame article has become a priceless antiquity.

"Now, the best of my purchases I keep for my own pleasure; the rest I sell. The trade goods repose in my warehouses, but those you see here are meant to stay. Not even the treasure of the Persian kings would persuade me to part with them. For I am at heart a romantic sentimentalist, no mere moneygrubber. I toil not merely to garner wealth but also to enjoy the sight of baubles like that sword of Alexander, to savor its touch and to relish its soul-stirring history."

"Such things have mighty magical powers," said Onas.

"Indeed they do," replied our host. "The gods grant that I never have occasion to use these powers against those whom I deemed my friends."

We went in to dinner with the wives of our host, as is customary in many foreign lands. Since Manethôs, as a priest, was allowed but a meager diet of certain plain foods and might not eat pork, mutton, fish, onions, and many other wholesome victuals, Tis had caused him to be given a special ascetic's repast.

During dinner I observed that Tis kept fussing over Thoueris, the younger wife, while ignoring Amenardis, the older. Although the latter made no comment, her looks revealed that she did not relish such treatment. Thoueris kept saying something in Egyptian, over and over in a high whining voice. I asked Amenardis what this meant.

"She want to spend the day in town," said Amenardis in a rich, throaty voice that made each word of her garbled Greek seem like a caress. "Tomorrow day of bullfight at the temple of Apis. She want to see."

"Who fights whom?"

"Two bulls fight. Poke with horns."

"Is one of these the sacred Apis bull?"

"*Oser hena Iset*, no! Just common mortal bulls. Great crowd come, see which bull win. Bet much money. Make much noise."

"I shouldn't think a pushing, yelling crowd would be any place for a pregnant girl."

Amenardis shrugged, her full, jutting breasts straining the front of her thin, tight gown, which clung to the contours of her small virginal nipples as faithfully as a casting in beeswax. "Pregnant women get strange desires."

"I've heard of their lusting for curious foods, but this is the first time I have seen one lust for a bullfight."

"Also want Tis to buy her necklace. He promise one if she pass third month without—how you say—miscarriage. Now he try to put off; she say he must."

"That, at least, I can understand," I said, and went on to converse with Amenardis. Although her Greek was poor, we managed. She urged me to tell her of my achievements and ambitions; so, naturally,

I found her charming. She could also jest in a tongue whereof she was not master. She said:

"And when you build the most big statue man can make, what you do then?"

"I don't know. I had not thought beyond that."

"I tell you. When you finish statue, you climb up to the head, jump off, and kill self."

"In Hera's name, why? That were the time for rejoicing!"

"Ah, but if this statue the most big that man can build, you can never make one more big. So you have nothing to look forward to. I think you should wait until you are old before you build statue. You nice boy. I not like to see you dead soon." She drew back her head and looked at me from under lowered lids. The effect was somehow as if she were looking up from a pillow.

"I'm a bit older than I look!" declared I.

"You know, I tell you secret. It other way round with me! Living with Tis make me look more old than I am."

"Come, madam, you are no older than I." (I judged Amenardis to be above five years older than I, in fact.)

"Ha! How nice if true. But I not mind being old lady. Modern Greek sculptors make statues of beggars, old ladies, and ugly things like that. So maybe you make statue of me."

"When the war is over," I said, "I shall be glad to. You would make a fine statue, having a strong bone structure."

"Strong bones not what men like in Egypt, alas! Like little soft plump girls, like kittens." She shot a lethal glance at Thoueris. "Nobody mistake me for kitten, even if I say *mêou, mêou*."

So went our chaff. By the end of our repast we were so absorbed in each other that we ignored the other diners in a way that was neither courteous nor prudent. Tis, though too much taken up with Thoueris to pay much heed to his older wife, and too self-controlled to show his emotions readily, still cast me a veiled glance that reined in my spirit.

After dinner the ladies withdrew. My eyes followed Amenardis out while my heart pounded. Tis called for more wine and said:

"Now to business, gentlemen. Seek you a robe, once belonging to Demetrios Antigonou, stolen from you at Tamia—this a few days past?"

I spoke: "That's true, sir. But how did you know?"

"The bats whispered a rumor in my ears as they fluttered through the dusk, and I got further details from Manethôs and Onas whilst you so charmingly entertained my wife. Can you tell me of this garment in more detail?"

"It's a silken robe of Persian cut, with long sleeves, made for a powerful man over six feet tall. It is a light grayish blue, with a purple strip one digit wide along the edges, and with stars and astronomical symbols worked in golden thread and spangles all over it."

"What say you it were worth if bought in the mart?"

"I don't know; those who deal in textiles can tell you better. I think I could have it copied for—say, five pounds."

Tis: "It were more in Egypt, because we have as yet but little domestic manufacture of silk, and there is an import tariff to pay. Know you our Egyptian custom for the recovery of stolen goods?"

"Yes. What is the going rate?"

"For centuries it has been one-fourth of the value of the goods. A thief who asked more would deem himself dishonest. However, we have here more to consider than mere market value. This is a special robe, destined to special uses. It were worth more to Rhodes than a similar robe, not made by Demetrios' wife for her husband on his assumption of royal rank. Do you understand?"

"You're saying that this robe's sentimental associations would give it more than its ordinary value."

"Aye, sir."

"How much more are you thinking of?"

"Oh—perhaps a total value of a hundred and twenty pounds."

"Two talents!" I cried, 'That's fantastic, sir! I'm sure you would never get so much from Rhodes. Anyway, I brought no such sums with me, but only enough to pay the expenses of the journey. Our orders were to recover the garment, by force of arms if need be; not to ransom it."

Tis shrugged. "Remember, I am but an agent, and I have not yet even found your robe. I expected not that you would bear such a sum upon you. However, you could, once a bargain had been struck, return to your ship and obtain the money from your captain, who no doubt carries funds for emergencies."

"I don't think this plan is practical, sir. Even if Python would pay so fabulous a price, our city is under siege. There is no time for me to travel up and down the Nile between Tamiathis and Memphis, bearing offers back and forth while you and Python come together on price. If you locate your thieves and learn what they demand, why can't you come to Tamiathis with us and do your chaffering face to face?"

"My business affairs do not permit. It were easier for your Captain Python to come hither."

"But he must stay with his ship, to oversee its repair and keep his crew in order. All I really need to know is where the polluted gown is, and my comrades and I will get it or die trying."

Tis looked shocked. "My dear sir, are you suggesting that I betray my clients? That were dishonorable!"

I decided to take a worldly line with this dubious antiquarian. "Look, old boy," I said, "you get a commission on these deals, don't you?"

Tis smiled. "You cannot expect me to engage in so speculative a business without recompense, though in Egypt it is considered more polite not to bring the matter up so baldly."

"Excuse my foreign crudity, but what's the going rate for making such arrangements?"

"One-third of the sum paid to the thieves."

"So the higher the price, the better for you?"

"Aye, unless the price be set so high that the whole deal fall through. In that case I lose my time and risk my person for nought."

"Perhaps if you enabled us to locate and recover the robe by force of arms, we could pay you good round sum, which you would not have to divide with anybody. Either the thieves would all be dead, or we should be."

"By Bakchos, you horrify me, young sir, with such bloodthirsty talk! I know not how the Ionians can consider themselves cultured, so long as they take so readily to throat-cutting." (Egyptians have a habit of calling all Hellenes "Ionians," whether they be such or not.)

"Aside from that, what about it?"

"Nay, Master Chares, you misjudge me. I have a position and a reputation, which I hope will continue to serve me long after you have departed from the land of Chem. I will not risk all of that for a single quick gain. However, perhaps I could send a trusted agent to Tamiathis with you to negotiate.

"In any case," continued Tis, yawning, "this is all bootless speculation. I know not where your robe is, or in whose hands. It may have passed on into the south—to Kenê or Koptos or Neth-Ammon—and thus be out of my jurisdiction. However, if you will make yourselves at home here, I will put out inquiries and consult certain occult sources of knowledge. Within a few days we should know better where we stand."

We retired. Manethôs, being a priest, and I, as the commander of the expedition, had rooms to ourselves. The others shared a large guest room. I slept ill, although I was tired from hiking about Memphis, and the bed of ivory and ebony was the most luxurious that I had ever occupied.

When I read over the foregoing account of my talk with Tis, I am struck by the impression I have given of my own brisk competence. This is false. While I spoke those words—or at least words much like them—to Tis, my speech was mechanical. Half my mind was on the dialogue while the other half whirled in confusion about one thought: the thought of Tis's wife, Amenardis.

That night I cared not a copper half-farthing about Demetrios' robe, or my art, or even the fate of beautiful Rhodes. All that really concerned me was to see this fascinating woman again and to speak to her.

Perhaps, even, to touch her.

Book VII

TIS

I was eating my morning sop when Manethôs and Phiôps, the workman from his temple, came into the courtyard. The latter bore a pick and shovel, which he gave to Tis's head gardener.

"We have dug a grave for my poor little Satenbastis," said Manethôs. (This meant that Phiôps had dug while Manethôs directed, for the youthful priest was not the sort of man to lay hand to tool if he could help it.) "This afternoon I shall fetch a fellow priest to assist me with the sacred rites."

"Who is for town with me?" said Tis, dipping his sop. "This morning will be given to buying Thoueris' necklace; this afternoon to the bullfight. You, Onas, must come with us this morning, as I trust your judgment in jewelry beyond my own."

"I shall be glad to help," said Onas. "But I wonder why you buy not a piece for your wife at wholesale in the course of your business."

Tis spread his hands helplessly. "You know women. She has set her heart upon a collar displayed by Men the goldsmith, made of amethysts in a golden setting. It is up to me to chaffer Men down without letting him know that I simply must have this bauble. Your duty, my dear Onas, will be chiefly to sneer at Men's goods and find fault with them."

I said: "Sir, you won't forget to pursue our special inquiry?"

"Patience, patience, my dear young man! With patience is the baboon taught to gather coconuts. Come you with us?"

"I thank you, but what I really need is to meet some Egyptian sculptor who can tell me about the techniques employed on those colossi in Memphis."

"I can help you there," said Manethôs. "This morning go I to the shop of Harmaïs the tombstone maker, to order a stone for Satenbastis. If you take not too long, I can interpret for you."

Berosos announced his intention of going with Tis, while Dikaiarchos said: "Thank you, but I have had my fill of sight-seeing for the nonce. Besides, yesterday's tramp made me realize my age. May I lurk in your library? Some of the titles there I have not read."

And so it was arranged. After a delay (caused, as usual, by Onas' tardiness) we climbed into a large four-wheeled carriage of the Persian type, drawn by a pair of whites with ostrich-plume crowns affixed to their crownpieces. Tis's coachman drove us across the canal, through the groves and gardens of the suburbs, through the Great White Wall, and into Memphis. Here the traffic slowed us to a crawl.

"It waxes worse every year," said Tis, mopping his broad face. "Ever harder it is to find a place to leave one's carriage. The police and soldiery harry one to move on, lest traffic be blocked." He spoke in Egyptian to the coachman, then said: "Psammos will drop us here, as we can walk the rest of the way faster than ride. He will leave the car at a public stable and wait upon me at Men's shop. If we get our errands done in time, let us all meet at Zer's inn for lunch, eh? It is a respectable place."

While the rest followed Tis toward his goldsmithery, I accompanied Manethôs to his stonecutter. Harmaïs was a burly man, blind in one eye, with whom Manethôs held a long conference on the monument to Manethôs' lamented pussycat.

Then, with the priest interpreting, I tried to learn something of Egyptian methods of sculpture. I will not repeat this labored and halting conversation. Manethôs, for all his fluency in Greek, had never learnt the technical terms of sculpture either in my tongue or his own and was at his wits' end to convey Harmaïs' and my meanings, one to the other.

Although the Egyptians are marvelous draftsmen and excellent masons, I soon discovered that there was little for me to learn, professionally, in this ancient land. For one thing, the Egyptians have a rigid and absurdly detailed set of canons of proportion, arrived at thousands of years ago and never changed since.

They also employ a limited set of inflexible, formal stances to which all statues conform. These poses are like those one sees in very old Greek statues, such as are kept as holy relics in some temples. This is natural, as we Hellenes first learnt the arts from the Egyptians. But we have gone far beyond them. An Egyptian sculptor would deem it shocking to portray a subject in a lifelike pose or to make a statue look like the individual depicted.

"Look!" said Harmaïs, proudly unrolling a sheet of papyrus. "This is a sketch of the new relief of King Ptolemaios, which I shall execute on a wall of the temple of Phtha."

I should have laughed had not good manners forbidden. Here stood this Macedonian adventurer—in real life a short, stout man—in the guise of a conventional Egyptian king: a slender, delicate-looking person, wearing only a linen loincloth, a towering crown, and a broad Egyptian necklace, raising his hands in the Egyptian gesture of homage to the gods. Over his head and beneath his feet crawled those little processions of men, beasts, birds, and flowers wherewith the Egyptians write their language.

I thanked Harmaïs and took my leave. For a time we lingered about the colossi at the temenos of Phtha, brushing off the guides who swarmed about us like flies about offal. Then we joined our friends at Zer's.

"The polluted necklace is not yet bought," said Tis. "Though fleered and sneered we for hours, Men has not yet met my price. Onas' fault is that he is too honest and open. When he likes a piece, it is hard for him not to show his true feeling. Howsoever, we will have another try this afternoon, after the bullfight. Are you with us, Master Chares?"

"Thank you," I said, "but if you don't mind, I will return to your house. I'm still stiff and sore from being thrown as from a heavy catapult yesterday."

"By the gods, what is this?" said Tis. "I saw that you bore bruises but did not think it polite to ask about them."

I told of my reception by the strategos Alkman.

"I am sorry to hear that," said Tis. "Many a time and oft have I warned Alkman—" He paused.

"You must know him well," said I. "I should think twice before admonishing this two-eyed Polyphemos."

"I have met him," said Tis shortly.

"Do you and he do business together?"

"Not really. Have some more wine, will you not? And try these honey scones. Have another sardine!"

Manethôs' eyes and mine met in a brief glance of shared suspicion. Soon the priest arose, saying: "I must be off to arrange the funeral."

Berosos said to Tis: "With due respect, sir, never have I seen a folk so mad about funerals as your countrymen. Since men die not often enough to suit them, equally sumptuous rites they hold for bulls and cats and other pets."

I also took my leave. Instead of returning at once to the house of Tis, I wandered down to the waterfront and found the *Hathor*. In the boat, Horos played checkers with a fellow boatman while Zazamanx mended cordage.

"You go back to Tamiathis now?" said Horos.

"Not yet. But I want you to stay close by your boat for the next day or two. We may wish to push off in a hurry."

"You kill somebody, maybe?" said he, grinning brightly.

"Not yet," I said.

For part of the return journey, I solicited a ride in a two-horse chariot, driven by a sporting young gentleman on his way to the desert for a shot at a lion. Although the ride saved me a weary walk, the youth drove at a pace that reduced me to speechless terror. I have never been at ease around horses, and to go bouncing and banging along in this flimsy little car at full gallop frightened me more than all of Demetrios' spears and missiles.

My heart pounded as I neared the house of Tis. In truth, my bruises were nothing. My real reason for returning ahead of the others was to see Amenardis alone.

The Nubian giant admitted me. As I entered the house, Dikaiarchos' deep voice boomed from the library.

"O Chares!" he said. "Look at this."

In the library Dikaiarchos showed me a roll. "It looks like Thoukydides' *Peloponnesian War*," I said.

"Ah, but look there!" He pointed a knobby finger.

I read, in small neat writing on the yellow papyrus: "Property of the Library of Kôs."

"Are there any more like this?" I asked.

"I think not, or at least not many. I have been through many of these rolls, and this is the only such legend that I have found. However, I have discovered evidence that somebody has erased similar legends on some of the other books with pumice."

"The men of the phalanx begin to take their proper places," I said. "By a slip at lunch, Tis admitted that he's intimate with Alkman. I think we have here one of those archthieves whereof Tauros and Manethôs have told us. Semken and Alexis, I doubt not, work for him, stealing books from far and near. I'd wager that, had we the librarians of Kôs and Rhodes with us, they could identify many of their stolen scrolls. And this explains why Alkman used me with such barbarity; he knew at once whom I was after and foresaw trouble for his private dealings with Tis, were I encouraged to pursue my quest in Memphis."

"Had he been cleverer," said Dikaiarchos, "he would have smiled sweetly and sent you upriver to Thebes and beyond on a false scent. But now, what shall we do?"

"I don't know; be prepared for anything. I've told Horos to stand by for a hurried departure. The polluted robe may be in this very house."

Said Dikaiarchos: "If Alkman be hand in glove with Tis, I don't think it would get us far to complain to the strategos."

"On the contrary, he'd probably hang us all for blasphemy." I caught my breath. "Excuse me."

Having glimpsed Amenardis in the garden, I went out to her. We fell into talk, walking slowly among the flower beds. At first we exchanged conventional greetings and compliments, though when we looked into each other's eyes I do not think either of us was deceived about what was going to happen.

"Did Tis get necklace for Thoueris?" she asked in her deep, caressing voice.

"He hadn't when I saw him at lunch, but he means to beat down Men some more this afternoon. It must be a costly piece."

"That so. I see it in shop of Men. Tis never give me one like that."

"Why not, dear Amenardis?"

"Because I never bear child. I drink Nile water; I pray to Isis; I take medicine the doctor give. Nothing do any good. So now Thoueris get all the—how you say—attention."

I was tempted to remark that the only effect of Nile water on me had been to give me a flux, but I did not know if such a jest would offend. I said:

"It must be hard for you, after giving him all those years."

She muttered: "*Neterou nophrou!* Sometimes I think I endure it no more. Run away."

"If the right man offered to take you with him, would you consider it seriously?"

She looked at me sidelong. "Maybe. What think you, Chares?"

"I think that if I get out of here alive, I might be the right man."

"Alive? What you afraid of?"

I smiled. "Come, my dear, not everything is what it seems in the house of Tis."

"How you mean?"

"Oh, you know as well as I. Tis calls himself a trader in used goods, but I don't think he pays for all the things he sells."

"You too smart for own good, Chares. You let Tis know you think that—" She made a clucking sound to indicate a throat-cutting, and her voice sank to a whisper. "He suspect you know, now, I think."

"It's true, though, is it not?"

"Maybe. What would you do? Alkman no help you."

"I had already figured that out."

"I no help you if I stay here with Tis. While I his wife, Tis's fortune my fortune."

"Help me to get Demetrios' robe back, and flee with me to Rhodes!" I urged.

"Oh? You like me?"

"Darling, I—I'm mad with love of you. I'm no orator, but from the moment I saw you I haven't been able to think of anything else."

"You nice boy. Maybe I love you, too, a little. We see." She looked at the sun. "Bullfight already started. Must hurry to show you where the robe kept."

I followed her into the house. First she went into the kitchen and lit a rushlight from the hearthfire. She fixed this in a holder and brought it into Tis's bedroom. The sight of Tis's broad bed drove me nearly mad with desire. I caught Amenardis' eye and indicated the bed.

"In house full of servants? You crazy?" she said.

Amenardis went to a wooden panel at one side, ornately carved with reliefs of coiling cobras. She twisted an ornamental knob, which turned out to be the handle of a latch. With a quick look at the door to make sure that none was near, she opened the panel and stepped in. I followed. She closed the secret door behind me.

The rushlight discovered walls of brown brick and a stair leading down. I descended cautiously until, I judged, we were wholly below ground. Then the tunnel ran almost straight; the brick gave place to solid rock, roughhewn.

Amenardis moved slowly so as not to extinguish the rushlight. I could see little but her silhouette against the feeble yellow light and a few feet of wall, floor, and ceiling. With a gown of gossamer and the light on the far side of her, she might as well have been nude.

The tunnel ran on and on, now and then bending a little. Something like a cobweb brushed my face; I almost cried out, snatching at the stuff with my fingers. There was no sound but our breathing and the scuff of our shoes on the dusty stone floor—and, perhaps, the faint rustle of some creature of the underground, surprised out of its burrow.

We walked for at least five or six furlongs. Then Amenardis said: "Watch step!"

We passed a couple of side tunnels, and our passage bent this way and that. Then it seemed to come to a blank end.

Amenardis pushed open a door. The rushlight wavered as she stepped down.

We stood in a spacious underground chamber, perhaps twenty by fifty feet. Three sides were hewn from soft rock while the fourth was closed by a wall of brick.

The door through which we had come was a thin flat wooden structure, coated with plaster on the chamber side and modeled and painted to look like the rock, with an irregularity that would serve as a handle to open it. In a strong light I do not think it would have befooled anybody, but by rushlight, especially if you were not looking for it, you would never have noticed it.

The central part of the chamber was taken up by a colossal sarcophagus of sable stone, such as might have held the body of a Titan or a Kyklops. It towered up over our heads.

"What *is* this?" I whispered. "I've never seen the like."

Amenardis waved at the sarcophagus. "Coffin of Apis bull. You in rooms under the temple of Osiris. Tis have men dig tunnel, take over this room for his band and loot. Nobody ever come in here, since the coffin was rolled in and entrance closed up."

I looked more closely at the sarcophagus. It was made of one single piece of polished black granite with a close-fitting lid. It was, I should judge, over twelve feet long and eight wide, and almost as high as it was long. The thing must have weighed hundreds—nay, thousands—of talents. I could see why "all Memphis" had to turn out to haul such monstrous objects from the city to this temple in the desert.

"Is the bull in there?" I asked. In my excited fancy the vast lid rose up and an angry deity issued forth.

"No. Tis cut hole in the sarcophagus, make door. Cut up mummy of bull and take out to make room for loot. I not see for years, since Tis marry Thoueris."

She searched along the end of the sarcophagus, low down. At last she said: "Here door!"

I slid my fingers along the granite and felt the crack. The door was big enough for a stooping man to go through. The insetting of this door, too, had been a masterly job. My fingers found the gamma-shaped slot for the key.

"Locked," said Amenardis in a despondent tone. "No have key. Can you pick this lock?"

"Alas, no! Do you know where Tis keeps the key?"

"Keep one on string around neck. Have other, spare, but I not know where he hide. Sorry. I no good to you after all." She began to weep quietly.

"On the contrary, my darling, this is a great stride forward. Now that I know where the accursed robe is, perhaps you can find that spare key, or I can learn how to pick the lock, or something. Everything is fine and I love you."

"You do? You not just say that to make me help you?"

"Of course not!"

I took the rushlight from her, set it on the floor, and took her in my arms. Her rich, thinly clad body seemed to melt into mine with a gentle but irresistible gliding, writhing motion.

When passion drives, a floor of rock thinly covered with sand is as good as a golden couch.

Later Amenardis said: "Chares! Hurry! Tis come back from city any time!"

Feeling magnificent, albeit a little lightheaded, I made myself presentable and picked up the rushlight. As I neared the door of the tunnel, something moved at floor level. When I stooped to see, I got a shock. There crouched a large black scorpion, hoisting its tail over its back and spreading its nippers.

I gave a grunt of dismay and stepped back, bumping into Amenardis.

"Is—is Tis a sorcerer who keeps familiar spirits to spy upon his people?" I said, trying to keep my teeth from chattering.

"Oh, that!" said Amenardis. "Step on it. Your shoes thicker than mine."

The scorpion scuttled. I brought my foot down upon it, albeit with loathing. "Let's get out of here," I said. "*Rhou-ek.*"

She gave a low laugh. "You mean *rhou-en*, unless you want to stay here while I go."

"The gods forbid!" I found the plaster-covered door and blundered through.

"Your friend Onas," said Tis at dinner, "has been at me all day to give him a glimpse of the dread *Book of Thôth*. In sooth, he drove a hard bargain with me, that he would not help me in the final haggle with Men unless I would fulfill his desire." The dealer in antiquities cast a possessive glance upon the splendid gorget of gold and amethysts that gleamed on Thoueris' neck.

"So," continued Tis, "I have—perhaps rashly—agreed to show it to him, this very night. For magical reasons, which as fellow wizards you all appreciate, this book must be scanned only at midnight."

"Are we all invited?" said Dikaiarchos.

"Certainly, my dear sir. I should be unhappy if any of you failed to come."

Berosos said: "Against rash adventures tonight the stars have warned me."

"Oh, you and your stars!" said Onas.

"And who won twenty drachmai by betting on the red bull, on whom he had cast a rough horoscope and so knew it would win?"

Manethôs: "Berosos, if the Divine Wisdom watches over me, I think it will also watch over you—even though you worship it with corrupt Babylonian rites."

Onas, Berosos, and I had brought our short artilleryman's swords on the journey, but Berosos had left his in charge of Horos. He pleaded that he would be unable to use it, and he disliked its weight and inconvenience. Before midnight Onas and I strapped our swords to our thighs and donned our military kilts, which hid the weapons. Then we went forth to meet our host.

Tis handed me a bronzen lamp, which sputtered and sent forth a powerful stench of castor oil. Dikaiarchos, wrapped in a voluminous cloak against the chill of the desert night, got another; so did Berosos, while Tis bore one himself.

"Come," said he. "You are about to see something few men know of."

He led us into his bedroom and opened the secret door. "In you go; watch the steps. Go straight along the tunnel."

Holding my lamp high, I descended the steps for the second time. Tis followed.

Ahead, my people trudged in single file, like a procession of ghosts. The lamplight flickered and flared, throwing weird shadows on the rough dun walls, as if the animal-headed gods of Egypt were keeping pace with us.

As we came to the first fork in the tunnel, Tis called out: "Stand, pray. Let me by."

He squeezed past us and took the lead. I passed the side tunnels with an uneasy glance, wishing I knew whither they went and whether indeed they were empty.

Tis opened the door at the end of the tunnel and ushered us into the burial chamber. While my comrades gasped at the sight of the vast black sarcophagus, Tis explained where we were, adding:

"You must all swear secrecy about what you see here. The priests of Osiris might not like my making so free with their catacomb for warehouse space. Will you hold this lamp, pray?"

Tis handed the lamp to Manethôs and brought out a key from his bosom. It was a short, heavy, forked bronze key of the new type, which throws the bolt by a single twist of the wrist instead of by teasing it across by stages. He slipped the ring on the end of the key over his-middle finger and felt along the sarcophagus until he found the little door. He thrust the key in and turned it with a click. The door opened.

Standing behind Tis on tiptoe, I raised my lamp and moved my head this way and that, to see as much as I could of the inside of the sarcophagus. I had a glimpse of shelving piled with goods: precious metals, jewels, silks, and above all with books, great stacks of them.

Tis, bending double, reached inside. Then he backed out and straightened up. In one hand he held a folded piece of textile; in the other, a scroll.

"Here, Onas," he said, proffering the scroll.

Onas took the scroll and began to unroll it. "Hold your lamp steady, Berosos," he said. "I cannot see to read. By the First Ennead, it is the genuine—"

I spoke to Tis: "Sir, what's that in your other hand?"

The mass of fabric which he held, pale blue-gray with a glint of golden thread and spangles, looked in the dim light like that which we sought.

Tis did not try to deny it. "Careless of me, is it not? Being my latest acquisition, it was on top of the pile."

"But, if—" I began.

"It matters not," he said. "You shall not have this back. I am fain to keep it for my collection, and you will have no use for it where you are going."

Tis nodded toward the door. In through the portal filed a group of men. Some wore Egyptian skirts; some, Greek shirts. Some bore lanterns or links, but all carried knives in their hands.

"So much protection for your guests?" I said. "Or for you?"

"O Chares, almost I like you! Alas, that you should be so inquisitive as to learn more than is good for you to know!"

"I know nothing."

"A fine performance, my boy, but came I down here before dinner and traced two sets of fresh footprints. There were also marks other than those of feet."

The last of the newcomers, about ten in all, had now filed into the chamber. Among them I recognized Alexis and Semken. One hardy-looking rogue put his back to the door.

I said quickly: "O Tis, I can make it worth your while to forget your grudge and let us go."

The archthief shook his head. For an instant I thought he assented, but then I recalled that among many foreigners this gesture means "no" instead of "yes."

"Again you misjudge me," he said, "I have never forgotten a favor or forgiven a wrong."

"But, as a practical man—"

He smiled. "I told you that I am not a practical man. I am a romantic sentimentalist. But enough of talk." Stepping away from me, he raised his voice: "*Chatboutken sen!*"

I hurled my lamp at Tis's head. There was a thud of lamp on skull and a flash of spilt and flaming oil. Tis fell at Onas' feet while the lamp rebounded clanking against the wall of the chamber. The spilt oil begun to burn with little dancing flames.

At the same time I shouted: "*Onas!* Grab the robe and run!" I snatched at my kilt to get my hands on my sword.

Onas looked up with a vague, far-off expression, as when he had talked in his shop in Rhodes of the mystical powers of gems. "Eh? Robe? This book—"

Berosos squealed like a slaughtered pig as a knife flashed and buried its blade in his fat. He stumbled and floundered heavily toward the door.

I got my hand on my hilt. Dikaiarchos, with one sweeping motion, whirled the cloak from his body and around his left arm, leaving bare his right arm, which grasped his sword.

A man stepped between me and Tis's body, drawing back his arm for a stab.

Dikaiarchos lunged at the man holding the door. The latter made a parrying motion, but the geographer's long blade skewered him through the guts.

I got my sword out at last, wondering how many I could take to the land of the shades with me. With odds of two to one, I had little hope of getting away.

There was a blinding flash, as of lightning; then a whole sequence of them, which lighted up the chamber with a ghastly, glaring, bluish light. Men cried out in terror. I glimpsed Manethôs, holding his lamp out from his body with one hand while he tossed something into the flame with the other. Then I could see nothing but whirling splotches of color.

I had started toward the robe, which lay beside Tis, and had begun an overhand slash at the man before me. Blindly I felt the blade bite meat and heard a hoarse yell. Blindly I stumbled over a body and groped on the ground. The fingers of my left hand touched silk. I snatched the garment up, whipping it about my left forearm for a shield.

A knife flashed close to me, and I heard the rip of cloth as it grazed me but sliced my garments. I struck out and missed; struck again at a hand that came out of the whirling spots of color to grasp my arm, and cut into something.

As my vision cleared, I saw Dikaiarchos holding the door, keeping two thieves in play with his sword; Berosos stumbling through the door into the tunnel; Menethôs throwing his lamp at Alexis; near him, Onas, like one walking in sleep, starting for the door at last; and some of Tis's thieves rubbing their eyes, being still unable to see after Manethôs' tame levin bolts had blasted their sight. Blades flashed yellow in the lamplight.

I may be small but in those days I was not slow. I sprang toward the men who were closing in on Manethôs and Onas. I cut, thrust, and caught stab after stab in the folds of Demetrios' robe. Though my longer blade gave me an advantage, I had to keep whirling and shifting as if I were dancing the rhoditikos, to keep three or four from closing in upon me at once. I could not press an attack on any one far enough to finish him, lest the others pull me down from the rear.

I got a thrust home into the back of a man who was about to stab Manethôs, who in turn was lunging at another man with his knife. Tis stirred and made as if to rise.

Then Onas was through the door, and Manethôs after him. I had almost reached it when a man caught the fluttering end of Demetrios' robe. I cut at him and missed, pulled with all my might, heard the fabric tear, and fell over backwards as it parted. I leaped up and ran down the tunnel. After me pounded Dikaiarchos, shouting:

"Faster! Hurry!"

The only light in the tunnel came from the few lamps in the chamber that had not been extinguished in the fight. As we went farther from the door, this light grew dimmer and dimmer until we groped in darkness. Ahead, I heard the footfalls and heavy breathing of my comrades.

Then light came after us again: a faintly winking yellow gleam.

"They're after us with the lamps," panted Dikaiarchos. "But they cannot run too fast for fear of blowing them out. Keep on!"

As the fight in the chamber of the bull sarcophagus had seemed to take no time at all, the flight down the tunnel seemed to take forever, though in fact it cannot have used more than the tenth part of an hour.

We burst through the door into Tis's bedchamber. Amenardis and Thoueris, drawn to the room by the noise, screamed at the sight of our tattered garments and streaming blood. Dikaiarchos again showed the greatest presence of mind. Dashing around to the other side of Tis's great ivory and ebony bed, he gasped:

"Help me with this! Pile things against the door!"

With mighty grunts Dikaiarchos and Onas pushed the bed against the secret door, while the rest of us piled chairs, vases, statues, and other movables on and around the bed. As we did so, there came a pounding on the door. The points of knives appeared through the thin paneling as the thieves stabbed at it from the other side.

"What happened?" said Amenardis. "Tis dead?"

"No, a bump on the pate only," I said.

"You take me like you promise?"

"Surely. Tell our servants to gather our gear."

"You not wait," she said. "Tunnels have other entrances, out in the desert. Soon these thieves think of them."

"Grab your stuff and run, boys," I said. "Can anybody harness and drive Tis's wagon?"

"I can," said Onas.

While the rest of us cowed Tis's servants with our blades, Onas and Manethôs hitched up the whites by torchlight. We threw our belongings into the carriage and tumbled aboard. Onas cracked the whip; out of the stable we clattered.

At the gate the giant Nubian barred our way, waving a cudgel and shouting. While Onas disputed him, Dikaiarchos and I dropped out of the carriage on opposite sides. Dikaiarchos menaced him with a sword in front, and I threw myself against the backs of his knees from behind. Down went the giant with a yell. Dikaiarchos smote him smartly with the flat of his blade on his shaven crown. We dragged the unconscious man out of the way, each tugging on a leg, and resumed our journey.

When we leaped aboard the *Hathor* and awoke Horos and Zazamanx, the boatmen screamed with terror.

"You dead!" cried Horos. "Ghosts! All blood, blood, blood!"

"You'll be a ghost if you don't get this boat under way," I said. "Push off, quickly! Manethôs, I fear you must sacrifice your spare tunic for bandages."

"Take it," said the priest. "Berosos, I think, is the worst hurt."

The Babylonian, presenting the broadest target, had been stabbed in three places: arm, buttock, and a grazing cut along the ribs. In the flickering light of our link he looked greenish under his swarthiness. He groaned and cursed in guttural Syrian as Amenardis washed and bound his wounds.

Every one of us who had been in the fight had at least one cut or prick of some sort. Mine was a small stab through the skin over the shoulder blade.

"Tychê favored us tonight," said Dikaiarchos. "A digit this way or that, and some of these wounds had been mortal. Manethôs, what Thessalian wizardry did you work to make those flashing lights?"

The priest gave a quiet chuckle. "O Hellene, not meet is it that laymen should penetrate these arcane secrets. But since we are comrades in arms, I will tell you.

"Know that betimes we priests need a miracle to strengthen the faith of the unthinking masses. If the gods provide one not, we must do our poor best in their stead. Now, there grows a swamp moss which, gathered in due season, sheds seeds like fine impalpable powder, and this powder burns with the levinlike light you saw. Only, in my haste, I blistered my own hand somewhat with the flame, Seth take it!"

Although the etesian wind now blew against us, we moved more swiftly than on our way up the Nile. We left the mast down, as the sail would be usable only on a few sharp bends. Instead, we manned all four oars. The boatmen and the two servants, being unwounded, did most of the rowing, but we relieved them all from time to time. We kept to the middle of the stream to take advantage of the swifter current, to avoid shoals, and to keep out of range of bowshots from the bank.

Sleeping cities drifted darkly past: Troia, Babylon, Kerkesoura, and the village of Delta, where the Nile casts off its first fork, the small Pelusiac branch. The glittering stars wheeled closely overhead, brilliantly white with glints of red and green and blue. They paled as a horned moon came up from the east.

We all knew, I think, that our problems were far from over. But, what with wounds and weariness and fear of arousing attention, we held our peace and caught what sleep we could through the dark hours. Despite all, I was as happy as I have seldom been. I was in love; I had my loved one; and we had escaped, at least for now, from our common foe.

As the eastern sky turned to green and gold, Manethôs said: "O Chares, were it not well to look at the robe, to see what is left of it?"

"I've been afraid to look," I said, unfolding the garment. "*Oimoi!* What sort of ragged relic is this to give a king?"

The robe was in much worse case than I had thought. It was slashed in every direction, and about a third of it was missing altogether, where the thief had torn off a piece. Onas whistled and said:

"It is too bad, Chares, that you used the garment for a shield."

"Listen to him who speaks!" I cried. "If you'd snatched it up and run when I told you to, instead of mooning over your silly old book, we should have gotten through the door before the thieves could close in upon us. As things fell out, it was use the robe as I did or perish and lose it anyway."

"The book was just as important," said Onas. "With the *Book of Thôth* in our hands, it recks but little what our enemies do. We can amend any plight and retrieve any loss."

"Well, let's see you cast a spell to put the robe back into its pristine condition! Go on, what are you waiting for?"

Onas gave me a look wherein defiance struggled with apprehension. He got out the scroll, unrolled a cubit of it, and scanned its opening lines in the ruddy light of the rising sun. His lips moved. He frowned. His face fell, running down into despondent lines like a casting pattern of beeswax left too near the furnace.

After an instant more he silently handed the scroll to Manethôs and buried his head in his hands. As Manethôs scanned the book, his solemn, shaven face broke into a smile. He even gave a low laugh.

"Poor Onas!" he said. "This concerns the fabled *Book of Thôth*, forsooth, but it is not quite what he thought."

"What in the name of Herakles is it, man?" I asked.

Said Manethôs: "We have here a version of an old tale, long current in the land of Chem: the story of Sethenes Chamoïs. I will give you an abridged translation.

"There was a prince named Sethenes, surnamed Chamoïs, a son of the mighty King Rhameses Osymandyas. This Sethenes had made his life's work the study of the magical books in the Double House of Life, at the then capital of Neth-Ammon, which you Hellenes, for reasons I cannot fathom, call 'Thebes.'

"One day, fell Sethenes into talk with one of the king's sages. Now, Sethenes was a skeptic, like our friend Dikairachos here. 'All this talk of the vasty powers of magic,' quoth he, 'is nought but mummery wherewith to cozen the simple. Never have I seen a wizard whose thaumaturgies were aught but sleights and tricks prestigious.'

"'Be not so hasty, my son,' said the sage. 'Deeply into the arts theurgic have I delved; long have I pondered; far have I fared. I have read awful spells writ in blood on crumbling scrolls of human skin; I have talked with gibbering ghosts in ruined fanes by the light of the gibbous moon; I have communed with demons dire in secret ways beneath the pyramids. And I know better than to sneer at magic.'

"'Faugh, sirrah!' said Sethenes. 'An thou wouldst convince me, thou must needs monstrate to me.'

"'That I will,' said the wise one. 'I will tell thee of a place where lieth concealed a book of portentous power, writ by the great god Thôth himself: Thôth, scribe of the gods, orderer of the universe, record keeper of the dead, viceroy of the supreme Ammon-Ra, and god of wisdom and learning.

"'This book comprehendeth two fell spells. The first of these enchanteth heaven and earth, sea and sky, mountain and river. Whoso readeth it shall understand the birds as they fly and the serpents as they crawl, and shall call fishes to the surface of the sea. The second enableth one stark dead in his tomb to come to life; to rise into heaven; to see the sun traversing heaven with his company of gods; to see the moon in her courses, scouring the sky with her company of shining stars; and to see the fishes as they swim in the depths of the sea.'

"'And where lieth this marvelous volume, grandfather?' quoth Sethenes.

"'It reposeth in the tomb of the princely wizard Nepher-kaphtha of Memphis, my son. Go, an thou wilt, and wrest it from the shade of Nepher-kaphtha.'

"So Sethenes prevailed upon his brother, Inaros, to come with him unto Memphis. There, for three days and three nights, searched they for the tomb among the necropoleis that lie west of the city. And at last, behold, they found that for which they sought.

"Thereupon uttered Sethenes magical words of power, whereat the earth opened before him. Into the tomb descended Sethenes and his brother Inaros. Within the tomb there glowed a radiance that paled their torches. For in the tomb lay Nepher-kaphtha's sarcophagus and in the sarcophagus lay the veritable *Book of Thôth*, blazing with silvery light, like that of the moon when she standeth at full above the desert.

"Within the tomb, also, Sethenes descried the form of the *ka* or shade of Nepher-kaphtha; and not only that of the wizard but also those of his wife Aoura and his young son Meros as well. Sethenes knew from his pervestigations that Nepher-kaphtha's wife and son had been buried at Koptos, far up the Nile. Nonetheless, their shades had come down the river to dwell with that of their beloved husband and father.

"As Sethenes gazed upon the three shades, the shade of Nepher-kaphtha spake: 'What wouldst thou, mortal?'

"'I have come for the *Book of Thôth*, quoth Sethenes.

"'Thou shalt not have it,' said Nepher-kaphtha. 'It is mine, bought with my life and the lives of my family, and here by all the gods shall it stay!'

"'It will do thee no good to bluster,' said Sethenes, 'for I am stronger than all of you and will take the book for all that ye can do.'

"Then spake the shade of Aoura, the wife of Nepher-kaphtha: 'Take not the book, O Sethenes. Its possession brings woe and calamity. Already it hath done us such scathe as it could, and wherefore shouldst thou suffer in thy turn?'

"'Even so, I will take it,' said Sethenes.

"'Take it not until thou hast heard our tale,' said Aoura. 'Then, haply, wilt thou be less rash and rapacious.'

"'Speak, woman,' said Sethenes.

"'Know,' began Aoura, 'that my noble husband, Nepher-kaphtha, dedicated his life to the study of magic. Wide, vast, and deep were his investigations. He hath read texts so ancient that none but he could grasp their import; he hath taken counsel with hoary sages, haggard mystics, and faceless presences from other planes.

"'At last, for an hundred pieces of silver and two magnificent sarcophagi, he bought from a priest of Phtha the secret of the hiding place of the *Book of Thôth*. He learnt that the ibis-headed one, when he had written the book, inclosed it in a golden box. The golden box he placed in a silver box. The silver box he shut up in a box of palm wood. The wooden box he inclosed in a bronzen box. The box of bronze he placed in a box of iron, which he fastened round about with stubborn chains and sank in the Nile. By his magic he surrounded the box by serpents, scorpions, and other vermin, and coiled about the box lay a deathless serpent of gigantic size.

"'Taking us with him, Nepher-kaphtha proceeded to Koptos. There, after Nepher-kaphtha had offered sacrifice in the temple of Isis and Harpokrates, the high priest of Koptas wrought for Nepher-kaphtha a waxen model of a raft and workmen with their suitable tools. Whenas Nepher-kaphtha recited a cantrip over these things, they came to life and bore him out into the river. After three days and three nights of searching, a spell enabled Nepher-kaphtha to find the box. Another cantrip caused the waters of the Nile to part, so that he could clamber down a ladder to the bottom. A third spell put to flight the venomous vermin—all but the deathless snake, which reared and struck at him.

"'With his sword of burnished copper Nepher-kaphtha doughtily fought the supernatural serpent. Twice he cut it in twain, but each time the sundered parts clove together and the serpent resumed the conflict. A third time Nepher-kaphtha cut asunder its body. This time he sprinkled sand on the severed ends, so that, though strove they to join again, they could not by reason of the sand. Thus died the deathless serpent.

"'Then opened Nepher-kaphtha the boxes, took out the golden box, and returned to his raft. There he opened the golden box and drew forth the *Book of Thôth*. He read the first spell, which revealed to him all the secrets of heaven and earth. He read the second spell, which enabled him to see the sun rising in the heavens with all its company of gods. To make certain his memory of these spells, Nepher-kaphtha wrote out a copy thereof on papyrus, washed the ink off the papyrus with beer, and drank the beer.

"'But alas! The great god Thôth was wroth with us because of our act sacrilegious. He delated us to the Sun, the great Ammon-Ra, the chief and king of all the gods. Ammon-Ra therefore caused me and our son Meros to fall from the raft as it returned to Koptos and to drown.

"'Nepher-kaphtha mourned us and buried us at Koptos. Then he set off down the Nile to his home; but, or ever he reached Memphis, his grief became too great for him to bear. So cast he himself into the

Nile and was drowned in his turn. His kin recovered his body and buried it, together with the *Book of Thôth*, in the tomb wherein thou standest. I warn thee, therefore, that nought but disaster dire awaiteth thee if thou take the book.'

"'I will have the book, for all of that,' said Sethenes.

"Then up spake the shade of Nepher-kaphtha. 'Wilt hazard possession of the book on a game of draughts?' said he.

"'I will,' said Sethenes.

"So they began to play. Now, Sethenes was a mighty player of draughts, whom none could vanquish save only the great King Rhameses himself. When the shade of Nepher-kaphtha saw that he would surely lose, he essayed to win by cheating. He endeavored to move a piece out of turn when Sethenes was not looking.

"After this had happened twice, Sethenes cried: 'Out upon thee, false shade! This is not to be endured. Brother, fetch me my scroll of spells and cantrips.'

"And when his brother Inaros had fetched the scroll, Sethenes laid upon the shade of Nepher-kaphtha, and upon the shades of his wife and son, such an incantation that they were rendered powerless to let him from taking the book.

"Grasping the book, Sethenes read the two mighty spells and ascended unto heaven with a swiftness wonderful to behold. But as Sethenes departed, the shade of Nepher-kaphtha said to the shade of Aoura his wife: 'Not helpless yet am I, little sister. Yon jackanapes will soon be back with a knife and a rod in his hand and a pot of fire on his head, and glad to be rid of the book, I will warrant you.'

"Sethenes returned to his home at Neth-Ammon and took up again his study of magic. Now, however, came upon Sethenes the doom that Nepher-kaphtha and Aoura had foreseen. For he fell in love with a beautiful and evil woman, Taboubo. Such was the blindness of his passion for her that when she commanded him to slay his own children, he did so.

"When this dreadful deed became noised about, King Rhameses heard of the matter and straightway discovered all that had befallen Sethenes. So the king commanded Sethenes, that he should forthwith take back the *Book of Thôth* to the shade of Nepher-kaphtha, ere worse befell him. And this Sethenes did, with a knife and a rod in his hand and a pot of fire on his head, as the shade of Nepher-kaphtha had commanded him in a dream.

"When Sethenes came to the tomb of Nepher-kaphtha and descended thereinto, he found the three shades awaiting him. As he placed the book back in the sarcophagus, the shade of Nepher-kaphtha laughed and said: 'What said I erst to thee? Next time be not so hasty to spurn good counsel.' And Sethenes went away, and the tomb closed up again, and for aught any man knoweth the *Book of Thôth* lieth there yet, illuming the interior of the tomb by its silvery rays. So endeth this tale."

Manethôs rolled up the scroll. "That, my friends, is the story of Sethenes Chamoïs. As you heard, it speaks portentously of mighty spells but tells not how to cast them. I had heard the tale before and supposed the *Book of Thôth* to be but a figment of a storyteller's mind. After all, a priest of Thôth and temple scribe should know whether such a thing exists, if anybody does. However, when I heard Tis speak so confidently of possessing this book, I held my peace, wondering if I might not be mistaken and the book exist after all.

"Now, as we can see, Tis merely used a copy of this ancient legend as bait to lure us to his lair where he could set his bullies upon us. Had we not had some good men of their hands among us, our friends and colleagues had known nought of our fate, save that we went up the river to Memphis and there disappeared."

I said: "Let's forget about restoring the robe by magic. The problem remains: what shall we do? I don't think Captain Python will be any more pleased by getting back his robe in this condition than by not getting it back at all." To Onas I said: "Stop blubbering, man! We all commit blunders. If you'd atone for yours, help us think our way out of our plight."

There were mutterings about darning and patching, but nobody held out serious hope in that direction. It would take more than a clever housewife's needle to make this tattered bobtail into a kingly garment again.

We reached the first of the sharp-angled bows which the Nile describes between Delta and Athribis. Here we shifted places to relieve

Zazamanx at the oars, so that he could watch the channel. I asked Manethôs:

"Are we likely to be pursued, and if so, how far?"

"I know not. It would take time for Tis to recover his wits and set the pursuit in order. And how would his thieves pursue? I have seen no river boats following upon our wake.

"The swiftest way would be by horse; and, even so, the horses would have to be shipped across the river, because of our taking the Phatnitic fork. To get horses, Tis must needs arouse his crony Alkman and persuade that lion in human form to send forth a troop of cavalry. Mmm. Also, we have long since left the Province of the White Wall, where runs Alkman's writ. I doubt that even so forceful a fellow as he would send his horsemen galloping athwart his fellow strategoi's jurisdictions without their leave. To win their permission would consume precious time; nor is it easy, without guidance, to pick one's way among the labyrinth of canals that divides up the Delta. By noon today, the gods willing, shall we have two entire provinces on either bank between us and Alkman's land.

"So, provided that we row blisters on our hands and then row them off again today, we should be beyond immediate danger. But think not to settle down quietly anywhere in Egypt for a lengthy stay without being smelt out by Tis's knaves. I know something of how these archthieves work. One will send stabbers and poisoners after those who cross him, or persuade or bribe one of his fellow lords of the underworld, in whose territory a foe has taken refuge, to take up the quarrel on his behalf. Especially"—Manethôs dropped his voice and cast a glance toward Amenardis, who was looking at the robe—"if his unfriend has taken something that the archthief considers his."

"How far can we get today?" I asked.

Manethôs spoke in Egyptian to Horos, then said: "At this rate we should be in Bousiris by dinnertime."

Amenardis, holding up the remains of the robe, spoke: "Chares, no use trying to mend this thing. Must have another one made. Who you know who make things like this?"

Although as a man in love I was not inclined to find fault with Amenardis, I felt a slight stir of resentment at being told what to do in so peremptory a manner. However, an idea struck me with such force as to leave no room for pettier feelings.

"Zeus!" I cried. "The very thing! Azarias lives in Bousiris; he weaves silk; and he's promised to help me whenever I need assistance."

Manethôs looked as if he had tasted something sour. "Must you resort to this Judaean?" he said. "With a little time I could find you an Egyptian weaver who could do the work better."

"One who could weave silk?"

"Belike not; this is a new craft in the land of Chem. Only, I pray, believe the Judaean not when he fills you full of lies about our holy religion."

"What sort of lies?" I asked.

"That we perform abominable rites, that we worship brute beasts instead of true gods, and so forth. Foreigners who have never studied our religion often entertain mistaken notions about it. They hear the myths of Seth's cutting Osiris in pieces, and Isis' causing a serpent to bite Ra, and they suppose that we take all these tales literally."

"Why, don't you?"

"Well, that is true among the lower classes, who must have simple stories, literally believed, to strengthen their faith and to keep their feet on the path of virtue. But, I assure you, not true is it among the better educated, or among the priesthood—save, perhaps, among a small group of literal-minded reactionaries. The rest of us know that these tales are allegories, embodying symbolic truths. The sacred animals symbolize various aspects of divinity. The real Thôth is not a man with the head of an ibis; he is the symbol of cosmic intelligence. Isis and Osiris represent the moon and the sun respectively.

"Know, O Hellene, that the universe is ruled by a single super-agency or godhead, whom you call Zeus. This divinity, however, manifests itself in multiple ways. Ammon is the soul of the godhead; Ra is its head; Phtha is its body. Three in one; unity in triplicity."

"Do you mean that God is one and three at the same time?" said I. "That sounds like a paradox."

"Ah, that only shows you have not studied these mysteries. I will explain this holy trinity." Manethôs brought out his bronze drinking cup, which he always carried lest he be polluted by using common vessels. "Behold this cup. It is one, yet has it an inner surface, and an outer surface, and the metal which fills the space between the two. Therefore it, like the godhead, has a threefold manifestation...."

The priest went on in that vein for some time. Puzzled but thoughtful, I left him to take my turn at an oar. We swept again through the Delta, with its hazy air, its rustling palm groves of emerald green, its black wet earth, its creaking swapes, and its humming mosquitoes.

At Leontopolis we stopped to buy food and stretch our legs, presenting an ominous sight in our bloody bandages. At my request, Manethôs took us to the temple of Sechmetis, where the sacred lion and his mate are kept, for I had never seen a live lion. Two lazier-looking cats I never saw, sleeping in the sunshine and not moving save to flick their ears when the flies assailed them. We were told that they were the earthly incarnations of the god Sous and the goddess Tephnis. I suppose the fees the priests collected from us went in part to keep the god and goddess in beefsteaks.

Amenardis squeezed my arm. "Darling," she gurgled, "they beautiful. Someday you get me lion."

"Ye gods, woman, what would you do with a lion?"

"Make him obey."

"I'll wager you could, at that."

On the way back to the *Hathor* I asked Dikaiarchos: "Did you hear that sermon from Manethôs?"

"I couldn't help hearing, on so small a ship."

"I must be stupid," I said. "I don't doubt that his talk is full of profound hidden truths, but I find it terribly hard to understand."

Dikaiarchos laughed. "I'll tell you a secret, Chares. I cannot understand it, either."

"You, sir?"

"Yes. It may be that we are both stupid, or it may be that there is nothing to understand. It is a good practical rule that, if a man cannot explain himself in terms that any reasonably intelligent listener can comprehend, he doesn't know what he is talking about himself. So you need not feel that your orthodoxy is threatened by these finespun speculations."

"Oh, I'm not really orthodox, sir. Once I tended toward Theodoros' atheism."

"And what happened to change your course?"

"Well, certain of my prayers to Helios, in time of peril, were answered in a way that inclines me to return to the faith of my fathers. Theodoros' viewpoint may be logical, but it leaves one with none but mortal men to take as one's ideals; and men, I find, seldom merit such devotion. An artist needs such an ideal to give him stability and direction. Do you think that foolish of me?"

"Not if your religion really helps you to wisdom and virtue. I manage to be reasonably virtuous without a religion, but then we are not all made alike."

"Are you of Theodoros' opinion, then?" I asked.

"Not quite. I think he may be right about there being no gods or spirits, but I'm not so cocksure about asserting it as a proven fact. You might call my view 'agnosticism.'"

"Don't you find it disquieting never to know where you stand?"

Dikaiarchos chuckled. "I am often asked that question. The fact is that I like to live floating in a sea of doctrinal uncertainty. It is a good state of mind for a philosopher. Although most folk find it terrifying, it enables a man of thought more readily to seize upon small bits of authentic truth as they whirl past. The reason is that such a man's perception is not limited by a preconceived credo as one's physical vision is limited by the eye slits of a closed helmet.

"On the other hand, for lives of certain kinds the philosophical equivalent of a closed helmet is an expedient thing to wear, despite its inconveniences, for it softens the bangs and bumps which we frequently take from Fate's cudgel."

Long after dark, exhausted from rowing, we reached Bousiris. Because of the lateness of the hour, I put off my visit to Azarias until the following morning.

The weaver was overjoyed to see me again. When I explained my secret errand and showed him the remains of the robe, he lifted up his hands and invoked his god Iao.

"How lucky I am that I can try to repay you for saving my life!" he cried. "If it can be done, it shall be done. Come with me, my dear friend."

He took me to his storeroom and pulled down several bolts of undyed silk. He compared them, one after another, with the goods of the robe.

"This is the one," he said. "Feel it. How fortunate that you came not later! For I have an order for this bolt, and in a few days it had been gone. Remain here whilst I fetch my fellow workers."

Soon Azarias came back with men whom he presented as Isakos the dyer, Abramos the goldsmith, and Iesous the tailor. So swiftly flew the talk that I was unable to follow the Judaean dialect. At last Azarias turned to me.

"We can make you a duplicate of the original robe, closely enough like it so that none but an expert could tell them apart, in less than a ten-day."

"How much will this cost?"

"It shall cost you nought, save for some gold thread and sequins, which I must needs buy. Nay, nay, my friend, press me not, or I shall be offended. I will take care of all other expenses. Now you must stay for dinner."

"I must first go back to the boat, to tell my comrades of our good fortune. And may I bring a friend to dinner? A lady?"

"Surely, surely, anyone you like."

At the boat I said to Manethôs: "Your home lies less than an hour's sail from here. Why not have Horos run you and Phiôps down to Sebennytos and then return hither for us?"

"I suppose I ought," said the priest with a glum look. Remembering Onas' remark about Manethôs' domestic life, I surmised that he would have deferred his homecoming if he could have thought of an excuse. "Ere I go, O Chares, let me warn you against Judaean tricks! This fellow may be as virtuous as he pretends, but I would not trust one of them."

At dinner the weaver asked many questions about our adventures. I answered guardedly, not wishing to give away news that might help to put Tis on our track. Among other things he asked:

"Was it the Egyptian priest who betrayed you into the hands of your foes? It is what I should have expected of a slave of one of those false beast gods."

"No, on the contrary, Manethôs rendered us invaluable services."

"*Heach!*" he said. "You wait; he will forelay you yet. And then, say not that Azarias ben-Moses failed to warn you."

I said: "Be that as it may, he told me an interesting history of your people's having once conquered his and later being driven out."

"What pack of lies is this? Tell me!"

I repeated, as well as I could, Manethôs' tale of the conquests of Egypt by the Hyksôs. As I neared the end, I could see that Azarias was hard pressed to contain his emotions. He flushed, bounced in his seat, and muttered: "Lies! Lies!"

When I finished, he burst out: "Never in my life have I heard such an amass of slanderous falsehoods! I call on Iao to witness!" He waved his fists above his head. "It is false! It is a vile calumny! It is the utter opposite of the truth! Cursed be they who give currency to such a lying tale!

"Let me tell you what really happened. There was a Judaean named Ioseph, who was carried off to Egypt as a slave...."

It transpired that this Ioseph was thrown into jail as a result of trouble with his master's wife. Then, by several strokes of improbably good luck, he was freed and raised to the post of king's minister as a reward for interpreting the Egyptian king's dreams. In this exalted position he devised a scheme by which the king was enabled, during a famine, to get title to all the land in Egypt, save only that belonging to the temples. The grateful king permitted Ioseph to invite in his fellow tribesmen, who settled in Egypt. As in Manethôs' story, the Judaeans were shepherds, as many of them are to this day.

In time these shepherds so waxed in power and number that the Egyptians began to fear that so vigorous and warlike a folk would seize the mastery of the land and rule the Egyptians as slaves. So the king, a successor to the one who had befriended Ioseph, enslaved and persecuted the Judaeans, until a Judaean prophet and politician named Moses arose to their leadership. This Moses led them to revolt and flee across the Arabian wastes to Judaea.

In the meantime other tribes had occupied the land vacated by the Judaeans. The latter, however, exterminated the other tribes with great and bloody slaughters and re-occupied their former homeland, as their god directed them to do.

"And that is the absolute, literal truth," said Azarias, waving his forefinger under my nose. "Baseas! Fetch the sacred scroll of the Five Books to show our guest."

Azarias' eldest son went out and quickly returned with an embroidered cloth container, from which Azarias took a small scroll.

"Here, do you see?" said Azarias, unrolling the scroll and pointing to the lines of Judaean writing, which of course meant nothing to me. "These are the words of the lord Iao himself, so there is no question about their truth. Would that you were here longer, that I might convert you to the true religion! Of course you would have to be circumcised and give up your iniquitous trade of making graven images, but those are minor matters compared to the grace of the one true God.

"That fantastical tale about the Shepherd kings is the sort of libel those vile beast worshipers would devise," he continued, rolling up his scroll. Then he ranted on for an hour about the depravities of the Egyptian priesthood. Nothing that Amenardis or I could say diverted him from this subject.

Azarias, I decided, was a good man. He was, in Homer's words, a friend to human race, and most of the time was not bad company. But when he embarked upon this particular subject, he could be the biggest bore in the land of Chem.

I took my leave early, not only to escape the tirade but also to be alone with Amenardis. Onas had taken space at Kenamon's inn, so that Amenardis could better nurse poor Berosos, who suffered a fever from his wounds. My sweetling proved a vigorous and vigilant nurse who stood for no nonsense from her patient. For her and myself I obtained a private room. Onas himself went off to visit his kin.

There was little to do while waiting for Azarias and his fellow tradesmen to finish their copy of the robe. Twice a day I went to their houses to see how the work progressed; but to stand over a craftsman and breathe down his neck makes him nervous and causes bad work. I know.

On the morning of the third day after we reached Bousiris, Amenardis, Dikaiarchos, and I were lounging on the waterfront and watching the Nile flow past. I repeated to Dikaiarchos the story I had from Azarias about the Egyptian captivity of the Judaeans.

"Now here," said I, "we have two histories about the same set of peoples, flatly contradicting each other. Which should I believe? It's no use appealing to ancient records, because each disputant has his own records, and the two sets of writings disagree."

Dikaiarchos yawned. "I suppose one might settle the question by twenty or thirty years of independent historical research," he said. "Had I nothing more urgent to do, I could settle down in Egypt, learn to read this writing that uses snakes and owls for letters, and compose my own history. In fact, both the stories you heard are probably wrong, or at least much distorted. That is the way with historical traditions; they suffer sea changes in the handing down.

"There are, you will observe, some curious features of these stories. For instance, why should it take the Judaeans forty years to cross the land of Sinai? According to all the geographers, whereas this peninsula is certainly hot, barren, and rocky, it is no larger than the Peloponnesos, and so could be traversed in a ten-day or two, even afoot."

I said: "If the Judaeans' forebears were truly a race of blind, crippled, and leprous beggars, as in Manethôs' tale, it might take them forty years."

"Ah, but if they were, they could never have escaped the pursuit of the Egyptian king! No, what we have here are probably a few scraps of authentic fact, boiled up with a lot of myth and legend and patriotic fiction. And how, in this stew, shall we tell the false from the true? The answer is: We cannot."

"Whatever be the truth," said I, "all this happened long ago. So why should Manethôs and Azarias hate each other so, despite the fact that neither really knows the other? Each, taken by himself, is a pretty fine fellow. Yet each of them snarls like an angry dog at the mere mention of the other."

"You cannot expect men to be rational about national enmities," said Dikaiarchos. "As everyone knows, people like to have friends, but they also like to have enemies. A hereditary foe is a useful thing to have. It gives you somebody to feel superior to; it provides a handy target for all the furies and hatreds which you have boiling around inside you but which you dare not direct at those nearer you. So, if you truly convinced either one of our friends that the other was really a good, honest, and kindly man, you would do him no service, for you would rob him of his dearly cherished enmity."

"Do you think such enmities a good thing, then?"

"Herakles, no! They cause all the hideous massacres and cruelties and destructions that I have set forth in my book. I merely state that this is how most men seem to be made, and I see no easy way of changing them. Even the godlike Platon, when he imagined his ideal states, assumed that they would be at intermittent war with their neighbors, and he therefore bestowed upon them strength in arms enough to defeat all comers. Of course he did not live to see such mighty captains in the field as Alexander and Demetrios. If he had, he might not have been so sure that his little city-states could be defended by virtuous valor alone."

"We're testing that theory in Rhodes right now," I said. "Come around in another year and see how we made out—*Papai!* Here's Manethôs again."

The lean priest rode up on the back of one of the big white Egyptian asses. "Rejoice, O Chares!" he said, dismounting. "At my temple I found news which so nearly touches you that I thought it my duty to warn you."

"My dear Manethôs!" I said, springing up to take the ass's bridle. "Tell me, by all means. Could I first get you something to wash the dust of the journey from your throat? Pray excuse us, O Dikaiarchos."

Manethôs let me steer him to a tavern and pour beer into his private bronze cup. When he had quenched his thirst, he whispered:

"Word has come to my temple of the battle in the bull-burial chamber. It seems that we left two men dead and one gravely wounded, though Tis has no worse than a pigeon's egg on the side of his skull. Moreover, Tis, with Alkman's help, has dispatched a band of hardy rogues in a rowing barge to slay you and your comrades."

"How has word come so quickly, in such detail?" I asked.

"We have our methods," murmured Manethôs.

"Go howl! Is it by familiar spirits, or tame falcons, or that extra-sensory perception of which Dikaiarchos speaks?"

Manethôs only smiled and went on. "Now, the cult of Thôth is not the only one to learn of these events. Some busybody of a bat whispered the tale in the ear of a priest of the temple of Osiris at Memphis. This was the first that this exalted college knew that Tis had been using one of their sacred sarcophagi as a locker for his loot. A shocking sacrilege, of course." Manethôs tried without complete success to suppress a smile.

"Anyway," he went on, "the priests of Osiris, with unseemly haste, knocked down the brick wall that parts the chamber from the corridor leading up into the temple. They found the secret door in the taurine coffin, but, lacking the key, they could not open it, nor would it yield to blows and bumps. They also found and explored the tunnels excavated by Tis.

"In fact, they encountered Tis and his rogues therein. I take it that there was a battle in the dark, with heads broken and knives fleshed. In the end Tis's band fled back to his house and barricaded the door into his bedroom, even as we did when they pursued us. Then the priests carried stone and rubble into the tunnels to block them and bricked up the secret entrance to the chamber.

"Then appealed Tis to his crony Alkman to compel the priests to vacate the bull-burial chamber whilst he took away his loot. So the strategos came clanking up to the temple with a score of soldiers. But the high priest refused them admittance. Nay more, he even defied this mighty man, averring that Alkman's jurisdiction, by express command of King Ptolemaios, did not extend one digit into the temenos, and that if he forced his way in he should rue it. This he said, with his temple guards around him, trying to look fierce behind their wicker shields and caps of crocodile; but not, I do fear, presenting too martial an array compared to Alkman's bronze-blanking hoplitai.

"Further, the high priest threatened Alkman with assorted curses and nocturnal ghostly visitations. This the strategos, being a superstitious wight for all his ferocity, took much to heart.

"Although he desisted from trying to invade the temenos, Alkman did demand to enter the chamber through the tunnels to remove the loot, which, he said, was governmental property. Not so, said the high priest; it belonged to great Osiris, having been deposited under his holy ground. Much talk brought no solution to this impasse. The upshot was that, whereas Alkman has posted soldiers at the entrances to the tunnels and all around the temenos of Osiris, lest the priests smuggle out Tis's loot, the priests keep watches of temple guards in the bull-burial chamber, lest Alkman or Tis again gain access thereto. And all the while the sarcophagus cannot be opened save by Tis's key, or by boring through a cubit of granite, which were a tedious task.

"Withal, the several parties to this contention quake in terror lest news of their wrangle come to the ears of the king, who would then seize the stuff for himself. Were it not that our knowledge of the matter were like to get us all murdered, I should find it a most risible affair."

"Suppose," I said, "that Alkman did lay hands upon the loot. Would he then return it to Tis?"

"That know I not, though I doubt it. If the imbroglio became noised abroad, Alkman were more likely to turn on Tis and slay him quickly, ere his dealings with the arch-thief become known to the king. Then he would plead: Why, certes, he had known Tis, but only as an honest merchant. Never dreamt he that so foul a soul underlay so fair a seeming! On the other hand, if Tis's knaves succeed in slaying us, Alkman might well continue his profitable partnership with this villain, who is now the undisputed lord of the criminal classes of the Province of the White Wall."

Amenardis burst out: "Ammon-Ra! How can you talk so calmly about being killed?"

"Faith in the immortality of the soul, madam," said Manethôs.

"Me, I no want to be killed, soul or no soul. We must get to the sea, Chares, right away. You order Horos to take us down river tonight!"

"My dear, that's impossible," I said. "We must wait for the Judaeans to finish the robe. And please keep your voice down."

"Seth eat up your robe! My life more important. You promise me you take care of me and take me to Rhodes. All right, do this. You not getting anywhere, sitting in Bousiris waiting for throat to be cut."

"Look, dearest. In the first place, I'm a soldier carrying out an order. In the second, when we get to Tamiathis, we're going next to

Alexandria. I shall have to make some special arrangement for you to follow on a merchantman, as my captain would never let me bring a woman aboard the trireme."

"Why you not put me on merchant ship for Rhodes? Then I wait for you there."

"Because it's the end of the sailing season, and we shan't find any merchantmen sailing for Rhodes for months to come."

"Why not?" she demanded.

"Because we have deadly winter storms on the Inner Sea, and even when the sea is calm, how can a ship find its way over open waters when clouds veil the sun and the stars? Moreover, no ordinary merchantman will be sailing to a city under siege."

She frowned. "I cannot go to Rhodes on merchant ship because none sail until war and winter are over. I cannot go on this warship because captain not allow women. How you expect me to go? Ride on back of fish?"

"Well—ah—darling, to tell the truth, I hadn't thought enough about the matter when I urged you to come. What I can do I will. If you can't get to Rhodes now, I'll see you comfortably settled in Alexandria until the war is over. Then I'll send for you."

Amenardis struck the table with a force that made the beer dance in our mugs. "Oh, you silly boy! You stupid little fool! I put my life in your hands; what happen? 'We cannot do this,' you say; 'we cannot do that; I sorry I did not think sooner; but anyway I cannot do what I promise.' Think you I sit in Alexandria for maybe year, two year, with no money, no man, no nothing, waiting to hear from you? Not knowing if you dead or living with some other girl?"

"Now look here, by Zeus the Savior, that's enough!" I said, angry because there was more truth in her words than I liked to admit.

"Not enough at all. You think you stay in Alexandria safely while Tis live? Ha! You even more big fool than I thought. He send man, stick knife through your rotten, lying heart! And I happy! I laugh!"

"Hold your tongue, hussy!"

Amenardis said: "I go take care of Berosos. He have more sense with fever than you without!" She slammed out of the inn.

Manethôs murmured: "One would think you an old married couple."

I sat down, breathing hard and trembling. After a few deep draughts of beer I got myself under control. I said:

"I see I've been much too casual about our pursuers."

"Love, no doubt," said Manethôs. "In that state even the wise Thôth would lose his judgment."

"Be that as it may, what shall we do about this barge-load of ready-for-aughts? Kenamon would never let us turn his inn into a fortress. If I were Tis, I should have obtained a description of the *Hathor* and passed it on to my villains to assist their search. Perhaps we ought to hide or disguise the boat."

"The best place to hide it were an irrigation canal," said Manethôs. "I would choose that which opens into the Nile near Sebennytos. However, I have a better proposal to make, not conflicting with the first."

"What's that?"

"That you and your comrades come down to Sebennytos and hide in the pilgrims' chambers at the temple of Thôth until the robe be ready."

"Would that be allowed?"

"Aye. I have already consulted with my high priest, the holy Thothises. Besides, you told me that General Thorax gave you no reason to expect his help when erst you called upon him here, whereas General Neon might afford you at least the pretense of protection."

"I'm tempted," I said. "But why should your high priest trouble himself on our behalf?"

"Partly because I, his favorite nephew, asked him; and partly to spite those high and mighty hierophants in the temple of Memphite Osiris, who would like nought better than for you to be quietly slain so that they could strike a secret bargain with Alkman for division of Tis's loot."

Thus Manethôs revealed that, despite his lofty theological talk, the priesthoods of Egypt were riven by jealousies and intrigues like those in which other men engage. I said:

"I'm most grateful. But we had better move secretly. We'll rouse Kenamon at midnight and then slip down the river."

"I will meet you on the waterfront at Sebennytos," said Manethôs.

We clasped hands on it, and the priest added, with a wistful smile:

"Do you know, O Chares, that I seem to have grown talents for intrigue and adventure that I never suspected in myself? Almost you make me regret my holy vows!"

After dinner I found Amenardis in our room. We had a tearful and intense reconciliation. When I had proved my passion for her, I told her of the impending move. At once she began to tell me what to do.

"Must tell Judaean weaver where you go," she said. "Then tell Kenamon you go to Boubastis or Saïs, so thieves go the wrong way looking for you. Tell Horos—"

"Now, darling, please, I'm running this expedition!"

"You no like advice? Remember what happen to Sethenes Chamoïs when he not take good advice!"

"When I want advice, I ask for it."

Perhaps this was unwisely petty of me, for some of Amenardis' suggestions were shrewd and, moreover, were things that I should not have thought of myself. Her forward and positive manner, however, made it hard for a Hellene, used to a becoming meekness in his women, to accept her counsels gracefully.

Berosos groaned when awakened. "Go away! I will not move this night for all the gold of Persepolis. A poor invalid hovering on the brink of death am I. Besides, the stars foretell disaster should I stir forth."

"To the crows with your stars!" I said. "You'll be over the brink of death for sure, if Tis's ready-for-aughts catch you here after we have gone."

"Blaspheme not the divine stars. Foretold they not truly the scathe that fell upon me in Tis's crypt? Three ghastly wounds have I to prove that they lied not."

"The reason you were nicked is that you had, against my orders, left your sword behind. Now get up or I'll empty this over you."

"Istar! Do not so! I come."

Uncle Thothises, high priest of Thôth at Sebennytos, was a large fat man who, I suspected, did not take the ascetic rules of Egyptian priestly diet too much to heart. Over a bountiful lunch he explained:

"This morn, just after Ra's arrows had put to flight the demon dark, a fast twenty-oared barge stopped at Bousiris. Men went ashore and asked for news of a band of adventurers under command of a small but handsome Rhodian with curly black hair. Not finding such persons, they took to the river again."

"*Ea!*" said I. "They didn't miss us by much. Where are they now?"

Thothises shrugged his well-padded shoulders. "Would that we knew. For aught that my sources can say, they might have been snatched up into heaven to ride the solar ship in the company of the deathless gods—though, from what I know of these knaves, their fate in the next world is likely to be somewhat different."

I said: "Perhaps I should ask the strategos to post a few soldiers near the temple, in case of a sudden onslaught. Would that suit you, sir?"

Thothises gave me a broad, bland smile. "Well thought of, my son. But think a little further. As you are a stranger in our city, your entrance into the chambers of General Neon might well be noted in quarters where it would do you no good. Let me send my nephew with a bottle of wine wherewith to sweeten Neon before swallowing, as physicians do their potions."

"Sir, words cannot express my gratitude. If there is anything I can do for you, without disloyalty to my city, name it. Although our flights and fights have been costly, I think I could squeeze a modest offering to your temple out of the funds my captain entrusted to me—"

Thothises held up a hand. "Let it not disturb you, my son. Ere you depart, you shall know of some valued service that you and no other can perform for us."

Days dragged by while we durst not venture forth from our cells. Some played checkers while others plumbed the mysteries of Egyptian theology. Dikaiarchos filled sheets of papyrus with notes on his travels.

I modeled statuettes of brick clay: figures in poses of frantic action, fighting with knives as I had seen men fight in the bull-burial chamber. I suppose the priests threw them all out after we had gone, so alien were they to the spirit of Egyptian art; although, baked and painted, they would not have made bad household ornaments.

The temple servants served us excellent meals—the Egyptians are superior cooks—in cheap earthenware dishes and cups. These, I learnt, they carefully broke after each repast, lest they be polluted by our foreign touch.

During this time I missed Amenardis, who was housed in another part of the structure. The priests took care to keep us apart, because Egyptians forbid sexual intercourse in temples, deeming it a pollution.

As, however, I yearned for Amenardis' deep-curved, tawny body with a lust that drove me frantic, I began to make discreet inquiries in hope of finding somebody among the servants of Thôth who could be cajoled or bribed into arranging a tryst. Here, however, I found my ignorance of the Egyptian language a hopeless handicap. The priests, with most of whom I could converse, pretended with bland smiles not to know what I was hinting at; whereas the temple servitors of low degree, such as Phiôps the handyman, could not understand a word I said.

Then Manethôs came to me with that look on his face as if he had been sucking a citron. "Your Judaean friend is here," he said.

"With the robe?"

"He bears a bundle. Were I you, I would scrutinize it with utmost care ere letting him go."

That proved unnecessary, for Azarias, proud of his fellow craftsmen's workmanship, unfolded the robe himself. And indeed it was a splendid piece of work.

"Here," he said, handing me a small and tattered role of silk, "is what remains of the original garment. We snipped off the gold thread and sequins to use on the new robe. Were I you, I would either destroy this remnant or hide it with such care that none should see it and ask embarrassing questions."

"Sir," I said, "you have more than repaid our small service to you. You have saved, if not our lives, at least our careers. If ever you come to Rhodes, ask what you will of me."

With much expression of eternal friendship and mutual esteem, we parted. As I came back into the temenos—for Azarias would not put foot on what he deemed unholy ground—Manethôs said:

"Will it suffice?"

"I'm sure of it. If the original, intact, were compared with the substitute, one could see differences. But if we hold our tongues, Python won't be any the wiser."

"Are you off for Tamiathis?"

"As soon as I can gather my people."

"Will you stop to see my uncle Thothises ere you go?"

The fat high priest, sprawled in a huge chair, said: "O Chares, two things have I to say ere we part. One is that the twenty-oared barge has been seen on the lower parts of the river, where the Province of the Ibis lies on the eastern bank. Meseems they lurk to ambush you. Down there in the swamps it were easy to hide behind a clump of reeds, whence one can see a long stretch of river, and then sally forth when the prey appears."

"What should we do? They have us much outnumbered and outweighed. They could cut us in two by ramming and let the crocodiles finish off the swimmers."

"Three and a half leagues below Sebennytos, past Iseion, the Mendesic branch of the Nile parts from the Phatnitic branch and wends eastward into Lake Tanis. Doubtless your boatman knows it. You could cross Lake Tanis, issue into the sea by the Mendesic mouth, sail west a few leagues to the Phatnitic mouth, and then sail up the river to Tamiathis. Though roundabout, this seems the readiest way to avoid your foes."

I foresaw a battle with Horos over the extra money he would demand, but I said: "An excellent suggestion, sir. And your other matter?"

"I should like Manethôs to go with you to Tamiathis. Thence he will find commercial transportation to Alexandria."

"Delighted! But may I ask why?"

"He has two missions. First, to save his life, which I think will be in less danger from Tis's ruffians at Ptolemaios' court than here. Second, to open direct negotiations between the king and the priesthoods of Thôth, instead of our being compelled, as now, to deal with Ptolemaios through the Osirians."

"I'll do my best to get him to his destination safely—though your nephew seems a young man well able to take care of himself. Would that the gods enabled me to make a more adequate return to you for the debt of gratitude that Rhodes and I owe you!"

Thothises smiled broadly. "You have your share of the celebrated eloquence of Rhodes, I see. Well, your gods have heard your prayer. There is something more you can do."

"Yes, sir?"

"At royal courts all goes by favor and machination. You will reach Alexandria first, and when Manethôs comes, you should be well acquainted. Make the introductions and recommendations that shall further our holy aims, and we shall be well repaid."

Book VIII

PTOLEMAIOS

Pointing to the shore of the Province of the Catfish, beyond which the morning sky was paling, I said: "The Mendesic branch ought to fork off soon. Everybody watch."

I did not trust Horos to point out this fork when we reached it. He had raised a terrible outcry when Thothises' plan for going down to the sea by the Mendesic branch was broached. We should, Horos assured us, lose our way in the swamps of Lake Tanis, or be capsized by a hippopotamus, or be slain by the brigands of the Pasture. Although he had subsided into surly mutterings, I was sure that he would try to slip past the opening of the smaller branch without a word and then present us with an accomplished fact.

Zazamanx and Sambas were at the oars. The sky turned from dark blue to light blue, then to apple green, then to gold. As the first red limb of the sun appeared above the palm trees, Berosos said:

"Yonder it lies, methinks!"

I shaded my eyes against the low ruddy rays and made out a gap in the bank of the river. At the same time Horos called out:

"Look, ship!"

We looked in the direction of Horos' pointing finger. A boat, larger than ours, detached itself from the shadows along the western bank and headed out toward midstream. Berosos, peering with puckered brow, gave a little squeak and said:

"O Chares, surely it is the boat of the thieves! Nine or ten oars on the nigh side I do see, pulled by sinister-looking knaves."

Several of my comrades exclaimed: "Whither shall we go?"

I thought swiftly. On the wide waters of the Phatnitic branch the thieves could, with their greater oar power, easily catch us and run us down. The Mendesic branch, being narrow and tortuous, would give us a chance to keep ahead of them by dodging around bends.

"Horos!" I said. "Run us into the small branch, quickly. Onas and Dikaiarchos, take the other oars; you're the strongest. Where is that old crocodile spear? Row, curse you!"

The *Hathor* leaped toward the fork of the Mendesic branch, A yell floated across the water as the thieves perceived that their prey had sighted them. Their leader called the stroke with shouts. Their oars rapidly rose and fell; water foamed about their bow. Despite our efforts, they were plainly making twice our speed.

Nearer we came to the Mendesic branch, but nearer yet came the barge. A little group clustered in the bow with knives and short swords, ready to leap. I prayed to the Bright One that they should have no missile weapons.

So close were the cutthroats that I could see the gleam of their teeth and eyeballs in the rising sun. I poised the spear to spit the first who should try to jump the gap. Manethôs muttered prayers and exorcisms.

"Berosos!" I cried. "Stop dithering and get your sword out. Cut off any hands that grasp our gunwale."

"I will t-t-try," said Berosos.

A heave of her oars brought the pursuing craft almost within arm's length of our stern. As a man started to reach out, I jabbed and got home. The man snatched back his bleeding arm; another struck at the spear shaft with a sword, nicking but not severing it. Their leader kept shouting a command, but nobody seemed eager to be the first to impale himself.

A man in the bow rose up and threw his knife. Amenardis screamed. I dodged but felt a blow on the side of my head and the sting of a cut on my right ear. There was a thump, and I glanced behind me to see Manethôs tumble on his back with his paper shoes in the air. He had been rapped on the crown by the knife handle.

The priest bounded up, prayer and exorcism forgotten, and shouted furiously to Horos. The latter threw down his paddle. The two squeezed forward between the rowers to where the mast lay. They picked it up and pushed their way aft.

"Get out of the way!" cried Manethôs.

Berosos and I ducked. The priest and the boatman grasped the mast near the butt end, one from each side, so that its thin end projected out over the water. Manethôs counted:

"*Oua! Sen! Chemet!*"

They swung. The ten-cubit pole hurtled round in a horizontal arc. Most of those clustered in the bow of the barge ducked as they saw it coming, but it struck one man. Splash!

Gabble and curses burst from the thieves. The barge slowed down and fell behind. Someone in the rear of the barge caught the hand of the man in the water and hauled him back aboard.

The quick stroke began again. This time the barge pulled up abreast of us to port, as if to ram us in the waist or to board us from the side.

"Pull!" I cried. "We're nearly there!"

Up forward, Amenardis stood by to strike with Onas' sword. Horos and Manethôs thrust the mast out to fend off the barge.

The barge angled in toward us; our oars fouled theirs with a clatter. Thieves mustered in bow and stern. The chief shouted a command. Some thieves gathered themselves to leap while others snatched at the mast, trying to seize it and wrest it from us.

Then there was a slight shock. I felt the drag of our bottom on ground, and the slowing of the *Hathor* staggered me. After two heartbeats we were free again and rowing into the Mendesic branch.

The barge, however, grounded firmly on the sandbar, with a grunt of strained timbers and a swirl of muddy water. Three thieves in the bow were pitched off into the river, while those erect in the stern were hurled into the laps of the rearmost rowers.

Our four rowers, with sweat streaming down their faces, gave a few more strokes and then dropped their oars, letting their heads fall forward on their knees.

Screams of rage came from the barge. Fists were shaken, and one man tried a long-range knife throw. The blade whirled across the water but fell short with a small splash. A Greek-speaking thief yelled:

"Dirty, greasy Greeks! Run away, you lying, boy-loving cowards!"

Dikaiarchos raised his head, mopping his face with the sleeve of his shirt, which was plastered to his torso by sweat. "My poor old heart! I never realized how wide that polluted river is."

A bend in the smaller branch of the Nile carried us out of sight of the barge. When I last saw the thieves, most had gone over the side and were wading around knee-deep, trying to push their boat off with random efforts and many cries.

Onas conferred with Horos, then said: "It will not be long ere they are again on our trail. Horos urges that we take to the canals, for they will surely catch us if we continue down this branch."

I said: "Ask him whether we can work our way back to the Phatnitic branch through the canals."

"He says he knows a way," said Onas.

"Let's take it. We should be able to lose them in the canals."

Horos cheered up at not having to face the hippopotamus-haunted swamps of Lake Tanis. An hour's row brought us to the opening of a large canal on our left.

Then we rowed through the countryside of the Delta. Naked peasants on the banks halted their labors to give us those stony stares wherewith peasants the world over confront outsiders. After a few turns and forks we were wholly in Horos' hands.

All day we wandered among the canals. At times the banks came so near on either hand that we had to unship the oars and use them as poles and paddles. Once we had to retrace our path for several furlongs because we had come to a bridge too low for the *Hathor*'s little cabin to clear. Moreover, as the canal was too narrow to turn the *Hathor*, we had to back the whole way.

At last, when the westerly palms showed black against the ruddy disk of the setting sun, we came again upon the broad Phatnitic branch of the Nile. As the scarlet sphere vanished, I breathed a silent thanksgiving to Helios-Apollon.

* * *

The next dawn saw us pulling up to the waterfront at Tamiathis. There lay a big merchantman whose squat form I recognized as that of the *Ariath* of Sapher of Sidon. There stood Sapher himself, long black beard and all, ordering the loading of cargo into his ship.

"I'm happy to see that fortune favors you, Captain Sapher," I said.

"Fortune is right, young fellow!" said the Phoenician. "The accursed brigands had not burnt my ship after all. And why? Because they wished to take out my load of timber first, for their own use. But these great beams of cedar took much pulling and hauling to get up through the hatch and over the side, so that when Tauros' triremes reached the spot, the knaves had not unloaded more than the half.

"Now, my agreement with Tauros was that he should pull me off in return for my cargo of lumber, and only half the shipment was left for the use of his station. However, being a good fellow, he agreed to pull me for what there was, and this proved not difficult once the remaining load was taken out."

"How soon will you sail?"

"I can go almost any time. I did but delay a little to attend Dikaiarchos' return."

"I think I have two more passengers for you." I introduced Amenardis and Manethôs.

"I am delighted," said Sapher. "For, despite the rescue of my ship, this voyage is like to lose me money."

News of our arrival brought Captain Python on a run. His first words were: "Did you get it?"

"Yes, sir," I said.

Python took my arm, walked me aside from the others, and spoke in a low voice. "Good, good! I will see that you and the other two are rewarded. But one thing: Say nothing about this expedition, nothing about the fact that the polluted robe was ever stolen at all."

"Herakles! Why not? I thought I could boast of this feat all my life."

"Well, don't. It makes me look foolish for letting the thing be stolen in the first place."

"How about the crew? They'll surely talk."

"I have sworn them to secrecy. I daresay the tale will leak out someday, but I mean to keep it dark at least until we have left Egypt. So curb that saucy tongue, young Chares, or it will go hard with you."

At first I was indignant that Python should obscure my small glory to avoid any risk to his own. Further thought, however, reminded me that if tongues started wagging freely, my dealings with Azarias might also come to light. Perhaps one should let well enough alone.

"Fetch the robe aboard the *Halia*," he concluded.

We rowed out and climbed the ladder to the deck of the trireme, which lay in the river. When I bore my burden to the captain's cabin, Python unfolded the garment and scrutinized it.

"Divinity! It seems to have faded a little," he said. "But I suppose that is to be expected after all its adventures. I see that some of you bear scars and bandages. Tell me what happened."

I told my tale, omitting the fact that this was not the original robe, the remains of which reposed at the bottom of my duffel bag.

"Would I had been with you!" exclaimed Python—a sentiment which I privately doubted. "But if what you say be true, then the rogues may still be after the thing, eh?"

"I suppose so, sir. Hadn't you better post a guard over it?"

"I will do better than that. I will have this ship on its way by sundown. Let's get the polluted rag into the king's hands and let him worry about his criminal class."

Python carefully folded the robe and placed it in a large box with a lock, which already held Demetrios' hat, tunic, and shoes. When he had locked this box, he put the box into a chest, like the god Thôth with his boxes of gold, silver, and so on, one inside the other. He locked the second chest—a new one, bolted to the floor—hung both keys about his neck, and ordered the four marines who happened to be within earshot to arm themselves and mount guard over his cabin.

"Let them try to steal it now!" he said.

The flat, sandy shore of Egypt, with the endless forest of palms behind it, becomes a weariness to the eye long before one reaches Alexandria. Past Kanopos and Boukiris the last stretch of shore rises in a slight ridge or hill—or what seems like a hill in the mirror-flat

Delta. Then the palm forest breaks up into groves, with fields and farms, villas and gardens, and then comes the wall of Alexandria.

Here, in contrast to the deadly peaceful monotony of the Egyptian littoral, all is bustle and building and change. This became evident as we swung to seaward to pass around Cape Lochias, whence rose, inside the wall, the temple of Artemis and the royal palace. From the end of Cape Lochias a string of islands forms an arc, bowing out from the coast and swinging back at its western end to meet another point of land beyond the city. These islands comprise the large isle of Pharos, several islets, and some mere points of rock.

Cranes and scaffolding rose from these isles; barges lay alongside them; and everywhere men toiled to extend the harbor works. Some were joining the end of Cape Lochias on the left to the nearest isles by a mole, while others strove to unite the farther isles with the Pharos, leaving but a single channel into the Great Harbor.

A little pilot boat, flying the red-lion standard, came bobbing through the chop. The pilot yelled and gestured until the *Halia* followed him through the Bull Channel into the harbor. Inside the harbor the king was making an even nobler improvement: a vast five-furlong mole, connecting Pharos with the shore and dividing the whole harbor into two huge basins.

We moored at the quay in the naval district, between the base of Cape Lochias and the islet of Antirrodos. Captain Python conferred in his cabin with the commandant of the local naval station. Then, gleaming in freshly polished armor, he drew us up on the deck and said:

"Boys, you are on leave for three days, so you may take life easy." (Cheers.) "Collect your pay from the boatswain and find yourselves quarters. Everyone shall report back to the ship at muster time each morning; that is, one hour after sunrise. Anybody who misses muster shall have his pay docked. After this three-day leave, we shall have exercises every day save feast days and days of bad weather.

"One more thing: Keep out of trouble. If anybody is caught fighting or stealing or otherwise misbehaving, he shall have trouble with me as well as with the local authorities, and he will find me the harder of the two. Dismissed!"

The commandant climbed down the ladder into a waiting boat. After him went Python, and then Python's cabin boy, carefully carrying the box containing Demetrios' garments, and lastly all ten marines as an escort.

I plunged into the bustle of this burgeoning city and gaped at the new tomb of Alexander and the other public structures a-building. Having avoided by a hair's breadth being run over by carts lurching through the broad, straight, swarming avenues with mighty beams and stones for the king's vast construction projects, I arrived at the shipyards on the morning of my fifth day in Alexandria. When roll had been called, Python said:

"See me after dismissal, O Chares."

Some of my shipmates chaffed me, calling: "What have *you* been up to?" Python, however, explained:

"The king has invited the officers of the *Halia* to dine with him tomorrow night. As our most junior officer, you are included. Be at the main gate to the palace, properly shaved and oiled and in your best civilian dress, an hour before sunset."

"How goes the mission, sir?"

Python grunted resentfully. "I had to wait three days for an audience, sitting in the king's waiting room and clutching the robe to my bosom like a shipwrecked man clinging to an oar. That Athenian exile, Demetrios of Phaleron, seems to be in command of arrangements at court. He's the rascal who imposed upon the Athenians those austere laws regulating conduct while wallowing in Persian luxury and filling Athens with statues of himself."

"No wonder the Athenians kicked him out! Then what?"

"When I finally got in to see Ptolemaios, he seemed mightily pleased with the garments—so much so that he invited us all to dine—but he evaded my requests for aid. Despite the good omens, I fear that our trip may be wasted. At best it will be too late in the season to return to Rhodes, so we shall have a three months' layover."

When we were all gathered in front of the palace—Python, his executive officer, his first lieutenant, the marine officer, the boatswain, the coxswain, and myself—an usher led us in. It was a large complex of buildings, decorated in what seemed to me like overly ornate taste. The usher took us into the main building, where a stout middle-aged man with long hair of a startling yellow hue awaited us.

A closer look showed the hair to be dyed and the full, jowly face to be rouged and powdered. His perfume was overpowering. The usher said:

"The king's guests, my lord!"

The man smiled. "Ah, my good Python! Rejoice, dear friends! I am Demetrios of Phaleron, sometime Athenian scholar and politician and now fixer-in-chief to the Great King."

Python presented us, and Demetrios Phalereus led us into a banquet hall, gaudy with gilded plaster wreaths and painted rose gardens all around the walls. Here were an Admiral somebody-or-other, and the king's brother Menelaos, and several other officials and military personages. Presently a trumpet blew, and in came the king with a golden wreath on his balding head.

Ptolemaios son of Lagos was a short, heavily built man with a paunch, in his early sixties. A thick bull's neck jutted forward from heavy, fat-padded shoulders. His jaw was massive, in keeping with his general build. Across his receding forehead ran a strong flange or bar of bone, and from this sprouted bushy gray brows that shadowed his deep-set eyes. His nose was short, albeit high-bridged, hooked, and prominent, so that it had the look of a parrot's beak. He wore Demetrios' spangled robe, with the hem curtailed to suit his stature.

The king strolled in, nodding and flipping his hand in response to our bows, smiling easily and casting polite comments as he was introduced around. To me he said, in a strong Macedonian accent:

"Chares of Lindos, catapultist? You must talk to my chief engineer, here. Perhaps you can tell him something new about catapult design; we cannot let others get ahead of us in military science. Are you a professional soldier or a militiaman?"

"The latter, sire."

"What do you in civilian life?"

"I am a s-sculptor, sire, of good repute."

I flushed and stammered because, as everybody knows, a sculptor works with his hands and, therefore, cannot aspire to be deemed a true gentleman. Ptolemaios' deep-set eyes looked keenly at me from under the beetling brows. The king said:

"A reputable trade, O Chares; to quote the Poet:

"An honest business never blush to tell."

"Your statues may outlast the fame of politicians like myself. Do you work in stone or in bronze?"

"Both, O King, but I prefer bronze."

The king clucked. "Then your pieces may not last so long as all that."

"Why, sire? With decent care, bronze—"

He chuckled. "Has it ever occurred to you that the first thing a tyrant thinks of, when pinched for money, is to melt down all the bronze in the land?"

"No, sir, it has not." I took a deep breath. "I hardly dare suggest it, sire, but—"

"Well? But what? Speak up, lad! I have never yet eaten an artilleryman; they are too tough."

"Would you—would you like me to make a statue of you while we are here in Alexandria?"

Ptolemaios cocked his head. "Mmm. Possibly; the idea bears thinking on. Take it up with Demetrios, and we shall see."

He waddled off to speak to another guest, leaving me atwitter. I knew that in theory one man is much the same as another, and that a king catches cold when he gets his feet wet as readily as a common man. I also knew that it ill becomes a citizen of a free Hellenic city to grovel before any king.

Still, an artisan like me never, in the ordinary course of events, gets a chance to hobnob socially with a king—even though the king be no scion of an ancient royal line but the son of a backwoods baron from the Macedonian hills. Ptolemaios had progressed from boyhood companion of Alexander, to bodyguard and general in his armies; then, by guile and foresight, he had obtained Egypt for his satrapy at the first division of the Empire. Now he had arrogated the title of royalty unto himself.

Still, legitimate ruler or upstart, wise or foolish, kind or cruel, none can deny that a king is somebody. Withal, Ptolemaios was a not unattractive monarch: shrewd, genial, and unaffected, with a great deal of canny Macedonian peasant peering out from under his bushy brows. Were I not a stout republican, I could think of worse men to give my loyalty to.

The talk at dinner was mostly concerned with the siege of Rhodes and with the disaster of Cyprus, when the island fell to Demetrios Antigonou. Ptolemaios' brother Menelaos and son Leontiskos had both fallen into the conqueror's hands; but then Demetrios, with one of his sudden gestures of generous gallantry, had sent these royal captives, together with their immediate friends and baggage, back to Egypt scot-free.

I fell into earnest talk with the chief engineer on the relative merits of balls of stone and of brick for stone throwers. When these subjects had been well covered, the king remarked:

"O Python, what sort of voyage had you hither?"

Said Python: "We fell afoul of a westerly storm, O King, which nearly sank us. After we sighted Egypt's shores, however, all went smoothly."

"Had you no further difficulties or delays?"

"None, sire, save for a stop at Tamiathis to have my ship's leaky seams recalked."

"Was that all that held you up?"

Python, looking more and more uncomfortable, said: "Yes, O King, indeed it was."

"That is odd," said Ptolemaios. "I have a report that this robe, which you were so kind as to bring me, was stolen in Tamiathis; that you sent a party of your men after it; and that they recovered it in Memphis from an archthief, one Tis of Hanes. I am surprised that you did not enliven our feast by telling of these dramatic events."

Python looked as if he wished the earth would open and gulp him down as it did the hero Amphiaraos. He mumbled:

"O King, I thought that so small and sordid a matter would bore you."

Ptolemaios wagged a finger. "All that occurs in my kingdom interests me, my good Python. Also, I like people who tell me the full and exact truth, even though it make them look something less than demigods." The king turned to me. "Were you in command of this raid, lad?"

"Yes, sire."

"Then tell us about it."

I told the story, enlarging on the battle in the bull-burial chamber but omitting the replacement of the robe and ignoring the venomous glances from Python. My heart was in my mouth lest the king know also of Azarias' part in the drama. However, he merely said:

"That confirms my report. You did well. When the siege of your city is over, if you would seek your fortune here, I think a place could be found for you in my government. I can use shrewd, daring, and conscientious young men."

I said: "Did you catch him, sir?"

"Catch whom?"

"Tis, the robber chief."

"Alas, no! His loot, hidden in the bull sarcophagus, and his house we have, but the man himself slipped through our fingers. No doubt he is hiding somewhere in that Memphite rabbit warren, to reappear anon under another name. It was a most ingenious idea, this international book-stealing ring, for next to precious metals and jewels, books combine the greatest value with the least bulk."

Menelaos put in: "Brother, if you catch this Tis alive, I am sure you can find him useful employment in your Department of Taxation."

I asked the king: "How about the strategos, Alkman?"

I caught a warning frown from Python, as if to say to keep quiet and not stir up unnecessary enmities. However, I could not miss a chance to do an ill turn to one whom I hated so bitterly.

"What about him?" rejoined Ptolemaios.

"He was in on it, too, sire. He used me in outrageous fashion to keep me from finding the robe—"

Ptolemaios: "Mayhap our good Alkman is not made to withstand the temptations of governing a great city. Yet he has many soldierly virtues, which will be put to better use in chastising a Nubian tribe that has been raiding my subjects across the border."

"Sire, are we safe from the vengeance of Tis and his gang here in Alexandria?"

Up went the shaggy brows. "In my own capital? I should think so!" Then the king laid a finger beside his nose. "But better safe than sorry, eh, lad? Belike you and your comrades had better not wander the town alone o' nights. Demetrios, pass word to the prefect of police to watch for Tis or members of his band, stealing into the city. Now tell me, O Chares, what said the folk you met on your quest about their government? An honest report now: no sweetening or omission to soothe the old man's vanity." He cast an ironic smile at poor Python.

I thought a moment, then said: "I did not meet many Egyptians, sire. But those I talked with frankly expressed resentment that they should be made an inferior class in their own land while all the posts of profit and power go to Hellenes."

Menelaos, the king's brother, broke in: "Let them resent. As Aristoteles has shown, it is nature's law that the strong and brave shall rule the weak and timid: for example, that the Macedonians shall rule the Egyptians. And who are we to go against the will of the gods?"

Demetrios Phalereus said: "It is not quite so simple as that, Lord Menelaos. The Egyptians are neither so weak nor so cowardly as we are wont to believe. According to Xenophon's books, their soldiery had a high repute for valor before the Persians conquered them. Therefore, say I, they are potentially dangerous, and we must be on our guard lest we all awaken some morning with our throats cut."

"Who cares what books say?" snorted Menelaos. "Experience is the only true teacher, and it tells me that the Egyptians are nought but a pack of soft, sly poltroons."

"Do not scorn books, my dear Menelaos," said Demetrios Phalereus. "Many a man who will not say what he thinks to your face will set forth his honest thought in books. For example," he turned to the king, "with the best of intentions the friends of a king seldom give him the exact truth, because they wish to please the king, and they know that kings, like other men, are not pleased by bad news or unwelcome advice. So, say I, a wise king will buy and read all the books dealing with the office of king and ruler, since those things his friends are not rash enough to tell him are set forth in manuscript."

The king said: "There is sense in what you say. We have had an example here only this evening. However, when those books in the hoard of Tis the archthief arrive, they will keep me busy for some time. I need to learn the finer points of the literary art, as I, too, am thinking of writing a book."

Everybody asked him what this was to be.

"A history of the campaigns of Alexander," said he. "I have the divine Alexander's own journal in the archives here, and many of his great deeds I myself saw or took part in. It were a shame to let these memories perish with my mortal frame, think you not?

"But let us back to our Egyptian problem, which has plagued me for years. I like to think of myself as more than a mere exploiter and tyrant, holding a conquered people in subjection by force. You may scorn the Egyptians, but they have crowned me with that monstrosity of red and white felt and have formally presented me to their gods. Hermes attend us, but I shall never forget that ten-day in Memphis! I have never been so uncomfortable in my life, standing for hours while they droned through endless rituals. Still and all, I am now their king as well as yours, and I ought to treat them kindly and justly, just as Alexander felt he owed kindness and justice to the Persians when he had conquered them."

"The Persians at least put up a gallant fight," said Menelaos.

The king ignored this remark. "However," he said, "it is one thing to talk about using the Egyptians kindly and another to bring them into the government. I tried arming some of them, and they began stealing the arms and hiding them for use in a revolt. I have met some of their priests and nobles, but most of them speak no Greek, and those who do are full of such strange ideas that there is no understanding them."

"You might learn Egyptian, Brother," said Menelaos, whereupon all laughed.

I saw my chance. "Sire, I know an Egyptian priest, fluent in Greek, who is on his way hither to represent the priesthoods of Thôth at your court."

"Good," said the king. "When he arrives, turn him over to Demetrios. It may come to nought, but it is at least a step forward."

He clapped his hands. The dancing girls came in, hung wreaths of red and blue lotus flowers around our necks, and began their act.

Days passed without word of the *Anath* and Amenardis, until I feared that some additional woe had befallen the merchantman. A gust of rain swept the city, proving that it does rain after all in Egypt.

One day Python called a conference of officers after muster. We sat in a circle in his cabin while he paced back and forth in the cramped space and chewed a fingernail.

"I am getting nowhere with my quest for aid for Rhodes," he said. "I have seen the king again, but again there are only polite excuses and postponements. He has made it plain that any further requests would have to be submitted to that painted-up literary character, Demetrios Phalereus."

The executive officer said: "Perhaps he's afraid of throwing good troops after bad."

"Whatever the reason," said Python, "he seems to have made up his mind not to send us any more aid. I am beating my head against a stone wall—a wall hidden behind soft cushions, but a wall nevertheless. What shall I do?"

There was a murmur of suggestions, most of them worthless. Then Python said:

"Chares, were there not some words between you and the king about your making a statue?"

"Yes, sir. I have an appointment with Demetrios Phalereus tomorrow to confirm the final arrangements."

"Get a commission to portray the king, at all costs. This Demetrios Phalereus is said to be quite a boy-lover; yield to him if you must, so that you get in to see the king. Then take up the matter of help for Rhodes."

Luckily, Demetrios Phalereus made no such advances to me. He merely said that the king had approved the proposal for a statue.

"However," he said, "it is plain that you will not be here long enough to erect anything large. Nor does the king care for a full-length statue. His shape, as he says, would never win beauty contests, and it were silly to mount his head on the body of an Apollon. So, not wishing a statue showing him either as he is or as he isn't, he will have a simple bust in bronze, for which we will pay you five hundred drachmai. Is that agreeable?"

"Yes, sir."

When I was taken in to sketch and measure the king, I found him seated at a huge table littered with papyrus. A swarm of secretaries sat about. Some read letters to him; some brought messages; some took dictation. Officials came and went. He was the busiest king I had yet seen. When I had a chance, I said:

"O King, you are paying me a fair price, but I would do the work ten times over for nothing if it meant aid to my city—"

I went on in that vein for a few sentences until the king raised his hand.

"Lad," he said, "perhaps you have not dealt much with kings, so your ignorance is excusable. But let me explain something to you. Have you seen me stop work since you began your sketching?"

"No, sire."

"Nor will you. On all but a few days of the year I work like this from sunrise to sunset. And why? Because a king can never fully trust anybody to carry out his orders faithfully unless he keep his officers in a state of salutary apprehension by inquiring into matters for himself. You know what Alkman was doing in Memphis, because I was not looking over his shoulder.

"Besides, half the people in Egypt—which, they tell me, has several millions of inhabitants—want to get in to see me about their complaints and personal problems. If I give audience to none, I lose touch with my people and suffer some of my officers to abuse them without redress. On the other hand, there are not enough hours in the day to see all who wish audience. That is why I have Demetrios Phalereus, or another like him, to pass on all requests for audience and to decide which to send in and which to turn aside.

"As you see, a king, if he would really rule, must be as niggardly of his time as a miser of his gold. Every hour must be devoted to certain things and those only. Almost every person he sees during the day has some request to press upon him, and the king must hold them off in order not to be driven mad. And that is why a king takes it ill when a man admitted to his presence on one pretext begins dunning him over some wholly different matter. Do I make myself clear?"

"Yes, sir," I said. Biting my lip with mortification, I went back to my sculpture in silence.

The *Anath*, after being held in Tamiathis by adverse winds, reached Alexandria late in Maimakterion. I had a passionate reunion with Amenardis. I had moved out of the officers' quarters in the barracks, next to the palace inclosure, and taken a small apartment in the Beta district. As I was paying the landlord his deposit, the idea struck me to give the man a false name, to make it harder for any ill-wishers to find me. So I became, for the nonce, Nikon Charetos of Kôs.

I also took Manethôs, Theodoros, and Dikaiarchos into the palace to meet Demetrios Phalereus. Manethôs had become quite cheerful at the prospect of an indefinite leave of absence from his wife. His temple council had promoted him from scribe to wing-bearer to lend more weight to his words.

On fair mornings we of the *Halia* spent a few hours in exercises: rowing and practice in arms. Captain Python chewed his nails and paced the deck in anxiety over the seeming failure of his mission.

"It is unfair!" he moaned to me in his cabin. "I am no magician, able to bend the king's will to mine by subtle spells. Before that accursed bust is finished, Chares, you must have another go at old potbelly."

"Sir," I said, "as I've explained, the king warned me not to do that. If I defy his warning, he will have me at least tossed out of the palace on my arse."

"You will have to take that chance. I have been working on Demetrios Phalereus, but all I get from him is a request for a new formula to restore his virility. The man who can furnish him with a drug or a spell to stiffen his yard can command the wealth of Egypt. His other main concern is literature. 'How about soldiers and food and arms for beautiful Rhodes?' say I. 'Listen to my plan for a new anthology of the early lyric poets,' says he. *Phy!*"

When I got to my lodgings, I found Amenardis brooding. She burst out:

"You must not sit here in Alexandria, darling. You go somewhere else."

"Why?"

"Because Tis still alive. He send somebody to kill you. I know him. He kill me, too. Take me away!"

"As I've explained, I cannot. I have to wait for the *Halia* to sail, two months hence."

"And what about me? You think you leave me here?"

I thought hard. "How would it be if I sent you to one of the Ionian islands out of the present war zone: Kôs, say, or Samos? Then we could be reunited as soon as the war is over."

"How soon you send me?"

"About the time I sail in the *Halia*."

"That not much better than Alexandria. What chance has poor lone foreign woman? Somebody seize me, sell me to slavers." She began to weep noisily. "You no love me! You get me by trick! All you want is one good futtering...."

We had another of those horrible scenes, which ended in my stamping out of the house. As I issued into the mild afternoon sunshine, I met Manethôs.

"Rejoice!" said the priest. "*Ē!* Where are you off to in such haste?"

"To the harbor, to drown myself! Life has become unbearable!"

"You will find the water unpleasantly cold at this time of year, my friend. More trouble with your true love, I suppose?"

"Of course. I cannot live with her or without her."

"Well, nought endures forever, even life. Pray, stop sputtering like an overheated frying pan and listen. I bring an invitation to a feast in the chambers of Demetrios Phalereus, in the palace, tonight."

"I'm grateful, but I don't think I could bear human company just now."

"Be not absurd! How better to cool off after such a bout than by means of sweet wine and witty converse with congenial comrades and learned colleagues? All the intellectuals of the city will be there."

"Hm," I said. "Maybe you will persuade me, after all. But what do these fine gentlemen want with a mere artisan like me?"

"You are known for your feat in recovering the robe, and the king has praised you. Besides, your knowledge of engineering and the arts qualifies you as a man of intellect. Demetrios has invited Berosos and me, who are not even Hellenes. After all, he is the son of a slave himself, so why should he be snobbish?"

As things fell out, I already knew most of Demetrios Phalereus' guests. There were Dikaiarchos, Kasandros' roving geographer; Theodoros, the atheistical philosopher; and Apelles, the great Koan painter. As I arrived, Apelles was telling of a fantastic thing that had befallen him.

"...so, because of our ancient rivalry over this lady," he said, "I thought it wise not to obtrude upon the king. Naturally I was astonished to receive an invitation to dine at the king's table; but, also naturally, I went as commanded. None challenged me as I entered the palace, and the butler announced me to the king as if all were in order.

"Ptolemaios looked at me with a puzzled expression and consulted with his minions. Then he confronted me, saying: 'O Apelles, tell me, pray, how you come to be here in this room.'

"'A man from your palace called at my lodgings with an invitation this afternoon, while I was painting, sire,' I said. 'Why, is anything amiss?'

"'Only this,' said he, 'that I never issued such an invitation. While I bear you no grudge after twenty years, meseems that somebody has played a joke upon us. Describe the man who spoke to you.'

"'I can best describe with a board and a piece of charcoal,' I said, and when these things had been brought, I sketched the face of my inviter.

"'Ah!' said the king at once. That is Pathymias, my second palace steward. He shall rue the day he thought it were fun to play a practical joke on his king. Meanwhile, since there is plenty to eat and drink, you shall remain and tell me of your rise in the world of art.'

"After that all went smoothly, and Ptolemaios even commissioned me to paint his portrait. 'In spite of the fact,' said he, 'that you painted that old temple robber Antigonos first.'

"'He asked me first, sire," I said, 'and your portrait will be all the better for this previous experience. Moreover, I hope you will do nothing drastic to Pathymias, whose jest has turned out well, at least for me.'

"'I will neither lengthen nor shorten his neck, if that is what you fear,' said Ptolemaios with a smile. 'I think, however, that six months of peeling onions in the kitchen will do much to season his flighty character.'"

Another guest was Philemon of Syracuse, a dramatist whom Ptolemaios had lured from Athens to write a comedy for the opening of the new Alexandrian theater in the spring. There was also a scholar, Hekataios of Teôs, who became embroiled with Manethôs in a heated argument on Egyptian history.

"I know not who gave your Herodotos his information," said the priest, "but either he or his informant got things fearfully confused. Imagine, placing the kings of the Fourth Dynasty two thousand years out of their proper time!"

The king dropped in for a short visit after dinner, to greet those whom he knew and to meet the others. He spent a while in private converse with Manethôs and then withdrew.

Demetrios Phalereus asked: "My dear Chares, how is your bust of the king coming?"

"I shall be ready to pour in a ten-day, sir."

"Good. Be warned not to prettify the king in his statue; he prefers to be shown as he is, bald spot and all." Lowering his voice, he continued: "Speaking of the effects of age, do you know any good methods of restoring youthful vigor to one's masculine parts? I've eaten bulbs, eggs, and snails until they run out my ears, to no avail. Why, but a few days ago I had to send one of the most beautiful courtesans of the city home untouched."

"I fear not, sir. But I have heard it said that faith in certain foods for this purpose is faith misplaced."

"Then what hope is there? I am even willing to try magic, which I once scorned as mere vulgar superstition."

I said: "I know no magicians, unless you count the Egyptian priest yonder. But wait.... An Egyptian of my crew, who is always talking of Egyptian wizards and their spells, might know somebody."

"Then pray send him to me."

"Gladly. And now, sir, may I ask you a candid question?"

"Surely, dear boy. What would you know?"

"As you are well aware, my captain and I have long tried to secure a commitment of more aid for Rhodes, and we have gotten nowhere. Are we wasting our time?"

Demetrios Phalereus smiled blandly. "I shouldn't say that. You are making your bust, safe for the nonce from war's alarums; and Captain Python is drilling his crew, so they should put up a mighty battle on your homecoming."

"Come now, sir, you know what I mean."

"I suppose I do. I cannot answer flatly, because I do not know myself. On one hand, we are loath to disappoint our faithful friends. On the other, our finances have been pulled and strained from many directions of late. And suppose the City of Roses fall, despite all that we can do? Antigonos wants the Isle of the Three Cities as a base for a descent upon Egypt. Should such an invasion take place, we shall need every man and every drachma. They are a formidable pair, the crafty and ruthless old king and the daring and ingenious young one!"

"The time to stop them, then, is now while they are afar off, not when they come sailing into your fine new harbor with a thousand ships." I thought I sounded wise, but Demetrios Phalereus rejoined:

"Dear boy, don't you suppose that we have been over all these arguments a hundred times, the king and his councilors? If the answer were easily had, we should have come to it long since. I will confide to you that Ptolemaios grows yearly more cautious, and his disaster in Cyprus inclines him to shun foreign adventures, like a turtle that has pulled its head into its shell."

"Well, then, is there nothing we can do to tip the scale in our direction?"

Demetrios Phalereus cocked his head and squinted a painted eyelid. "Let me think.... The king does cherish one ambition that few know of, and I am not without influence with the king. If somebody wanted something badly enough to reveal to me how the king might achieve his ambition, without claiming any credit for himself—well, something might be done."

"What is the royal ambition?"

"Do you understand that if you have any useful thoughts on the matter, you will speak of them to my ear alone?"

"Yes, yes, I understand. But what's this mysterious yearning? To fly to heaven on the back of a gryphon?"

Demetrios Phalereus looked at me with displeasure. "You are an irritating young man at times."

"I'm sorry, sir. Impatience is one of my many shortcomings."

"Very well. If we clearly understand each other, there need be no recriminations later. And don't doubt that I can cause trouble for those who play me false." He reminded me of Kallias at this juncture. "Well, what the king wants is this: to set up, here in Alexandria, some thing, or building, or institution that shall be wholly new in the world. That, he thinks, is the one sure way of being remembered forever."

"You mean something that doesn't yet exist?"

"Precisely. It is to be invented."

I pondered. "How about a colossal statue—say, of Zeus, overlooking the harbor?"

"My dear Chares, don't you think we have heard of Lysippos' colossi at Taras?"

"Well, let's make the new statue twice as tall as the Tarentine Zeus—on which I had the honor to assist the great Lysippos."

"You do not seem to understand. The king wants something new in kind, not merely an old idea enlarged."

I thought some more. "How about a great lighthouse? You could erect it on Pharos Island, tall enough to be seen a thousand furlongs at sea."

"That is a better try. Unfortunately we have already thought of that. The king has even had architects' preliminary drawings made. It will be years, however, before we shall have the funds to start it."

"I give up," I said, "at least for now. If Helios-Apollon vouchsafe me any more suggestions, I'll let you know."

"Do so. And now, let me tell you of my plans for a new anthology of the early lyric poets...."

Despite the dyed hair, the cosmetics, and the dubious reputation, Demetrios Phalereus was a most stimulating dinner companion. He had been a pupil of the all-knowing Aristoteles and had taught in his school. He seemed to have read everything and could discourse with equal fluency on history, philosophy, politics, warfare, poetry, and rhetoric.

When the time came to leave, I approached Manethôs, who was still arguing with Hekataios: "…nay, nay, it was not *that* King Rhameses but a later one of the same name. Oh, is it time to go already?"

"I fear so," said Hekataios. "What we need is some central place where all this information, such as we have been discussing, is brought together, so that a scholar can study it all at once, instead of having to travel all over the Inner Sea to find the needed scholars and books."

Demetrios Phalereus had bid his guests good night at the main gate and disappeared into the palace grounds, and we were dispersing into the dark of the Broucheion district—the richer preceded by their own link boys—when an idea struck me with the force of a thunderbolt.

"Demetrios!" I shouted. I tried to rush back through the gate, but the sentries stopped me.

"Get Demetrios Phalereus!" I cried. "It's urgent! I must speak to him at all costs!"

So excited was my manner that the corporal of the guard said: "Kleon, go tell Lord Demetrios. And you, young man, your errand had better be worth his lordship's while if you don't want a beating for making a disturbance."

Soon Demetrios Phalereus arrived, looking old in the torchlight with the paint and powder washed off.

"What is it, Chares?" said he in a rather brusque tone.

"I have it! I have it!"

"You have what?"

"You know, that idea we were talking about. If you don't wish it made public property, show me to a place where we can talk."

When Demetrios Phalereus had led me back to his chambers, I said: "What Ptolemaios needs to immortalize his name is a library. Don't wave your hand at me until I have finished, please, sir. I don't mean an ordinary library, such as many cities now have, with a couple of hundred scrolls and one sleepy slave to sort and mend them. This would be a library of a wholly new kind.

"I have in mind a vast collection of copies of all the books that have ever been written: books not only in Greek but also in other tongues, such as Egyptian and Babylonian, with word books whereby scholars can translate from one language to another. These books should be arranged in logical order: by languages, and within each language by the author. At one end of the racks should be all books by authors whose names begin with *alpha*, then all those beginning with *beta*, and so on through the alpha-beta. Do you follow me?"

"I begin to," said Demetrios Phalereus.

"Then, there should be a permanent staff of well-paid scholars to care for these books. They would not only keep the books sorted and mended, but they would also direct the slaves to copy the books before they wore out. The copyists would make extra copies for the reserves of the library and for outside sale. There would also be employees whose sole business it was to know the contents of the scrolls and direct inquiring scholars to the books they want. Say, a fellow drifts in from Syracuse. 'I hear there is a copy of Pittakos' *On the Laws* here,' he says. 'It is a lost work in our part of the world.' The librarian says: 'Right this way, sir; third stack, fourteenth case, sixth row from the bottom.' Such a librarian could even help with the research."

"Is this so different from the libraries of today?" asked Demetrios Phalereus.

"Herakles, yes! What happens now? Suppose a geographer wishes to know where the Nile comes from and what makes it rise and fall with the seasons. He goes to Athens, where he hears contradictory opinions by various philosophers and perhaps reads two or three treatises. Then he goes to Megara and reads a little more; then he takes ship to Kôs, and so on. By the time he has reached one city, he has forgotten most of what he heard or read in the last one he visited. And, needless to say, all this travel is too costly and time-consuming for all but a few.

"But with a universal library our inquirer can compare all these opinions at once and decide whether to accept one of them or to set off up the Nile on his own to find out. Now there is no place on earth where such comparison is possible. The king who made such a library a reality need never be forgotten, unless the world be overwhelmed by another flood like that of Deukalion."

"But books are costly," said Demetrios Phalereus thoughtfully.

"Of course they are, but you can still buy hundreds of books for the cost of one trireme." As I paused, the unseen powers furnished me with a clinching argument. "You already have the core of your library in the stolen hoard of Tis of Hanes, which includes thousands of rolls. Don't try to do the whole thing at once. Start with Tis's books, then add a few hundred scrolls a year. Make copies of all books coming into the kingdom, and before many years have passed you will indeed have the world's wonder."

Demetrios Phalereus rubbed his chin. "I say, Chares, I think you have something! Remember our agreement, however. Go your way, and in due course you shall hear of the outcome of your proposal."

I finished the bust of Ptolemaios, drilled with my catapult crew, and quarreled with Amenardis. These quarrels reached a pitch where the landlord of my little apartment threatened to throw us out if we did not stop disturbing his other tenants.

One of our sources of discord was my refusal to take Amenardis along when I dined with Greek friends. She refused to believe that among Hellenes it simply wasn't done. When I carefully explained that it was a compliment to her to omit her, as a Hellene would bring with him a woman of only the lowest class, she remarked:

"I always know Greeks dirty, faithless, immoral people. Now I find out they also cruel to their women. Should come to Egypt to be civilized."

I also killed much time with Onas and Berosos in the drink shops of Alexandria. When not worrying about our friends and dear ones in Rhodes (which, Python said, still stood) or weighing the complications of our personal lives, we engaged in the great Alexandrian sport of gossip.

We heard about the king's women, for instance. He had four: two wives, Eurydikê and Berenikê; an ex-wife, Artakama; and a mistress, Thaïs. All dwelt in Alexandria, and the amiable monarch somehow managed to keep on good terms with all of them.

There was also gossip about the king's eldest legitimate son, Ptolemaios called "Thunderbolt."[7] (Leontiskos, captured by Demetrios Antigonou at Cyprus, was a son by Thaïs and hence illegitimate.) Thunderbolt was a wild, violent, cruel, and gloomy stripling who, it was said, had already murdered several people for the fun of it. It is not surprising that the king chose a younger son, also named Ptolemaios, as his successor, when he resigned the throne a little before his death a few years ago.

When this happened, Thunderbolt, fearing to be brought to book for his crimes, fled from Egypt. He murdered old Seleukos the Victorious, who was so foolish as to befriend him, and seized the throne of Macedonia. Now, within the last month, I am told, he has been slain in a battle with the invading Kelts when he somehow fell off his war elephant into the midst of the foe.

Then, one day in the month of Poseideon, Python appeared at muster with his long narrow face split by a smile. He called an officers' meeting after dismissal.

"Well, boys, we have made it at last," he said. "Thanks to my persistence and powers of persuasion, the king has decided to help us. He can spare us, he says, few soldiers, but he will send three hundred thousand medimnoi of wheat and other foodstuffs. Now we can sail for home as soon as winter breaks."

We cheered our captain—I, a little ironically. Later the same day I returned to my quarters to find Berosos in converse with Amenardis. The Babylonian said:

"O Chares, have you heard of the king's wonderful plan for a universal library? Strange it is that no potentate has thought of it hitherto! They say that Demetrios Phalereus first broached the idea."

I said nothing, because of my promise to Demetrios Phalereus and my knowledge of the harm he could do my city if I betrayed him. However, as he and his king are now dead, I do no wrong by revealing my part in the instigation of the great Library of Alexandria.

Elaphebolion came on; shipping began to revive. The crew of the *Halia*, trained to a fine pitch, looked forward to their homecoming,

7 Keraunos or Ceraunus.

even though it might mean battle and death. I think we could have returned to Rhodes more promptly than we did, and that Python's affected concern for the safety of his ship was a mask for his higher esteem of his own precious skin.

My relations with Amenardis had gone smoothly for several days; so smoothly, in fact, that I suspected that something was amiss. Then, one evening, she beset me over dinner:

"Chares, I think."

"Yes, dear?"

"You say I cannot go with you to Rhodes, so I must stay here or go to some other dirty Greek place. You no think enough. I have the answer."

"Well?"

"You not go back to Rhodes. You and I go on ship together to Kôs."

"What? Dear Herakles, woman, are you suggesting that I desert my city?"

"What difference? One Greek city just like another. You take me to Kôs, make statues there. Or if you know other city not in siege, we go there. No more war, no more being afraid of Tis."

"Listen, my dear. If Tis had been going to do anything to us, he'd have done it by now. And while I don't claim to be nobler than Kodros, nobody has accused me of disloyalty to my city, and I don't intend to begin now. So forget your clever little plan."

"If you love me, you do this. Ship leave tomorrow; the *Amphitritê* of Halikarnassos. Easy; put on false beard—"

"Go walk! I won't, and that's that!"

"Stupid boy! I know better than you what good for us...."

Off we went again. In the end I slammed out and got drunk in taverns. I remember boasting in my cups, in a place run by a fat, dirty Hellene in the western part of town, of my great artistic ambitions. Then I fell asleep in a corner.

I awakened to the sound of a voice saying in a strong Egyptian accent: "Is this the man?"

My guardian spirit warned me not to start up. As I lay, shamming, the voice of the taverner said:

"He said his name is Chares, and anybody can tell he's a Rhodian from his speech."

"Aye," said the first voice. "He fits."

I opened one eye a slit. Three hard-looking knaves, with blades in their hands, were peering at me by the light of a single taper that my host, standing to one side, held aloft. Otherwise the shop was dark and quiet. I could not tell in the dimness if these were men I had seen before in connection with Tis of Hanes, but that was a minor detail.

"I want no blood shed in here," said the taverner.

"All right, we will rap him on the sconce and carry him out. Here is your money—"

I set both feet against the edge of the narrow table behind which I lay and pushed with all my might. The table flew over against the thieves, who sprang back with oaths to avoid it. Before they could recover, I was up and at the taverner, knife in hand.

This traitor had not taken the precaution of arming himself. He backed away with a cry, trying to fend me off with his left hand. Quick as a leopard, I dodged past his hand and sank my knife in his flesh. He screamed and dropped the taper, which went out.

In the instantaneous blackness that descended upon that shop, I barked my shin on a bench in trying to reach the door. However, I reached it a digit ahead of the clutching hands of my would-be murderers. Once outside, I filled my lungs and ran for my life through the moonlit streets. At every corner I took a turn, now this way and now that. Soon the footsteps of my pursuers faded away.

Then I found myself lost. The tavern stood on the edge of Rhakotis, the native quarter of Alexandria, and in my flight I had plunged into the winding alleys of this region. When the moon set, navigation became impossible.

I therefore found a nook in a vacant lot, whence I could see the approaches without easily being seen. There I sat shivering (for I had lost my cloak) through the long hours after midnight, while the countless cats of Rhakotis gamboled and quarreled about me and sang sad threnodies to the wheeling stars.

Toward dawn I fell asleep, with the result that I missed muster. With four heads instead of one, I returned home from a wigging by Python, ready to admit that I had been wrong about Tis's harmlessness. At my lodgings I found an indignant landlord with another complaint about my noisy home life, but no Amenardis.

Her absence did not alarm me until the dinner hour had come and gone without her. A knock on the door brought me bounding up, prepared for our usual tearful reconciliation. Instead of the Heraean form of Amenardis, however, there stood a small brown boy with a note in his hand and a mongrel at his heels.

"You Master Chares?" he said with an Egyptian accent.

"Yes." I gave him his half-obolos and took the papyrus. As boy and dog scampered off into the dusk, I read:

BEROSOS OF BABYLON WISHES CHARES NIKONOS WELL.

Know, dear friend, that Amenardis and I have left Alexandria on a ship for foreign parts. It wrings my liver thus to make off with your loved one—nay more, to leave the service of beautiful Rhodes. But like wet clay am I in the hands of this wonderful woman, whom I have loved with a passion that passes description ever since she nursed my wounds at Bousiris. When she commands me to go, I go.

Moreover, truth to tell, I am weary of being frightened nigh unto death, as I have been by the fighting at Rhodes and again on our venture to Memphis. No Gilgamos or other mythical hero am I, but a timid, indolent, self-indulgent man of scholarly tastes, who asks for nought but to be left alone with his philosophical studies. I simply cannot face the prospect of more death and danger. Besides, the stars foretell that certain disaster awaits me if I continue in this ill-chosen career.

Should we ever meet again, I hope that your just wrath against me will by then have waned. Come what may, to Mardoukos and Istar and Nebos on your behalf I shall pray. Farewell.

Never have I undergone such a variety of emotions as I did in the hour after I received that letter. I crumpled the papyrus and threw it across the room. I raved and cursed and stamped. I threw myself on the couch and beat it with my fists. I wept with self-pity. I swore to follow Berosos to Kôs—for I was sure he had gone thither—and cut his heart out.

Then, realizing that I was waxing hungrier by the heartbeat, I got my own dinner. I ate with a curious feeling of relief that I could not at first account for, as I assumed that my spirit was dissolved and that life was virtually over.

As I finished the rough repast, it struck me that I was fortunate, after all, for the strain of these daily quarrels had told on my nerves. From that I passed to the thought that Berosos had really done me a favor. While I roundly condemned his desertion of my beautiful Rhodes, I owed him thanks for resolving an intolerable personal situation.

Anyway, I thought with malicious satisfaction, for any wrong that Berosos has done, he will be amply punished by this Erinys in mortal form whom he has taken unto his bosom. Folly is mortals' self-selected misfortune.

Smiling in that empty little rented room (which I should give up on the morrow to move back to the safety and economy of the barracks) I poured an extra cup of wine and raised the mug in a toast to my fugitive colleague.

"Good luck, old boy," I said. "You'll need it."

Book IX

DIOGNETOS

Before the dawn of a blustery day in Elaphebolion, when Kaikias blew boisterously, the *Halia* swept into the Great Harbor of Rhodes under sail and oar, the spray curling from her ram. We cheered and waved from her deck as our beautiful city opened out before us, for the dawning light soon showed that King Demetrios had not had his will of the City of Roses. The solar-disk standards still rose from the fortifications around the Great Harbor, while the king's ships still lay, by scores and hundreds, in South Harbor and in the coves along the coast. A fiver had put out to intercept us, but our speed and the direction of the wind had rendered her effort futile.

Trumpets blew as soon as we were within recognition distance, and continued to blow as we pulled up to the quay. Soldiers trotted through the harbor gate and lined up on the waterfront A group of plumed officers walked out in front of them; among these I recognized President Damoteles, Admiral Damophilos, General Ananias, and my old commander, Bias the carpenter. A straggle of civilians also issued from the gate, forming a crowd behind the line of soldiers. There were many women in the crowd; I was astonished to see that most of them had their hair cut short, like a man's.

Python climbed down the ladder. He brought his heels together, saluted with his sword, and cried:

"Sirs, I have returned from Egypt to report success in my mission. Ptolemaios has promised us three hundred thousand medimnoi of wheat and other provisions, and perhaps some more soldiers to follow later."

The soldiers waved their spears; the crowd cheered, albeit the cheers had a thin sound. The President said:

"That is good news, Captain. How soon will these supplies arrive?"

"When the seas are calm enough to sail from Alexandria, perhaps within the month."

The officers looked at one another. Damophilos said: "We shall be dead of starvation by then. We've hanged six men in the last ten-day for stealing from the public stores of food."

Python said: "We brought what little grain we could carry in the ship."

Bias grunted. "I've been starving on a roll of lentil bread a day so long I'm used to it. I guess I can hold out a while longer."

Our executive officer motioned us to start leaving the ship. We climbed down the ladder and mustered. Python made a speech, ending:

"You have all done well by your city, which is the greatest single virtue a man can have. A cheer, now: *Iai* for beautiful Rhodes!...You have one day at liberty; then report to your regular officers for assignment. Dismissed!"

Everybody started to mill about and greet his friends and dear ones; the uxorious Onas set off for his home at a run. "*Ē*, Chares!" said a soldier in the line.

"Glôs!" I cried. "I didn't know you!"

"I hardly know myself," he said, looking down at his shrunken form. "I almost fit my armor now. We must get together, and you shall tell me all about the beautiful food you had in Egypt. That's all we think about here."

"What in Hera's name have the women done to their hair? Is this some new Scythian fad?"

"No, they've given their hair to the city for catapult skeins."

My father pushed through the crowd. We fell into each other's arms. He looked wan and drawn, like all the others, but still his competent, self-reliant old self.

"You've had one of your wishes granted, son," he said.

"How so?"

"Your mother's flower garden is no more. Every space like that in the city is given over to the growing of food. We are hoping for a crop of peas and beans, if neither birds nor burglars get them first. You didn't bring a sack of grain from Egypt, did you?"

"Alas, Father, I'm a selfish, thoughtless, worthless son! It never occurred to me. But Python brought a little to add to the city's store."

"Chares!" called Bias. "You'll have to give him up for a piece, Nikon. You know how it is. The more important they get to be, the less you see of them."

"When he makes general, I shan't see him at all, then," said my father. "Come home when you can, Chares. We can't give you much of a homecoming feast, but we can at least feast our eyes upon you."

"What's important about me?" I asked Bias.

"Oh, don't you know? But of course you wouldn't. You're a battery commander now. Come with me and I'll show you your command."

"By the! That's something. Then what are you?"

"General of artillery. Phaon is your battalion commander."

"Zeus, what a lot of promotion in three months! Have all the other officers been killed?"

Said Bias: "No. Matter of fact, there's been only a few deaths in action since you left, though we've all gone hungry. But we have a lot of new pieces, and a couple of our older officers dropped out from natural causes."

"If you're general of artillery, what has become of Kallias?"

Bias chuckled. "That's quite a story. Wait till we get to the South Wall. I'll show you."

As we crossed the marketplace, I saw that my statues of Antigonos and Demetrios still stood. "How is it that they haven't been melted down for arrowheads?" I asked.

"There was a motion before the Assembly to do just that. That fellow Lykon, your rival in the statue business, was all for scrapping them. But I stopped him."

"You?"

"Sure. I'm a full citizen now. When the rich bastards got wise to Kallias, they figured they needed a general of artillery who knew a skein shackle from a horse's arse. So they came to me. Not without citizenship, I said. I'm no mercenary soldier of fortune, I said. I'm a Rhodian, and I'm fed up with carrying out policies I don't have no hand in deciding. They had to bend the property qualification a little to squeeze me through, But they did it."

"But I thought you were for scrapping the statues! When we talked about it—"

"Sure, but I guess you kind of convinced me. Anyway, I know Lykon has a grudge against you, and I didn't like to see him put one over on you when you wasn't here. So I got up and told 'em what you had said to me: If we win, the statues will do credit to our generous spirit, while if we lose, the fact that they're still there might make the kings go easier on us."

As we neared the South Wall, I could see many changes. The animals that had pastured on the athletic field were gone; eaten, no doubt. Before the siege, a number of squatters' huts had cluttered the plaza between the wall and the city's houses. This space, thirty paces wide, was supposed to be clear of buildings, but our easygoing government had failed to keep it so. Now, however, the huts had vanished.

Behind the old wall Makar and his masons worked on a new wall, a lune parallel to the original one. They used material of all sorts: bricks, timbers, roofing tiles, broken catapult balls, and stones from the old theater and the temples. Some of these things were set in mortar, while others were only roughly fitted and piled up.

The original wall stood, but it was crazed with cracks. A line of sail-like squares of canvas had been erected on frames along the top of the wall to stop high-flying missiles from falling into the city.

Between the old wall and the new, east of the South Gate, rose two new structures: a pair of thick, squat, round towers, lower than the original wall but connected with it by a flight of steps. On each of these towers stood an enormous catapult. I recognized the three-talent stone throwers that Demetrios had erected on the South Mole, and which we had captured. One seemed complete, while men struggled to assemble the other under the direction of Polemon, the Captured Athenian engineer.

"Come on up," said Bias. He led me up a stair to the top of one of the towers.

"All right," he said, "here's your command: this pair."

He indicated the two stone throwers. I gasped. These were probably the world's most advanced catapults—Apollonios' masterpieces. The dearest wish of any engineer would be to command one, let alone two.

"By the gods and goddesses!" I exclaimed. "Bias, what have I done to deserve this? I know that many people don't like me, yet you've put me in a most responsible position. Do you think I can measure up?"

Bias: "Well, I had to push to get you the commission. Like you say, some don't take to you. But this isn't a contest in popularity. I wouldn't lay any bets on you to win the tide of the best-loved man in Rhodes; on the other hand, you've got your good points, too. You're smart, you learn fast, and you've got plenty of energy and initiative. And you've got courage. A fighter has to have courage like a boat has to float. Nothing else is any good without it."

I became absorbed in the technical details of the installation. The only major shortcoming of these colossal engines was that they were too heavy to train by ordinary means. But Bias had partly overcome even this difficulty. He had affixed posts to the corners of their frames, so spaced that men with long levers, applying them to these posts and to the crenelations of the round towers, could slowly rotate the catapults as if they were mounted on pivots.

"Don't you want a look at what the other team is up to?" said Bias.

We crossed over to the old wall. I looked across the leveled fields, where once had stood the suburbs of Rhodes. Now Protogenes' studio was almost the only structure still standing, in a cleared area four furlongs wide, measured parallel to the walls.

If I had gasped at the sight of the two supercatapults that comprised my battery, I almost stopped breathing altogether at the sight of Demetrios' engines lined up across the clearing, out of catapult range.

The sight that first caught my eye was the immense new belfry that Epimachos the Athenian had built for King Demetrios. This was the largest siege engine that the hand of mortal man had ever constructed. It was larger than the belfry that Epimachos had built for the attack on Cyprian Salamis, and larger even than the ill-fated sea tower, erected on six ships fastened together.

This belfry stood on a square base about forty cubits on a side and rose to a height of at least seventy cubits. From each corner of the base rose an immense squared timber, slanting inward toward the center, to the top of the belfry. Within the frame thus defined rose the tower. The belfry had nine stories, each smaller than that below it, so that the effect was a little like that of King Sosorthos' stepped pyramid at Memphis.

The front and sides of the tower were built of heavy timbers bolted together by broad iron plates, so that the engine appeared to be mailed in iron. On each story, in front, were ports for catapults. Before each port hung an enormous cushion of stuffed hide, with cords by which those inside the machine could raise the cushion to shoot the catapult and then lower the cushion again.

"Now you see why Kallias don't have his job no more," said Bias. "Remember that great sluing crane that was going to pick up siege engines? Well, he got a crane of sorts built over the gate tower. Then Demetrios put up that thing yonder. I figured it must weigh something like five or six thousand talents. When the Council asked Kallias how he expected to lift thousands of talents with a crane that could lift thirty or forty talents at the outside, he admitted he was licked. So they dismissed the temple thief."

"Who is municipal architect now? You?"

"No, son, I'm no architect, just a carpenter. The Council tried to get Diognetos to take his old job back, but he's still sore."

"Enough of the oak! What good would that hidebound old reactionary do?"

"Use your wits. We all know Diognetos' faults, but the point is, he can *think*. For all his dislike of anything new, he's still smarter than any three other architects you could name. He could think our way out of this mess if any man could."

I looked across at the engines. On either side of the belfry stood five tortoises: long sheds on wheels. The two largest of these, flanking the belfry, carried enormous rams, over a hundred cubits long. On either side of these stood four smaller tortoises for the shelter of sappers, who would fill the ditch outside our wall and undermine the wall itself, shielded from Rhodian missiles.

Men, small in the distance, moved about the belfry and tortoises. To our ears came the sound of hammer and saw and the bark of commands. I asked:

"How did our wall get into such shape? I see no signs of heavy assault."

"Mining. Demetrios ran galleries under our walls."

"How has it taken him so long to get ready?"

"Those contraptions take much longer to build than you'd think. And the wind and rain have slowed him up."

"Good for Helios-Apollon! I knew—"

A hand smote me on the back with such force that it nearly felled me. "Chares!" said a lusty voice.

"Phaon!" I embraced my new battery commander.

"Have you seen your new battery?" he asked.

"Yes. Aren't they beauties? I don't yet understand why I got them."

"Well, confidentially, old boy, all the rest of us in the artillery are afraid of those monsters. Moreover, it seemed only right to give the biggest catapults to the smallest officer in the corps: to balance things out, you know."

"How about ammunition?" I asked.

"That is what I wanted to speak to you about...."

Bias left us, and I spent the rest of the day organizing my crews and arranging for the manufacture and supply of balls. I had eighty-odd stone balls from the previous fighting, but these would not last a day once the battle was joined again.

For more ammunition I had to settle for balls of brick with cores of stone, as Makar could not spare his masons long enough to chip down balls of solid stone. Besides, he needed all the large stones he could get for his walls. It did not much matter; brick is about as effective as stone except against stone walls. Brick also has the advantage that the ball usually breaks on impact and hence cannot be picked up and shot back.

I named my catapults *Skylla* and *Charybdis*, after the Poet's mythical monsters. They were commanded, respectively, by Onas and by Mys.

Toward sunset the pangs of hunger reminded me that I had forgotten to eat my lunch. I went home and was made much of by my mother.

"I'm only sorry we cannot give you a decent meal, dearest Chares," she said. "I'll warrant you haven't eaten properly during all your journey. You were always the worst eater of any child I ever heard of."

"Don't worry, Mother," I said. "So long as I keep my health and strength, my diet must be adequate. The people to worry about are those like Glôs and Genetor, who lug all that extra weight around, Why, Father, what's this?"

My father came in, carrying a cuirass, a helmet, and a pair of light greaves. "A little surprise for you," he said. "I made them with my own hands. We cannot have a battery commander running around in the cap and jack of a private soldier."

"Splendid!" I cried, wriggling into the armor. It fitted perfectly, even though made in my absence. The helmet was one of those with a plume holder that rises straight up for nearly a cubit before curling over forward at the top.

"I thought it would make you look a little taller," said my father proudly. "You will also notice that the cuirass is not all tricked up with reliefs of Herakles rescuing his wife from the centaur and similar subjects. This is a fighting corselet, and such irregularities merely afford places for the foe's point to catch and lodge.... Why, Chares, what are you crying for? Don't you like the suit?"

"It's that you are t-too good to me," I said. "In spite of my being headstrong and selfish and cross-grained—"

"You're coming along," he said. "When do we eat, Elissa?"

My hunger was partly appeased by a miserable meal of barley porridge, with a few greens and one small fish as a treat. I told of my adventures in Egypt—or as much of them as I thought my parents should know—and asked for news.

"The big event," said my father, "was Demetrios' attempt to invade the city through tunnels. He began these tunnels inside his stockade, so that we could not see their entrances. It meant much delving, but he has plenty of men. He ran several tunnels across the cleared space, dipping deeply to pass under the ditch.

"Hermes only knows what would have befallen us had not a deserter warned the Council. Our people found the tunnels by setting bronzen bowls along the base of the wall—bowls made in my foundry, I'm proud to say—and watching the water in them ripple from the vibration of the sappers' picks. Then they dug a trench inside our wall, so deep that when the first tunnel emerged from under the wall, the sappers broke out into the trench. Our men jumped down and pushed into the tunnel, and a stubborn fight raged back and forth in these burrows. Your cousin Herodes was killed in this brawl.

"In the end the Antigonians were unable to force their way into the city, but neither could we force them very far back into the tunnels, because they had cross drifts by which they could feed men from one tunnel into another and cut us off. So each side piled a barrier of stones, we at the entrance of the tunnels into the trench and they farther back, and kept a sharp watch on the ends of the tunnels.

"Now, the commanding officer of the mercenaries sent by Ptolemaios is Athenagoras of Miletos. One night, when Athenagoras had the guard, the Antigonians, by hissing and whispering, persuaded him to come into one of the tunnels for a parley. An officer was there with an offer of a magnificent bribe if Athenagoras would betray the city.

"It transpired that there was one tunnel the Rhodians did not yet know of, because its crew of sappers was slow and had not yet come near the trench at the time of the breakthrough. The Antigonians wanted Athenagoras to shoo his men away from that tunnel on the appointed night, so that the sappers could break through and pour soldiers into the city.

"Athenagoras pretended to fall in with this scheme. But, he warned them, the Antigonians must scout the city first. Otherwise they would mill around in the dark, get lost in the strange streets, and be destroyed piecemeal. The Antigonian officer, a Macedonian named Alexandros, agreed to come up on a certain night and be shown over the ground.

"Then honest Athenagoras went to the Council with the story. Alexandros was captured as he came up out of the tunnel, and the Council voted Athenagoras a bonus of five talents of silver.

"Knowing that they had been foxed, the Antigonians tried to enlarge their tunnels, setting props in them, so that they could burn the props and cause the wall to fall with the collapse of the tunnels. Our men drove them out with smoke and red-hot clay and hornets' nests, though not before they had done our wall some damage. That's why Makar has been working so frantically to build a secondary wall, because we don't trust the present wall to stand for long against Demetrios' engines."

I got my battery organized none too soon. Less than a ten-day after the *Halia*'s return, Demetrios' trumpets sounded the advance.

With a tremendous groaning and creaking, as of ten thousand oxcarts with ungreased axles, nine of the eleven great engines lurched into motion; the ram tortoises stood still for the time being. A quarter of Demetrios' entire army was engaged in pushing these machines, within and at the sides and rear. Thirty-four hundred of his strongest soldiers pushed the great belfry alone.

"Herakles!" said Phaon, beside me on the wall. "Isn't that a sight?"

"It's like a whole army in armored war machines," I said.

Trumpets from the harbor told us that Demetrios was also attacking from the sea. Now thousands of soldiers marched across the plain, filing between the slow-moving engines. First came men carrying wicker mantlets, two men to each mantlet. Next came archers and slingers and scorpion men in small straggling groups.

Then came men bearing ladders over twenty cubits long. After them the infantry, brave in polished cuirasses, marched in time to the flutes, with golden eagle standards bobbing in front of each company. The sight of this vast mass of men and machines brought my heart to my throat. Nothing, it seemed, could withstand such an overwhelming assault.

A little group of mounted men cantered out between the engines: several officers, a trumpeter, a standard-bearer, and couriers. As they came nearer, one forged to the front: a big man with a purple cloak floating behind him. Although I could not make out his features at the distance, somebody cried:

"Demetrios!"

At once men up and down the wall began to shout: "Temple robber! Dung eater! Filthy sodomite!" A catapult discharged with a crash; then another. A few archers loosed shafts at an angle halfway to the vertical, in hopes of bringing down the king by a lucky long-range shot.

Most of these missiles fell short, and the archers' officers shouted to hold their shooting. One of Bias' long-range dart throwers, however, sent a dart close over Demetrios' head, so that the king flinched at the screech. He did not check his course but spurred toward the walls, passing between his archers and guiding his horse to right and left in a zigzag to throw off his enemies' aim.

Now I could make out the too-handsome features under the gleaming steel helmet. His cuirass, too, was of steel, polished until it shone like silver. Ignoring the missiles that whizzed about him, he drew rein well within catapult range and waved at us—rudely, with his palm turned toward us. The rising sun flashed on the splendid teeth which he bared in an insolent grin. Then he touched spur and headed back out of range at a leisurely canter, weaving among his advancing companies. His soldiers cheered as he passed.

Now the men who carried the mantlets came within missile range. As arrows and bullets began to fall among them, they broke into a run, carrying their defenses up to within a hundred paces of the wall before setting them down and running back. Other men set more mantlets in slanting lines extending back to the limits of missile range, to provide covered ways by which the archers could reach their shelters.

The archers rushed forward, jostling and shouting, to pick the best-placed mantlets for themselves, like a disorderly crowd scrambling for seats in a theater. Soon there was not an archer to be seen, save where a steel cap and a pair of eyes appeared in the arrow slit of a mantlet as the archer drew bow. Arrows whistled past us and skipped from the masonry; one stuck quivering in the timbers of *Skylla*.

"When shoot we, O Chares?" queried Onas.

"Not until the big engines are in range. We won't waste three-talent balls on single foes."

A trumpet blew; commands resounded. A company of foot charged clattering across the plain, shouting: "*Eleleu! Elelelew!*"

Catapults on the wall were trained with rope and crowbar to bear upon this company. The catapults crashed and their darts streaked.

Our own trumpets blared. Rhodian footmen hurried past along the wall; I glimpsed Kavaros. An officer shouted:

"Do not let them frighten you! Remember, a man on top of a wall is worth ten at the bottom!"

"Cock your piece," I told Onas. "Make the men who aren't cocking keep down." Then I went over to *Charybdis* and repeated my commands to Mys.

Other Antigonian companies advanced. Soon the dreaded cry rang up and down the wall: "Ladders! Ladders!"

Wherever a ladder appeared, Rhodians rushed up with forked poles to push it over, while missile troops showered those below with arrows, bolts, javelins, and basketfuls of stone. The Cretan archers were especially active, screeching in their unintelligible Greek and racing back and forth like boys in a hockey game. Such was the din that I had to put my mouth to a man's ear and shout to make myself heard.

The groaning, creaking mobile engines now passed through the lines of mantlets. I could see the bottoms of the huge iron-tired wheels, with rims two cubits wide, on which the belfry advanced. Seeing that *Charybdis* bore upon it, I passed the word to Mys to shoot.

Charybdis discharged with a thunderous crash. The three-talent ball struck the belfry with a thump that shook the whole structure and caused dust to fly from its joints. But the thick leather cushions, with which the front of the belfry was hung, absorbed the blow. Other catapults hurled smaller stones against it until the sound of their impact was like the roll of a gigantic drum, irregularly beaten by a mad Titan.

The tortoises moved up to the edge of the ditch. Men set up mantlets from the rear of these tortoises in rows to provide covered ways. Then, despite the hail of missiles around the open front ends of the tortoises, men began popping out to cast bundles of faggots and brushwood into the ditch before ducking back out of sight.

The belfry groaned to a stop. The cushions hanging down in front all swung up as those inside reeled in the cords. It was as if Argos son of Agenor opened all his hundred eyes at once.

The vast frame quivered as the twenty-odd catapults within discharged at once, with a mighty roll of crashes; the recoil made the belfry roll back a few digits. I risked having my head taken off to watch the flying missiles.

Each story had three or four ports. On the lowest story Epimachos had placed two three-talent stone throwers, like those we had captured. Between them, in the center, was a single smaller stone thrower, casting one-talent balls. The second story bore three one-talent stone throwers. The middle stories carried smaller stone throwers, while dart throwers shot through the ports of the upper stories.

Our wall quivered under the impact of this mass of missiles. Clouds of dust arose and chips of stone flew. Down went the cushions in front of the ports. Soon the small ports of the dart throwers opened again, but it took much longer to recock and reload the heavy machines.

Onas bellowed at his crew, which was levering *Skylla* around to bear upon the belfry. This, however, was a dishearteningly slow process, and the Egyptian cursed the day he let himself be placed in command of so immobile an engine.

The battle raged on. Little by little, Demetrios' companies of foot gave up their attacks on the wall. Their officers knew that such assaults are fruitless unless the defenders be cowed by lack of spirited leadership or laid low by plague or starvation. Short of food though we were, nonetheless the soldiers had first call on our dwindling stores and so had energy yet to spare. The Antigonian infantry fell back, leaving scores of soldiers writhing or lying still, with blood running out from under their armor.

I looked at the sun and thought: Herakles! Since when has the sun risen in the west? Then it struck me that the sun was not rising but setting. The entire day had slipped away in missile fighting. Of the sails mounted atop the wall to check missiles, some had been overthrown, while others were tattered rags. But no Antigonians had pierced our defenses, from the land or from the sea.

During the night, despite harassing archery, Demetrios' men filled up the ditch in two places. The next day, as the missile fight resumed, the ram tortoises moved up to the wall at these points. By noon they were in position. A thousand men heaved on each ram inside its shed. The great iron head drew back....

Boom! The wall shook like a man with the ague.

Boom! went the other ram.

My memory of that day is confused. I dashed about, slipping in pools of blood. I inspected my two stone throwers, helped to carry a wounded artilleryman to safety, and harassed the manager of the brick kiln to get my catapult balls baked sooner. I also did what I could to help in the defense against the rams.

Against these engines we first lowered straw-stuffed mattresses by ropes to cushion their blows; Demetrios' engineers burnt the mattresses. Then we lowered an iron hook on the end of a chain, to try to catch the beam of the ram and haul it up; the Antigonians fended the chain aside with a pole. We tried the same trick with a length of ship's cable, lowered by two men at once to catch the head of the ram in the bight; the Antigonians cut the cable.

We dropped heavy stones on the ram tortoises; the stones bounced off their strong sloping roofs. We dropped incendiary jars and javelins on them; the green hides with which they were covered shed the fire like water, though a horrid stench arose. When we did get a small fire started, the Antigonian engineers, despite the loss of several men, put it out by slapping it with a rolled-up hide.

The wall shook and wavered until we feared even to stand upon it. Then, when overthrow seemed inevitable, two muscular stevedores from the waterfront appeared with a heavy beam on their shoulders. Another pair followed them. Each pair placed his beam atop the battlements over one of the rams.

Timing their actions to the swing of the ram, one pair pushed their beam off the wall so that it fell straight down. This first beam missed the head of the ram, which drew back just before it struck.

The second pair narrowly watched the swing of the ram. One gave a short, deep shout. Over went the beam.

This time the beam struck the ram's head squarely. There was a crash and a jangle of snapped chains inside the tortoise. The ram ceased moving, with its head lying on the ground. We danced and cheered on the wall. The Antigonians pulled the damaged ram back for repairs.

The other ram continued to pound as the sun went down. As dark came on, a long chain of our men came up to the wall, each carrying a bundle of faggots or brush. These bundles they dropped over the wall above the remaining ram. As the brush piled up, it got between the head of the ram and the wall, cushioning its blows. The Antigonians stopped pounding the wall to pull the brush aside, whereupon we dropped more upon them before they could resume. When they brought out links to see by, the Cretan archers feathered them with shafts and drove them back to cover. Lastly we fired the mass, so that, to save their ram, the Antigonians had to pull back the tortoise.

The next morning, as a gusty rain slanted over the battlefield, an Antigonian trumpeter blew "parley."

Our general of infantry, Ananias, put his head over the wall and bawled: "What do you want?"

A herald called back: "The Great King, Demetrios Antigonou, at the behest of the envoys from Knidos, requests a conference."

General Ananias sent a messenger to fetch President Damoteles. When things had been explained, the President called:

"We will come by sea into the South Harbor. Expect us within the hour."

The President went away, and I saw no more of high politics that day. The President collected some Councilmen, and a fisherman rowed them around the end of the South Mole into Demetrios' territory.

The long closure of Rhodes's port had begun to hurt the other maritime Greek cities, whose favorite transshipment port it was. Moreover, they were not insensible of the benefits of our long campaigns against the pirates. Therefore the city of Knidos, nearby on the Karian coast, had sent a delegation to Demetrios, asking him to moderate his terms and promising to try to persuade the Rhodians to accept them.

So, for a ten-day, fighting was suspended. Antigonian soldiers strolled by within easy bowshot. They caroused and gambled and shouted taunts up to us, but Ananias sternly forbade us to reply.

Meanwhile Makar's masons worked furiously to raise the secondary wall. Our sentries patrolled with two spears apiece, to give the foe an impression of greater numbers than we truly had.

On the fifth day of the truce a squadron of ships loomed up. The Antigonians went out with a couple of battleships to intercept them, but to no avail. Surely the god who had wind duty that day fought for us. In came the ships, the red lion blazing on their sails. This was the shipment of three hundred thousand medimnoi that Ptolemaios had promised us. Next day we ate heartily.

Drooping spirits revived; shrunken bellies filled out. The following night a ship arrived from Kasandros with ten thousand medimnoi of barley; two nights later in came a squadron from Lysimachos with forty thousand medimnoi each of wheat and barley. I never realized how good a loaf of wheaten bread can be until I had spent half a month on barley porridge.

Then the word was passed: The king has called off the conferences; prepare for another attack. From friends with political connections I learnt that Demetrios had refused to yield a digit from the terms he had originally demanded, nearly three years before.

Skylla and *Charybdis* now had an ample supply of brick balls. On the other hand, Demetrios' engineers had also repaired their engines.

On the morning when the trumpets blew the assault, the ram tortoises rumbled back up to the wall. One moved up a little east of its former position, so that it attacked a big square tower.

Boom! Boom!

All morning the pounding went on, despite our countermeasures, from the rams and from the heavy stone throwers in the belfry. Early in the afternoon Ananias and Makar appeared on the wall in heavy, frowning conference. The general said quietly:

"Get off this section, boys. It's going any minute."

Boom! went a ram. There was a deep rumble.

With a frightful roar the wall gave way, carrying several men shrieking to their deaths. When I could see through the cloud of dust, it transpired that the curtain wall had fallen in front of *Charybdis*, down to a height of a mere ten or twelve feet.

Trumpets blew; the Antigonian infantry rushed into the breach. Spears, gilded standards, and long ladders bobbed amidst the flood. The foe swarmed over the pile of debris and down the other side—to be stopped by Makar's lune. Fighting swirled around the bases of the towers on which my stone throwers stood.

These continued to bombard the battered belfry. Several of its catapults were out of action; half its shutters hung awry with the woolen stuffing dribbling out of them.

The other ram and the stone throwers continued their attack on the wall. One more boom, another roar, and the square tower crumbled. One side fell away, leaving half the tower's interior, with stairs and storerooms, exposed to view.

More trumpets, trampings, clangor of arms, and screams of rage, fear, and death. Again I prayed to the Bright One.

I know not how we did it, but the setting sun saw every Antigonian slain or driven from his lodgment in our works. Some of our men collapsed, lying listlessly with sobbing breath. Many bled or limped; the slain were carried off. Blood was everywhere; red and slippery, or brown and dry, on shoe and kilt and skin.

Bias appeared, followed by a baker with a sackful of loaves, which he passed out. The carpenter said:

"Looks like so much of the hides and ironwork of the belfry are knocked loose that we can try a fire attack. Beginning at the second watch, on signal, all stone throwers are to throw incendiaries while dart throwers are to maintain a barrage around the belfry to keep their fire fighters away. Catch some early sleep if you can."

Despite our exhaustion, sleep was hard to come by, because during the evening Bias moved several smaller catapults to the sections of the wall near the belfry. There was a continual chatter of commands, grunting of men, creaking of ropes, and rumbling of rollers.

The second watch was nearly over when the preparations were complete. Then Bias cried: "Shoot!"

Crash! Off went *Skylla* and *Charybdis*, hurling jars of the largest size; off went all the other catapults on the South Wall. The jugs struck home with crashing, splashing sounds.

Then incendiary darts and arrows cut fiery arcs toward the dim black shape that towered into the stars. Flames sprang up its sides.

The Antigonian camp sprang to life, with torches and trumpet calls. Men poured across the field toward the burning belfry. Our dart throwers laid down a bombardment; men screamed and fell in the flickering light.

"Shoot faster!" cried Bias.

We cranked and shot until our cockers were ready to drop. But it was like trying to beat down a swarm of flies with a cudgel. The Antigonians swarmed into the engine. Hundreds began pushing, while others climbed around the narrow balconies with water buckets. With a mighty groan, the engine lurched into motion away from the wall.

"Bear a hand with those ropes!" called Demetrios' powerful voice. "You men, take hold and pull! More men on the buckets!"

Away went the belfry, shuddering, rocking, and creaking. It left a hundred little spots of fire flickering on the ground behind it, where burning incendiary mixture had dripped. The tower itself burnt for half an hour, before the fire fighters doused the last coal.

Meanwhile a party of men sallied forth and laid fire to the tortoises. The Antigonians came back, and there was confused fighting in the dark. One smaller tortoise went up in a blaze, but the Antigonians drove our men back inside the wall, pulled the other engines back, and put out the fires.

Dawn showed scores of bodies and hundreds of missiles littering the field, and all Demetrios' siege engines back out of range.

Another ten-day passed; Persephonê's flowers bloomed once more on the flanks of the akropolis. Bias, some other officers, and I stood on the newly finished lune, watching our artillerymen dig deep ditches on either side of the mound of debris where the main wall had fallen. Behind us, Makar's men, with volunteers from all corps and classes, worked on a second lune, longer than the first and reinforcing all parts of the main wall weakened by Demetrios' attacks.

Across the field the sound of tools came to us as Demetrios' workmen repaired his fire-damaged engines.

"He's a hard man to discourage," said Bias. "He'll be back again tomorrow, with more power than ever."

I said: "You once told me that old Diognetos could think our way out of this. Has anybody worked on him lately?"

"I guess not. We've had our hands full here." The carpenter wrinkled up his face. "You know, you may have said something. I'm going to speak to the President. See you later."

Two hours later Bias was back. "Phaon," he said, "you and Chares come with me. I hope you're not too proud to kneel in front of the old bastard when your city's safety demands it."

We followed the carpenter down from the wall and into the city. In the Town Hall, we found President Damoteles, the Council, and a couple of the generals; Nereus, the high priest of Helios-Apollon, and his subordinate priests; and a group of young people of both sexes. These last had apparently been picked for birth and good looks. I exchanged shy smiles with my affianced bride Io. She looked much prettier than I remembered her, even with her hair cut short. Damoteles said:

"We are going to the house of Diognetos to make a last plea to him to save us. Nereus shall make the actual appeal while the rest of us kneel humbly before him. If anybody mislike this plan, let him withdraw now."

Nobody did, and the procession wound up the hillside to the house of Diognetos. The porter fled into the house at the sight of us, and presently the old man appeared.

"By Earth and the gods!" he exclaimed. "Have you come to murder me, or what?"

Nereus, who was almost as old as Diognetos, stepped forward. "O Diognetos," he began; "we have come to you, not as murderers, but as humble petitioners...."

I do not remember Nereus' speech well enough to write it down. Nevertheless it was a cursed fine sermon, full of the loftiest Rhodian eloquence. Before he finished, the priest had everyone weeping. Everyone, that is, save old Diognetos, who stood leaning on his stick with his mouth shut in a hard line. When Nereus had finished, Diognetos looked out over our bowed heads.

"Fie!" he said. "A fine performance: free Hellenes, even your President, kneeling and sniffling! Get up, all of you. Although you do not deserve it, I will do what I can for you, on one condition."

"What is that, sir?" said President Damoteles, rising.

"Just this: that, if I capture Demetrios' oversized belfry, I shall have it as my share of the booty. Agreed?"

"Certainly, it is agreed," said the President.

"Very well, then, lead me to the scene."

When he had walked the walls, Diognetos turned to the knot of notables that trailed him. "The solution is obvious," he said. "You could have saved yourselves much trouble and many lives, had you kept faith with me in the first place, instead of spurning me for that Phoenician cutpurse."

"We have long since regretted that rash act," said Damoteles. "But what, sir, shall we do now?"

"Do you see that ditch down there, along the outer side of the pile of tailings?"

"Yes. We have dug it in the past few days, to hinder the Antigonians from climbing through the breach."

"Well, I want every vessel in Rhodes to be mobilized; every jar, jug, bucket, chamber pot, or what have you. And tonight I want everybody who can walk to carry anything wet he can find up to the breach and down to that ditch. And I want that liquid dumped into that ditch. Anything you have: water, mud, sewage, or anything at all. Be sure also to collect the jars that the dyers set out at street corners for urinals. Then we shall see what we shall see."

At dawn the trumpets blared. Once again Demetrios' engines, fully repaired, rumbled across the field. This time, I thought, we were in for it. Our defenses were steadily weakening, while Demetrios, like Antaios in his wrestle with Herakles, seemed to derive additional strength from each fall. Again I prayed.

As the engines approached to within range, our catapults were cocked and loaded. Onas said: "I fear your Diognetos, too, is but a mountebank. See, they come on as ever. What you need is a good wizard—"

"Speed up your cockers," I gritted. "There's more magic in a well-aimed three-talent ball than in all the wizards of Egypt."

On came the armored engines. Then somebody cried:

"What ails the belfry?"

Little by little the great tower slowed. The shouts of the officers, urging their thirty-four hundred men to greater efforts, rang across the field. Slower and slower went the tower.

Hundreds of infantrymen added their strength. When there was no more room around the base of the tower itself, the Antigonians belayed ropes to the engine and put more men on these.

In spite of all their efforts, the tower stopped dead.

While other Rhodians were still crying: "Why is this? A miracle!" I saw what had happened. The liquids which, at Diognetos' behest, we had spent the long night pouring into the trench, had spread out into the field, converting it into a bog. Under the weight of thousands of talents, the eight wheels of the belfry had sunk deeper and deeper into the ground, until the engine stuck fast.

Moreover, as the front wheels had reached the soft ground first, the front end of the machine sank more deeply than the rear, so that the tower was tilted forward, thus reducing the range of its catapults and rendering them useless.

On the walls we danced and yelled and embraced one another. But Demetrios was not yet finished. When his tortoises, also, began to sink into the wet earth, he had them pulled back, jacked around, and sent forward against a more easterly section of the wall. His mechanics began removing the smaller catapults from the belfry. This, however, was a very slow process, as the engines had to be taken apart and reassembled outside.

I spent the day levering my two heavy stone throwers around to bear upon the new scene of action. We sweated and strained while the roar and dust of battle rose and fell. All afternoon and into the night the rams boomed. Toward morning, despite all our counter-measures, two more sections of wall collapsed.

With the coming of light I kicked my crews awake and drove them to their stone throwers. With a few ranging shots we got the range of the ram tortoises and stove them in. By now, however, Demetrios' armored foot was already swarming into the breaches.

The fight raged for hours. Our General Ananias fell fighting like a common soldier, while the Antigonians, fighting without artillery support, suffered even more severely than we.

Then something raised our spirits wonderfully. A squadron of Egyptian ships arrived, bearing not only another shipment of food but also fifteen hundred more soldiers from Ptolemaios. The soldiers were no sooner off the ships than they were marched across the city to the battle.

The sight of all these fresh men, in spotless armor trimmed with gold, pouring in upon them, cast down the spirits of the Antigonians. They gave ground, then suddenly ran. Many threw away shields and spears. Jeering and cheering, we chased them away from the wall and drew long breaths of exhaustion and relief.

Next morning another truce was called. More than fifty envoys had arrived from Athens and other Greek cities to urge peace upon the contestants. A day's argument in Demetrios' camp, however, showed that the king had not receded from his former demands: to go to war with Ptolemaios, to give hostages, and to let his forces into the city. And why should we, who had defied him in our darkest hour, yield to him now that we were stronger?

I bathed and slept at home that night. I dreamt I was standing on the wall when it was overthrown by Demetrios' rams. I tried to escape by running along it, but each section toppled under my feet, so that I was tossed about like a leaf in a gale. . . .

It was my father, in cuirass and helmet, shaking me. "Chares!" he said. "Wake up! They blow the alarum!"

I gathered my weary wits and heard, afar off, the thin sound of trumpets and, fainter yet, the cries of men. Dogs barked furiously all over the city. My mother came in.

"They say the Macedonians are in the city!" she said.

"How can that be?" I mumbled, still more asleep than awake. "We chased them—no, that was two nights ago. What—"

My father brought in my armor. "Get into this, son."

I dressed, armed myself, and went out with my father. The sounds of conflict were louder now. They seemed to come from all directions, from near and far. People flitted about in the dark like ghosts.

At a street corner we found a bearded officer answering questions and directing people. "If you have a place on the walls, go to it," he said. "If you belong to the inactive reserve, muster under your precinct captain in the marketplace. Avoid the theater; that is where the enemy is gathered. The password is 'Helios the Savior.'

I parted from my father and headed south, giving a wide berth to the area of the theater. On the round towers I found about half my crews. The sounds of battle came more loudly.

I waited, toying with the wild idea of trying to turn *Skylla* and *Charybdis* completely around so as to bombard the theater area. But I gave it up as impractical. It would take the rest of the night to move my monsters into position, and then I should only squash a few good Rhodians by wild shots.

The cry of "Ladders!" rang out, close at hand. I led my men in a dash to the first lune. I helped to push over a ladder, while Onas (who had just arrived) split the helmet and skull of an Antigonian who popped up in front of us.

The sounds of battle came, now near, now far. We waited for at least an hour before Bias appeared.

"Chares!" he said. "You're battalion commander now. Appoint somebody to command your battery."

"Why? What's become of Phaon?"

"Dead. He got caught without a shield in the fighting around the theater."

"What shall—" I began, but Bias was gone, leaving me in command of all the catapults on the South Wall.

I strode up and down the wall, asking how many of the engines had full crews and checking supplies of ammunition. As nobody could see to shoot, I told my men to stand by and help the other soldiers beat off attempts to scale the wall.

Several such attempts were made but were not pressed home. I think Demetrios launched them in the hope that all the defenders had left the walls and rushed down into the city to deal with the group in the theater, as indeed a less seasoned and well-organized army of defenders might have done.

Toward morning I made up scratch crews for two unmanned dart throwers, with Onas in command of the pair. We lowered the engines down a stair, found rollers for them, and towed them off toward the theater.

As we neared the theater, we came upon knots of spearmen waiting for daylight to close in upon the enemy. I had to shoo them aside to let my catapults pass. Somebody said:

"Who is this? Chares?"

I recognized the voice of President Damoteles, in armor and leading the reservists. "Yes, sir," I said.

"A good idea, bringing these engines. Between the reservists, and the Ptolemaians, and the Cretans on the roofs, and now this, we ought to smash them."

"How did they get in, sir?"

"Some sentries at the westernmost break in the wall decided that the war was over and they might as well take things easy. The Antigonians cut their throats as they slept, climbed the stairs of the ruined tower, gained the top of the first lune, and thence marched down the stair and into the city. They had reached the theater when the alarum was sounded."

"How many are there?"

"We do not know, but it seems like a couple of thousand. Place your catapults where the Street of Dyers opens on the Square of the Theater."

"Good luck, son!" came my father's voice out of the darkness.

A little farther on we reached the designated spot and set up our dart throwers. When I saw that the general aim was right, the supply of missiles adequate, and a squad of spearmen at hand to protect the pieces, I bid Onas good luck and returned to the South Wall.

As dawn lit the oriental sky, attacks on the walls came with increasing frequency and vigor, while from within the city arose a vast uproar as the Rhodians attacked the Antigonian force in the theater. I could see nothing of this fight except for some of the Cretan archers moving about the roofs of the houses on the near side of the Square of the Theater.

The din kept up for hours. Again and again the Antigonians surged up into the gaps in the outer wall, and again and again the artillery poured balls and darts into their crowding masses while the infantry drove them back with arrow and javelin and thrusting spear. Demetrios had set up two more catapults from the belfry, which sent darts whizzing at us in high arcs, but we had the advantage of being mounted thirty feet higher than they. Our long-range dart throwers drove the unprotected Antigonian crews from their engines. Demetrios' great belfry, which might well have tipped the scale in his favor, stood silent and abandoned.

When the sun stood at the top of its fiery arc, the fighting slackened off. The Antigonians straggled back behind their mantlets or out of range. We wolfed our lunches, expecting them to renew the attack.

The attack did not come. Instead, the uproar from inside the city increased. Wondering if the Antigonians had broken in at some other point, I sent a messenger down toward the theater to find out. When he did not return after half an hour, I appointed a deputy battalion leader and went to see for myself.

The streets were so crowded that it was all I could do to worm my way through. As I got closer to the theater, pools of blood became common. Wounded were helped away; corpses were borne off. The most astonishing sight that met my eyes was six disarmed Antigonians, roped together with their hands tied behind them, being prodded on their way by a spear in the hand of Genetor, my prospective father-in-law.

"Did you capture them all yourself, sir?" I asked.

"Not exactly, Chares, not exactly. To tell the truth, I think Damoteles deems me more useful at this task than at fighting in the front rank."

"Are they broken yet?"

"By no means. Some have given up and many have been slain, but hundreds are still massed in the square, defying us to do our worst. The captain who leads them, an Epeirot named Alkimos, is a very fiend."

I kept on pushing until I came to the square. Here I could see nothing but the backs of our foot, pressing in upon the Antigonians with a deafening din. I worked around until I came to one of the dart throwers. Onas helped me to climb up on the structure, so that I could see over the forest of plumed helmets.

"This is the fourth attack," shouted Onas. "The foot goes in and works on them for a while; then they are withdrawn while we and the Cretans ply them with missiles. There goes the recall now!"

Trumpets blasted, and the Rhodians drew back, breaking up into their separate platoons. Their officers herded them this way and that to get them out of the way of the missile troops.

"Cock your pieces!" said Onas.

The square was littered with bodies and weapons. On the far side, where the old theater had stood before it was demolished to reinforce our walls, stood the mass of Antigonians, clustered close, with their shields in line. Even at this distance I could see that their armor was battered and bloody.

"A most obdurate foe," said Onas. "Shoot at will!"

The dart throwers discharged; their darts whistled on flat courses across the square, to plunge into the packed ranks. There was a movement among the Antigonians as those on the outside knelt and those inside raised their shields to form a tortoise. At the same time came a bark of commands from the roofs around us; hundreds of Cretan arrows streaked toward the invaders. The arrows skipped from shield and helm; here and there one found an opening, and a man fell clanging. Off went the dart throwers again.

"Faster on the cocking!" said Onas. "Had we a hundred of these, Chares, we should have cleaned out the miscreants long since.... *Ech!* Guard yourself; here they come!"

Suddenly the mass of Antigonians moved, shaking out into a regular formation as it advanced, with spears in the front rank. Our trumpets blasted madly; a platoon of Rhodians ran clattering to take the enemy in flank. In front of the Antigonians trotted an enormous man, six feet tall and built like a Scythian bear, wearing an iron cuirass like that of the king. Over the rising din I heard Onas' shout:

"Chares! Take a shield!"

I darted forward to pick up one of the discarded shields that littered the pave. Two Rhodian spearmen rushed against the giant leading the Antigonians. With two swipes of his huge sword he smote them both to earth, and an arm flew off one of them. On came the Antigonians, shouting:

"The Empire! King Antigonos! *Eleleleu!*"

I ran back to the catapults, just ahead of the Antigonians, who were trying to break out through the Street of the Dyers. The catapult crews clustered around their pieces, lightly armed and not looking too resolute, but held to their posts by Onas' powers of command. Arrows rained upon the Antigonians, and Rhodian footmen hurled themselves upon their flanks with spear and sword; but those in front pressed on, mowing down all who strove to stop them.

I do not know quite how it happened, but I found myself engaged with the giant Antigonian captain all by myself. I had no time to think on the ridiculous spectacle that this fight must present when the giant's sword, striking my shield, hurled me headlong to the ground by sheer impact.

Then the bronze-clad legs of the Antigonians were all around me, as in that fight on the mole. I rolled over and got my shield over me.

Two cubits away Onas and the steel-clad captain traded Homeric blows. Onas, though not so big as his foe, was still one of our largest and strongest soldiers. For three heartbeats they faced each other, their swords clanging like blacksmiths' hammers. Then an Antigonian spear took Onas in the ribs from one side, and down he went.

Blind with rage, I rolled to hands and knees and sent a backhand cut at the Antigonian's ankle. The blade bit into the hamstring. Like a felled oak, the giant tottered, swayed, and toppled. A rush of Rhodians swarmed over him, jabbing and hacking. A body fell across me, and another.

By the time I crawled out from under, the last armed Antigonians had pushed out of the square; the only living foes left were the wounded and the prisoners. The sounds of fighting receded down the Street of the Dyers.

Onas was dead. Blinking back tears for a brave and true comrade, I rounded up the catapult crews and started them hauling the engines back toward the wall. It took an hour because of the press in the streets and the litter of bodies and weapons.

By the time we reached the wall, the Antigonians who had broken out had long since limped and staggered across the field to their camp. Perhaps two hundred had escaped, compared to three hundred captured and nearly a thousand dead. Of those who got out, nearly every man bled.

On the wall I found Bias with blood on his armor. "General!" I said. "Fie upon you, you've been fighting! Is that any way for a general to act? This isn't the Trojan War, you know."

"Look who's talking!"

"Why, what's wrong with me?"

"Your face!"

I put my hand up and found that my face was covered with blood from a cut that had laid open one cheek. Now I understood why I had found it hard to talk clearly, though I had no remembrance of the blow itself. I was also soaked with the blood of those who had fallen on top of me at the Square of the Theater.

"President Damoteles is dead," said Bias. "Your catapults helped a lot. I don't think the boy wonder will try any more attacks today. His men balked this afternoon, and the sight of those troops that broke out finished off their warlike spirit."

"Have you any news of my father?"

"I wouldn't know about him. Get along home and have that wound sewn up. We can't have the handsomest man in Rhodes going around with his face laid open."

At home I found my father, with a leg wound that lamed him for the rest of his days. My mother and Io were nursing him. The women gave a little shriek at the sight of me.

"It's only a scratch," I said, "but I shall appreciate it if you ladies will wash it off and sew it up." I spoke thickly out of one side of my mouth.

When I had looked into my father's wound, I asked him how the battle had gone with him.

"We broke them!" he said. "It was hard work for us old fellows who hadn't wielded a spear for years, but we did it. A lot of reservists fell besides Damoteles; Giskon's friend Nikolaos, for instance.

"The Antigonians had a captain, Alkimos, six feet tall and wearing one of those iron cuirasses you tell me about. He led his men again and again, roaring and smiting like a lion. But somebody—some little fellow—got him in the leg and brought him down, and then we all surged over him. I wish I could have gotten my hands on that steel corselet, but somebody else made off—why, what's funny?"

As Io was cleansing my face, I could only laugh out the side of my mouth and point to myself.

"Oh," said my father. "So it was you? I wasn't close enough to see. Son, if I've castigated you in the past, forget it. You're the bravest hero we have."

It did not seem politic to argue that I had gotten into handplay with Alkimos because I had been too stupid to get out of his way. I said:

"If those steel corselets become common, it won't be good for the bronze-founding business."

"My thought exactly. I remember when the steel helmet first began to come in, when I was apprenticing to my father in Lindos. He was sure that steel would never prove practical for armor. A steel helmet would be too brittle, or would rust away unless cleaned every day, and so forth. Well, the steel helmet is now common; but we nearly went bankrupt before the old man would admit it was here to stay."

I said: "Oh, well, I suppose we can always sell lamps and trays."

My mother said: "Chares, if you'll stop talking, I will sew up your wound. Hold still; this will hurt. . . ."

The wound left a conspicuous scar on my cheek; but, to tell the truth, I have been proud rather than regretful of that scar.

Io bathed me and scrubbed the dried blood off me. Later, when the women had left us alone for a moment, my father said: "What are you going to do, son, when peace finally comes?"

I spoke in a muffled voice through my bandages: "I'm going back to my studio. But I'll still help out with the foundry; don't worry about my abandoning the business. Where's Io?"

"She'll soon be back. What's the hurry?"

"I like to see her around. I never knew she was so good at nursing."

After my father and I had been put to bed for the night, I said: "Father! If peace come, I should be glad to wed Io as soon as it can be arranged."

"Oh? Why the change?"

"Put it this way. I once had a friend who did not wish to wed any Greek girl. They were, he thought, too tame and subdued, and would bore him. His mind was full of romantic notions of mating with some foreign wench of more wit and spirit, who would make life interesting.

"Well, he had a chance to know such a woman—quite well—and learnt that a very little of a vigorous, domineering dame goes a long way. In the end he was glad to settle down with a sweet, docile Greek girl of good family, earn a decent living, and rear a family."

"Oh," said my father. "Your friend learnt wisdom at last. Well, I shall see Genetor one of these days and take the matter up with him."

As it fell out, Genetor came to see us, wig awry and wringing his hands in piteous fashion.

"*Oimoi!*" he moaned. "Woe and destruction! Have you heard the conditions of peace that those god-detested politicians of ours have agreed to?"

"Surely not to let Demetrios' forces into the city!" I exclaimed.

"No, no, nothing like that. They have agreed, however, that we shall be allies of Kings Antigonos and Demetrios against all foes except Ptolemaios."

"Why," said I, "those are just about the terms we offered him before the siege!"

"But that is not all. They have also agreed to give him a hundred hostages—the hundred richest citizens of the city. And naturally that includes me!"

"You poor fellow!" said my father. "That's the price of wealth."

"But still that is not all. Do you know what stipulation those intriguers and windbags have made? That no officeholders shall be included among the hostages! Oh, the perfidy of it! The rest of us must waste our lives in durance vile while these polluted rascals strut and swill, free men, in our beautiful city! They have taken care of themselves, all right!"

"Perhaps you ought to have run for office," murmured my father. The dexterity with which Genetor, when he had been made a full citizen, had nevertheless avoided all public offices and liturgies because of the financial burdens that these entail in maintaining ships, staging drams, and feeding the poor was a common joke in Rhodes.

"However," continued my father, "before you sail off with Demetrios, we ought to consider our children's wedding. This betrothal has run on more than long enough."

Genetor: "True, true. It were better to push it through now, before I am carried off into shameful captivity. In Ephesos, where I am not known, how could I make a decent match for my little girl?"

The beginning of the first year of the 119th Olympiad, when Pherekles was archon at Athens, saw the wedding of Chares of Lindos to Io daughter of Genetor. The marriage turned put exceedingly well, considering that the groom was not the easiest man in the world to live with.

A few months later I was sitting in my father's house, watching Io go about her wifely duties, wearing a blue-gray veil made from the remanent of Demetrios' original robe—nay more, actually going out of her way to try to please me, despite my shortcomings—I thought, what a fool you have been, Chares! This is the true love, built up piece by piece by time and mutual effort. That other thing, that emotional storm that seizes one on first sight and all but tears one to bits, is all very exciting, but it cannot compare with this for solid comfort. Treat the little creature well and she will repay you at a higher rate of interest than Elavos the Syrian ever charged.

The same season also saw Genetor and his wife, with the other hostages, departing on an Antigonian battleship amid many tears and lamentations. It saw King Demetrios sail away toward Hellas in his great two-masted elevener, followed by his whole vast fleet, still gorgeous with purple and gold. This mighty force, despite the skill of its sailors, the number and hardihood of its soldiers, and the demoniac ingenuity and determination of its dashing sea king, had been fought to a standstill by the people of one small, free, republican city.

We learnt that Demetrios might not even then have raised the siege but that his father had written urging him to make peace. King Antigonos had gotten wind of another alliance among Ptolemaios, Seleukos, Kasandros, and Lysimachos. These satraps, all of whom now called themselves kings, were determined to quash, once and for all, the boundless claims and pretensions of the Antigonids.

The pirates had already scattered, fearing the vengeance of Rhodes. Of those whom they had enslaved, few ever came home again. The war left many gaps in the ranks of my foes, my friends, and my kinsmen.

An embassy arrived from Rome, now a rising power, to congratulate Rhodes on her victory. In gratitude for Ptolemaios' help, the Assembly conferred upon the king of Egypt a series of honors almost as extravagant as those bestowed by the Athenians on Demetrios. The Rhodians addressed Ptolemaios as "Savior," which title seems to have taken his fancy, for he adopted it officially.

Book X

KAVAROS

When I re-entered my studio for the first time in more than a year, I saw that I had my work cut out for me. My tools I had taken home, but other equipment too heavy to move—furnaces, anvils, tubs, troughs, and the like—was mostly broken or stolen. Refugees had camped here, using my scanty furniture for firewood, and gangs of boys had broken things up.

I was poking at the litter in a futile sort of way when I heard a step behind me. Before I could turn, a large hand grasped my shoulder and whirled me around. There stood Kavaros, wearing a plain but decent tunic, with wine on his breath and murder in his eyes.

"This for you!" he cried.

A fist crashed into my jaw, and down I went. The next thing I knew, he was cradling me in his arms and weeping over me.

"Ah, the poor little man!" he moaned. "Bad cess to me that struck him, and him so brave and clever and all!"

I tore loose. "Before I cut your heart out," I said, "would you mind telling me why you did that?"

"It was only to get even with you for all the times you beat me, sir. My honor demanded it."

"Honor! But you were a slave then!"

"Maybe I was to you, Master Chares, but to me I was still Kavaros son of Ortiagon, a chief's son and a Keltic gentleman. And I did not like the beatings any more than you would."

I was filled with mixed emotions. On one hand, I was furious with Kavaros, but on the other I had to admit the logic of his feeling as he did.

"Go walk! The wild Keltic race is too much for me," I said, rubbing my jaw, picking up the broom, and resuming my work. "I shall never understand them."

"It is truly sorry that I am, sir," he said. "If you would like a bit of a knock at me, go ahead and take it. Here, young master, indeed and you are doing it all wrong. Give me that broom."

The Kelt fell to work with a will. I think he stirred up twice as much dust and caused twice as much commotion as he needed to, but that was ever his way.

"It is like my great-grandfather and the enchanted bear," he said. "My ancestor was hunting in the Rhiphaian Mountains once when he came upon this big brown devil, who knocked the spear out of his hand with one paw and my ancestor into a snowdrift with the other. When my great-grandfather dug himself out, there was the bear standing over him and growling like a thunderstorm that had got out of bed the wrong side that morning.

"'Well, bear, get on with it,' said my ancestor. 'If I am to be ate, I do not want to be wasting time with preliminaries.'

"'Who said anything about eating you?' said the bear. 'People have always disagreed with me. I want to know what you mean by trying to poke me with that little pointed straw.'

"'That is no straw but a spear, and I am after trying to kill you, because you are a bear and I am a man, and it is right and proper for the likes of me to kill the likes of you.' Then something about this conversation struck my ancestor as curious, for he was a clever man. 'And what are you doing, my good bear, talking to me like this? Is it that you are an enchanted bear?'

"'I wondered how soon you would notice,' said the bear. 'Know that I am Prince Tasios of the Bastarnians. I was betrothed to the daughter of the king of the Elves, but Morrigana the witch, who loved me, changed me into this shape in a fit of jealousy. And I cannot recover human form until I find a man who is willing to exchange shapes with me.'

"'Indeed and it is a pleasure to meet you, sir,' said my great-grandfather. 'Know that I am Gargantyos of the Tektosages, who married the daughter of the king of the Elves.'

"At that the bear began to growl and roll back his lips, until the big white teeth of him stood up like the snow-covered peaks of the Rhiphaians. My great-grandfather saw that the bear would soon eat him out of simple jealousy, even though he suffered a bellyache afterward. So my forebear said: 'Did you say something about finding a man to exchange shape with?'

"'And would you be willing, now?' said the bear.

"'I might,' said my great-grandfather. 'What sort of arrangements have you here for bearing it?'

"The bear waved a paw, pointing out where there was berries to be found in the fall, and the stream that the salmon came up, and the woods that had deer and rabbits, and all the other things needed for a bear's comfort. 'And my wife is sleeping in a cave on the north side of this hill,' said the bear.

"'Is it a good wife that she is?' said my great-grandfather.

"'A bear could not ask for better,' said the bear. 'How is dear Brigantia these days?'

"'She grows more beautiful every day,' said my great-grandfather, omitting any further description of the lady, to whom he had now been married for above two years and so knew her better than when he had first met her in the halls of the Elf-king.

"Well, the bear's eyes began to roll with thoughts of his lost love; so he and my great-grandfather each drew a drop of blood from his arm, and they mixed them. When they stood up, Prince Tasios had my great-grandfather's form, while my ancestor had the shape of the bear. And they parted with expressions of esteem.

"Now my great-grandfather thought: I have loved many a woman, but never a bear, to do which in my human form would be indecent not to mention unsafe. And he galloped off to the northern side of the hill and found the cave. There inside was the lady bear asleep with two little ones curled up beside her.

"When my great-grandfather had had his fill of looking upon this scene with eyes full of tender sentiment, he tried to wake up the lady bear. He had a terrible time getting her to waken at all. When she did and saw what he had in mind, she roared in bear language: 'Are you out of your wits? You know it is not the season!' And she set upon my poor ancestor and nearly clawed and bit him to death before he ran howling and bleeding out into the snow.

"Well, my ancestor recovered from that reception, except that a piece was bit out of one of his ears permanent. And he spent a dull winter digging mice and squirrels out of their holes to eat. But before the snow was all gone, who should come back but Prince Tasios, wearing my ancestor's body.

"'What a dirty liar you are, Gargantyos!' he said. 'Why did you not tell me what I was getting into?'

"'Liar yourself!' said my great-grandfather. 'I told you the true answer to your question, which is more than you did for me.'

"So Prince Tasios threw his spear at my ancestor, who knocked it aside and chased the prince up a tree. After much mutual roaring of insults, the prince called down: 'What is the matter with my wife? The bear one, that is. She was always a good wife to me, you ungrateful spalpeen!'

"When my ancestor told Tasios what had happened, the prince laughed so he nearly fell out of the tree. 'Of course not, your poor loon; bears have but one season for love, and that in the summer. I am the one with cause for complaint. No sooner did I put foot in your castle than dear Brigantia scolded me for tracking mud in on her clean floors. Then she scolded me for not bringing her a fur coat. Then she scolded me because at dinner I held the roast in place with my paws and put my mouth down to it, as any well-behaved bear would do. Then she scolded me for going to bed with my clothes on, as I had forgotten about this business of dressing and undressing. And when I finally got to bed, she kept waking me up by saying: 'Well?'

"The third time this happened, I said: 'Well, what?' And then she began to cry and say I did not love her any more.

"'Now that I bethink me, I begin to understand what she was complaining about, for I had forgotten your beastly human habits in the years I lived out here. And, if you like, I will gladly be changing shapes with you again.' So they did: and each lived, if not happily ever after, at least wiser than they had been, which is the best that mortal creatures can reasonably expect. And the moral is that, if you cannot have what you think you want, it is often just as well."

When I got my breath from laughing, I said: "What are you going to do now?"

"I will be going back to the land of the Tektosages; a ship to Macedonia leaves tomorrow. To be sure, a fine thing it is to be a free man and an enrolled Rhodian tribesman, but it is well to live among your own people, too. Here, sir." He pulled out a heavily laden wallet and handed it to me. "Keep that for me, please, and let me not have any until I am after boarding my ship. It is my mustering-out pay. I know myself, and if I try to keep it, it will be all drunk up."

"Excuse me, O Chares," said another voice uncertainly from the doorway. Who should stand there but my old foe Kallias! I hardly knew him. His hair had grayed completely, and he had lost twenty or thirty pounds. The siege had aged him by decades; his skin had a grayish hue in lieu of its former ruddiness.

"Well?" I said.

"Well—ah—know, dear friend, that I am planning to leave Rhodes," he said. "As you are aware, I have run into difficulties here. They are not really my fault; the disfavor of Lady Luck and the conspiracies of jealous competitors caused them. However, you know how people talk. I doubt that I shall be able, therefore, to get good commissions in nearby cities like Knidos and Kôs.

"What I must do is to go far afield—say, to Byzantion or Syracuse—where none has yet heard these calumnies. And there is a difficulty. To move myself and my family, such a distance takes more money than I have. So I wonder if I could not persuade you to lend me a little, just till I get established in my new home—"

"No," I said.

"Just a few drachmai? You are going to be successful, Chares, as I always said you would. You will never miss—"

"Not a half-farthing. Get out!"

"After all, I did give you your start—"

"Go!" I shouted, taking a step forward.

Kallias turned away with a sigh. As he disappeared, Kavaros said: "Master Chares, could you let me have a little silver out of that wallet I just gave you?"

"What for?"

"To give the poor man."

"That liar, faker, and grafter? I should say not! Anyway, you just told me not to give you any of this money until you were on your ship, and that's what I shall do."

Kavaros sighed in his turn. "It is a hardhearted fellow that you are. But perhaps you are right."

The Rhodians were mystified when the Council told them to assemble on the plain south of the city, on the fifth of Hekatombaion. They were more puzzled when the new President commanded:

"Lay hold of those ropes, men! The rest of you go behind the belfry and under it. Place your hands against the crossbeams."

When five thousand Rhodians were clustered around the engine, the President cried: "Now, all together, *heave*!"

As the earth had been dug away to make a ramp in front of the sunken wheels, the belfry groaned up the gentle slope and began rolling toward the city.

Being one of those commanding the men who pulled and pushed, I was in on the secret. We headed the engine toward the place where the South Gate had stood. It was not hard to maneuver, as the eight huge wheels were mounted on castors and so could be swiveled.

Once the Council was sure that Demetrios had sailed away for good, they had most of the South Wall torn down. It was in such tumbledown condition from the battering of Demetrios' engines that it was cheaper to build a whole new wall than to try to patch the old one. Makar and his masons were already at work on the new wall, but a fifty-cubit gap had been left where the gate had stood.

Makar himself was among those pulling. As the machine rumbled toward the city, he cried: "O Chares! Be sure to look inside this thing. Remember what happened to the Trojans!"

A half-hour's pull brought the belfry into the city. We halted inside the ruins of the old wall, on the open plaza.

As the monstrous engine groaned to a stop, old Diognetos stepped forward, wearing the golden crown surmounted by rayed solar disks, which the Council had conferred upon him along with every other honor they could think of. He held up a hand for silence.

"When I undertook to save the city," he rasped, "I demanded this belfry as my share of the spoils. Now that I have it, there is a question of what to do with it. It does not look edible, nor could it easily be turned into a comfortable dwelling house, even by so accomplished an architect as myself. 'Well then, you will say, why do I not disassemble it and sell the parts? The timber, iron, and hides must be worth many talents.

"However, I am old. I am comfortably off now, and I do not wish to spend the rest of my days seeking out customers for these materials. Nor have I the true huckster's gift, as has a certain colleague of mine, now happily departed from this land. Therefore, it seems to me that the best thing to do with this monstrosity is to give it to Rhodes. Chares, where is that sign?"

I held up the bronzen placque (which I had cast the day before in the foundry) against the timbers of the base of the belfry, while Diognetos drove two bronze nails through the holes in the ends. Then we stepped back and read:

DIOGNETOS DEDICATED THIS TO THE PEOPLE
FROM THE SPOILS OF WAR

"There you are," said Diognetos. "You do not deserve it after the way you treated me. But," he added, wiping away a tear, "you have suffered for your fault, and I cannot help loving you, at least a little. Let's go."

He tottered off on his stick, amid cheers that shook the blue sky above. Then we swarmed into the belfry to examine it.

Most of the catapults were still in place. Demetrios had provided two sets of stairs, with signs indicating that one was to be used by upward-bound traffic only and the other by descending traffic. Thus was confusion among the crews avoided.

Also, profiting from the loss of Epimachos' previous belfry at Cyprian Salamis, the king, or his engineer, had placed a huge tub of tarred leather on each story, hung about with leathern buckets for fighting fires. This, then, was how the Antigonians had saved their belfry the night we set it afire. What a pity that Demetrios was not satisfied simply to practice engineering! He had made a far better technical man than a king.

When it transpired that the sale of the war materials left by Demetrios would come to scores or even hundreds of talents if shrewdly handled, the Council asked among the citizenry: What to do with this money? Some were for saving it; some, for putting it into defenses; some, for distributing it to the people. As I was now a person of some standing, albeit not a full citizen, the Council also sought my opinion. I said:

"Gentlemen, know that I was not, formerly, a religious man. But several times during the late war I prayed to Helios-Apollon to save us. Each time he responded magnificently. Some of my philosophical friends may tell me that my logic is faulty, but it is good enough for me. As you know, I have returned to the faith of my fathers and joined the Board of Sacrificers of our chief temple.

"Since you ask me what to do with this money, I would honor the true savior of our beloved city by building him a statue: the greatest statue that has ever been erected. I personally swore to Helios-Apollon that if we won the war and I survived, I should urge this plan upon you and devote my life to the building of this memorial."

"Do you mean," said one Councilman, "a statue like the Tarentine Zeus of Lysippos?"

"Oh, no. I would make this one twice as tall—as tall as Demetrios' great belfry, which is about seventy cubits high. Lest the commercial-minded among you hesitate, I might add that from a secular point of view this money were not ill spent. Many cities profit from having some wonder to draw travelers, as the pyramids draw them to Memphis. This statue would spread our fame throughout the world and thereby attract business."

Several ten-days passed while they wrangled. I appeared again and again to repeat my arguments. When the Council adopted my plan and presented it to the Assembly, a citizen named Evarchos read an hour-long speech against the proposal. Since my old antagonist Lykon had written this speech, you can imagine its tenor:

"...Fellow citizens, must we be stupid? Anybody can see that Chares has proposed this plan because he knows that if it be adopted, he will be in a position to secure the contract for himself. Now, we all know what sort of person Chares is: a mere baseborn artisan, and not even a real Hellene; vulgar, quarrelsome, pushing, self-conceited, and implacably ambitious; a climber if ever I saw one. Why, if given a chance, he would make this statue an eidolon of himself, with his own face atop it! If that be his aim, let him do it with his own money, not ours! Shall we bob at the end of this grasping Phoenician's string, like a bait on a fishing line?..."

However, my friends in the Assembly defended me doughtily. Bias said:

"Look here, Rhodians. We've voted to build statues of Kasandros and Seleukos and Lysimachos. For Ptolemaios we've voted not only a statue but also a temple. That's all very nice, but if we're going to load these honors on our mortal helpers, we ought to do something special for the immortal one. Someday these Macedonian warlords will all be with the shades, but Helios will still be here when we need him. So it don't make sense to be stingy with the god...."

In the end the proposal passed. There followed months of discussion about the site and the appearance of the statue. At one session of the Council they threw some fantastic proposals at me. One said:

"Let the statue bestride the harbor, with one foot resting on each of two moles, so that ships shall pass between its legs!"

"That were impossible," I said.

"Why so?"

"It's a matter of elementary engineering. A statue of this size must be braced by columns of stone, rising through the legs. If the statue straddled the harbor, the legs would rise at a slant, and the columns would not stand up; they would collapse of their own weight. Moreover, the space between the statue's legs would not allow enough clearance for the masts and yards of the larger ships. And, lastly, I should have to close the harbor to traffic. This would ruin our city, since the statue will take years to build."

In the end we chose as our site the high ground west of the Great Harbor, where the foreign quarter lies.

Then there were the financial details. As nobody had ever built so large a statue, none knew what it would cost. The estimates started low and kept climbing as each new expense transpired. In the end I undertook to build the Helios for the cost of materials plus a fixed fee of two hundred talents, to be paid in installments.

The Council and I agreed that it were better to take my time in beginning the statue until I had learnt everything I needed to know. Meanwhile I had plenty to keep me busy. The new theater was taken in hand again, and I was told to go ahead with the statues of the playwrights. The city also ordered a statue of King Ptolemaios for the Ptolemaeion, as well as several smaller statues to decorate this edifice. Business was so brisk that I hired a couple of full-time assistants for the studio.

Summer had come again when a familiar voice spoke through the door of my busy studio: "Is it that Master Chares still works here now?" There stood a tall, red-haired, mustached man wearing Keltic trousers and tunic of a gaudy checkered pattern, with squares of red, yellow, and blue.

"Kavaros!" I cried, clasping his hand. "I thought you'd gone back to live among your wild countrymen in Getika."

"That I did, that I did. But things are not what they used to be. My poor father was dead. Some dirty murtherers from the Trokmoi had slain him, and for no reason at all, just because he had taken a few heads from their tribe to hang over his gate. A new chief leads the clan, so it is no longer a chief's son that I am. Then there was a bit of an argument with a man who thought that my wife Grania here"—he indicated a tall, beautiful, golden-haired woman in the doorway—"ought to belong to him. And besides, sir, to tell the truth, I am after being spoilt by life in a great city. A man can buy so many nice things that he cannot get in the Keltic country."

"But what will you do in Rhodes?"

"I am thinking you will need a pair of strong arms to help with the heavy lifting and moving for your new statue. I will work as I did before, but as a free man, of course. I leave the pay to you; as a gentleman you will be fair."

So I took on Kavaros at two and a half drachmai a day: a fair rate of pay for a starter. Although he still had his old faults, he soon made himself indispensable nonetheless.

After the contract with the city had been signed, you might think that I could start work at once. But as Hippokrates the physician once said, art is long, life short, opportunity fleeting, experience deceptive, and judgment difficult. I did not intend to spend years in putting up my statue, to have the first blast of Boreas tumble it down. Hence it took eleven years of painstaking preparation before I could actually begin the construction of my Helios.

After months of work on my lesser contracts, of wandering about the foreign quarter to see just where the Colossus would look best, of making and discarding models, and of covering tablet after tablet with calculations, I set sail for Argos. It was spring of the second year of the 119th Olympiad, when the allied kings were closing in upon Antigonos and his son Demetrios.

I had to wait over three days in Argos for a party for Corinth to be made up. Brigandage was rife in Hellas, and few roads were safe for solitary travelers.

A hard day's muleback ride through the rugged, scrub-covered hills of Argolis brought us into sight of the Gulf of Corinth. Here I left the party and, with my new Colchian slave, took the coastal road westward. The first stars to light their tapers saw me banging on Lysippos' door in Sikyon.

"Well, well!" cried the old man, with a gap-toothed grin, "Do not tell me that Chares of Lindos has gone all these years unhanged! I remember you well. Talent you had, but you were the snottiest little bastard I ever dealt with."

"I still am, you old tyrant," I replied, "but I've learnt to hide it. Have you reached your goal of fifteen hundred statues yet?"

"No, but I shall, even though age has slowed me. The boys do most of the work now." He raised his voice. "Daïppos! Boêdas! Euthykrates! Here's one of our old apprentices, grown famous!"

The three young stalwarts rushed out and fell to wringing my hand and pounding my back. In the time of my apprenticeship my relations with Lysippos' sons had not been friendly. I suppose they feared that I might gain a lasting influence over their sire, to the detriment of their own careers. Now, however, their greeting was as hearty as one could have wished.

"Dinner is over," said Lysippos, "but our cook shall scramble something up for you. Come in, man, and tell us all about the great siege! Is that how you got that scar on your face?"

An hour and a skin of wine later we had finished with the siege and were asking about fellow artists. I said:

"What has become of Eutychides? You remember, he and I invented the revolving workstand when we apprenticed here."

Daïppos replied: "He has been in Samothrace, sculpturing a winged Victory for King Demetrios."

"Surely not to celebrate his Rhodian war!"

"No, this monument commemorates the defeat of Ptolemaios off Cyprus. They say this statue is a wonder; one expects it to soar away any instant. But what brings you to us?"

"I need advice," I said, "and if there be any articulates freer with advice than Lysippos and his sons, I have yet to hear of them." I told them of my contract for the Colossus.

"My main concern," I went on, "is whether so large a statue be possible. As the geometers have proved, when we expand a work, the areas increase as the square and the weights as the cube of the linear dimensions. At that rate, a point should be reached where a statue's ankles, if made to normal human proportions, could no longer support the statue."

"What you must do," said Lysippos, "is to concentrate the weight in the lower parts. You might make the feet and ankles of solid bronze; then the legs of thick bronze, say, a palm in cross section; and so on down to mere sheeting for the head and arms. Thus you will put the most strength where it is needed. You will also render the statue less liable to be blown over, as a pyramid is more stable than an obelisk."

"There's another thing," I said. "You erected a pillar on the windward side of your Tarentine Zeus, to break the force of gales. But it were hardly practical to put up a hundred-foot column beside my Colossus. So how shall I brace it against overset?"

Boêdas asked: "First tell me, what pose have you planned?"

"Erect, shading its eyes with its right hand, as I saw the god on that day of the siege."

"Any drapery?"

"I hadn't planned any. What wants a god of clothes?"

"Well, why not hang a cloak over the god's left arm, trailing to the ground? Then you can run up a third pillar through this cloak and tie it to the others by architraves. That will give three points of support, making the structure far stronger than one with only two."

"That's it!" I cried. "And I can make the third column thicker than the other two, for it will not be limited by the proportions of the human ankle. Moreover, I can run a smaller column from the architraves up into the head...."

The discussion raged far into the night. The next day it continued while we paced about Lysippos' court, a swarm of Lysippos' grandchildren frolicking about our legs. We adjourned to Lysippos' studio, where I sketched in charcoal and clay while Lysippos and his sons criticized—and none too gently, either.

My stay lengthened into days and the days into ten-days. When we got the pose right, there still remained an ominous question:

"But how, my friends, am I to put this thing together? Remembering all the trouble we had with the scaffolding of the Tarentine Zeus, I doubt if a scaffold so high as this statue could even be built."

We mulled over this question for days until Daïppos proposed: "Why not erect a mound around the statue, raising it little by little as each part of the structure is completed? Then, when all is finished, the earth can be shoveled away."

I said: "Hm... That means that the statue must be far enough back from the waterfront so that the earth shan't spill into the harbor. Let's see, what is the normal angle of repose?..."

When Lysippos had shared his wisdom to the full, I returned to Rhodes and took up work on my lesser commissions. I could do nothing definite on the Colossus, because Rhodes had experienced difficulty in selling the timber, rope, and hides from Demetrios' engines. We kept the iron and bronze for use in the statue.

I told the Council: "To provide wood for his stockade and his engines, Demetrios has denuded whole mountains. He felled as much timber in the year and a quarter of the siege as we should normally have cut in decades. The only market that can possibly absorb so vast a store of timber before it rots is Egypt, which has no hardwood to speak of. Why don't we send an embassy to Ptolemaios to arrange a deal? I shall have to go thither anyway, to take measurements for his statue."

Although I tried to push this proposal through, the discussion took several ten-days, because every Councilman had to have his say several times over. When the embassy was finally approved, it was too late in the season for the voyage. Besides, we heard that Ptolemaios was marching up the coast of Palestine to join the allied kings in their invasion of the Antigonid lands. Demetrios, who had been campaigning against Kasandros' forces in Hellas, hastened to Asia to his father's support.

As things fell out, Ptolemaios heard a false report that Antigonos and Demetrios had crushed the allies. Thereupon he scuttled back to Egypt without accomplishing anything of military value, while the opposing armies maneuvered on the Anatolian plain until the mud and snows of Poseideon drove them into winter quarters.

With the coming of spring the armies stirred again. Seleukos arrived from India with his five hundred elephants.

Then came the great battle of the kings at Ipsos, where Seleukos' elephants turned the tide against the royal father and son. Antigonos commanded the foot. When Demetrios had gone off in pursuit of the allied cavalry, and some of Antigonos' men went over to the allies, his friends cried:

"Sire, they are coming upon you!"

"Well," said old One-eye, "what do you expect them to do? But Demetrios will come and save me!"

But Demetrios could not come, being cut off on his return to the battle by the impassible line of elephants. Antigonos fell beneath a shower of javelins.

So ended Antigonos' successful thirty-year rule of Asia Minor. For all his cruelties and treacheries, his subjects missed him, especially those who fell under the harsher rule of Lysimachos. They say that one of the latter, a Phrygian peasant, was seen digging a pit on his farm. When asked what he did, he sadly replied:

"I seek Antigonos!"

Soon after the battle of the kings, Lysimachos' soldiers freed Demetrios' Rhodian hostages at Ephesos. My father-in-law Genetor returned home, bemoaning his two years' sufferings but looking like a stuffed pheasant at a banquet.

Demetrios escaped from the battle of Ipsos. Still having powerful forces of his own, and bases in Hellas and Phoenicia, he spent several years in wild adventures around the Inner Sea until the death of Kasandros enabled him to seize the throne of Macedonia.

But although Demetrios could conquer, he could not rule. He never learnt the lesson that Ptolemaios taught me, to wit: that ruling is hard work. He spent his years in endless carousals and amours, leaving his people to fend for themselves against his officials.

Once, when a number of Demetrios' subjects had presented petitions to him, he accepted them graciously and put them in his riding cloak; then, coming to a ford of a river, he dumped them all into the stream and rode on. It is not the wont of Macedonians tamely to accept such contemptuous treatment, even from kings. So, when Lysimachos combined against him with Pyrros, the warlike young king of Epeiros, Demetrios' people deserted in droves, and he had to flee.

After further campaigns, Demetrios finally fell into the hands of Seleukos the Victorious, who kept him in genteel confinement and hospitably invited him to drink himself to death. And this the great adventurer soon did.

When things had settled down after Ipsos, Rhodes dispatched its embassy to the king of Egypt. Although the nominal head of the embassy was Admiral Damophilos, everybody knew that, as I had the widest acquaintance at the Alexandrian court, I should lead the negotiations.

We were paraded into the palace with trumpeters blowing flourishes and an usher announcing us in a voice to awaken the dead. I know not whether this formality was a tribute to the honor gained by Rhodes in her struggle or simply part of the pomp of the Egyptian court. In years gone by, while Ptolemaios claimed to be only one more Macedonian general, he adhered more or less to the rustic simplicity of his forebears. Now, however, Egyptian ceremoniousness was taking over.

The stout old king sat on a throne of gold and jewels, flanked by his minions. One of these was the aging Demetrios Phalereus, on whom the yellow hair looked more and more grotesque. Another was the priest, Manethôs of Sebennytos, a little heavier but as grave as ever.

Damophilos made his speech and presented the king with the inevitable gift: a small bronze of a dancing satyr, which I had executed for the occasion.

After the audience officially ended and everybody began to mill around the court and talk, Manethôs touched my arm. When we had exchanged warm greetings, I asked:

"Did Nembto get home safely?"

"She certainly did, and she told us how the members of Onas' club had come forward to help her. There are good men in Rhodes."

After Onas' death in the siege, it transpired that his stock of gems barely paid off his debts. The Seven Strangers, of which I had become a member, had accordingly taken up a collection to send his widow and child back to Egypt.

"What has become of her?" I asked.

"Well—ah—as a matter of fact, she keeps house for me here. But what has your embassy really come for?"

"To sell your king some wood."

Manethôs lowered his voice. "You will work through Demetrios. We must get together, but discreetly, so that he shall not know."

"Why the secrecy?"

"Because Demetrios hates me. If we openly showed our friendship, it would harm your chances. I see him scowling at your back now."

"By the gods, what has Demetrios Phalereus against you?"

"Simple jealousy. I have risen to equal him in importance on the civil side of the administration, as I am the king's personal representative in dealing with the Egyptian priesthoods, with the rank of prophet. So the Athenian has become bitterly anti-Egyptian. He hates all us 'natives,' as he calls us, and hobnobs with young Prince Thunderbolt, who is of the same mind."

Demetrios Phalereus entertained the embassy the following night, along with several Alexandrian intellectuals. One was a thin, sickly-looking man whom Demetrios Phalereus introduced as Straton of Lampsakos. The thin man was the new tutor to the king's younger legitimate son, the eight-year-old Ptolemaios Ptolemaiou.

"He is also a former student of the great Aristoteles," said Demetrios Phalereus.

"Do you then know Dikaiarchos of Messana, or Eudemos of Rhodes?" I asked the scholar.

"I knew both well," said Straton. "I fear, however, that they would disown me now."

"Why, sir?"

"My researches in physics have led me far from the master's doctrines, in particular his teaching regarding the vacuum—"

Straton went into a fit of coughing. Demetrios Phalereus presented a young man with a shy look. "This is Eukleides, a schoolteacher and my reader," he said. "Ah, woe! Age has lengthened my sight until an ordinary manuscript is but a blur to me, so I must be read to aloud like an unlettered lout. In return, I give my young friend the run of the books yonder."

He indicated the next room, jammed with bags, boxes, and single rolls. "My living space grows more cramped with each month as books for the Library pour in upon me. I have talked myself hoarse, pleading with the king for funds for an adequate library building, but something more pressing always supervenes. Therefore I must store these books here, where they are rapidly crowding me out of house and home. Of course I have only myself to blame for proposing the enterprise!"

Demetrios Phalereus dropped a painted eyelid in a subtle wink. He continued: "However, the king has definitely promised that construction shall begin this year. And high time, too, for our plans have gone far beyond the original proposal. I am urging the king to build a temple of the Muses to house the books, and to hire scholars and scientists to study them, to compose critical works upon them, to test their claims by experiments and expeditions, and to teach the younger scholars the lessons thus learnt. This policy, I aver, will make

Alexandria the intellectual and educational center of the world. Now, my dear fellow, what's the purpose of your visit this time?"

I told Demetrios Phalereus of our plans for selling the timber.

Demetrios Phalereus doubtfully pursed his lips. "I fear we are well supplied with timber from the Lebanon, but we shall see."

My heart sank. Eukleides and Straton questioned me about my plans for the Colossus, news of which had spread far and wide about the Inner Sea. Soon we had forgotten the other guests as we scribbled computations on a waxen tablet.

Eukleides proved to have an extraordinary grasp of mathematical matters. He suggested some geometrical formulae that bade fair to simplify the design, and he promised to write them out in permanent form on papyrus.

"You should write a book on geometry," I told him.

"Perhaps I shall," quoth he. Now I hear that he has, and a masterly work, too.

Straton asked me: "What sort of stone will you employ for your columns?"

"I thought to use our ordinary Rhodian brownstone. It's not very pretty, but it works, and who cares what columns inside a statue look like?"

"Sandstone doesn't weather very well," said Straton.

"But the columns will be shielded from the weather by the statue's skin."

"Ah, but the skin will leak, unless you provide means for inspecting it and calking the seams. And how will you do that with so tall a statue? Nobody will pay to put up a seventy-cubit scaffold every few years, and thus neglect and decay will have their will of your masterpiece. Besides, your iron bracing will corrode away even faster than the stone if it be not well protected."

"Now that you mention it, I ought to give more thought to maintenance," I said. "The gilding on the crown may also need to be renewed. How would it be to provide a set of ladder rungs, running up the inside of the drapery and the left arm to the shoulder? With a few additional handholds and a rope tackle, one could reach all parts of the statue."

Thus swiftly fled the evening. The next day I spent in working on a copy of the bust of Ptolemaios, which I had made on my previous sojourn. This was for the statue of the king in the Ptolemaeion at Rhodes. I also measured the king, after persuading him that if the statue showed him seated on his throne, the squat build about which he was self-conscious would not be evident.

That evening I dined in Manethôs' apartment on the palace grounds. The apartment was decorated, in contrast to those of the king's Hellenic officials, with frescoes of Egyptians in linen skirts, animal-headed gods, and ritual texts in sacred picture writing.

Nembto rushed up and touched her nose to mine. "How nice see you, Chares!"

Manethôs showed me around. He was living well, with two servants. In one small room sat Onas' son, doing his homework. Manethôs' bedroom including a double bed and an obviously feminine dressing table. Following my glance, Manethôs said:

"Know, my friend, that an Egyptian priest is allowed but one wife. How was Demetrios' party?"

I told the priest of my discourse with Eukleides and Straton, adding: "Philemon and Hekataios were there, too."

"That Hekataios!" said Manethôs indignantly. "His book on Egypt is so full of error and inaccuracy that I shall have to write one myself, as once I swore to do, if I can ever get enough time off from my duties."

He explained what a busy fellow he was. To unify Ptolemaios' subjects, he and the king had some mysterious plan, at which he would only hint, for merging the Egyptian Osiris and the Greek Plouton into one god, to be worshiped as Sarapis by the folk of both races. I wondered what the gods thought of it, but then nobody asked them.

"And speaking of my oath to write a history of Egypt in Greek," he said, "have you heard aught of Berosos?"

"At last accounts he was still in Kôs. My father's friend, Tryphon the silk weaver, knows him slightly."

"I must write him. Is he still living with Amenardis?"

"I suppose so. And, speaking of her, was the rascally Tis ever caught?"

"Not he! There is a rumor that he is in Alexandria, having changed his name and appearance. They also say that he is the new archthief of the Province of the Western Harpoon, the old one having been murdered last year."

"Hm! Of course, Alexandrian gossip is not notorious for accuracy, but perhaps I had better not go strolling down dark alleys at night."

We passed on to other matters. I mentioned the remark of Demetrios Phalereus about the lack of any pressing need for Rhodian timber.

"Let him not daunt you," said Manethôs. "That is but his opening move, to beat down your price. In confidence, the kingdom starves for good timber, because King Demetrios controls the Phoenician ports through which the Lebanese timber comes. Moreover, King Seleukos is busily founding cities in Syria and buys up all the Lebanese timber to be had." The priest smiled wryly. "Of course, as a faithful servant of King Ptolemaios, it is my duty to help him to buy the timber cheaply. But, as your friend, it is my duty to help you to sell it dear, and I knew you first. Ah, here comes dinner. Nembto, my dear, you have outshone yourself."

The next few days were occupied, first, in copying the bust of the king in clay and, secondly, in haggling with Demetrios Phalereus over the sale of our timber. Fortified by Manethôs' words, I held out for a stiff price.

The bargaining was not made easier by the official Rhodian ambassadors. They had assigned me the task because I knew Demetrios Phalereus. Then, in our private meetings, they harangued me, urging me not to hold out for too high a price and spoil the deal, not to let Demetrios Phalereus beat me down too quickly, not to let my notorious impatience sway me, and so on.

"Zeus ruin the lot of you!" I burst out at last. "If you think you can do better, take over the task. I'm an artist, not a shopkeeper, and I'll thank you not to make any more snide remarks about my Phoenician blood, either. To negotiate with you bags of wind bawling advice in one's ears is like trying to chisel a marble with people jogging one's elbow."

Thereafter Damophilos and the rest let me handle matters in my own way. I finally got a good offer and closed the deal. When we had shipped all the timber that had not otherwise been disposed of, it brought us around ninety talents.

The king, who had been on a short vacation, returned and gave the inevitable banquet of state for the Rhodians. Damophilos pledged the prosperity of Egypt, and the king pledged the beauty of the City of Roses. Then Damophilos said:

"What ails you, O Chares?"

A sudden pain in the viscera had made me wince. Soon I was holding my belly and groaning. People helped me out of the banquet hall. I have a blurred remembrance of lying on a couch while the king's head physician bent over me and said:

"He has been poisoned, forsooth. Drink this, Master Chares!"

For two days I hovered on the banks of the Styx. Then I mended and in another ten-day was none the worse. The physician's promptness with an emetic had saved me.

The king made a studious inquiry among the servants of the palace, but nothing did he learn of who had slipped the potion into my victuals. With such a swarm of servitors, it might have been any of fifty people.

Manethôs said: "It is Tis, I have no doubt. When he told us, in the chamber of the Apis bull, that he never forgave a wrong, he meant what he said."

"It's just as well we're sailing soon," I said. "For all the attractions of Alexandria, I don't care to give him another try at me."

The next few years were occupied with the execution of the statue of Ptolemaios the Savior and many smaller commissions, including some from King Seleukos the Victorious. I traveled to his new city of Antiocheia, in Syria. Here my old colleague Eutychides was making a magnificent statue of the Fortune of Antiocheia, in the form of a beautiful seated woman.

I also began to buy materials for the Colossus. I traveled to Cyprus, Kilikia, and Syria for copper and iron. I bought only a little at a time, to keep the price from soaring. Nevertheless, such was the total quantity needed—eight thousand talents of bronze and three hundred of iron—that bronze was scarce and dear for several years around the Inner Sea. My journeys were interrupted by wars, as when

King Demetrios, in the fourth year of the 120th Olympiad, fought with King Seleukos for control of the Phoenician cities.

There were also delays over the choice of the site for the Colossus, as several magnates owned land in the foreign quarter and each tried to push me into selecting a site that would profit him.

Moreover, I could not proceed with my main task until the city advanced me enough to pay my workmen. Rhodes could not pay me until King Ptolemaios paid her for the timber, and this money was slow in coming.

Notwithstanding all these good reasons for delay, I had to endure unbridled ridicule from Lykon and his friends for taking so long in getting started. People made jokes about Chares and his never-to-be-finished Colossus as they had in years before about Protogenes' painting of Ialysos.

At last, in the second year of the 121st Olympiad, the site was officially chosen, condemned, and cleared. The following year I sub-contracted the pedestal to Makar.

The year after that, when the pedestal was completed, I set up my furnaces on the site and put my crew to work. I employed as many as five hundred men at a time, most of them engaged in moving earth for the mound. This mound grew in the form of a cone, with a spiral path coiling around it to reach a flat working space on the top.

As the mound arose, my crew assembled the three forty-cubit stone columns, fastening the drums together with huge iron cramps set in leaden sockets, and inserting iron braces into holes in the drums. When the braces were in place, the bronze plates of the skin were cast, hammered into shape, and riveted to one another and to the bracing.

As Lysippos had suggested, I made the skin thicker at the bottom. Around the ankles, where the bronzen skin of the god closely surrounded the columns, I cast thick solid sections to give the greatest strength at that point.

As the mound arose, the columns arose above it, then the bracing, then the skin, and then the scaffolding. The first year was occupied in making the feet and ankles alone; the second, in building the legs up to the calves. The third year saw the statue complete to the knees;

the fourth, to the crotch. Meanwhile the fall of drapery rose beside the legs.

It was eleven years after I had begun work on the feet of my Helios. This was the second year of the 124th Olympiad, the year in which King Demetrios Antigonou died as a prisoner of King Seleukos. About the same time, Demetrios Phalereus died in Upper Egypt, whither the new King Ptolemaios had banished him.

My men were assembling the bracing for the head and the right arm. This arm presented a difficult problem. I had to extend the scaffolding out at an angle into the air, in order to assemble the iron bracing and then the pieces of bronzen skin. To strengthen this otherwise flimsy structure, I ran a stout iron brace from inside the head, out through a lock of the god's hair, and into his right hand, where it joined the bracing that extended up from the shoulder. The hand was so close to the head that the spectator could not see this connection save from certain limited angles.

One person in Rhodes had certainly profited from the construction. This was Aktis, the waterfront loafer who guided visitors. So many travelers stopped off at Rhodes to see the statue, even before it was finished, that Aktis became prosperous on the fees of those he guided. He now wore a decent shirt, shaved regularly, and bathed at least once a month.

There was not really much for visitors to enjoy at this stage. They saw the mound stretching from the waterfront three plethra inland and towering up more than a plethron in height, like a miniature volcano. A tangle of scaffolding and iron bracing stuck out its top.

One day Kavaros and I were strolling up the spiral path toward the top of the mound, arguing a technical point. (Let me give credit here to Kavaros, to whose vigorous but good-humored foremanship much of the success of the enterprise was due.) I turned at the sound of Aktis' calling my name.

"Hey, Chares! Can I have a word with you?"

I started down the path as Aktis came up, leaving the party he was guiding. When he came close, he spoke in a low voice:

"Say, I thought you ought to know. There was a man in town yesterday trying to hire somebody to kill you."

"What?"

"That's right. He didn't come right out and say: 'I'll pay you to stick a knife in Chares.' Oh, no! He asked about you, and then asked a lot of sly questions about was there a good man in town who could make accidents happen to people. When I told him 'no,' he seemed to think this was an awful dull little town."

"What did he look like?"

"A kind of dried-up little old fellow, very dark, with a big round head. He sounded like he was an Egyptian."

This could well be Tis, allowing for the effect of years. I rewarded Aktis and went to a magistrate with the story. That night the magistrate, a pair of his guards, a couple of men of the night watch, and I made the rounds of the taverns, wineshops, and brothels. But no sign of our man did we see. He must have slipped away on an outgoing ship as soon as he learnt that Rhodians were, by and large, too law-abiding to serve his fell purpose.

Still, the incident gave me pause. I bought a dagger with a broad fourteen-digit blade, a weapon fit for disemboweling an aurochs. I also resolved that if I ever again ran off with another man's wife—which the gods forbid—I would choose one whose husband was not a romantic sentimentalist, full of notions of honor and the duty of vengeance. Or perhaps, I thought, Tis was now too old to enjoy the simpler pleasures of the flesh, so that the only joy remaining him was that of tracking down and killing those who had wronged him years before.

The next year saw the completion of Helios' head and arm and the casting and the gilding of the crown of solar rays. This was the year when old King Lysimachos fell in battle with Seleukos the Victorious, and King Pyrros of Epeiros invaded Italy to help the Tarentines against the Romans.

It was also a year of sadness for me. For one thing, my father died. For several years he and I had been very close. He caught some disease of the lungs during a wet winter and never recovered.

Then my younger daughter died. I am no mainland Hellene, to toss girl babies on rubbish heaps; I grieved almost as much as if this child had been a boy.

Lastly I found myself more and more pressed for money. I had contracted to build the statue for two hundred talents, not including the cost of materials. At the time of signing the contract, all my calculations showed that I should clear a profit of at least twenty or thirty talents, which would make me independent for life.

However, delays and accidents and miscalculations drove my costs up and up, beyond my estimates. For one thing, I had computed my costs on a basis of the level of wages prevailing in Rhodes at the time of the signing. But the withdrawal of several hundred men from our small labor force had the effect of raising the wage level, even though a number of workers came from the mainland.

Strive and save as I might, it looked as though I were going to end up several talents in debt. At interest rates of ten to twelve per cent per year, I did not dare to get into the clutches of the moneylenders unless I could foresee a quick repayment, as by a big new contract. However, no king or republic seemed eager to give me such a contract until I had finished the Colossus, on which I had been working so long that few believed I should live to complete it.

My friends were sympathetic, but they had their own worries and expenses. The few thousand drachmai they could have raised would hardly have made a dent in my obligations. My father-in-law, Genetor, had the money to rescue me, but he had become queer in his dotage. One could not compel him to talk about any single subject long enough to get an aye-or-nay from him.

I will not detail the bitterness of those final months of construction, when I trailed from one magnate to another, seeking a loan at low enough interest—say, eight per cent—to allow me to work off my debts. They were politely regretful, but none would risk an obolos until he saw whether the statue stood when the mound was taken away. Then, if all went well and I would put up my foundry as security, he would see. The ordinary moneylenders, like Elavos the Syrian, wanted fifteen to twenty per cent, because my real property did not even come near to covering my debts.

At last, twelve years after I had begun, I stood on the peak of the mound. With my own hands I riveted into place the last of the gilded spikes of the god's crown of solar rays. I stepped back and swept my hand to indicate the scaffolding and the mound.

"Take it away, boys," I said.

"A cheer for the best boss that ever was, and the greatest statue that has ever been made!" bellowed Kavaros.

"*Iai!*" cried the men. Since their pay was in arrears, I suspect that it was as much their fear of the Kelt's fist as their admiration for me that elicited the cheer.

Then they began to shovel the earth into baskets. Standing silently by the great graven face, with a curiously lost feeling, I uttered a silent prayer that the god should find my offering good.

It was a cool evening in Pyanepsion, when the full moon was breaking through the clouds, after the first rain of the season. Kavaros and I were on our way home from a meeting of the Seven Strangers, of which the Kelt had just become a member on my nomination.

We were both a bit drunk. The talk of the evening had run to famous suicides, such as that of the Assyrian king, Sardanapalos, who is said to have burnt himself up with his palace, treasure, wives, and concubines when the Medes defeated him.

As our way took us past the square of the Colossus, we stopped to look at the statue. Kavaros said:

"Is he not the grand sight now, with the moon shining on his golden crown and all?"

I said: "Do you remember that woman I once got involved with in Egypt?"

"I am after hearing about her, sir. What about her?"

"She gave me one useful piece of advice."

"And that was?"

"When I had finished the statue, to climb up to the head and jump off, because I could never look forward to a greater moment. In fact, I think I'll do it right now, while my resolution holds."

"Sir, I do hope you are not saying that serious-like!"

"I've never been more serious, old boy. Any fool can see that I shall be ruined. I have struggled every way I can think of, short of selling myself into slavery, to get out of this snare of debt, to no avail. I am sick of it, and my main task is done. To the afterworld with everybody! They'll be sorry when I'm gone."

I started purposefully up the remains of the mound. Kavaros threw himself in front of me, crying:

"You will not, sir! I will not let you! It is just that you are feeling bad tonight. You need another drink; Grania can get us one at my house. Please, sir—"

I dodged around the Kelt with the agility that had served me on many a hockey field in my youth. Kavaros seized my cloak, but I shed the garment and ran on to where the fall of bronze drapery rose from the earth. With Kavaros pounding after me, I grasped the rungs of the maintenance ladder and scampered up like a monkey.

"Come down, Master Chares!" cried Kavaros. "You can have everything I own, only do not be doing this foolish thing! If you do not come down, I will climb up and pull you down!"

"You can't! You're afraid of heights. Take care of my family, will you?"

I resumed my climb. Kavaros stood in perplexity for a few heartbeats, then ran out of the square.

When I reached the crook of the statue's left arm, my racing heart and laboring breath reminded me that I was, after all, a middle-aged man. I paused to rest. The cool air and the exertion had cleared the fumes of wine from my head.

As I sat there holding the handgrips, my conduct did begin to seem absurd. After all, I was still eating and drinking regularly, I had a loving family, and nobody was threatening me with torture or slavery. The money matters might somehow work themselves out. Besides, if I died in debt, my sons would inherit my debts, and what sort of legacy was that to leave them?

I swung back over the ladder and began to descend. When I got to the level of the statue's knees and glanced down, however, I saw that several figures were grouped about the foot of the ladder. Thinking them Rhodians aroused by Kavaros, I continued my descent.

The next time I looked down, though, the figures seemed too still for my taste. Rhodians would have been gabbling and crying out to know if I was all right.

"Kavaros?" I called. There was no answer.

I lowered myself a few more rungs, till I could see their upturned faces. Although the moonlight was strong enough to make recognition possible, I saw nobody whom I knew. They were just a group of men in nondescript clothes.

"Who are you?" I demanded.

"Come on down, O Chares," said a creaky old voice.

"Is that you, Tis?"

"Come down and see."

"Do you think me mad? If you want to talk, do so now."

Instead of replying, the voice spoke in Egyptian. Two men sprang to the base of the ladder and began to climb, with blades glinting in the moonlight.

I drew my large dagger and reached down to strike at the first. The man parried my thrust with his short sword. Then he swung himself to one side of the ladder, allowing the other man to crowd up abreast of him. Both of them thrust and hacked at me until I was forced back up the ladder.

Rung by rung they drove me up. I shouted: "Help! Rhodians! A rescue! Help!" But, what of all my climbing, my voice came out as a feeble croak.

My assailants were well-trained killers. Whenever I made a stand, the leading man held me in play with his longer blade until the other could lend his weight to the attack. My efforts to kick them in the face or stamp on their fingers only got me a wound in the calf.

I reached the statue's left arm again, bleeding from a cut on the forearm and another on the leg. I cried:

"Help! Rhodians! Murder! I'm beset!"

Up came the other two. They pulled themselves up over the turn of the drapery, blades first. Holding a bronze fold with one hand, I made a furious thrust at the leader's breast. He struck at my darting blade; his edge bit one of my fingers to the bone. My dagger spun out of my grasp. It struck the statue's skin with a clank and fell away into darkness.

I darted up the rungs that extended up the statue's left arm. I could not move so swiftly as before, between fatigue and the cuts on my right arm and hand. My breath came in great gasps, so that I had none to spare for shouting.

I pulled myself up on the broad curving surface of the shoulder. I had not been up on top of the statue since the mound had been carried away. A look downward showed a drop to appall even one with my head for heights. Moving carefully, I walked the length of the shoulder and grasped a handhold on the statue's left ear. My last hope was that my pursuers would fear the height more than I, and that I could use this fear.

If I had had a proper tackle of rope, I could have rigged a sling to the cleats on the head and swung myself around the head to the other shoulder, where they would have had a hard time coming at me. But I had no such gear.

The leading pursuer reached the shoulder. His breath, too, came in gasps. As he stood up, I saw that he was not more than half my age: a dark, powerful youth, probably Egyptian. He paused to catch his breath. Then, after a downward glance, he moved with exaggerated caution. But still he came toward me.

If, I thought, I could land one good solid kick, while holding the ear, he would have nothing to clutch....

The man came closer, in a half-crouch, his short sword out. I launched my kick, but too soon. The man swayed backwards, so that I missed him. As my leg fell back, the assassin lunged.

On solid ground he would have spitted me, but caution slowed his movements. As his arm snaked forward, my own right hand came around in a snatch. I caught his wrist and deflected his thrust far enough to miss my midriff. His point struck the bronze behind me with a faint bell-like sound. With the same motion I carried his right arm up to my face and sank my teeth into his forearm.

Never have I bitten into anything with such earnest effort. I tasted blood and felt it running down my chin. The man's breath came in gasps in my ear. His left hand clutched at my face with gouging thumb and raking nails. I fended it off with my right hand and drove my right elbow into his face and midriff. I also tried to kick him in the crotch.

His left fist pounded at my left hand, trying to break my grip on the ear. It occurred to me that I had only to let go and we should both hurtle to our deaths. A short while before, the idea might have appealed to me. But now my blood was up. I thought of nothing but saving myself and killing this murderous lout. I silently cursed my smallness and the years that had sapped my strength.

Battered, bleeding, and gasping, I hung on. I beat, kicked, and clawed at the man while he assailed me in the same manner, all the time trying to wrench his arm free from my teeth.

There seemed to be an uproar from somewhere, but I supposed this to be merely the sound of blood in my ears. I did not even have time to wonder when the man's comrade would join the struggle.

The man suddenly screamed in my ear. I was dragged toward the swiftly steepening downward slope of the statue's chest. My assailant clutched me as if to keep from falling.

I rolled my eyes, which had been squinted almost shut against my enemy's clawing hand. Someone, on hands and knees, had a grip on the Egyptian's ankle and was trying to tear him loose from me.

I released my jaws from the man's arm, pivoted, and struck his face a backhanded blow. At the same time, the crouching person gave a heave. The Egyptian dropped his sword, made a wild clutch at the air, and toppled from the shoulder. A long diminishing shriek came up as he vanished into the darkness below. The scream was cut off by the smack of a body's striking the ground.

I straightened painfully up, gulping air. My rescuer now lay prone on the convex upper surface of the shoulder, pressing his flattened hands against the bronze as if to glue himself to it.

"Master Chares!" whimpered the apparition. "It is frightened to death that I am. I cannot move from this cursed spot!"

"Kavaros! Get up on your hands and knees. Don't look at the ground; look at the places where your hands and feet will go. Now back slowly toward the top of the ladder. That's it, old friend. Another step. Now feel with your toes for the topmost rung...."

A quarter-hour of guidance brought Kavaros back to the ground. Here was a crowd of Rhodians, with several prisoners. Two bodies lay at the statue's feet.

The Kelt and I nearly collapsed when we stood on solid ground again. My shirt was half torn from me, and I could feel the blood trickling down from a score of cuts, bites, and scratches.

Kavaros gasped: "I found the watch—and fetched them—and here were all—these murtherers."

"You're the bravest man in Rhodes, for coming up to help me in spite of your fear of heights. What befell the second man who followed me up?"

"That is him, there. I caught the omadhaun by the leg and plucked him loose from the ladder, as easy as taking a little bird from the nest. But some of them got away, I am thinking."

"Here's one who didn't," said another voice. "Chares, do you know this fellow?"

I went over to where men with links bent over a third body. Though withered and wattled with age, it was unmistakably Tis.

"I quarreled with him once in Egypt," I explained. "How did he die?"

One of the watch spoke: "We ran to the square after Kavaros, thinking to stop you from slaying yourself, and these fellows drew steel against us. After we had knocked a couple down with our staves, the rest ran away. Of course we ran after. This one had reached the entrance to the alley when he clutched at his heart and fell down, as you see him now. Nobody touched him. The god must have struck him dead."

"He was too old to take such an active part in his murders," I said. "What will be done with these desperadoes?"

"If convicted, they'll be sold. Would you buy one?"

"Zeus forfend! They're cut out for a short but useful life in the mines."

A surprising event took place a few days after the death of Tis. After all, there was nothing surprising in Tis's raid when you think about it. The archthief was merely acting in character, fantastic though that character may seem.

It was much more astonishing that my old foe Lykon the sculptor, now a full citizen, should carry a bill in the Assembly to pay off the debts that I had incurred in completing the Colossus. These came, all told, to a little over nine talents. Thus the Colossus cost Rhodes altogether about three hundred talents.

When I learnt of this amazing act, I went, still bandaged, to Lykon's studio to thank him. He heard me out, looking me through with cold gray eyes. Then he said:

"Chares, I have never liked you and I still don't. If you will keep out of my way, I'll keep out of yours, and we can thus avoid a contact that must be as irksome to you as it is to me.

"As for this bill to indemnify you, I did that, not for your sake, but for my own honor and that of my city. Men would say: 'Shame on the Rhodians, who so niggardly used the man who showered fame on their city that he was almost driven to suicide by monetary worries!' While I could bear your departure without uncontrollable grief, I would not have the City of Roses thought hardhearted and ungrateful. Does that satisfy you?"

All I could think of to say was a quotation: "Wonders are many, but none is more wonderful than man!"

Two months later the remains of the mound and the scaffold had vanished. The Helios-Apollon towered proudly over the waterfront, shading his eyes against the rays of the rising sun. On a clear day he could be seen from elevated points on the Asiatic coast, and mariners a hundred furlongs at sea caught the golden blink of the sun on his gilded crown. I had slightly changed Lysippos' canon of proportion, enlarging the head a little to cancel the foreshortening effect of viewing so tall a statue from below.

When it became evident that the statue was going to stand securely, the Rhodians began to look upon it with quiet pride, as if some of the virtue of the god had entered into the statue and, through it, into them as well. I found that they even looked with quiet pride upon Chares the Lindian. When the rich, the noble, and the learned went out of their way to pass the time of day with me, I had to ask myself: Am I really the same man as that boastful, runty, testy, friendless, part-Phoenician youth who had so set everybody by the ears when he arrived, twenty-seven years before? I had so long struggled for respect and recognition that it took me a while to realize that I need not battle for them any more.

Then I turned the statue over to the city at a great public ceremony, at which I was at last made a full citizen of Rhodes.

"By the gods!" said old Admiral Damophilos, craning his neck. "I never realized it before, but the statue's face is the spit and image of the Besieger!"

For so they now call King Demetrios Antigonou, from his many famous sieges.

"I didn't intend it that way," I said. "I merely tried to get my idea of perfect beauty and virtue into those features. But the Demetrios was a man of godlike beauty and presence—whatever one say of his character—so I suppose some resemblance is inevitable."

"Well, I daresay we ought not to hold grudges," said Damophilos. "Demetrios' attack and our defense did give Rhodes more glory than anything else could have done."

"There's a certain logic about the statue's looking like him, too," I said, "since it was built with the spoils from his siege."

The admiral gave a cackling laugh and slapped his thigh. "That is right! He paid for it, didn't he? That's good! Oh, Chares, how about dinner at my house tonight?"

I accepted this and many other such invitations. I ought to have been ecstatically happy; the richest and best-born men in Rhodes accepted me as an equal and even paid social court to me, just as if I had never worked with my hands and bore pure Hellenic blood in my veins.

I soon found, however, that most of these parties bored me to tears. These magnates are not really such villains as the poor are wont to think them; their worst fault is dullness. They talk about their games and sports, their children and relatives, their purchases and sales, their aches and pains, and they talk about them over and over.

When I burn to learn about the progress of the arts and sciences, about new engineering techniques, high politics, and distant lands, what do I get? So-and-so's roof leaks; so-and-so seeks a divorce; so-and-so's slave has run away. To the crows with it!

So back to the Seven Strangers, of which I had long been a member, I went, starving for food for the mind as well as for the body. Shortly after I had finished the Colossus last year, Giskon called a meeting of the club at his house. To this meeting I brought my oldest son, who wanted his first taste of club life. When I entered, there stood a fat bald man who looked somehow familiar.

"Chares!" he cried. "Know you me not? Berosos of Babylon?"

"By Zeus! I didn't recognize you without your hair."

"Well, I scarce knew you with your hair all gray. You are not, I trust, still angry with me—ah—"

"On the contrary, old boy, I'm delighted to see you." We embraced and burst into talk. Berosos said:

"...I settled in Kôs, sold some more sundials, cast horoscopes, and started a class in the science of the stars. I was never in danger of starvation"—he glanced down at his paunch—"and happy I should have been, but for that woman."

"Amenardis?" I asked innocently.

He shuddered. "Speak not that name! From morn to night it was: 'Do this! Do not do that! What a fool you are!' Nearly mad was I driven."

"Why didn't you throw her out? She had no legal claim on you."

"Oh, you know me, Chares. No liver for combat have I, and she frightened away what little valor I have. For nigh unto ten years I submitted."

"Herakles, man! My heart bleeds for you."

Berosos: "Well it may. Would to Mardoukos that I had a flinty streak in my soul, as you have! At last, having secretly hoarded a goodly sum from my earnings—for she demanded the monetary management of our home—I quietly took ship for Athens. For aught she knows, I went for a swim in the Aegean and was swallowed by a shark."

"What became of her?"

"May I never know! In Athens I prospered and married a jolly wench, the daughter of a Syrian metic. She knows how to protect a man of intellect from the shocks of this rude, rough world. When I left, the Athenians put up a gilded statue of me, belly and all. Recall you that queer Phoenician youth, Zenon of Kition, who dined with the Seven Strangers at the first meeting you attended?"

"Vaguely. What about him?"

"He has settled in Athens, audited the sundry philosophers, and become a teacher on his own account, with a sizable following. "The

Man of the Porch'[8] they call him, from his lecturing in the Painted Porch. Although he claims to have based his doctrines in part upon my celestial science, I cannot say I ever truly liked him. When sober, he is haughty and irascible; when drunk, he chases every boy and youth in sight; and his teachings seem to me a tissue of windy rhetoric. Howsomever, Athens was lovely."

"Then why did you leave?"

"Oh, a better prospect have I. The new king of Syria and Persia, Antiochos son of Seleukos, wrote asking me to come to his court at Antiocheia as official historian. Do you remember that oath that Manethôs and I swore, to write the histories of our peoples in Greek? Well, here is my chance to carry it out." He lowered his voice. "And, speaking of queer young Phoenicians, who is this that Giskon has dredged up from the Syrian Sea?"

"This" was a young Phoenician from Akê, Abdemon by name, who had gone Greek in the biggest possible way. He dripped oil, fluttered his eyelashes, made sexual advances to all the men, and spoke with the most extreme Atticisms.

"This whacking great statue of yours," he said, "is all very well as a monument, but is it art? Is it in the best taste? Rather, I should compare it to the sign over a tradesman's shop. Jolly useful, but hardly esthetic. You might as well have the god hold a banner reading, 'Come to Rhodes, commercial center of the Inner Sea!'"

Talk died down; eyes turned toward me. Although I have learnt with the years to control my temper, I still have a name for touchiness.

"Oh, I say!" said Abdemon, glancing round the circle. "Is this the man who put the thing up? I'm frightfully sorry—"

I gave a short laugh. "Never mind, you may have something there, son. Do you want to know the real reason I erected that statue? It wasn't the money—in fact, I'm a poor man tonight, because my costs far outran my estimates—nor was it an excess of piety, though I am a good conventional worshiper of the Bright One. The reason is that I'm a small man, so I have always wanted to be remembered for building the largest thing of its kind.

---

8 *Ho* Stôikos, the Stoic.

"Well, now I have done it. I won't say I am sorry, because it has been a lot of fun. I have learnt some useful technical lessons, and I have fulfilled the vow I swore to the god and garnered some slight glory. But I agree with this young fellow that it's time I got back to art of a more normal kind. Besides which, I have a living to earn. Kavaros, tomorrow we must clean all the models for the Colossus out of the studio. We're going to do some sculpture better than anything that has yet been seen!"

AUTHOR'S NOTE

The following characters in this story were real persons: Alkimos (or Alcimus), Amyntas, Ananias, Antigonos, Apelles, Apollonios, Aristodemos, Athenaios (or Athenaeus), Athenagoras, Berosos (or Berossos, -us), Boêdas, Chares, Daïppos, Damophilos, Damoteles, Demetrios Antigonou (later called Demetrios Poliorketes, "the Besieger"), Demetrios Phalereus, Dikaiarchos (or Dicaearchus), Diognetos, Epimachos, Eudemos, Eukleides (or Euclid), Euthykrates, Eutychides, Evagoras (or Euagoras), Hieronymos, Hekataios (or Hecataeus), Kallias (or Callias), Lysippos, Manethôs (or Manetho, -on), Menedemos, Menelaos, Philemon, Protogenes, Ptolemaios Lagou (or Ptolemaeus or Ptolemy I, later called Ptolemaios Soter, "the Savior"), Theodoros, and Zenon (or Zeno).

In a few names, where it might make a difference in the Anglicized pronunciation, I have indicated the long Greek vowels ω by *ê* and *ô* respectively. Thus, in Anglicized form, "Kôs" and "Thôth" rhyme with "dose" and "both," while "Tychê" rhymes with "my key." "Dikaiarchos," not being a well-known name, has no established Anglicized pronunciation; for those not up to tackling the Greek, "dick-IRE-cuss" will do. "Chares" is adequately rendered as "Carey's."

In the Egyptian sequence, the Sosorthos, Imouthes, Souphis, Sesostris, Toutimaios, Amosis, Amenophthis, Rhameses Osymandyas, Sethenes Chamoïs, and Apries mentioned by Chares and his informants are the Zoser, Imhotep, Khufu (Herodotos' Cheôps), Senusert III, [Dedu]mes, Aahmes I, Amenhotep III, Rameses II (Shelley's Ozymandias), Setekhnakht and Khaemwaset (two separate men confused by later generations), and Wahabra II of Egyptian history. The spellings are mostly those of Manethôs himself, in the surviving fragments of his work, as Chares would naturally have obtained most of his information from Manethôs.

Berosos and Manethôs both wrote histories, in Greek, of their respective peoples, as in the story they vowed to do. Both works are lost, though a good idea of their contents can be obtained from the numerous fragments (quotations, citations, and outlines) in the works of later writers. All that is actually known of these authors is as follows: Manethôs was a priest of Sebennytos who was active at the courts of the first two Ptolemies, took part in founding the Graeco-Egyptian cult of Sarapis, and wrote his Egyptian history at Heliopolis. Berosos was a priest of Marduk, probably a little older than Manethôs, who invented the hemicyclic sundial, taught astrology and astronomy at Kôs, lectured at Athens, and wrote his Babylonian history at the court of Antiochos I. Sending Berosos to Rhodes and Egypt and having him meet Manethôs are fictional contrivances.

Manethôs' tale of the invasions of the Hyksôs is, probably, a wildly inaccurate account of the Egyptian history of the time in question. But it represents the real Manethôs' beliefs (Josephus: *Against Apion*, I, 14-31) and is perhaps no wider of the mark than the Hebraic tradition. The legend of the *Book of Thôth*, as told by Manethôs, occurs in a papyrus of Ptolamaic times.

Likewise, the opinions attributed to Dikaiarchos of Messana on such subjects as war, prophecy, and the soul, though they may sound a trifle anachronistic, are opinions the real man held. Although Dikaiarchos' original works have all perished, some of his doctrines have been preserved by Cicero and other ancient authors.

The "scorpion," mentioned by Chares in connection with the siege of Rhodes, is the crossbow, also called in ancient times the *cheiro-ballista*, "hand catapult," and *gastraphetês*, "belly weapon." The crossbow was well known to the Classical from the fourth century B.C. on, although it never attained the popularity it later achieved in medieval Europe.

Subsequently, to confuse matters, the name "scorpion" was applied to a quite different stone-throwing catapult, invented after Chares' time. This later engine had a single throwing arm, with a spoon or sling on its end, which flew up in a vertical plane against a stop. It was also called an "onager" (wild ass) from that animal's mythical habit of kicking stones back at its pursuers.

I was tempted to call all catapults "guns" and their crews "gunners," since the original meaning of "gun," like that of the Greek *katapeltês* and *ballista* and the German *Geschütz*, is simply "shooter" or "thrower"—that is, any missile engine, firearms included. However, such usage might have bewildered some readers.

The precise nature of the *triemiolia* (literally, "triple one-and-a-halfer"), the antipirate cruiser built by the Rhodians, is open to question. One opinion is that it had two banks of oars, with two men on each upper oar and one on each lower; another is that it had the regular trireme's arrangement of three banks of one-man oars, but with special facilities for removing the oars and benches from the after half of the upper deck to make room for the sail and rigging when these were stowed for a fight. See the Loeb Classical Library: *Diodorus Siculus*, Vol. X, p. 389, n. 3; and the *Journal of Hellenic Studies*, Vol. 78, pp. 14-18.

I used "lune" as a convenient equivalent of *τειχος μηνοείδῃς*, "crescentic wall."

The months of the Attic calendar were, in order: Hekatombaion (from late June to late July), Metageitnion, Boedromion, Pyanepsion, Maimakterion, Poseideon, Gamelion, Anthesterion, Elaphebolion, Mounychion, Thargelion, and Skirophorion.

Getika, the land overrun by the Kelts in Chares' time, corresponds more or less to modern Wallachia in the Balkans.

The story of the siege of Rhodes in 305-4 B.C. is told by Diodorus Siculus: Book XX; Vitruvius: Book X; and Plutarch: *Demetrius*. The three accounts are not altogether consistent. Minor details are added by other authors, such as Aulus Gellius.

Most of the information on the building of the Colossus is in *Of the Seven Wonders of the World*, by Philon of Byzantium. Shorter accounts occur in Pliny the Elder (XXXIV, xviii, 41-42) and Strabo (XIV, ii, 5). Minor allusions to it appear in the works of other classical authors.

Pliny gives most of our information about Chares and his fellow artists Lysippos, Apelles, and Protogenes. In the story of Apelles' purchase of Protogenes' pictures, Pliny says that Apelles paid Protogenes fifty talents (300,000 drachmai). This seems to me wildly improbable, as the sum would be the rough equivalent, in purchasing power, to half a million or a million dollars. I therefore reduced the price to fifty pounds (5,000 drachmai), equivalent to ten or twenty thousand dollars.

Almost nothing is definitely known about Chares of Lindos save that he studied under Lysippos, worked mostly in bronze, built the Colossus, and also made a colossal head, later taken to Rome. Eutychides, mentioned in the first book, was the sculptor of the Fortune of Antioch and possibly of the Victory of Samothrace.

The Colossus is said to have been 70 cubits high. This may mean 90, 105, or 120 feet, depending on which of several different cubits is assumed. It may be compared with the Statue of Liberty, which stands 151 feet from base to torch, or 111 from heel to crown. In the first century A.D., Nero had a statue of himself, as large as the Colossus of Rhodes, erected in Rome. Vespasian later turned it into a statue of Helios by putting a crown of solar rays, like those borne by the Rhodian Helios, on its head.

Chares' Colossus stood for 56 years and then, in 224 B.C., was overthrown by an earthquake (Polybius V, 88). The "colossal wreck" lay on the ground until the Saracen conquest. In 656 A.D., an Arab general, Mu'ôwiyah, scrapped it and shipped the bronze to Syria. There a Jewish merchant of Edessa bought it and carried it off on 900 (or 980) camels, presumably to be turned into trays and lamps.

Here is a puzzle. Philon says that the statue contained 500 talents (15 tons) of bronze and 300 talents (9 tons) of iron. As a healthy camel can carry 500 pounds without strain, either the weight of the bronze in the statue or the number of camels must be wrong, because the number of camels given could carry 225 (or 245) tons. If the statue contained only 15 tons of bronze, the bronze would have to be about one-sixteenth of an inch thick, which seems like too flimsy a structure to withstand wind pressure.

More likely, the number of camels is right, but the weight of the bronze is grossly understated, and the bronze averaged about an inch thick. This inference is supported by Philon's statement that building the Colossus caused a temporary scarcity of bronze. Compare the

Statue of Liberty, of the same general size, which weighs 225 tons, including 100 tons for the copper sheeting. As Chares' Helios and Bartholdi's Liberty were of about the same size, one would expect the latter to weigh somewhat less, because Bartholdi had steel girders to work with while Chares did not.

Some well-known stories about the Colossus, which appeared long after the statue was built, can be more or less safely rejected. One is the statement of Sextus Empiricus, who wrote about 500 years after Chares erected the statue. Sextus (*Against the Logicians*, I, 107-8) said that at first the statue was planned to be half its eventual height. When the city decided to double the height, Chares asked for only twice the original fee, forgetting that the material would be increased eightfold; this error drove him to bankruptcy and suicide. It seems incredible that a man with the engineering skill that Chares must have had should not have known the square-cube law. A similar story, probably no more authentic, was told of Lysippos.

More stories appeared in the Middle Ages, more than a thousand years after Chares' time, and several centuries after the remains of the statue had been junked. The best-known of these says that the Colossus bestrode the harbor:

> "*...the brazen giant of Greek fame,*
> *With conquering limbs astride from land to land.*"

Its feet rested on the ends of two moles, so that ships passed between its legs. This legend, impossible for engineering reasons, was perhaps suggested by the remains of fortifications on the ends of the moles. While the exact location of the statue is not known, some scholars think that it stood either near the site of the existing Mosque of Murad Reis or near that of the Castle of the Knights of Rhodes.

Other medieval tales averred that the Colossus was 900 feet tall (also technically impossible) and that it had a beacon in its head (not impossible, but unlikely because of the difficulty of getting fuel up to the beacon).

The only circumstantial account of the founding of the Library of Alexandria (aside from a brief statement in Diogenes Laërtius' *Demetrius*) is at the beginning of the so-called *Letter of Aristeas to Philokrates*, used by Josephus (*Jewish Antiquities*, XII, ii) and other later Judaeo-Christian writers. While this is a work of fiction, written at least a century after its fictive date, it preserves a few historical facts. Like the works derived from it, it confuses the first two Ptolemies.

The Library was founded by the first Ptolemy and reached its definitive form under the second, but all of the rulers of this dynasty (save perhaps the seventh Ptolemy, who favored the native Egyptians against the Greek ruling class) added to it. At its height, it held nearly three-quarters of a million rolls. Most of these, however, must have been duplicates, as there were not enough authors in the ancient world to produce so many separate titles.

A series of fires and depredations during the Roman period gradually destroyed the Library. As the books were stored in two or more buildings, no single fire accounted for all of them. When Julius Caesar occupied Alexandria in 48 B.C., Cleopatra urged him to help himself to the books, and he took away hundreds or thousands to be shipped to Rome. Then Alexandria revolted against Caesar and Cleopatra. In the fighting, either the books that Caesar had taken or those still in one of the libraries, or both, were burnt. When Antonius formed his connection with Cleopatra, he stole and gave her the 200,000-roll library of Pergamon to replace the losses.

The Library probably suffered further damage when Aurelian suppressed the revolt of Firmus in Alexandria in A.D. 272; again when Diocletian put down another revolt in 295; again when the Bishop Theophilus, a bloodthirsty fanatic of the Hitlerian type, led a Christian mob to the destruction of the Serapeion in 391. The remains were finished off by the Arabs of the Muslim general 'Amr ibn al-'Âs when he captured the city in 646. A story relates that when 'Amr wrote his Khalif, asking what to do with these books of the infidels, he received the reply that if they agreed with the Qur'ân they were superfluous, whereas if they disagreed with it they were pernicious, so it were well to destroy them: a suitable maxim for all true believers.

Modern apologists for the Arabs have denied this story and put all the onus of the destruction on the Christians. Christian apologists, on the other hand, have striven to exculpate the godly Theophilus and put the blame back on the Muslims. In fact, we shall never know just how many books were destroyed at each predation, nor to what extent the destruction was due simply to the agents of time and neglect—mice and mold, thieves and termites—suffered to work their will unchecked when, with the rise of Christianity, governments lost interest in the preservation of mundane writings. All we can say for sure is that monotheism proved as deadly a foe to learning as war and barbarism. *Tantum religio potuit suadere malorum.*

For the weights, measures, and coinage of the time and their modern equivalents, see the Postscript to my previous historical novel, *An Elephant for Aristotle.* During the twenty years between the fictive dates of the two novels, inflation, caused by Alexander's spending of the treasure of the Persian kings, more than doubled the prices of commodities in the Greek world.

CPSIA information can be obtained
at www.ICGtesting.com
Printed in the USA
LVHW092325210721
693373LV00014B/118

9 781612 421445